Amadis de Gaule
AND ITS INFLUENCE
ON ELIZABETHAN
LITERATURE

11/11/81

Amadis de Gaule

AND ITS INFLUENCE ON
ELIZABETHAN LITERATURE

by JOHN J. O'CONNOR

RUTGERS UNIVERSITY PRESS
NEW BRUNSWICK, NEW JERSEY

The woodcuts in this volume are reproduced from rare sixteenth-century folio editions of *Amadis de Gaule,* with the kind permission of the Folger Shakespeare Library and the New York Public Library.

For Martha

. . . namque tu solebas
Meas esse aliquid putare nugas.

Preface

The purpose of this book is twofold: to recall the romance of *Amadis de Gaule* from its literary limbo and to examine the influence of the French version on Elizabethan literature. This is a new venture, for though several books in various languages discuss bibliographical problems of *Amadis* or its influence on manners and morals in France, no other book focuses on the romance itself. Nor is there a complete discussion of the influence of the romance in sixteenth-century England. The dearth of prior literary studies accounts in large measure for the emphasis here on describing rather than interpreting or evaluating.

I begin with the assumption that most of my readers have not read, even in substantial part, the twenty-one volumes that comprise the sixteenth-century *Amadis de Gaule*. I try to give an idea of the texture of the whole romance—its length, complexity, style, characters, motifs—so that some may be tempted to read it for themselves and that others who remain untempted may acquire some information about *Amadis* in relatively painless fashion. My consideration of the influence of the romance in England attempts also to inform. The problem of influence, however, is inevitably subjective, and writers of books like mine tend to exaggerate the importance of what they have done. The appendices are meant to give every reader a chance to measure for himself the degree of exaggeration.

I confess to a certain fondness for *Amadis de Gaule* that will be readily understandable to anyone who has read other sixteenth-century romances of chivalry, but I make no claims for it as a great literary work. Its imperfections are great, obvious, and endearing. With those who consider all chivalric romances hopelessly trivial I sympathize. I can suggest only that the trivial has its uses and say, with Dr. Johnson: "There is nothing, Sir, too little for so little a creature as man."

I have attempted to regularize the names of characters. Thus I give one character's name as Sphéramonde, although it can be found also in such spellings as Spheramond and Sferamund. On occasion, however, I am obliged to use Spanish forms as well as French, so that, for example, Amadis and Oriane appear as Amadís and Oriana. Where macrons appear in the French or English texts I have silently modernized; so rēdre becomes rendre. Since ligatures do not occur in the sixteenth-century texts I used, I have omitted them. In a parenthetical notation indicating the source of a passage in *Amadis,* such as V, viii, 27, the arabic number may indicate either a folio or a page.

I am much indebted to the work of scholars living and dead. I owe special thanks to my friend and colleague C. F. Main and to B. J. Whiting, both of whom read this book at an early stage and suggested ways of improving it. Clarence E. Turner kindly read my translations and offered numerous emendations and improvements. I am grateful to the Rutgers University Research Council for numerous small grants over many years and for making possible the year's leave during which the book was written.

John J. O'Connor

February 20, 1969
New Brunswick, New Jersey

Contents

Amadis de Gaule

AND ITS INFLUENCE
ON ELIZABETHAN
LITERATURE

Ode au
Seigneur des Essarts
sur le discours de son Amadis

Celuy qui chanta jadis
En sa langue Castillane
Les proësses d'Amadis
Et les beautez d'Oriane,
Par les siecles envieux
D'ung sommeil oblivieux
Ja s'en alloit obscurci,
Quand une plume gentile
De cete fable subtile
Nous a l'obscur eclerci.

   *   *   *   *   *

Or entre les mieux appris
Le chœur des Muses ordonne
Qu'à HERBERAY soit le pris
De la plus riche couronne:
Pour avoir si proprement
De son propre acoutrement
Orné l'Achille Gaulloys,
Dont la douceur allechante
Donne à celuy qui le chante
Le nom d'Homere François.

—Joachim du Bellay

I

The Literary Background
of *Amadis de Gaule*

The romance of chivalry is a literary genre that was as close to the hearts of sixteenth-century readers as it is distant from ours. Never before or since has this kind of prose fiction appealed so strongly and so generally. The vogue for marvelous tales of knight-errantry that began in Spain and Portugal in the latter part of the fifteenth century continued almost unabated up to the fateful year of the Armada. Beginning with the publication of *Tirant lo Blanch* in 1490 and continuing up to 1588, Spanish and Portuguese writers produced some two score prose narratives of knightly adventures.[1] Some of them were translated into French, Italian, German, Dutch, and English. In these tongues they were read with a passion sometimes surpassing that they excited in their native peninsula, and inevitably they inspired imitations and continuations. In several European countries in the sixteenth century chivalric romances ranked second in popularity and bulk only to devotional literature.

Renaissance romances evolved out of verse and prose narratives of the Middle Ages, and in sentiment and technique they have a

3

decidedly medieval flavor. They often pretend to be the newly discovered chronicles of an ancient sage or prophet, and their background is vaguely historical. Their claims to historicity were accepted by some readers, but the romances seldom attempt to maintain the illusion of a basis in actuality. Most of them spring from tales out of the Arthurian or Carolingian cycles, freely embroidered with matter from the Crusades or from classical mythology. The real centers of interest are of course the fictional loves and wars of heroes. Knights like Lancelot and Tristan and ladies like Guinivere reappear, and the fading traditions of chivalry and courtly love take on new life. The interlaced style of narrative so common in the Middle Ages is favored, and the most cherished figures of speech are the commonplaces of medieval writers like Chrestien de Troyes. Although an important source of sixteenth-century fascination with such tales must have been nostalgia, a resurgence of interest in chivalric customs and polite manners made the romances fashionable and relevant.

In general, the longer a chivalric prose narrative, the better and more influential it was. This kind of tale was written in such a way that, if popular response warranted, succeeding books could easily be added. Hence the number of volumes a romance finally attained is an approximate gauge of its popularity. Many of the Spanish and Portuguese romances had no discernible literary impact elsewhere, for they were never translated; however, the influence of individual titles is hard to establish, since all chivalric romances have a marked family resemblance and within the genre there is a great deal of intermarriage and adultery.[2]

The most important of the long romances are *Amadís de Gaula, Palmerín,* and the *Espejo de príncipes y cavalleros (The Mirror of Knighthood)*. In pattern each is more like the others than different. Each grew large by accretions over a considerable period of time, and each attracted a number of authors and translators. The earliest extant edition of the first four books of *Amadís de Gaula* was printed in 1508, and *Palmerín de Oliva,* the first of the Palmerín cycle, appeared in 1511. By 1546 the Spanish *Amadís* had grown to twelve books, and Spanish and Portuguese additions to the Palmerín cycle continued until 1602. The English translation of *Palmerín,* a selection from among the many volumes available, runs to five full tomes. The first part of the *Espejo de príncipes* did not get into print in Spain until 1562. It was continued in 1581 and brought to a coy conclusion—in which another continuation is suggested—in 1589. In English translation the work dragged out its weary length in nine volumes, from 1579 to 1601.

Of the Spanish and Portuguese romances of chivalry the best and most influential is the cycle held rather loosely together under the title of *Amadís de Gaula.* This enormous work is much longer than either *Palmerín* or the *Espejo de príncipes.* Moreover, since it was first in print, it exerted a great deal of influence upon the other two cycles, and indeed most other romances produced in the sixteenth century were written in its expansive shadow. In his nineteenth-century edition of the first five books, Pascual de Gayangos has pointed out some of the ways in which both *Palmerín* and the *Espejo de príncipes* imitate *Amadís,* and Sir Henry Thomas notes among the many relationships of the great cycles that the names of the heroines rhyme: Oriana (*Amadís*), Griana (*Palmerín*), and Briana (*Espejo de príncipes*).[3]

There is no question of the literary importance of *Amadís,* for ten of its twelve books quickly found their way into other languages. In the major countries of Europe it was one of the most widely read secular works of the entire sixteenth century. The defeat of the Armada in 1588 took some of the joy out of the chivalric tale for Spanish readers, and after the first part of *Don Quixote* appeared in 1605, the romances could never again be read with quite the same devotion. Nonetheless, scores of editions

appeared in the Peninsula and on the Continent during the sixteenth century—*Amadís* was even translated into Hebrew—and
the vogue continued well into the seventeenth.

Largely because the cycle is so long and the various books were
in such demand, an exact reckoning of the publication of *Amadis*
cannot be had. The bibliographical problems, especially in Italy
and France, are to be explained in part by the history of the cycle
in Spain. There, multiple authorship, the extravagant length of
the cycle, and the many years that elapsed between the writing
of the first four books and the twelfth combine to create inconsistencies and confusions in the narrative. Garcí Ordóñez (or
Rodríguez) de Montalvo, whose name is most commonly associated with *Amadís de Gaula,* wrote (or reworked) only the first
five books. Book V, relating the adventures of Amadís' son Esplandián, came out in 1510. In that year also, a much maligned
sixth book was added by Páez de Ribera, and the imaginative and
industrious Feliciano de Silva produced a seventh in 1514. After
more than a decade, in 1526, Juan Díaz added Book VIII. This
book shocked and infuriated admirers of Amadís and his lively
brother Galaor, for in it Amadís dies, and Galaor turns monk out
of repentance for his sins. Díaz' continuation surely ranks as one
of the great literary betrayals of the century. But Amadís and
Galaor were soon restored to the world in Book IX, which appeared in 1530. The author, Feliciano de Silva, carried on with
Book X in 1532 and Book XI in 1535 and 1551. Meanwhile, someone else—perhaps Pedro de Luján—added a twelfth book in 1546.

The Spanish *Amadís* is long and rambling—words of praise by
some sixteenth-century standards. It is marked by the differing
views and styles of at least five authors and reflects the changes
in manners and ideals of perhaps half a century in Spain. The
cycle concerns the adventures of Amadís, his family and friends,
and their children through several generations. By Book VII

Amadís is already a great grandfather. Moreover, even when Book VI and Book VIII are disregarded, as they habitually are in Spain and other countries, there is some confusion about what happens and who is who. Since neither Amadís nor scarcely any of the other chief characters is permitted to die, there is a grotesque accumulation of characters who have to be reviewed and reexplained periodically. Both Pascual de Gayangos and Sir Henry Thomas supply genealogical tables designed to help the modern reader clarify the relationships among the chief personages.[4]

That this vast romance, which jumbles the minds of modern readers and drives them to such epithets as "confusing," "fantastic," and especially "unreadable," should have been so widely read in Spain and other countries in the sixteenth century is understandable largely in social and political terms. The world of *Amadís* is not entirely chimerical, and the book was not read simply as entertainment or escape from bleak reality. Rather it gave its readers a reflection of the world they recognized— heightened, to be sure, but seldom wholly distorted. Many of the characters became household names, and the romance was widely regarded, both by its champions and its critics, as a practical guide to manners.

In Spain, where a long struggle against the Moors had culminated in the fall of Granada in 1492, *Amadís* reflected a background that seemed familiar. The military virtues of strength and skill, courage and loyalty, shone here in fictional triumph over the forces of evil, and a parallel—not very exact, of course— with the Spanish victory was easily made. To a nobility faced with the absolutism of Ferdinand and Isabella the troubled relationship between Amadís and his lord, King Lisuarte, must have seemed relevant.

Like the Spanish aristocracy, the romance had its roots in the medieval past. If we may judge by allusions to *Amadís,* at least

7

three books were well known in the Peninsula in the fourteenth century; [5] hence the sixteenth-century redaction of Montalvo combined nostalgia for a vanished age with pride in a victorious present. The emphasis in *Amadís* upon ceremony and refined manners was bound to seem appropriate in view of the new emphasis at court upon the social graces. On the other hand, Amadisian insistence on a life of action must have appealed to sixteenth-century Spain, now deeply engaged in exploration and conquest of the New World. The first sight of Mexico City reminded Bernal Díaz del Castillo of those enchanted cities he had read about in *Amadís,* and Spanish explorers along the Pacific coast called the land California because it reminded them of the Amazonian kingdom described in Book V. [6] As the chivalric ideal slowly decayed in Spain, gentlemen were drawn all the more to the romance, in which that ideal gleamed untarnished, and their highest praise of a lady was to call her an Oriana. [7] Although not much in *Amadís* was exclusively Spanish, it mirrored with sufficient fidelity the Spanish gentleman's dream of himself.

Montalvo's *Amadís* and the other romances offered not only a national but a personal ideal. The avowed intention of Spenser's *Faerie Queene,* "to fashion a gentleman or noble person in vertuous and gentle discipline," might as easily apply to *Amadís de Gaula* and its offspring. Amadís is the ideal knight, faithful in love and gallant in war, and his conduct was regarded as worthy of imitation by young Spanish nobility. Ignatius of Loyola was as a young man much influenced by his reading of chivalric romances, and St. Teresa of Ávila grew so infatuated with them that she and her brother Rodrigo de Cepeda composed a romance.

Although Ignatius and Teresa are scarcely typical examples, it would have been a rare young nobleman in sixteenth-century Spain who had not heard of Amadís and did not want to be like him. As Menéndez y Pelayo has said of *Amadís:* "The ideal of the Round Table appears here refined, purified, and ennobled. Without the amorous giddiness of Tristan, without the adulterous passion of Lancelot, without the ambiguous mysticism of the heroes of the Holy Grail, Amadís is the model of the perfect knight, the mirror of courage and courtesy, the pattern of loyal vassals and of pure and constant lovers, the shield and refuge of the weak and needy, the strong arm set to the service of moral order and justice. His slight frailties declare him human but do not dim the luster of his admirable virtues. He is pious without hypocrisy, in love without prudery, although a bit of a weeper, brave without cruelty or boasting, courteous and discreet always, loyal and infrangible in friendship and in love." [8] Don Quixote, whose judgment in such matters is surely worth consideration, says to Sancho: "I would have thee to know, that the famous Amadis du Gaule, was one of the most accomplished Knights Errant. I doe not say well, saying hee was one; for he was the onely, the first, the unike and the Lord of as many as lived in his age." [9]

Although the early appeal of *Amadís* was to the Spanish upper classes, the romance soon percolated downward. Before mid-century it was being read widely by readers of all classes and was being imitated by other writers of chivalric romances. With the broadening of its popularity the chorus of criticism grew. Both critics and champions agreed on one point: the romance was widely read and was, for good or bad, very influential. Spanish humanists like Pedro Mexía, Juan Luis Vives, Diego Gracián, and Antonio de Guevara attacked *Amadís* and other romances because they considered such works inferior, unclassical, and unprofitable. Churchmen were concerned about the effect the secular morality of *Amadís* might have upon credulous readers. In 1531 a royal decree forbade the importation of chivalric romances into the Spanish colonies of the New World on the ground that the books were idle and profane, and a later edict banned their printing.

So great a fictional force for good and evil could not be kept long in the Iberian peninsula. *Amadís* was received warmly into other European languages and took on an international rather than a merely Spanish look. A Spanish edition of the first four books was published in Rome as early as 1519, and beginning in 1546 *Amadís* was available in Italian translation. Readers of Boiardo, Ariosto, and the Tassos were just as captivated by the cycle as Spanish readers, and all books went through many editions. Moreover, Mambrino Roseo da Fabriano added six books of his own devising to those translated out of Spanish and so brought the total number of books in the cycle to eighteen. He also created supplements to Books IV, V, VII, IX, X, XI, and XII. The hero Amadís and his numerous progeny were thus rendered effectively Italianate.

In Germany too *Amadís* became the rage. Since at first translation was made by way of France rather than Spain, the numbering of the German books of *Amadis ausz Frankreich* follows the order of the French version. Some of the Italian supplements of Mambrino Roseo were also introduced, and the cycle for a while seems to have outsold even Lutheran tracts. In 1594 and 1595 three further books, original in German, were added to the total number available. They continue the tale from the point where Mambrino Roseo had left it and extend the number of books in the German version to twenty-four.[10]

More than any other country France took to the Amadis cycle. French reaction must have been in large part patriotic. Amadis, after all, is *of Gaul,* and the French naturally assumed that Gaul was France. Translators were quick to suggest the correspondence of the heroic personages to the heroic royalty of sixteenth-century France. In a complimentary poem introducing Book VIII

Michel Sevin d'Orléans points out that *Amadis* can be read as prefiguring the royal family of France. After first explaining the deep sense of morality that informs the work, he continues:

> Semblablement si bien tu veux entendre,
> Tu y pourras vn autre sens comprendre
> Voulant louër par faitz clers aparens
> Le Roy, ses filz, & ses nobles parens:
> Car Perion, & Amadis, regnerent
> En nostre Gaule & de fait triumpherent,
> Par Perion, donques, & Amadis,
> Et leurs enfans si sages & hardis,
> Le puissant Roy de France est entendu,
> Et tout le sang Royal d'eux descendu. . . .

The sense that *Amadis* was in a fanciful—or even mystical—way involved with the destiny of France is not confined to prefatory material and commendatory poems. French translators occasionally added to the Spanish text in an attempt to further the idea that the romance could be read as a prophetic history of France. In Book XI, Chapter lv, for example, the two heroes Florarlan and Artaxerxes recover from their wounds in the Palace of Mars. They inspect the building, which contains all kinds of armor and engines of war from ancient times to the fictional present. They see depicted on stained-glass windows a history of a future kingdom. A nymph in a forest near a great city in western Europe sings in Latin and French. At one edge of the forest is a "chasteau de plaisance nommé de fontainebelleau." In a prophetic frenzy the nymph foresees a time when the world, especially Europe, is beset by crimes, wars, and desolation.

Florarlan and Artaxerxes then see a picture of a royal cock fighting against a serpent in Insubria (a Latin name for the region around Milan); afterwards the cock is shown in pursuit of three island leopards (apparently the British Isles), while a third fight against a Turkish horse remains to be fought. The royal bird of destiny is pictured as extinguishing with its wings the torch meant to set Europe afire. Finally, victorious, the cock reposes in a delightful garden "entre les fleurs de lis celestes" and a new age of gold ensues. Florarlan and Artaxerxes are greatly impressed by the series of pictures and wish they knew for what people so great a destiny is promised. French readers of the sixteenth century had, of course, no doubts about what was meant, but, if they thought about the matter, they should have been surprised to find this vision in a work translated out of Spanish.

When French destiny and French royalty could be found so readily in *Amadis,* it was inevitable that counterparts should be found also for prominent members of the court. In dedicating Book X to Marguerite of France, the sister of Henry II, Jacques Gohorry says that in her are conjoined all the virtues of such heroines of the romance as Oriane, Lucelle, Heleine, and Alastraxerée. Although in this case the fictional characters were being used merely as a means of passing an extravagant compliment, often the analogy between French and fictional nobility was made much more precise. At least one French gentleman compared Marguerite de Valois, Queen of Navarre, with the beautiful *Amadis* heroine Queen Niquée.[11] Nicholas de Herberay dedicated Book VIII to the powerful Anne de Montmorency, Connétable of France, because, he says, the Connétable who, as Keeper of the Royal Sword, can properly be called "le Cheualier à la grande Espée," obviously resembles the book's hero le Chevalier de l'ardante Espée. In similar fashion Books XI and XII, both dedicated to Diane de Poitiers, suggest at elaborate length the many ways in which she resembles the fictional heroine of those books, Diane, "la plus belle Princesse du monde," who is thus a prophetic delineation.

Analogies of this kind helped make *Amadis de Gaule* fashionable reading and fostered the tendency, already pronounced in Francis I and Henry II and their court circles, toward self-dramatization. The vogue of the romance coincided with the efforts of these kings to renew chivalresque pageantry and ideals. Francis I read *Amadis* for the first time while he was held captive in Spain, and he liked it so well that after his return to his own country he asked Nicholas de Herberay, Seigneur des Essarts, to translate it. The king and his courtiers read the French *Amadis* with delight and enthusiasm, and life at court sometimes took on a cast indistinguishable from that of chivalric fiction. Not only jousts and tournaments but court pageants were often reminiscent of episodes common in *Amadis*. The Field of the Cloth of Gold, whereon Francis met Henry VIII of England in 1520, probably the best-known instance of the French king's fondness for chivalric splendor, might have been taken out of the pages of *Amadis*.

This habit of seeing themselves in Amadisian terms continued among the courtiers throughout the reign of Henry II. The ceremonial entrance of Queen Catherine de Médicis into Lyons in 1548 was particularly reminiscent of events in *Amadis,* for some of her gentlemen disguised themselves as Amazons and passed out gold coins to the ladies of her retinue. This unusual disguise must have been prompted by the famous disguise of Amadis de Grèce as the Amazon Néreïde in Book VIII. Similarly other festive occasions gave rise to spectacles that have a strong flavor of the romance. As part of the entertainment at Fontainebleau in 1564, various lovely ladies were imprisoned in an enchanted tower, where they were guarded by two giants. Charles IX and his brother killed the giants and rescued the damsels, and the whole edifice went up in smoke. At a fête given by Henry III to celebrate the marriage of the queen's sister to the Duke of Joyeuse in 1582, the tableau opposite the king's loge presented a golden-robed Circe seated at the portal of her castle, framed by a pergola in the garden. After a gentleman escaped from her arms to recite a eulogy to the king, she delivered a lament full of grief and rage.[12]

A social historian of this period in France has called *Amadis* "the veritable breviary of the court of Henry II." [13] Not only did young French knights emulate Amadis by riding through the country in search of adventure, but the greatest duel of the century, between Jarnac and La Châtaigneraie, was fought in the presence of Henry II and his court, in the fashion of countless duels in *Amadis*. Some years after the death of Henry II, the old Calvinist soldier François de La Noue complained that everyone at court was accustomed "Amadiser de paroles," to talk in the style of Amadis.[14] Even the letters of cartel written by various French courtiers read as though they were paraphrased out of many such challenges in *Amadis*. One of the best sources of court gossip at this time, the Seigneur de Brantôme, frequently used the name Dariolette (the confidante of Queen Hélisène in Book I) as a generic term for bawd. *Amadis* also did its bit toward fostering at court an interest in neo-Platonic love. Diane de Poitiers, whose intimacy with Henry was piously cloaked under the name of friendship, was hardly averse to a demonstration, albeit fictional, that a lady and her knight might enjoy a relationship wholly spiritual. Since several books of *Amadis* stress such liaisons, French ladies and gentlemen must have perused them with more than passing interest. In a court thus given to the emulation of the chivalric heroes and heroines of *Amadis* it is a grim irony that Henry II himself died of an injury received in a joust.

As in Spain, criticism of *Amadis* in France was sometimes bitter, especially as the romance worked its way down into all levels of society. Although a common charge against it was that it was compounded of prodigious lies, all criticism assumed that it was an enormous force for either good or evil in the lives of its readers. La Noue was so upset by what he thought was the pernicious influence of the romance that in his *Discours politiques et militaires* he devoted an entire chapter to it. He is concerned lest young men believe that they can learn how to wield arms merely by reading *Amadis*. Moreover, he complains that the presence of enchanters in the romance and the attendant exaltation of magic may cause readers to investigate black magic and so lead to the loss of their souls. Clearly, La Noue saw in the reading of *Amadis* dangers that modern readers would not readily imagine. He and Don Quixote remind us that the boundary between the useful and the vain was not always easily made in the sixteenth century.

La Noue mentions also another reason for the enthusiastic reception of *Amadis* in France, the excellence of the French translation. Nicholas de Herberay, Seigneur des Essarts, the translator of the first eight books, was highly praised as a French Homer by Joachim du Bellay, and French literary historians still regard the translation as a literary milestone. Although Herberay's connection with *Amadis* ceased after Book VIII, the quality of his translation commanded such admiration that publishers of some of the later books expected their translators to come close to his standard.

Herberay's translation of Book I, with a prologue addressed to Charles, Duke of Orléans and Angoulême, "second son" of Francis I, appeared in 1540, and it is clear from the dedicatory epistles to succeeding books that the King himself has commanded the translation. Herberay worked systematically, for he added a book every year until 1546, when Book VII was published. Francis died in 1547, and with Book VIII in 1548 Herberay concluded his work on *Amadis*. In 1551 Book IX was made French in a joint translation by Giles Boileau and Claude Colet. The following year came Book X in a translation by Jacques Gohorry, and his version of Book XI followed in 1554. In 1556 Guillaume Aubert added his name to the growing list of translators with a rendering of Book XII. There was then a lapse of fifteen years in France before the work of translation went on.[15] In 1571 Jacques Gohorry returned to the task of turning Spanish into French and produced Book XIII. In 1574 Book XIV appeared in a translation by Antoine Tyron.

With this book the original Spanish *Amadís* was exhausted—the much-despised Books VI and VIII having been ignored—and French publishers now turned to the Italian continuations of Mambrino Roseo for the further adventures of Amadis and his descendants. Between 1576 and 1581 Books XV to XXI appeared in French translation from Italian—though some of the title pages continue to assert Spanish antecedents.

The bibliographical confusions that beset the French *Amadis* are well illustrated by the history of Book XV. There were in France three different versions. The earliest was translated in 1577, but the publisher, Jean Parant, did not like it. In a prefatory letter to the readers he apologizes for the work and says that its fault lies in its unfamiliar idiom, that Tyron is accustomed to "la langue du pays où il demeure." The extent of Parant's concern appears in Book XVI, which was translated by Gabriel Chappuys. There the first thirty-three chapters are a retranslation of Book XV, and Book XVI really begins with Chapter xxxiv. Chappuys' French clearly fell more pleasantly on Parant's ears. Where, for example, Tyron writes: "en quoy il rendit ses sens si fort occupez, qu'il fut par plusieurs foys prest à tomber du cheual," Chappuys renders it: "en laquelle [pensée] il estoit tellement occupé qu'il cuida plusieurs fois tomber de cheual" (*Amadis,* XV, x, 93; *Amadis,* XVI, x, 139). That Parant should have gone to so much trouble and expense emphasizes the high standard of French prose established by the translations of Herberay. In addition to the two versions of Tyron and Chappuys a third Book XV, entirely different, was translated by Chappuys in 1578. The gap caused by the absorption of Tyron's work into Book XVI was thus

quickly filled. Meanwhile the seventeen-year-old Nicholas de Montreux had brought out in 1577 a substantially different version of Book XVI.[16]

Gabriel Chappuys found Mambrino Roseo's Italian to his liking, for he continued his translations until he had brought the cycle in French through Book XXI. Other translators, however, were also at work, for in addition to the Tyron rendition of Book XV, Book XIX was translated by Jacques Charlot and Book XX by Jean Boiron. With Book XXI, advertised on the title page as "vingtvniesme et dernier livre," the French Amadis cycle came to an end. But years later French devotion to *Amadis* was such that three more books created by German writers in 1594 and 1595 were translated into French in 1615.

In all its ramifications, duplications, and inconsistencies the French *Amadis* was the version educated Englishmen read and on occasion imitated. The English translation appeared too late and was too partial to have much influence in Elizabethan or even Jacobean England. Anthony Munday followed Herberay's rendition with relative fidelity, but his first book of *Amadis* was not published until 1589. Book II came out in 1592, and then there were no further books in England until 1619, when an edition of the first four books appeared. Elizabethans who wished to read beyond Book II turned most readily toward France, and it is significant that the romance is seldom referred to in sixteenth-century England otherwise than by its French title or as *Amadis of France.*

As in Spain and France, *Amadis* appealed especially to courtiers, who found in it a mirror of the world as it ought to be. Although chivalric customs and ideals were not nearly so prevalent at the court of Elizabeth as at that of Henry II, she had many reasons for keeping chivalry alive. The Tudors, after all, according to popular legend were descended from King Arthur, and Elizabeth was just as willing to be flattered by the pseudonym of Oriana as by that of Diana, Cynthia, Astrea, or Gloriana. She liked spectacles, and jousts and tournaments provided plenty of pageantry and color.

Besides, the high place accorded to chivalric exercises at the French court inevitably affected the attitudes of Elizabeth and her courtiers. The great French poet Ronsard dedicated his *Elégies, mascarades et bergerie* (1565) to Elizabeth with a flattering preface upon her abilities as a ruler, and one of the poems is a cartel written by him particularly for the Amadisian entertainment at Fontainebleau in 1564. Sir Philip Sidney, who was proud of his knightly accomplishments and mentions them in several of the sonnets in *Astrophel and Stella,* makes a point of the fact that he was judged the winner of a tourney at court not only by his fellow Englishmen but by knights "from that sweet enemy, France."

November 17, Elizabeth's Accession Day, was normally celebrated by a tournament. In 1592 for some reason a tournament was not held, but the Earls of Essex and Cumberland issued a joint cartel to the effect that on the following February 26 they would maintain their mistress to be the "most worthyest and most fayrest, quoth *Amadis de Gaule*." [17] This challenge, in the tradition of chivalric romance, indicates that Essex and Cumberland under the dual guise of Amadis de Gaule stood ready to maintain the beauty of their mistress Oriana (that is, Elizabeth) against any pair of challengers.

Amadisian influence upon polite behavior in France has no parallel in Elizabethan England. Despite the invocation of *Amadis* by Essex and Cumberland, historians are not likely to call the book the breviary of the English court. The impression it made upon the populace was minor, except insofar as Amadis blended into the public mind with such heroes as Guy of Warwick, Bevis of

Hampton, and the Knight of the Sun. *Amadis* is important in England not as a social document but as a literary influence. The growth of English interest in pastoralism in the last quarter of the sixteenth century, the increased antichivalric temper, the style and structure of prose romances by such well-known writers as Robert Greene and Thomas Lodge—all owe something to *Amadis*. Since such major authors as Sidney and Spenser drew upon the romance for ideas and settings, it has to be considered a strong force in English literature.

Its influence in England emphasizes that for the purposes of this study the French *Amadis de Gaule* is central. If we ignore the German additions, we are confronted by a romance of twenty-one books, several of them in duplicate translation and two—Books XV and XVI—in two very different versions. The cycle, written in Spain by at least five authors over a period of about forty years and added to by the Italian Mambrino Roseo, was made French by ten different translators or adaptors, the process of translation extending over nearly as many years as the process of writing. Small wonder that the quality of both writing and translation is sometimes uneven. Moreover, the time of translation was one of vernacular uncertainty. In mid-sixteenth century the French language, under the influence of the Pléiade, was undergoing considerable scrutiny, and the translators of *Amadis* apparently felt under constraint, for there are grumbles about inkhornisms and the introduction into French of such nonnative words as *infanta*.[18]

One of the consequences of multiple authorship and multiple translations is a certain amount of confusion and contradiction in *Amadis*. In view of its history, the existence of noncanonical books, the large scope of the narrative, and the hundreds of characters, discrepancies were well-nigh unavoidable. One is surprised only that there are not more. In his version of Book XVI, for example, Nicholas de Montreux rights an old wrong in the tale by having Niquée die so that Amadis de Grèce can wed Lucelle. But this death does not occur in the Chappuys version of Book XVI, and those readers who happened to read the Montreux adaptation must have been startled to find Niquée blithely attending public functions in Books XX and XXI. The various French translators did not always see eye to eye on some Spanish words and phrases, and their differences affected the English translation. Exotic place names are predictably troublesome, and even the places Amadis habitually frequents are not always easy. Thus Firm Island of the first two books in English becomes suddenly in Book III Enclosed Island and then later, as though Munday was not at all sure, "Firme or Enclosed Isle."

The names of many of the characters are mouth-filling in Spanish—Salustanquidio, Famongomadan, and Brontajar Danfania, to name a few—and they sometimes suffer strange transformations from Spanish to French to English. Even in Spanish there is confusion, for Angriote's brother appears both as Grindonan and Grovadan.[19] Handwriting and careless typesetting were obviously problems in all languages. The Spanish Grinfesa becomes Gonisesa by the time it reaches England, and the formidable Brontajar Danfania becomes in Munday mere Brutaxat. The name of King Arábigo gave a great deal of trouble in England, and in Munday's books it is sometimes Aranigne, sometimes Aramyne, and only occasionally what it ought to be on the basis of the French rendition—Aravigne. The dwarf Ardian becomes somehow Dardan in Munday's Book I, a designation particularly confusing because of the presence in the same book of Dardan the Proud. In Book II the dwarf's name changes to Ardan and so becomes susceptible to confusion with Ardan Canileo (or Canila). In somewhat similar fashion Andalod becomes Andahod in English and the Spanish Gavarte becomes Garnate. One of the most vexed names of all is that of the famed physician Elisabat—whose name in Spanish is also given as Helisabat and Elisabad. Probably because it sounded like a variant of the name of the English queen it gave the English great difficulty. It appears in Munday in such spellings as Elisabet and Elisabel, and in Kirkman's late seventeenth-century translation of Book VI it becomes Mr. Elizabeth and then Mrs. Elizabeth.

Nor are the changes in *Amadis* merely a matter of names and spelling. In crossing the Pyrenees, Amadis became so French that Spanish readers would scarcely have recognized him at certain moments. French translators felt free to improvise, and they added to and subtracted from the narrative with license. A comparison of the Spanish, French, and English texts of the first four books suggests that the reader can never assume that what he finds in the French *Amadis* bears any relation to the Spanish or Italian originals. One scholar has pointed out that several episodes in Book XII of the French *Amadis* were borrowed more or less closely from Ariosto's *Orlando Furioso*,[20] and very likely many other such liberties could be found. Such literary detective work cannot, of course, be contained in this book.

Not only does the French *Amadis* differ from the Spanish in substance, but the French read it in another spirit and with new emphases. In praising Herberay's prose style, the sixteenth-century critic Etienne Pasquier has special praise for Book VIII,[21] and his preference is significant. French readers generally liked the later books, especially Books VII through XII, even more than the early ones. They found the narrative as well as the style more sophisticated. Moreover, accustomed as they were to satires on court life,[22] they must have found the strong antichivalric bent of some episodes in the later books particularly diverting. Unlike the early books, where the adventures of Amadis de Gaule are told in all seriousness, Books VII through XII often stress the ridiculous side of incidents involving Amadis de Grèce and other heroes. Indeed *Amadis* has been given a large share of credit for preparing the way in France for public acceptance of the much more sophisticated and antichivalric *Orlando Furioso*.[23]

Confused in origin, confused in translation, confused even in designation,[24] the French *Amadis* is a baffling work to describe. It resembles nothing so much as one of the composite beasts conjured up by its authors. In Book XIV, for example, Lucendus fights a strange animal that has the head of a dragon, the beak of a griffon, the front paws of a lion, the horns of a basilisk, and the body of a bull. Its hide is impenetrable. Like this beast, *Amadis* is a preposterous blend. It is huge, varied, unnatural, and formidable. If not quite impenetrable, it is at least difficult to get at.

Since an attempt to give a synopsis would be the last refuge of desperation,[25] it may be more sensible to describe what *Amadis* was taken to be in the sixteenth century. Readers then seem to have welcomed it in one or more of four ways. First it was read as a book of war, a record of valor in action, of exemplary deeds done by right-minded knights in the face of overwhelming physical odds. Second, it was read, especially by ladies, as a book of love, a history of the joys and vicissitudes of lovers of all sorts, and a key to the indecipherable mysteries of the heart. Third, it was read as a courtesy book, a guide to proper behavior and polite manners of knights and ladies in peace and war, and a compendium of speeches, challenges, letters, and rhetorical flourishes for different occasions. Finally it was read as a wonderful treasury of stories, exciting and varied, which ran the gamut from tragedy to farce.

II

Amadis as a Book
of War

The life of a knight in *Amadis de Gaule* is, above all, a life of action, and his virtue is almost always muscular. Before a great battle in which he must participate, Silves comforts his mistress Licinie by reminding her that fighting is what a knight exists for, and that "l'homme qui ne tasche d'estre vertueux, en ceste vie, & par sa vertu, d'aider & subuenir aux autres, est moins estimable que . . . bestes brutes" (XX, lxiii, 262ᵛ). Since the only way for a knight to achieve virtue and glory in this life is through combat, the twenty-one books of *Amadis* are saturated with fights. In Book VII, for example, there are more than forty of them, and this number does not include encounters with lions, bears, or other nonhuman opponents. The best knights are the best fighters, and the best fighters are the most loyal lovers, the most devoted friends, and the best rulers. Battle is the measure of a knight in a way that nothing else is.

Chivalric encounters occur in incredible variety and range in size from duels to great battles involving hundreds of thousands of soldiers. Battles are fought on horse and on foot, on shipboard and in the water, indoors and out, upstairs, downstairs, and in my lady's chamber. There are even examples of air combat—like that in which Agesilan of Colchos, mounted on his flying Grifaléon, contends with a flying dragon above the kingdom of the Garamantes (XII, xciv). All kinds of weapons are used, from tooth and claw to enchanted swords and to lances as great as shipmasts. Knights do battle with each other but also with Amazons, giants, magicians, centaurs, lions, bulls, and dragons. Such fabulous opponents as Jason, Achilles, and the Minotaur put in an appearance, since the Amadisian knight in his search for glory does not hesitate to beard even the Underworld.

All these combats fall roughly into two groups: regularized combats, that is wars, duels, tournaments, and enchantments, which have ground rules of some kind, and other combats of an irregular or extemporaneous nature. The first kind of fight is between peers, who recognize the rules and who struggle to conquer by courtesy as well as by force of arms. Christian knights may battle an army of pagans, as they often do in *Amadis,* but the pagans are also knights who observe the laws of chivalry. In the second kind of combat one of the principals may be a knight impelled by wickedness or depravity to disregard his chivalric vows, but more often the forces of evil are represented by wild men or giants or monstrous beasts. In this kind of fighting a knight must rely upon God and his strong right arm.

Since *Amadis* is in large part a book of war, a great deal of the narrative in its many books is devoted to the conduct of immense wars. In the first four books much of the fighting takes place in the British Isles and Gaul—wherever that may be [1]—and the wars are therefore somewhat localized. King Lisuart of Great Britain fights small wars against King Cildadan of Ireland, Queen Madasime, and King Aravigne. So chivalric is the war against Cildadan that both sides agree to settle their differences by a combat to be fought between a hundred knights from each army. Lisuart's war against Amadis in Book IV is not settled so easily. Lisuart's honor is at stake, for he has promised his daughter Oriane in marriage to the Roman prince, and Amadis has abducted her before the ceremony. The war is further complicated by King Aravigne's second invasion of Lisuart's kingdom.

Though the fate of Great Britain frequently rests upon the result of battles fought within the first four books, the scope of the wars in the later books makes the British battles seem mere skirmishes. As the center of activity shifts toward the East, the wars become more horrendous and the fate of all Christendom is threatened. Again and again Amadis and his descendants are called upon to save Europe from hordes of pagan invaders. In Book V the Turks attack Constantinople, and an enormous battle on land and sea ensues. In Book VI the Turks attack Constantinople again, and once more they are repelled after battles on land and sea. In Book VIII the besieged city is Trebizond, and the attacker the soudan of Babylon, but his forces too are routed. In Book XIII King Bulthazar of Russia with one hundred and sixty pagan kings attacks Constantinople, this time so savagely that the city falls. Reinforcements reach the Christian defenders in time to turn the tide, and the pagans are once again defeated. In another attempt to overthrow Christendom in Book XV, King Bultendus, the new king of Russia, arrives with a huge army to seize the Isle of Guindaye. In Book XVII the center of conflict shifts to the Château du Fort, and there once again the fate of all Europe depends upon the outcome.

In Book XIX the tempo of the wars is increased. Constantinople is besieged, Trebizond is threatened by a second army, and the Persian capital of Taurique also comes under attack. As the fury of the siege of Taurique increases in Book XX, prayers for a Christian victory are offered throughout the Western world: "Le pape à Rome, tout le consistoire des Cardinaux & le Clergé entierement prioient Dieu quasi continuellement pour la victoire des Chrestiens & par toute l'Europe se faisoyent plusieurs processions" (lxiii, 259ᵛ–260). In Book XXI there is a final all-out pagan attack upon Christendom. This time Dardanie and Trebizond are the chief centers threatened, but later the war shifts to the kingdom of Alape, where a last great battle takes place.

When Christian knights are not fighting off pagan invaders, they are often to be found fighting one another. In Book X, for example, the rape of Heleine of Apolonye sets off war between Rome and Constantinople that threatens to divide all Christian Europe. Both Rome and Constantinople look for allies, and many a neighboring king has difficulty in deciding on which side to fight. Nor are all invasions religiously motivated. In Book XI the king of Gelde invades the kingdom of Galdap simply in hope of conquest.

Since armageddons occur in almost every book, small wonder that so many of the pages of *Amadis* concern the strategy and conduct of war. The use of siege engines, artillery, and mines, the disposition of troops, the proper deployment of cavalry and archers, the mounting of night attacks, and similar technical matters make up much of the substance of the romance.[2] Before almost every great battle the positioning of soldiers is described, often in merciless detail. There are numerous catalogues of leaders, both pagan and Christian. Sometimes both sides hold reviews of their armies, a task of considerable magnitude when an army numbers in the hundreds of thousands. When Queen Persée reviews the pagan army in Book XIX, she requires two days, one for the cavalry and the second for the infantry, and the author requires two chapters to describe the appearance and equipment of the troops under review. Battles are described with relish and an apparent determination to account for every blow.

Battle details do not always conform to a particular time or place, and indeed the chronology generally is conveniently vague. In some books gunpowder is used, but in others the assumption seems to be that gunpowder is still unknown. In Book V, Chapter xxvi, there are many details about the use of mines to blow up walls, and in Book IX Florisel and his followers blow a hole in an abbey wall by using "pouldre à canon." But perhaps the anachronism bothered both readers and writers, for there is a tendency, particularly in later books, to equip armies with siege engines proper to the first or second century. At the siege of Taurique in Book XIX there is no mention of gunpowder. Instead archers on platforms mounted on elephants are used to rout defenders from the city walls, and there are "plusieurs moutons & instrumens a l'vsage ancien, pour battre & esbranler la muraille" (cii, 337^v).

So seriously are battles taken and so numerous are they that they inevitably assume for the reader a look of sameness. Archers habitually shoot arrows in such profusion that they hide the brightness of the sun, and the knights like Leonidas' Greeks have to fight in the shade. Sparks fly at the clash of sword on armor as from a smith's anvil. Opposing forces crash like thunderbolts, splinters of spears fly up out of sight, and the din is so great that the fighters cannot hear God's thunder. The fall of night usually halts the fighting, though in Book XIII the pagan attack upon Constantinople continues after dark, and the fighters see one another only by the light of sparks from the striking of steel on steel. Night attacks are a favorite device of besieged Christian knights, who wear white shirts over their armor so that they can distinguish friend from foe. Especially in later books the obsession with arithmetic is ruinous to the narrative, which again and again comes to a full stop while the troops of horse and foot are laboriously counted. Moreover, the outcome of battles is always predictable. However close the pagans may come to victory and however superior their numbers, they never win.

Occasionally in the battle scenes the reader comes upon inspired departures from normal procedure. The pagans besieging Taurique in Book XIX hit on the unusual idea of keeping the Christian defenders awake all night by making a great racket with "trompettes & tabourins" (cxxi). A more exotic device is employed in Book V by the Amazon queen Calafie when she uses her griffons —especially trained not to attack women—to help Armato at the siege of Constantinople. Released from their cages, they pluck the astonished and terrified Christian defenders from the walls, carry them high in the air, and drop them, "vne mort malheureuse & estrange!" (l, 141). Unluckily for the pagans, both innovations backfire. The "trompettes & tabourins" keep the pagans awake, while the Christian heroes, inured to the spirit-stirring drums of war, sleep soundly. Calafie's stratagem would have worked except for overeagerness on the part of the Turks. They have been warned to stay out of sight until the griffons, which cannot distinguish Christian from pagan, have cleared the walls of defenders and the Amazons, who have nothing to fear from their griffons, have secured the city. But, eager for booty, the Turks come out of hiding before the huge birds have been recaged, the griffons fall upon them, and the Christians throw back the unsupported Amazons.

Almost all the great battles are accompanied by sea fights, as the Christians seek to cut off the enemy's line of supply and means of escape. Like the land battles, they suffer somewhat from repetition. In a sea fight the usual objective is to grapple and board the enemy ship and then proceed to combat on the decks. An interesting variation in tactics occurs when Greek fire is employed as a defensive measure in the fight for Constantinople in Book XIII, and we are told that this is the first time it was ever used.[3] In the same war the Christian admiral Frandalo deploys more than a hundred frogmen, called in the story by the even more descriptive name of "urinateurs." These daring underwater swimmers "garnis de terrieres & vibrequins . . . allerent occultement percer les vaisseaux aduersaires, qui apres insensiblement faisoyent eau, & en combattant alloyent à font" (xxxvi, 241).

A considerable element of the fantastic pervades all these wars on land and sea. The reader is often asked to believe that a small handful of heroes can stand off an army. In one episode three knights—Fortunian, Lucendus, and Sphéramonde—hack their way through an army of 235,000 besieging the city of Taurique. Yet our heroes frequently display practicality and common sense. Both pagan and Christian princes rely heavily on diplomacy, for in the world of violence in which *Amadis* is set the future of civilized society perpetually hangs by as slender a thread as an alliance. Part of the preparation for great wars consists of writing letters to allies for help, such letters generally being given in full; and again and again great battles are decided by the last-minute arrival of reinforcements sent by a friend.

After a battle it is common for the victor to treat his conquered enemy generously. Knights are continually reminded that they ought to treat their enemies as though they may one day be their friends. Each side tries to outdo the other in courtesy as well as in strength of arms. Moreover, the problems of the common people caught up willy-nilly in the wars of their betters sometimes receive attention. After the pagans have been defeated at Taurique and the siege has been lifted, the Christian armies make plans to leave the kingdom of Perse as quickly as possible in order to relieve the people of the need of feeding so many.

When both sides respect the laws of chivalry and both armies include knights eager for personal glory, duels are to be expected.

Even in the midst of battle knights tend to seek out particular adversaries, and a description of a battle may turn out to be an account of a series of duels. During the truces that are necessary in a long and savage war, unwounded knights like to keep fit by challenging the enemy. On several occasions the outcome of a battle is allowed to rest upon the issue of a combat between champions. In Book XIX the pagans around Constantinople far outnumber the Christians, but after several battles and skirmishes they agree to let the victory hinge on the result of a combat between seven pagans and seven Christians. When the Christians win, the vast pagan army withdraws. The great fight for Taurique is also finally decided by a limited combat. The twin giants called the Cenofales Barbacans challenge any four Christians. Honor forbids the Christians to accept an advantage in numbers, and they choose Sphéramonde and Amadis d'Astre to represent them.

Such combats are almost always conducted under very strict rules. Judges are chosen from each army, and courtesy is carefully observed. When King Bulthazar leads his huge army against Constantinople in Book XIII, he allows a truce so that two of his champions, Mouléon and Mondragon, can challenge the Greek knights Rogel and Agesilan. In the fight Rogel rather quickly dispatches Mondragon, but courtesy and regard for the honor of Agesilan forbid his interfering in the other fight. However, since Mondragon has behaved in a most unchivalric and arrogant way, Rogel does him the final indignity of sitting on his corpse to watch Agesilan defeat Mouléon.

In a work like *Amadis,* wherein scores of challenges are delivered, the effort to avoid obvious repetition sometimes leads writers to fabricate combats of an unusual kind. In Book VIII, when Lisuart has to fight the Amazon Zahara, the agreement is that the first one to lose his weapons loses the contest. Lisuart's sense of propriety prevents him from striking a woman. He therefore

fights on the defensive, parrying her blows until at last he wins
when her sword breaks on his helm. What would have been a
relatively commonplace fight between Agesilan and the Amazon
Pentasilée in Book XIII becomes uncommon when his bellicose
mother Alastraxerée and her mother Calpendre join the fray. In
Book XX the pagan Amazon Cilinde and her brother Galard challenge the Christian Amazon Sauvage and her knight Dorigel. In
such a mixed combat the assumption is that Cilinde will oppose
Sauvage and Galard Dorigel, but Dorigel deliberately upsets ex-
pectation by moving against Cilinde, who loves him. This move
forces Galard to fight against Sauvage, whom he loves.

A good example of the attempt to provide variety in combats
of this kind appears in Book VII, Chapter xxiii, when the Knight
of the Burning Sword has to overcome seven different opponents
at seven towers. Not only do his opponents differ considerably in
size and strength—the knight at the fourth tower being particularly worrisome "car il auoit la teste ressemblante a celle d'vn
Dogue Anglois"—but each opponent insists on using a different
weapon. Burning Sword fights the first opponent with a lance, the
second with a sword, the third with a mace, the fourth with bow
and arrow, the fifth with a battle-axe, and the sixth with cape and
sword. This series of trials indicates clearly that Burning Sword
is a master of all the weapons a good knight should know.

Since wandering knights go often in disguise—a change of
armor suffices—it is not unusual for two combatants to fight on
for hours and then discover that they are friends or relations.
Moreover, since Amazons in armor are indistinguishable from
knights, two fighters frequently discover after many blows and
perhaps a good deal of gore that they are lovers or even husband
and wife. Since royal and noble offspring are often lost or stolen
in childhood and become known to their fathers only after a complicated series of revelations, it is an unusual hero in *Amadis* who

does not sooner or later fight his son. In Book V Amadis in disguise fights with Esplandian so fiercely and evenly that both are seriously wounded before the fight is stopped. Later, in Book VIII, Amadis and Esplandian clash again, though on this occasion their identities are known before either is hurt. In the same book Lisuart and his son Amadis de Grèce have a savage fight that goes on for thirteen hours. Even the onset of darkness does not stop it, for the fighters call for lights and continue "opiniastrez plus que vieilles Mulles, & eschaufez à leur ruyne, comme deux fortz Cerfz durant leur rut" (li, 93^v). The Sohrab and Rustum conflict, without the tragic ending, is a commonplace.

A popular, though less dangerous, form of regularized combat is the joust. Weddings, feasts, and celebrations of all kinds are likely to include tournaments of three or more days' duration. Or under somewhat less public auspices a knight may set up a tent at a bridge or on a forest path and challenge all comers. *Amadis* contains scores of tournaments and casual jousts, and a chapter may be devoted to a blow-by-blow recital of each day's struggle. So in Book VI, Chapter xxviii, a troop of fifty knights is stopped at a bridge by two knights and challenged to joust for passage, two at a time. The entire chapter is given to a detailed account of the action, which comes to a climax, or anticlimax, in the twenty-fifth combat when the challengers—Amadis and Esplandian in disguise—are discovered to be contending with their sons Périon and Lisuart de Grèce.

As in other kinds of combat, a considerable effort is made to render each joust memorable or at least distinguishable from the many others given equal attention. In Book VII Birmartes wanders everywhere fighting for the beauty of Onorie. He carries along a picture of his beloved and makes all his opponents present pictures of their mistresses. When he wins, as he usually does, he takes the portrait of the vanquished knight's lady as a trophy. Each joust thus becomes a beauty contest as well as a fight.

In Montreux's version of Book XVI there occurs a rather strange tournament in which a group of old knights led by Amadis de Gaule, now well over a hundred years of age, issues a challenge to a group of young knights. Since age cannot wither Amadis and sentimentality is strong in the romances, the old knights win. When Florestan jousts with a group of proud Roman knights in Book III, he defeats each of them in particularly ignominious fashion. One breaks a leg when his horse falls, one cries out in pain as Florestan beats him "about the pate," one hits the ground with his saddle still between his legs—whereupon Florestan mockingly awards him the saddle—and one is knocked "into a quagmire, full of stinking soyle and dirt" (xiii, 133).[4]

Another way of providing variety in the round of duels and jousts is through enchantments that can be broken only by combat. Enchantments do not usually endanger life, but the knight who fails may himself be enchanted. Conditions of combat are properly fantastic, for the enchantments are meant to be tests of courage as well as skill in combat. Opponents are sometimes invisible, or they may be automata, giants, dragons, bulls, lions, or composite beasts.

In Book XVI, when Sphéramonde attempts the enchantment of the Isle of Fire, he must first cross a river, which turns out later to have been an optical illusion. Then in succession he engages two savages, a bull and a lion, two giants, and a horrible serpent. The two giants prove invulnerable, and they burn Sphéramonde with their fiery swords. In desperation he leaps into a fountain, which, like the Well of Life in the *Faerie Queene*, rejuvenates him, cures his wounds, and even mends his hacked sword. When he throws some of the water at the giants, they disappear. The serpent, his next opponent, has the head of a dragon, the feet of a man, the legs of an elephant, and the body of a serpent. It has a long tail, a big mouth, sharp teeth, and only one eye—"brief c'estoit vn animal qu'auoit esté plustost formé en enfer qu'au monde" (XVI, xxxvi, 421). All this fighting takes Sphéramonde only past the first part of a three-part enchantment.

Sometimes the knight trying to end an enchantment must fight heroes and monsters of classical mythology or figures of biblical or historical significance. One of the opponents Silves fights in Book XIV is Antaeus-like and no sooner hits the ground dead than he revives as strong as ever. When Silves tries to enter the Château du Fort, he has to fight his way past Hector, King Arthur, Samson, and Hercules. It is interesting to note that Silves wrestles Samson and throws him. In Nicholas de Montreux's version of Book XVI Sphéramonde fights a knight who bears the designation "Achilles debellateur de la race Troyenne" and then faces the Minotaur and a three-headed dog like Cerberus. Opposition of this caliber gives the reader an inkling of the heroic stature of knights like Silves and Sphéramonde.

Combats to end enchantments, like wars, duels, and jousts, are fought in accordance with certain rules, however vague, but there is also in *Amadis* a great deal of fighting in which no holds are barred. Heroes are often engaged against unprincipled knights, savage giants, centaurs, dragons, serpents, and other improbable monsters, and in this kind of fight the amenities of chivalric combat do not apply. A knight who comes upon a damsel screaming in the embrace of an ugly giant cannot concern himself with rules, and even chivalric courtesy is likely to be forgotten. Amadis of Gaul has a special aversion to rapists and readily allows his horse to trample those he unseats. Some of the strangest and most exciting combats in *Amadis* occur outside the bounds of normal chivalric combat.

Adventitious combats are a severe test of a knight's mettle, for the odds almost always lie heavily against him. The character of his opponents, their frightful appearance, and their unorthodox style of fighting try his courage and ingenuity at every turn. Some opponents, like the dread Endriague, whom Amadis kills, are so horrific that any other brave knight could scarcely bear to look at, let alone fight them. Somewhat more human, but still ghastly, are monsters like Ardan Canile and Corneille le Furieux. The giants from the Isle of Cynofale, who keep reappearing throughout *Amadis,* are dog-faced. Alizar, "l'outrageux Roy," is scarcely a winsome opponent. Flat-nosed, with two long fangs protruding from his mouth like boars' tusks, he has a breath so vile that "qui ne le voyoit de pres, le pouuoit bien sentir de loing" (VIII, xcv, 178). Indeed, many giants have at least one animal characteristic. One has, instead of fingernails, claws like a lion "dont quelque fois il dechiroit & demembroit les hommes tous vifs" (XIII, xxvii, 175). Such opponents seldom observe chivalric rules, and their ability as fighters is inversely proportional to their beauty.

Fighting against such bestial and outsized enemies demands special skill and courage. Not only do giants have an advantage in size and weight, but they frequently ride into combat on elephants, camels, unicorns, or other unusual mounts and brandish immense battle-axes, scimitars, or clubs. During a fight they may foam at the mouth like boars, roar like lions or bulls, and blaspheme against their pagan divinities. When fully angered, they may emit fume. Brandinel grew so enraged that "il vomissoit l'escume comme vn vieux mastin enragé, remplissant toute la chambre d'vne vapeur & fumée qui luy sortoit de son horrible gueule" (IX, viii, 20ᵛ). When Madaran is unhorsed in a fight, he begins "à ietter vne fumée espesse de la bouche & des nazeaux" (XI, xiii, 25ᵛ). In another fight Corbalestre, who is even more furious than Madaran, throws "la fumee par les yeux"

(XVIII, vii, 58). The giant Scaranfe emits "feu & fumee par le nez, & par les oreilles" (XVII, xviii, 97^v).

A knight versed in combat avoids direct onslaught and tries to exhaust his huge, unwieldy opponent by feinting and dodging. It is good strategy to infuriate a giant so that his anger inhibits his reason. When Lucendus challenges Mondragon to come out of his castle and fight, the giant is enraged by what he considers the knight's impertinence. He rushes out and after several vain swipes at his opponent becomes so crazed "qu'il luy sortoit par les narines & par la bouche vne grosse & espoisse fumée ainsi que de la gueule de quelque fourneau" (XIV, lix, 81). When he misses Lucendus with his great "coutelaz," the knight severs the giant's right hand. Pain and the sense of irreparable loss add to Mondragon's already ungovernable rage, and he continues the fight "mugissant comme vn toreau enragé." But rendered awkward by his need to fight left-handed, Mondragon is gradually worn down by wounds and weariness, and Lucendus cuts off his head.

Fights against serpents, dragons, sea monsters, and composite beasts are often long and arduous. Silves fights a dragon for six hours. At first his blows are vain, for hitting the dragon is like striking an anvil. Finally Silves manages to run his sword into the monster's open mouth and kill him. Agesilan has an even more difficult time conquering a dragon which plagues the realm of King Trasathée. This unusual dragon has a head like a monkey and throws off "vn venim glué, puant." When Agesilan cuts off his head, two heads grow back. After two more strokes of his mighty sword, Agesilan finds himself confronted by a four-headed monstrosity, but he perseveres and ultimately kills the dragon by cornering it in a cave and burning it to death.

Agesilan's battle with a sea monster is even more frightful. The monster is so huge as to seem shapeless, and only its head and mouth can be distinguished. Mounted on his flying Grifaléon, Agesilan fights the beast for a long time in an encounter like that between a fly and a dog in a hot month. Finally Agesilan dismounts and, all else failing, throws himself into the sea beast's great mouth. There he sets his halberd upright so that the monster cannot close its jaws and then sets to work on its throat with his sword.[5]

The great number of combats and the considerable relish with which they are described suggest that the readers of *Amadis* were far from squeamish. In a fight between Périon and the Knight of the Duchess in Book VII, not only does the bright armor of both knights turn red but their blood dyes the grass underfoot. In Book VIII, in the great battle fought between pagans and Christians for the city of Trebizond, so much blood is spilled that it rises over the horses' pasterns. At the fierce siege in Book X combatants wade in blood up to the knee, and all become so stained that means of identifying friend and foe are utterly lost. In a great battle before Constantinople the carnage is so great that the ground looks as though it has rained blood for a whole day. In another fight before that much-besieged city blood covers the fields in such profusion that they seem to have been swamped by a river of blood. After repeated exposure to such gory hyperbole through many books a credulous reader is tempted to accept as unembroidered the account of a fight on shipboard during which so much blood is spilled that the sea around the ship reddens— especially since the blood proceeds mostly from three giants.

The rain of blood is often accompanied by a hail of severed arms, legs, heads, and assorted internal parts. When attacked by a dozen knights, the enraged Daraïde strews the grass with their arms and legs. Silves cuts off an opponent's head and, throwing it, "la faisoit tourner comme vne boule" (XIV, xiii, 55ᵛ). Anaxartes fights off an attack of twenty knights like a lion amidst a pack of dogs and "à l'vn faisoit voler le bras, à l'autre la teste, l'vn tombe vne iambe aualée, l'autre a la teste fenduë iusques aux dentz, l'autre chet tout estourdy comme s'il eust esté frapé du mal caduque" (IX, ix, 25ᵛ). At one attack on Trebizond a mine blows up and "plus de dix mile Payens volerent en l'air, bras, testes, iambes, & corps, escartez" (VIII, lxxvii, 144). The corporal parts of a notorious enemy may be sent to court as tokens of victory. When Amadis severs Arcalaüs' left hand and Lindoraq's head, he sends both parts as gifts to Lisuart (II, xv). Later Gandalfe's head is sent to Amadis "en vne quasse," and the gentle Oriane has it fixed over the main entrance to the palace (VII, xxxix, 103).

Harshest treatment is reserved for giants, who are disemboweled with unhappy frequency. When Amadis' lance enters Famangomad's body, "the tripes came out of his belly, and he tumbled ouer and ouer" (II, xiii, 87). The giant Astradolfe suffers a similar ignominy at the hands of Moraïzel, and the giant Madaran, wounded in his fight with the Knight of the Phoenix, has to fight with his entrails hanging to the ground (X, xlvi, 89; XI, xiii, 25ᵛ). Even ladies are not free of blood lust, for the princess Barraxa cuts off the heads of prostrate giants with her own hands.

Under such conditions the casualty figures are bound to be high. In one attack upon the Château du Fort the pagans lose more than ten thousand men, and a three-day truce is taken to bury the dead. Fortunately for the Christians in this fight their losses are quite low. In one surprise attack they kill "plus de mille cinq cens hommes" and lose only one knight, who is taken prisoner after his horse has been killed.

The one-sidedness of the casualty list underlines a recurrent moral note in *Amadis,* for in spite of all the blood and horror battle is ultimately terrible only for the mean in spirit. A description of a big battle before the Château du Fort makes the point clear: "En cest endroit voit on la mort pasle, aller auec sa faulx en rond, se tournant de tous costez, l'on entendoit les cris horribles des blessez qui mouroyent, les lamentations de ceux qui auoyent compassion d'eux, les cris de ceux qui demandoyent secours pour eux releuer & finalement le bruit des armes, le hannissement des cheuaux, & le son des trompettes, espouuantable aux craintifs, & agreable aux vertueuz" (XVII, lxiii, 322–322ᵛ).

If the sound of trumpets is sweet to the hero's ears, it is because he knows that in spite of all the blood of chivalric fighting the life of a knight is a life of glory. Though the blows may fall on his armor like the strokes of a blacksmith's hammer on an anvil, he can take some comfort from the fact that they are seldom fatal. Wounds, of course, are common enough, and all heroes spend a substantial part of their lives recuperating from loss of blood. Don Quixote notes sagely that most knights in the romances must be masses of scar tissue. But aside from Amadis' famous scar, by which he is recognized in his disguise as le beau Ténébreux, wounds cause no lasting damage. Nor do scars diminish the girlish beauty that enables knights like Florisel and Agesilan to masquerade as lovely maidens. In short, all the fighting, blood, and violence of *Amadis* seem to hurt only the wicked. The hero remains essentially unscathed, nigh immortal, secure in the love of his mistress and the honor of society.

III

Amadis as a Book of Love

Love and his lady occupy almost as much of the hero's attention as fighting, and there is little doubt that in the sixteenth
century *Amadis de Gaule* was read principally as a book of love.
Since a knight without a lady is unthinkable, all knights of consequence in *Amadis* have at least one. Ladies provide the incentive
for many a battle and are often the cause for war. Amadis and
King Lisuart fall out when the king, ignorant of Amadis' love
for his daughter Oriane, and bound to grant a boon, insists on
her wedding the Roman prince Patin. The great war between
Rome and Constantinople begins when Florisel de Niquée runs
off with Heleine de Apolonye, who is betrothed to the Roman
prince Lucidor. Indeed, love and war are closely related throughout the many books of *Amadis*, and heroes generally excel in both
pursuits. The enchantments make the point, for many are to be
broken only by the knight who is both the greatest warrior and
the most loyal lover.

Although the emphasis on love in *Amadis* attracted many sixteenth-century readers, especially women, it alienated others.

43

There was, at any rate, a great deal of criticism directed at the depiction of love among the knights and ladies in the various books. Some critics charged that the romance poisoned the minds, inflamed the senses, and corrupted the morals of its readers.[1] It is against such charges that Gabriel Chappuys feels obliged to retort in his translation of Book XVI. I confess, he says, that previous books have dealt with love, but it is a love "honneste & non lascif."

Despite Chappuys' reassurance, the debate did not end with the sixteenth century. Even among modern commentators on the work both approval and disapproval of the treatment of love can be found. Menéndez y Pelayo calls *Amadís* "the epic of faithfulness in love," but a more hostile critic, with the French version in mind, remarks that "the license of the amorous episodes is . . . pushed much further in *Amadis* than in the poem of Ariosto."[2] Both comments can be amply illustrated.

Love is endemic in the dream world of *Amadis,* and all its people are susceptible. With love in the air a knight need not even see a lady to fall in love. Through more than half of Book V Esplandian loves Léonorine and she him. He has trouble sleeping, and she is tormented by thoughts of him. Yet neither has set eyes on the other. Each has fallen in love by hearsay. Fie upon such love, says the king of Dace to Esplandian, for it is merely "feu de paille, aussi tost mort qu'allumé" (xxxiii, 87). But this sensible comment falls on deaf ears in the world of *Amadis.* Zaïr, the soudan of Babylon, asleep in his own bed, should be safe. He dreams, however, of the beauteous Onolorie of Trebizond, falls madly in love with his dream, and is led at last to attack the city to get her (VIII, i).

Love frequently reaches epidemic proportions and, plague-like, infects everyone. When Agesilan first sees Diane, he "fut rauie iusques au tiers ciel (qui est la sphere de Venus)" (XI, xx, 38).

He feels cold, he trembles all over, his heart pounds, and he cannot speak. He faints. Indeed many knights are so afflicted when they first glimpse their mistresses. Anaxartes, at first sight of the lovely Oriane, daughter of Olorius, faints and later faints twice more. Later still he faints again, but by this time Artymire "estoit acoustumée de le voir tomber en telles sincopisies" (IX, lxvi, 170ᵛ), and she helps him. When Mouton de Lica sees a portrait of Niquée and immediately falls in love with her, he does not faint. Instead love makes him so sick that his trip to see her has to be delayed a month (VIII, xxix). Amadis de Grèce in the throes of love "se iette sur l'herbe ou il se tourne & roule douloureusement." Finistée, who comes upon him in this plight, cannot understand at first what is wrong. Is he wounded? She finds that his hands are "mouillées d'vne sueur froide." Amadis can only describe his sensations in figurative language: "ie resemble à Prometheüs de qui le foye reuenant d'autant qu'il est rongé sert de continuelle viande à l'autour de Caucase" (XI, lxiv, 104ᵛ–105). Even so experienced a ladies' man as Rogel de Grèce finds that his previous conquests have not gained him immunity against the pangs of true love, for "le sang luy fuyt du visage, & deuint pasle comme vn trespassé" (XI, lxxi, 117ᵛ).

The end result of love sickness can be death, and in *Amadis* such an end is not rare. A damsel reports to Amadis de Grèce an occurrence at the court in London. There a knight very much in love with Lucelle heaved a great sigh and said, "Ah Dieu! Dieu! faut il que la recompense de loyale amour me soit telle?" and fell dead (VIII, xx, 37).

Amadis de Gaule, a paragon of devotion and sanity in love, has his share of difficulties. Early in his love for Oriane he has a decided reaction to the mere mention of her name: "his hart began to tremble in such sort, as he had fallen beside his Horse, but that Gandalin staied him" (I, vi, 37). Later he almost falls again when the Damsel of Denmark brings him a letter from his beloved. He sometimes slips into a trance as a result of mooning over Oriane. This is not a problem as long as the faithful Gandalin is near to look after him, but it can be a dangerous habit. In the midst of a hard fight against Dardan the sight of Oriane among the spectators so transports Amadis that he forgets all about his opponent and is alerted to his danger only at the last second by a shriek from the Damsel of Denmark (I, xiv). After he has been rejected by Oriane, he seeks solace in the life of a hermit. But even this austere discipline cannot cure him. He slowly wastes away, and "his continuall weeping made such furrowes in his face, that there was nothing to bee discerned but skin and bone" (II, x, 53–54). The disease of love brings him finally to the verge of death and so changes his appearance that the Damsel of Denmark does not at first recognize him—even though she is searching for him.

The havoc worked on heroic bodies mirrors the desolation wrought on heroic psyches. Jealousy is a recurring problem of chivalric lovers and their ladies. Mabile urges Amadis to be more careful of his conduct with other women, "for it is a very hard matter wholly to banish and extinguish jealousie from a woman after it is much rooted in her mind" (II, xvii, 127). Since the jealousy of Oriane has already led to a long separation between her and Amadis and almost to his death, her suspicions begin to look like obsessions. Ladies in *Amadis* are easily made jealous, and Amadis' troubles are paralleled by those of other knights in other books.

Yet jealousy appears to be only mildly irrational in comparison with some other conditions of the mind. Oriane more than once threatens to kill herself. Amadis de Grèce becomes so depressed as a result of his love for Niquée that he tries to commit suicide, and if Gradamarte had not prevented him "deux ou trois foys," he would have thrust his sword into his own stomach (VIII, lxvi, 120). Many heroes and heroines in the romance are tempted to give way to suicidal impulses, and only the fear of hell discourages the final act.

Madness, in spite of the example of Orlando, is somewhat less common, although there are several instances. The beauty of Niquée has an unsettling effect on her beholders, and her father is urged to keep her out of sight, for "quiconque la regarderoit (vaincu d'Amour) ou perdroit l'entendement ou mourroit sans longue demeure" (VIII, xviii, 31ᵛ–32). The beauty of Diane drives Daraïde to talk to himself in the garden and carve her name on the bark of trees (XI, xxxiii, 59). The loss of Sestiliane leads Arlanges to maunder "comme fol par le mond" in search of her. He suffers under the delusion that he has lost his soul. His attention wanders, and he does not respond sensibly to questions. He requires the constant supervision of his faithful squire (XIX, i–ii). Probably the most noteworthy instance of madness caused by love is the case of Galanides, the king of Galdap. He falls in love with Daraïde—who is really Agesilan in disguise as a maid. When Galanides proposes and the feigned Daraïde refuses, the king falls ill and goes without eating and sleeping. Soon "son sens se troubla, & se mit à faire tant de folies & grimaces hydeuses qu'on l'enferma en vne chambre" (XI, lxxxiv, 143ᵛ).

Sometimes the pangs of love grow so intense that they drive the sufferer to attempt ritualistic alleviation. Rituals involving a procession, obeisance to a statue of Cupid, and sacrificial victims occur in several books, and some lovers even try to quench love's fire by drinking blood. The most gruesome of these ceremonial acts require human sacrifices and a procession much like that in the Mask of Cupid in the *Faerie Queene*. Slightly less barbaric are the rites in connection with the worship of Alastraxerée on the Isle of Colchos. There the ruler Falanges has fallen so violently

47

in love with Alastraxerée that he builds a temple dedicated to her worship. The elaborate ceremony includes the sacrifice of the hearts of various beasts.[3] Marfire, who loves Filisel so devotedly that she keeps "vne effigie" of him, conducts another sort of ceremony wherein she wounds herself and sprinkles blood on the image to soften the hard heart of Filisel.[4]

All right-minded knights condemn these love cults as wicked and idolatrous, and they set out to abolish them, by force or by persuasion. There persist, however, peculiar religious overtones in many expressions of love for a mistress. She is a goddess who can do no wrong. When Oriane rejects him, Amadis will hear no complaints about her behavior from his loyal friend Gandalin. Oriane, he says, has never done wrong, and if he should die, his death will have been justified because she has commanded it (II, vi). And Bruno, when he thinks he is going to die of a severe wound, asks Lasinde to send to his lady Melicie "the right sleeue of my shirt, thus tincturde in my true heartblood, and seauen letters foulded vp therein" (III, xii, 123). In the context of *Amadis* this bequest seems the perfectly natural act of a knight who loves deeply, and it is described with approval. Yet it has distinct sacrificial overtones. Rogel clearly points out the dilemma of every good knight as he and Brianges discuss the nature of true love: "Auoir donné sa volunté à sa Dame (dist don Brianges) & ne se pouuoir gouuerner par autre volonté que par le sienne, en l'aymant entierement de tout son cueur. C'est en ceste façon (dist don Rogel) qu'il fault aymer Dieu, non pas les femmes" (XII, lxxi, 182ᵛ).

In spite of Rogel's reservation, *Amadis* is generally a celebration of love in Brianges' terms. When the pagan princess Sestiliane and the Christian knight Arlanges fall in love in Book XVII, she gives him "vne relique . . . qui a touché la chasse du corps de nostre sainct Prophete Mahommet" (lxviii, 342). He accepts it with delight, not because it has associations with Mahomet but because it has touched her. She is love's saint.

48

Amadis *as a Book of Love*

Again and again in the books of the romance the argument is made that love is all-powerful. Florisel runs off with Heleine quite against her father's wishes. She is, after all, betrothed to Lucidor. But in the view of the author and the other characters Florisel has clearly done the right thing. Heleine herself insists that love is absolute. "Amour n'est point suiect aux loix des hommes," she says, and points out how love has ruled Solomon, David, Aristotle, Demosthenes, Virgil, "& autres infiniz denommez es histoires tant anciennes que modernes" (IX, lvii, 149). When Amadis de Grèce, in disguise as the warrior maid Néréïde, arrives in Trebizond after eloping with Niquée, he confesses before the whole court. The power of love, he says, is shown not only in his readiness to assume the garb of the fair sex but also in his willingness to risk his reputation: "Car qui ayme . . . est du tout hors sa puissance, & subiet à faire la volonté de l'afection qui le gouuerne" (VIII, xci, 171ᵛ). In the world of *Amadis* everyone loves a lover—except, of course, the rival and the angry father.

The quasi-religious view of love so common in *Amadis* was not novel in the sixteenth century. The idea that because love is a law unto itself a lover is to be excused for crimes committed in its name met with vigorous dissent among those readers with limited tolerance for the sentimental excesses of chivalric romance. Nevertheless, righteous wrath was tempered by the realization that this view of love was a sin to which most romances were equally prone. Not the chivalric philosophy of love but chivalric practice bothered sixteenth-century moralists. They found that *Amadis* went far beyond *Palmerin* and *The Mirror of Knighthood* and other sixteenth-century romances in retailing in the most explicit terms the love of knight and lady. Chappuys' assertion to the contrary, *Amadis* was liberally salted with passages that are certainly *lascif*. Was this kind of writing to be excused by talk of love being above and beyond the laws of man?

In Book XVII Amadis d'Astre—in disguise as the Chevalier du

Feu—meets Emiliane, lovely daughter of the princess Alériane. Emiliane falls in love with him, and her mother obligingly consults a magician to find out who the knight really is. Whereas marriage is not in the stars, a son is; and therefore, on a night designated by the magician as auspicious, Emiliane, with her mother's blessing, steals into Amadis' bed, trembling as much out of fear of being rejected as out of shame. The startled Amadis tries to dissuade her from her purpose, but he is overcome in part by the fact that she knows his true identity and in part by her assurance that "il est ainsi ordonné des cieux." When she threatens to kill herself unless he consents, poor Amadis has no arguments left, and shortly "de Damoiselle elle fut faite femme." They stay the night "reiterans leur amoureuse guerre," Amadis disturbed only by the thought of his disloyalty to Rosaliane (XVII, xxxvii). Though his conscience later bothers him somewhat, he, like Emiliane and her mother, is impressed by the idea of being in the grip of a vast, unopposable destiny.

The Amadis-Emiliane episode, offensive as it may have been to strict sixteenth-century moralists—and some among them were well acquainted with the romance—contained very little to worry the conscience of the devoted reader of romances. The idea of love as an overruling force is, after all, very old, and there is nothing in the least lascivious in the description of the incident. The debate in bed is even mildly humorous and succeeds to some degree in intellectually sterilizing what follows. If all erotic encounters in *Amadis* were so handled, one could have little sympathy with sixteenth-century complaints about its lewdness. The truth is that the first fourteen books of the French *Amadis* contain numerous bedroom episodes, lavish in detail and evidently designed to titillate.

So explicit is *Amadis* on occasion that it almost seems to be intended in part as a guide for young men about town bent on seduction. At one point, for example, Amadis de Grèce finds himself alone with Lucelle and "prit tant de hardiesse sur l'heure, que, la baisant, auança sa main droite iusques sur le tetin, qu'il toucha à nu, s'oubliant pour ce coup, & non sans cause: car Amour, & bonne volonte, consentans à l'heur du desir qui s'ofroit, l'estomac d'elle luy faisoit repousser si haut vn gorgias de crespe, que l'oeil pouuoit iouïr a la desrobée de ce que l'acoustrement deuoit cacher" (VIII, lii, 96–96^v). A description of this kind couched in such direct and graphic language is relatively uncommon in Renaissance narrative and cannot easily be paralleled in chivalric romance.

On another occasion Amadis de Grèce attempts to seduce Lucelle on shipboard in the midst of a wild storm at sea. In her fear of drowning she clings to him, and he kisses her. The darkness and turmoil work in his favor, "de sorte que gaignant païs petit à petit, vint des baisers à l'atouchement du tetin: & si eust passé outre . . . si honte poussee par l'honneur ne s'en fust meslee . . ." (VII, xxi, 58). The phrase "gaignant païs" offers a clue to the spirit in which the episode was meant to be read. In addition to the wind and rain and the tossing of the ship Amadis has to contend with another unfavorable condition. He makes his attempt upon Lucelle's virginity virtually in the presence of her parents, who are prevented from observing the lovers only because of the darkness brought on by the storm.

Often the comic element in such erotic descriptions verges on the ludicrous or the coarse. In Book VIII Amadis de Grèce disguises himself as a maid in order to gain access to the tower in which the beauteous Niquée is kept under guard. He succeeds and is accepted among Niquée's attendants under the name of Néréide. Unfortunately his feminine disguise is so convincing that the old soudan falls in love with him and tries to seduce him. Will you marry me, asks the dotard, and "il vouloit en la baisant venir & au tetin, & plus bas" (VIII, lxvii, 122). The much-embarrassed Néreïde has to talk fast and protest girlish chastity.

One day the soudan manages to corner Néreïde. "Et à ceste cause estans eux deux seulz, & l'huis bien barré, entreprit, sans faire longue harengue venir au point ou il tendoit, si toutes choses eussent aussi bien tendu qu'il desiroit: mais d'autant que l'impotente vieillesse luy ostoit la force des braz, elle luy auoit encores moins laissé le pouuoir du surplus . . ." (VIII, lxvii, 124). And so that the reader can fully savor the episode, the author reverts to figurative language borrowed out of Ariosto: "Toutefois son courtaud desbridé & hors l'estable tresbuche à toutes heurtes, estant si amorty à cause des ans passez, que tant plus il luy secouë la bride, ou le trauaille, & moins se trouue à son commandement, sans quasi faire semblant ny de sauter, ny de regiber, tenant tousiours la teste baissée: car le corps debile ne corespond aucunement à tel desir" (VII, lxvii, 124).[5] Néreïde has to stifle his laughter, and many a sixteenth-century reader must have roared.

Amadis de Grèce's difficulties with the amorous old soudan are mild when compared with those of Agesilan. Disguised as the warrior maiden Daraïde, Agesilan is thrown ashore in Galdap, where King Galanides falls dotingly in love with him. Agesilan's problems are doubled when Queen Salderne penetrates his disguise and falls in love with him too. Poor Agesilan, already in love with Diane, has to fend off advances from front and rear. Galanides is not quite so persistent as Néreïde's soudan, but Salderne, pursuing the advantage of her sex, one night arrays herself in her most elegant nightdress and arranges her person "assez pour esmouuoir vn Narcissus, ou Hypolite, & tous les austeres & reuesches philosophes abhorrens les oeuures de nature." Failing to arouse Agesilan immediately, she throws herself upon him, and "le manioit dessouz les draps & luy redoubloit les baisers secz, moettes, en maintes manieres" (XI, lxxxv, 144ᵛ–145).

The Amadisian romancer, like Iachimo in *Cymbeline,* shows an indelicate willingness to number the turns. When Lisuart marries Onolorie, and Périon Gricilerie, the author protests that he is unable to describe accurately the joys of the two young married couples, but in the next breath he declares: "Ceux qui ont esprouué semblable auanture, supliront au surplus, & les autres aprentiz doiuent estimer, que pour la trois ny pour la quarte, & sixiesme rencontre, ne se voulurent tenir recreuz ou lassez, ains passans outre, & reprenans aleine, se mirent en diuers propoz." After a few words "la baisoit & mignotoit auec telle douceur, que le feu presque amorty par les efortz precedans, reprit sa vigueur, sans qu'ilz le sceussent du tout estaindre pour l'heure, que la recharge ne fust encores double." Lest anyone think poorly of knightly vigor, Lisuart arises next morning only "apres luy auoir donné le bon iour, ny plus ny moins qu'elle auoit receu le bon soir" (VIII, xliv, 81^v–82).

All told, sexual love is presented in *Amadis de Gaule* probably with more frankness, variety, and sensationalism than in any other European literary work of the sixteenth century. Where else can one find sex in such varied guise? Where find so single-minded a lover as Amadis de Grèce, who tries to make love to Lucelle on a ship in danger of sinking, and who tries to make love to Niquée by disguising himself as a girl? Where find so ingenious a lover as Esplandian, who arranges to see his mistress by having himself delivered in a coffin? (V, xxxvi). Or Agesilan, who is tempted to make advances to Diane while they are high in the air on the back of the Grifaléon?[6] Moreover, the presence in the work of Don Juan types—Galaor in the early books and Rogel in the later—indicates that the attempt to titillate readers was quite deliberate. Both Galaor and Rogel take an almost professional attitude toward seduction, and Rogel in particular has a long list of conquests.

Frank as it is in the handling of the erotic, *Amadis* shows not the least reluctance to treat love in its bestial or perverse aspects. The myth of Pasiphaë is frequently invoked. For example, a giant vassal of the king of Thrace falls in love with a cow and becomes so infatuated that "venant à auoir affaire à sa femme engendra en elle, par force d'imagination, vne creature si estrange & monstreuse, que depuis le nombril à bas, il se trouua ayant la forme de Thoreau, & le surplus d'homme hors qu'il auoit deux cornes en la teste, quatre bras, & quatre mains" (VIII, xcii, 173).

Incest is frequently another source of monstrosities. The awesome Cavalyon, the offspring of Gregaste and her son, is part horse, part man, with the limbs and claws of a lion. It runs on eight feet. Its birth was permitted by God as an example of the horror of incest (XI, lxxii). The dread Endriague is the product of incestuous union between the giantess Brandaginde and her father. "It was so full of haire on the face, feete and hands, as it appeared to be a Beare, all the rest of the body was couered ouer with scailes, so hard and strong, as no arrow shot from a Bow could pierce them. . . ." The nurses attending Brandaginde at the birth are stunned at the sight of her offspring. One of them attempts to suckle it, "at whose brest it drew so strongly, and without any intermission, as, notwithstanding all her loud cryes, he sucked the very heart blood out of her body, so that she fell downe dead on the floore" (III, x, 98–99). In Book VIII Niquée's father and brother both fall in love with her, and in the case of her brother emergency treatment—enchantment—is required for a complete cure.[7] The same treatment has to be prescribed in Book XVI for Clareneuf, who falls in love with his sister Daraïse and thereby causes the enchantment of the Isle of the Lake.[8]

Homosexuality, a rare subject in sixteenth-century romances, crops up on several occasions in *Amadis,* though always in cases of mistaken identity. The device of a knight disguised as a damsel or a damsel disguised as a knight—a favorite in some books of *Amadis*—lends itself readily to homosexual implications. The episode in which Amadis de Grèce in disguise as Néreïde excites the love of the old soudan has already been mentioned. Similarly Agesilan in disguise as Daraïde awakens love in the heart of Galtazar de Barberousse, who never for the rest of his life entirely recovers.[9]

Lesbianism occurs particularly in Book XI, where Agesilan in his disguise as Daraïde arouses strange feelings in the breast of Diane, and Agesilan's friend Arlanges, similarly disguised as Garaye, similarly perturbs Cléophile. Daraïde kisses Diane, "en luy succant le miel de sa bouche pourprée," and Diane finds herself deeply stirred. She cannot understand why she should feel so towards a woman and says: "Fille aymer fille, helas qu'est-ce sinon estre amoureux de la lune qu'il faudroit prendre aux dentz? Las Pasiphaë ne fut iamais si malheureuse pour auoir aymé vn taureau, combien que beste indigne de son affection. Ne Myrrha semblablement en son amour incestueux. Ne Pigmalion amoureux de son ymage que Venus luy viuifia & anima" (XI, xxxiii, 59ᵛ). The strangeness of the relationship between Diane and Daraïde is dwelt on at considerable length and in a variety of tones—wonder, vague alarm, mild horror, and amusement. Daraïde is described by Galtazire as saying that she is not the first woman who has loved another "& que Sapho la lirique l'auoit esté d'Amytone & Atthis, & que sa nation y estoit plus sugette que les autres" (XI, lxxxii, 139ᵛ). Daraïde goes so far as to compose and sing a song in which she likens her love for Diane to the perverted love of Pasiphaë (XII, xxviii, 77).

Although strange and terrible manifestations of love have a prominent place in *Amadis*, love wears also a more beneficent face. Lovers are generally loyal and speak of the union of souls rather than bodies. Many of the enchantments are tests of loyalty in love—the kind of test Amadis de Gaule passes by making his way successfully through the Arch of True Lovers in Book II— and knights who are constant to their ladies gain hereby a glory almost on a par with that gained by combat. When Galaor and Rogel fare badly in enchantments of this kind, their failures are understood to represent deficiencies in their characters. True lovers take courage in times of crisis merely from the remembrance of their mistresses. When Amadis in the midst of a difficult fight catches sight of Oriane, "hee felt his vertue augmented in such sort, that hee was as fresh and lustie, as if but then he entred the field" (I, xiv, 89). And love, even though it is a kind of sickness and sometimes causes death, can be curative and restorative. The wounded Daraïde recovers more quickly than the surgeons had anticipated, "tant eut l'ame de force à auancer la guerison du corps" (XI, lxxxiii, 140). True lovers generally find that love has its bright side.

Moreover, a large number of unrequited lovers, instead of languishing or committing suicide, seem to gain spiritual strength. Some ladies who fall in love with a hero already committed to another ask only to be allowed to remain in the loved one's presence and to help him—even in the courting of his true love. Artymire loves Anaxartes and follows him in the hope that he may learn to love her. When he confesses his love for Oriane, she feels at first desolate, but then, in a way characteristic of the type, offers to help him win Oriane. Finistée loves Amadis de Grèce, and Carmelle loves Esplandian, but each unselfishly gives up her dream of marriage upon learning that he loves another. The most famous of the type is probably Gradafilée, whose unselfish love for Lisuart is remembered by characters in later books. She falls in love with Lisuart although she knows that he loves Onolorie and that her love is hopeless. All she asks is Lisuart's permission to remain continually in his presence. When his life depends on a combat, she disguises herself as a knight and helps save him—"Qui," declares the author, "me fait estimer, qu'entre toutes les amours & fidelitez qui se ramenteurent onques, voyre entre les plus passionez des fleches du petit dieu, qui firent iamais preuue de leur fermeté, ceste Damoyselle doit auoir le premier lieu" (VIII, xv, 26).

Women like Gradafilée, who succeed in sublimating sensual impulses, have advanced part way up the neo-Platonic ladder of Renaissance love. They have reached the stage where the ideal has become preferable to the actual. Gradafilée still enjoys being in Lisuart's company, but he recognizes that her state of mind in no way depends on his presence. In fact, he thinks she has surpassed the Roman soldier who willingly thrust his arm into the fire. Whereas Mucius Scaevola burned only his arm, she has burned away "par force d'amour, le cueur, & le corps, ou repose l'ame gentile, & l'esprit si parfait" (VIII, xvi, 27). His statement strengthens the neo-Platonic implications, for it suggests a love that enjoys a higher existence divorced from the senses. Gradafilée is thus to be distinguished from ladies like Lucelle, who enters a nunnery after she has been abandoned by Amadis de Grèce. There she remains, bitter and brooding, until the death of Niquée finally allows Amadis to marry her.[10]

Other expressions of neo-Platonic doctrine are common enough in some books of *Amadis*, though they are not always pure and undiluted. They are sometimes so mixed with sentimentalism or Petrarchanism that they are hard to label. For example, the idea frequently recurs that a lover is a portrait of his lady. In Book IX Arlande says that the painting of Florisel is only partial, that she herself is the best depiction of him since she carries him whole in her heart (xlvii). Similarly when Amadis de Grèce attempts to explain to Lucelle the nature of their love, he says: "Nous sommes comme les deux lutz acordez en mesmes tons, tellement qu'en sonnant l'vn, les cordes non touchées de l'autre (qui est vis a vis) s'esmeuuent & branlent la paille si luy metz dessus" (X, liv, 107). The sentiments of both Arlande and Amadis may be labeled neo-Platonic, but such remarks are so commonplace in the literature of this time that the label is not helpful.

Other references more clearly show neo-Platonic influence. When Lisuart and Périon meet their ladies after a separation, their reunion is celebrated in the following words: "s'il est vray les corps auoir esté doubles, nous sommes les parties separées & à present reiointes, mieux qu'elles ne furent oncques" (VIII, iii, 6). When tempted by Queen Salderne, Daraïde tries to explain to her that he is not really a man since the masculine half of his soul has been given to a woman "tellement que ce qui me reste est vrayement feminin, n'ayant nomplus de puissance d'homme enuers les autres dames, que si i'estoys femme vraye" (XI, lxxxv, 145). And when saying farewell to Diane, Daraïde argues that only the body goes, the soul remains behind (XI, lvi).

The neo-Platonic allusions lead up to the central episode in Book XI. There the lovers Garaye and Cléophile are clearly intended as models of neo-Platonic love in inaction. Garaye assures Cléophile that his love for her is pure since it is the love of his soul for hers. Love begins, he admits, in the eye, and desire spreads through the senses, all the while "volons laisser l'ombre, & de tous noz sens embrasser la realle verité." He and she are born for each other. "Parquoy estans si semblables de corps & d'ames se ioignent en vnion pafaitte [*sic*], quasi de deux en vn, que les anciens ont appellé homfenin, qu'il n'est possible que chose du monde puisse iamais separer ne desioindre" (XI, lxxxviii, 151^v–152). Garaye and Cléophile share the neo-Platonic ecstasy in which their souls mingle outside their bodies.[11]

The neo-Platonic ecstasy experienced by Garaye and Cléophile is the high point in the spiritualization of love in *Amadis,* and nothing like it recurs. The lover in *Amadis* generally concentrates on the here and now and prefers the body over the soul. The ecstatic union of the lover with God or Universal Beauty, so rhapsodically described by Cardinal Bembo in Castiglione's *Cortegiano,* is nowhere to be found. In spite of all the holy wars, God and religion are overshadowed by Cupid. They represent the last refuge of a lady deserted by her lover or of a knight too old for the physical love that remains the central concern of all knights not yet superannuated.

If one were forced to choose an episode that best sums up the Amadisian attitude toward love, he would not choose the love of Garaye and Cléophile any more than that of Brandaginde and her father. A choice that better typifies love in the romance's twenty-one books is the episode in which Amadis d'Astre in his wanderings comes upon an old shepherd living quietly with his young wife and young child in a countryside otherwise deserted. Amadis is impressed enough to say: "si ie n'estois Amadis d'Astre, ie ne voudrois estre autre que ce Berger . . ." (XVII, lxxxv, 414). Amadis' wish is in part an echo of the sentimentalism that the pastoral life habitually invokes in sixteenth-century literature after Sannazaro; but Amadis also sees here the primary ingredient of the good life: love that, though quiet and peaceful, remains sexual even into old age.

The expression of neo-Platonic doctrines of love in *Amadis* is of particular interest to literary historians, for the romance has not been previously emphasized as important in the spread of neo-Platonic ideas.[12] Writers who, like Edouard Bourciez and Eugène Baret, have discussed its literary and cultural influence have stressed its treatment of sexual love and its influence upon the rise of the sentimental novel in France. The strong neo-Platonic strain strengthens their case for *Amadis* as a courtesy book, for neo-Platonism provides a link between the romance and Castiglione's *Courtier,* that great popular purveyor of the neo-Platonic gospel.

IV

Amadis as a Courtesy Book

As a series of marvelous tales of knights errant, as a book of war, and as a guide to the art of love, *Amadis de Gaule* captivated Renaissance readers of all classes, but among the aristocracy it was also esteemed as a courtesy book. This facet of the romance troubled the self-appointed guardians of French morality, and it has continued to provide a target for a large part of later commentary. In the opinion of many scholars the *Amadis* cycle not only reflected a continuing, if decadent, preoccupation with chivalric customs and ideals but also had a pronounced and sometimes pernicious influence on the manners of sixteenth-century France.

The studies of Edouard Bourciez and Eugène Baret have helped a great deal to put *Amadis* in reasonable perspective, but they have not ended the attacks upon it as a bad or inconsiderable influence. A modern critic, A. Cioranescu, in a disparaging vein, says: "This work was considered throughout the sixteenth century to be a book of war, morals, and virtue, quite the opposite of what it really was. It was one of the books that more often than not were put into the hands of boys and young people to open their eyes to the facts of life. This no doubt accounts in large part for the lax morality in the time of the later Valois." [1] E. B. Place does not agree that the influence of the work was entirely bad. He believes that *Le Thresor des liures d'Amadis*, a collection of speeches, letters, and soliloquies culled from the various books of *Amadis*, served as a refining influence. He lists the French editions printed between 1559 and 1605, and, after comparing the number with that of editions of Castiglione's *Cortegiano* and *Il Galateo* of Giovanni della Casa, he concludes that *Le Thresor* "had more influence on the uncultured French upper class of the Renaissance than any other courtesy book." [2]

In his dedication of Book XVI the translator Gabriel Chappuys specifically recommends the work as a guide to honorable and generous behavior and the language of polite intercourse and calls attention to "vne infinité de belles sentences seruans d'instruction qui y sont semees: l'ornement de nostre langue Francoise, la iustice qui s'y voit naifuement depeinte de la punition des geans, la generosité des princes & Cheualiers en l'aide, & subuention des affligez & de ceux qui sentent les fascheuses trauerses de fortune, la pitié des dames & damoiselles, & vne infinité de beaux traits d'honneur & courtoisie." If this advertisement sounds too sweeping and too obviously conventional, we must remember that *Amadis* is an enormous work, and it would be strange indeed if this claim were not made or had not some validity.

It might seem that the sixteenth-century arbiter of manners and morals had to overlook a good deal to make a case for a score of books filled with tales of chivalric blood and thunder and liberally sprinkled with eroticism. The main outlines of the case for *Amadis* as a courtesy book are well put by Jacques Gohorry in his dedication of Book X. *Amadis*, he says, does not sermonize but teaches by example. By reading it, the observant man can learn

which models to follow and which to avoid. Most people have no
stomach for plain moral instruction and resist it as a child resists
bitter medicine. But just as the addition of honey makes medicine
acceptable, so the addition of pleasant tales of strange adventures
and love intrigues makes the moral teaching of the romance palatable. As for those who complain that *Amadis* is not true but contains fictitious matter, they are in effect attacking Xenophon,
Herodotus, Æsop, and all comedy and tragedy. And what does it
matter whether the stories are true or false, as long as they are
concerned with things that are possible, good, and imitable? Ultimately, Gohorry falls back upon that last bastion of defense—the
allegorical level of meaning. He suggests that many incidents in
Amadis are to be interpreted allegorically and cites, among other
works of recognized allegorical validity, Apuleius' *Golden Ass* and
Boccaccio's *De genealogia deorum*.

Although the modern reader may have trouble swallowing the
notion that the honey in *Amadis* is only a flavoring for the medicine, Gohorry's argument doubtless pleased many already disposed
to believe that what they found so pleasant was also useful. Certainly, instances of moral and social instruction can be cited.
Proper behavior in war and peace is a recurring theme. Consideration for the oppressed and courtesy even in the teeth of an enemy
are the hallmarks of the gentleman. Amadis d'Astre is so courteous that the giant Corbon not only surrenders to him but changes
his whole way of life—"d'où lon peut colliger ou recueillir que les
meschans aupres des bons, peuuent à leur exemple estre induits à
bien faire, & changer leur mauuaise nature en vne bonne" (XVII,
xl, 211ᵛ). The kind of conduct that in time of war so often results
in the conversion of pagans has proportional benefits in time of
peace.

The heroes of *Amadis* are almost invariably knights of considerable intellectual attainment. They are excellent at languages,

accomplished as musicians and poets, and skilled in repartee. As in Castiglione, there is much discussion of education and the life of the cultured gentleman. The art of conversation is constantly praised for its civilizing effects on ladies and gentlemen alike, and the varied books of *Amadis* are laced with quasi-philosophical discussions in the manner though not on the level of the *Cortegiano*.

In *Amadis* all the rules of courtesy rest upon the chivalric concept of honor. Honor is a key word continually invoked. Although the word has spiritual and religious overtones, it is for practical purposes equivalent to good reputation. It is what every knight strives for, his reason for being. As Axiane says: "la vraye richesse non perissable est la renommee des faitz bons & heroïques de la personne vertueuse" (VII, xxx, 87). Honor for the knight is to be found in action, not in meditation; in the field, not in the study. Nothing should stand in the way of his pursuit of honor, not even the members of his family or his mistress. Honor leads Galaor to follow Lisuart and his cause, even though his decision means he must fight against his brother and his father. Galaor's moral courage in this instance is widely recognized, and his example is later praised by the Knight of the Burning Sword, who says that every man of good will is more obligated to his honor and his reason than to his father. Burning Sword's comment is quite proper within the context of *Amadis,* and so is his easy assumption that there can be no quarrel between honor and reason.

It is taken for granted that only the nobility have concern for honor, and in all books of *Amadis* it is rare for a common person to be mentioned by name. In its emphasis upon the requirement of noble birth *Amadis* is even more old-fashioned than Castiglione's *Cortegiano,* which considers low birth a flaw but not an insuperable obstacle for the courtier. All books of *Amadis* assume that a knight inherits nobility along with his brown eyes. When a commoner like Darinel has the temerity to attempt to break the enchantment of the Mirror of Love, he finds he cannot take even one step—for enchantments ought to be confronted only by the well-born. When danger threatens, Darinel's first impulse is to hide in the nearest bush, but the noble-born Florisel faces the same danger promptly and unflinchingly.

The instincts and impulses of a person nobly born belong to an order of sensibility quite different from that of commoners. When the Knight of the Burning Sword, who does not know his parents, falls in love with the princess Lucelle, he is tormented by the thought that he may be of low birth. He is cheered, however, by the way he feels and acts. That his heart "prend vn vol si haut" in loving Lucelle is itself an argument that he must be well-born. Moreover, would he act as he habitually does were he not noble? Assuredly not, he says, "si me reputay-ie yssu du sang royal, ou illustre: dont mon cueur me donne souuent tesmoignage, par les hautes entreprises & dangereuses, ou il me semond" (VIII, xxi, 40).

According to *Amadis* the inherited nobility that the Knight of the Burning Sword feels so strongly finds its natural outlet in chivalric deeds. A noble heart longs for honor, and the achievement of honor is recognized even by his lady as the main reason for his existence. A knight without a desire for honor—if such a one existed—would be a chivalric cipher. Not only must the noble knight go in search of honor, but once he has attained it, he must struggle to keep it.

In a life of action honor is always in jeopardy. A knight who wins fifty consecutive combats has attained considerable honor, but the loss of the fifty-first renders him as poor as a knight just dubbed. For honor, being fame, is quickly snuffed out, and the knight loses not one fight but rather fifty-one. So when Galtazar de Barberousse is defeated by Daraïde, he mourns because he has lost in one fight all the honor carefully earned over the years (XI, lvi). Because he is noble he accepts his loss gracefully, in accordance with the prescribed rules of conduct. To do otherwise would be to cast doubt upon his inherited nobility. It is this code that governs the search for honor. When the Knight of the Burning Sword breaks his weapon in a combat with Gandalfe and is left holding the hilt, his friend Gradamarte momentarily forgets the code and moves to help him. Burning Sword pauses to deliver a lecture on honor before going on to finish the contest with the remnant of his sword (VII, xxxviii, 102). It is clear to him that honor is more important than life.

One of the common duties of a knight is to avenge a wrong done to a kinsman, but he is not obliged to revenge an injury received by a kinsman in an honorable fight; and under some conditions revenge is wrong. When Amadis defeats Balan in a properly conducted duel, the defeated knight's son Bravor attacks Amadis with a large group of men. Balan, badly wounded, learns what his son has done and is much upset. He has Bravor bound and delivered to Amadis to punish as he pleases (IV, xxxiv). Honor is dearer to Balan than his son.

A knight defeated in an honorable battle can take comfort in the thought that honor is a secular concept and therefore subject to mutability. A loser still has his inherited nobility and must simply start from scratch again in pursuit of honor. Again and again *Amadis* tells us that true defeat comes only to the quitter. When Quadragant is downed by le beau Ténébreux and called upon to surrender, he says he is not conquered: "for hee is not ouercome that without shewing one iot of cowardise, hath defended his quarrell euen with the losse of his breath, and vntill that he did fall at his enemies feet: but he onely is ouercome, that for want of heart, feareth to doe what he may" (II, xiii, 81).[3] Since this idea is so prominent, it is not surprising that a knight will often go on fighting even against overwhelming odds. So Esplandian, trapped in the city of Alfarin and called on to surrender, announces his faith in God and fights on (V, xxix).

Courage is essential to a knight in pursuit of honor, but it is important that he understand clearly what courage is. Like honor, from which it is often inseparable, courage is frequently discussed throughout *Amadis,* and much of the discussion is clearly germane to sixteenth-century modes of thought. True courage can spring only from virtue, never from pride in oneself or contempt for an opponent. It is to be carefully distinguished from rashness, for courage is always reasonable. When Esplandian, Frandalo, and two other knights, riding back from Mélie's cave with her magic book, find themselves confronted by sixty Turks, they pause to consider their situation. Esplandian's pride will not let him run, and yet he recognizes the validity of Frandalo's judgment that a fight would be foolhardy since they are outnumbered by fifteen to one (V, xli). This kind of chivalric problem comes up often in *Amadis.* In some cases would not rashness be a sin? When Lucendus undertakes to kill a fierce serpent that has been ravaging the countryside, the duchess of Valeran asks whether a knight has any right to attempt what is manifestly impossible. She suggests that Lucendus' quest may offend God "comme dit tresbien vostre docteur de l'Eglise Romaine que celuy n'est pas inculpable, lequel s'expose à vn certain danger" (XVII, ii, 12ᵛ).

An interesting distinction between courage and rashness is made on one occasion by Agesilan. He says that the knight who has never known fear is a knight who has never been really brave— for true courage is nothing but the virtue of knowing how to conquer fear. Rashness is involved, he continues, whenever force is used without being tempered by the courage that arises from fear. Even though victory may follow, the action deserves the name of temerity rather than valor (XII, iv).

Since true courage arises from a clear-sighted awareness of individual weakness and is always ruled by reason, it follows that a reasonable knight may sometimes look cowardly to fools. On several occasions an Amadisian hero who is observing the spirit of courage draws jeers from those who observe only the letter.[4] Thus Rogel, riding on his way, makes a detour to avoid a large company of knights and ladies and is mocked as a coward (XI, lxix). Arlantes is also considered a coward when he refuses to accept an ungrounded challenge from a strange knight (XV, xv).

When Fénix of Corinth and Astibel of Mesopotamia, in the company of two lovely ladies, come to a bridge guarded by a knight, they learn that they can pass without a fight only if they surrender the ladies for one night to the pleasure of Grandoin le fier. If they fight and lose, the ladies must pay. Fénix refuses to hazard his lady's honor, and they bypass the bridge, though the ladies suspect the knights of cowardice. Later they come upon two knights also accompanied by two ladies and are challenged to a fight, winning pair to take all ladies. But Astibel objects that they lack a valid reason for fighting, and Fénix adds the practical observation: "Cheualiers il me semble qu'auez assez forte partie à vaincre sans vous mettre en danger d'auoir chacun à faire à deux pour vne" (XI, xxxii, 58). What is the point of fighting when victory will put you in a position almost as embarrassing as defeat?

Though a true knight has a vivid perception of courage that keeps him inwardly secure against catcalling and the charge of cowardice, affairs of honor can be on occasion extremely complex. Even knights well practiced in the pursuit of honor may become confused. After the long and bitter fight between Amadis and his son Esplandian, in which both are seriously wounded, the puzzled Lisuart asks Amadis why he engaged his own son. Because, says Amadis, even if Esplandian had defeated him, "sa gloire presente augmente la mienne passee" (V, xv, 40). In other words Amadis sees his honor or glory as passing relatively intact to whoever defeated him. Since a man's son is an extension of himself, there can be no loser in a fight between father and son.

A knight who has a proper regard for honor is very careful to keep his word. Once he has given it, he is bound to carry out his promise unless an obvious sin is involved. On one occasion an old lady comes weeping to court and asks a boon of Florisel. He is so touched by her apparent suffering that he promises to help her. She thereupon asks for his daughter Polixène. She threatens that if he does not hand over the girl, she will spread the news of his perfidy. Since to break his word would be to destroy his honor, and since to the noble Florisel honor is dearer than life or daughter, he can only give in (XIV, lxvii).

The boon trick is a very common device in *Amadis,* as it is in most romances. Néreïde uses it to escape from the amorous soudan (VIII, lxxiv). Amadis de Gaule is tricked into promising to help a sorrowful woman in black, only to discover that she is the wife of his worst enemy, Arcalaüs (IV, xxxvi). King Lisuart accepts a crown and a mantle from a mysterious stranger on condition that he return them on a given day or else grant a boon. As any reader of romances can guess, the crown and mantle disappear. On the dread day the mysterious stranger asks for Oriane, and Lisuart has no alternative but to hand her over (I, xxxv).

Sometimes the boon asked is quite improper, and here a knight or king has no hesitation in refusing. He is still left in the embarrassing position of having given his word. One woman to whom Silves grants a boon asks for his love. Silves refuses, but she follows him everywhere reviling him as an oath-breaker. She finally causes a fight between him and Rogel, who takes the position that a knight who makes a promise to a woman ought to keep it (XIV, viii). Similarly Esplandian grants a lady a boon, and she asks him to get a female dwarf with child. When he indignantly refuses, she pursues him with curses (XVI, xxiv).[5]

The authors of a work like *Amadis,* in which honor and chivalry are taken seriously, can scarcely afford to let their heroes look
foolish—at least not very often. Sometimes the tables are turned.
A boon is granted but in language so carefully worded that the
grantor has a way out. When Madasime releases Amadis and
Galaor from her prison, she does so only on condition that "both
of them forsake the seruice of King Lisuart" (I, xxxiv, 202).
Later, before the assembled court, Amadis and Galaor are reminded of their oath, and to Lisuart's dismay they immediately
leave his service. But then, having thus kept to the letter of their
oath, they rejoin the king—for their oath did not stipulate how
long they should remain away from him.

On another occasion Amadis, in disguise as the Knight of the
Green Sword, is embarrassed by Grasinde's request that he take
her to Lisuart's court and defend her as fairer "then any Maiden
there to be found" (III, xii, 120). Amadis is at first speechless, but
then he remembers that Oriane is not a maid but a mother and so
consents. Amadis' loyal servant shares his master's cleverness at
equivocation. When asked about his lord's identity, Gandalin says
he does not know because he has been with this knight only a short
while. His statement is literally true, for Amadis has not long
appeared in this particular disguise (III, ix).

Heredity is clearly a matter of first importance for all knights,
but the child may also derive character from his wet nurse, and a
recurring question is whether a mother should suckle her children.
Some of Esplandian's virtues are drawn from the diverse natures
of his three wet nurses. Found by the hermit Nascian, Esplandian
is suckled by a lioness, a ewe, and Nascian's sister. A letter from
the wise enchantress Urgande explains that Esplandian "partaketh
(somewhat) in the nature of those creatures that gaue him sucke"
(III, viii, 85). From the lioness he has drawn strength and mag-
nanimity, from the ewe gentleness, and from Nascian's sister gen-

tlemanliness. In some of the later books the reader is impressed with the idea that noble ladies should suckle their children. Born on a desert isle, Silves is nourished by his mother Finistée (XI, lxxvii). The six princesses seized by magicians in Book XIV all give birth at the same time and are forced to nurse their children (xxv). There are, of course, many instances—inevitable in a chivalric romance—when children are suckled by animals.

However whimsical its notions about the nursing of infants, *Amadis* reflects the new concern of the sixteenth century for education and learning. By 1540, near the end of the reign of Francis I, when the first book of the romance appeared in Paris, the French Renaissance was well under way. At least the ground on which the Pléiade was to build had been cleared. In contrast, the Spain of 1508, which saw the first four books of *Amadís de Gaula,* was essentially medieval in character in spite of the resurgence in fine arts under the patronage of Ferdinand and Isabella. Moreover, *Amadís* was clearly inspired by an unknown model of much earlier date.[6] It is not strange, therefore, that Herberay should have found Montalvo's depiction of courtly manners rather too old-fashioned for his taste. In his introduction to Book I he says he has taken certain liberties in his translation: "Et si vous apperceuez en quelque endroict que ie ne me soye assubiecty à la rendre de mot à mot: ie vous supplye croire que ie l'ay fait, tant pource qu'il m'a semblé beaucoup de choses estre mal seantes aux personnes introduictes en regard es meurs et façons du iourd'huy. . . ." Nor is it strange that the early books do not particularly stress education. Amadis de Gaule is a great and noble knight, but he is not unusually learned. Other knights in later books may not be his equal in arms or fidelity to a lady, but they often surpass him in erudition.

As the books of *Amadis* succeeded one another in French translation, they became more and more concerned with education.

The emphasis is especially evident in Books XV to XXI, which were adapted from Italian originals. Knights in the early books are not likely to be familiar with foreign tongues, but their descendants in later books become accomplished linguists. Lisuart, for example, in Book III does not understand Greek, and though Amadis de Gaule seems to have a smattering of the language, he apologizes to Queen Menoresse because his unfamiliarity with the language is such as to hamper his saying his thanks (III, xi). The apology, of course, may be ascribed to Amadis' habitual modesty, but it is not a likely explanation.

In Book VII, however, the Knight of the Burning Sword can speak not only Greek but "tous autres langages aussi" (vi, 10). The "tous" is apparently meant quite seriously, for later in the book he has no trouble in deciphering a carved inscription in "certains caracteres Caldeans" (xxii, 60). In the same book Florestan finds an inscription in Chaldean that he cannot read, but the author hastens to add that Florestan is a considerable linguist since "peu de langages luy fussent incogneuz" (l, 127).

Silves has an educational experience unusual even for a hero of chivalric romance. He is born on a desert isle, and his early education is undertaken by his mother and his father Amadis de Grèce. After their return to civilization Silves' physical and intellectual development becomes the responsibility of two tutors. The knight Perot instructs him in military and gentlemanly pursuits, and under his guidance Silves becomes the greatest hunter of all chivalric heroes.[7] For instruction in letters and poetry Silves has a teacher called Léon le Suave, who is a poet and translator of great note at court. As a result of Léon's tutelage and the early training by his father, Silves is, like other knights, exceedingly clever at languages. When he finds letters in Arabic in an enchanted chamber, he reads the language with ease, "pourtant qu'il entendoit fort bien ce langage, comme aussi faisoit-il plusieurs autres, lesquels des sa petite enfance il auoit apris de son Pere en l'isle Solitaire & deserte" (XIV, xvi, 20ᵛ).

At the age of six Prince Agesilan is sent to Athens to be instructed in polite learning, music, and the use of arms. He studies Latin and Greek and learns that work is pleasure and idleness pain. When he has occasion later to read Arabic, he does so readily, "comme celle qui entendoit toutes langues." Strongly imbued with reverence for God and the law, Agesilan, after he becomes king, "se monstra quasi plus suget que seigneur en l'obseruance des loix" (XI, iv, 8). Rogel is also sent to the best teachers so that he will learn how to be a good ruler. "Car telle estoit l'opinion du grand roy Amadis en l'institution des Princes de son sang, pour les rendre si bien douez & apris, que leurs sugetz leur obeissent voluntiers, en les cognoissant si dignes de l'estat & lieu qu'ilz tenoient: & a fin que quand ilz se trouueroient entre les estrangers, ilz gaignassent par tout le point de preëminence par leur vertu" (XI, iii, 6).

Further evidence of the scholarly attainments of chivalric heroes is presented in Book XVII, when Arlanges uses his extensive knowledge of theology to convert the princess Sestiliane and her mother from Mohammedanism. He is so learned that he can reinforce his arguments with numerous references to the Koran. He argues that Christ's divinity is apparent even there. What is the explanation for all this erudition? "Combien qu'il fust Cheualier errant par le monde, il desroboit tousiours quelque peu de temps pour vaquer à la lecture de quelque liure, estant si bien instruit es choses de la saincte Escriture, qu'il sembloit vn grand Theologien, il estoit pareillement bien versé es Histoires anciennes, au moyen desquelles en ses communs propos & deuis, il acqueroit grand honneur . . ." (XVII, lxxiii, 360ᵛ–361).

The acquisition of honor through learning is a relatively late innovation in the romances, and Arlanges is an unusual knight.

Generally in *Amadis* a hero seeks after honor in the medieval manner, and theological controversy—even when it results in such distinguished conversions—is not one of the traditional paths. The later books do not suggest that erudition is incompatible with the exercise of arms; rather, they take for granted that it makes a knight more attractive and more effective. They show how Renaissance ways of thought altered the figure of the ideal knight. Arlanges represents an intellectualized conception of the original Amadís de Gaula, and one cannot read many books of the romance without being aware of the evolution from medieval ideals to those of the Renaissance.

Though not all latter-day knights are as conspicuously learned as Arlanges, quickness of wit is much admired, and most chivalric heroes have in speech and in the composition of letters, orations, and poems a native facility and a readiness that were evidently intended to be exemplary. *Amadis* is a treasury of instances of knightly wit in action. On one occasion Amadis de Gaule turns what appears to be an embarrassing relapse into a minor social triumph. While he is telling the ladies of the court at Constantinople about some of the kingdoms he has visited, a sudden memory of Oriane almost causes him to swoon. While the ladies look on in some perplexity, he goes into one of the trances to which he seems prone. Finally Queen Menoresse takes him by the arm and brings him to his senses again. Whereupon Amadis makes as neat a recovery as one can imagine by saying that among so many beautiful ladies who would not lose his senses (III, xi).[8]

One of the most severe tests of a knight's wit comes when he is asked directly a question to which he cannot, for one reason or another, give a completely honest answer. His problem is to word his reply in such a way as to make it acceptable both to the questioner and to his own honor. The witty answer that holds literal truth but is very nearly a lie obviously fascinated the authors of *Amadis*.

Amadis de Gaule, like Hamlet, has a knack for framing the equivocal retort. Once, disguised as le beau Ténébreux, he comes to court with Oriane, who is also in disguise, to try a test for the perfect lover and lady. The queen, Oriane's mother, very curious about the lady's identity, questions le beau Ténébreux. "I am as little acquainted with her as you," says he (II, xv, 104). On a later occasion, after his identity as le beau Ténébreux has become generally known, the question arises at court again: Who was the lady with him? Oriane, who in her desire to keep her honor intact has to be as curious as everyone else, asks him in company who the lady is. "In faith Madame," he answers, "I know no more what she was then you doe, although I remained in her company sixe daies together" (II, xvii, 127).

Many are the problems in etiquette that arise to try a knight's native wit and courtesy. What should be Florisel's attitude toward the young knight who bears a letter from Queen Arlande indicating that he is Florisel's illegitimate son? (X, lviii). On another occasion Amadis de Gaule finds himself in the awkward position of introducing the bastard Florestan to their father King Périón. Amadis then introduces him to Queen Hélisène—up to this point wholly unaware of the existence of this byblow—and she proceeds to give a lesson in grace and kindness by offering Florestan "most gracious entertainment, as well for the Kings sake, as for his renowned fame thorow all Countries" (III, v, 45). And what should an honorable knight do when an amorous damsel creeps into his bed at night and "le commence a baiser & entreietter la iambe coquine?" Amadis de Grèce invents a way out that spares the damsel's feelings, for he tells her "qu'il estoit interessé d'vne maladie secrette, luy ostant la puissance de luy faire tel seruice" (XI, xliv, 73^{v}).

In such tight social predicaments chivalric wit—still loyal to honor, courtesy, and truth—must be at its quickest. But wit wears a more sustained and formal guise when it informs the speeches, letters, and poems that knights so often produce. The large number of such rhetorical outpourings and their great popularity in the sixteenth century are sufficiently attested by the vogue of *Le Thresor des liures d'Amadis*. Here the emphasis is upon the instructional function of the rhetoric selected from the romance. The table of contents in the English translation offers the selections as models: "A forme to giue thanks to one"; "A forme to write or to speake amorous and louely purposes"; "A forme to comfort one"; "A forme to defie one for him selfe, or for other." The English reader of the sixteenth century, who is here being urged to learn to speak and write as well as Amadis de Gaule, apparently felt no sense of the bizarre. In such a heading as this from the table of contents, "Orations to incite his vassalles, friends, or alies to take armes, and to encourage the souldiers readie to fight," the Middle Ages and the Renaissance blend indistinguishably.

Concerned as it is chiefly with princes, *Amadis* inevitably confronts problems of government. Since the education of a prince is a chief preoccupation of the sixteenth century, *Amadis* is in considerable part in the mirror-for-magistrates tradition. Henry IV of France is supposed to have read *Amadis* nightly before retiring.[9] In a complimentary poem that graces Book VIII Michel Sevin d'Orléans makes the point that, like Homer and Virgil, *Amadis* tries to describe ideal conduct: "Pour enseigner ceux qui voudront regner,/Le bon chemin de tout bien gouuerner." *Amadis* contains numerous instances of good and bad rulers, and where example and ideal conduct do not suffice, the authors are quick to supply pointed commentary.

The ideal ruler is described at length in Book IX, Chapter lix. Strong, healthy, and handsome, he is "non superflu en parolles, ny vsant de langage fardé ou de hault stile." He detests flatterers, "par ce qu'vn Prince ne peult auoir pire ennemy que le flateur."

He is just, merciful, law-abiding, and temperate and does not live "pour boire ou manger." He prefers to overcome his opponents by kindness rather than by force, but in war he is harsh and cunning and tries to take advantage of surprise. Because he works hard at leading his people, they try to obey him and love him.

Oriane is a good example of the princess who can inspire her people to trust and devotion, for "she was so humble, wise, and debonaire, that by her meere humility and courtesie, shee knew how to steale the heartie affections of euery one. A matter so apt and proper to heroyick persons, and them deriued from great place: as they haue no other powers or faculties, but such as make them to bee more honoured, praised and esteemed. . . . Gracious language, apprehensiue grauitie, and humble modestie, are so proper and peculiar to Princes and great persons, that whensoeuer they but speake: it begetteth their subiects cordiall loue, absolute obedience, with a generall feare of offending . . ." (IV, iii, 15–16).

Amadis would be a very dull work if it did not have many examples of bad rulers and several of good kings led astray by evil counselors. King Lisuart is misled by two evil flatterers into a break with Amadis and a ruinous civil war. King Aravigne appears as an example of the king who falls from high place. Defeated in war, and in the hands of his enemies, he comments sadly on the irony of his fate: "For, it is fully a yeare, since I stood vpon no meane tearms, of being the very greatest King in all the West" (IV, xxxvii, 184). Queen Persée commits a grievous fault when she permits her personal feelings to outweigh her duty as ruler. As a result of her bitterness toward Rogel, she invites several pagan kings to help her attack him. Her country becomes a gathering place for pagan armies, and she awakes one day to the realization that since the armies she has invited greatly outnumber her Persians, she is in fact no longer the ruler of her kingdom (XIX, xcv). *Amadis* is hard on usurpers. When Rogel leads a successful plot to restore Griande to her throne and kill the usurper, he has no trouble finding help among Griande's people: "Ce qui deuroit estre vn bel exemple aux Roys, à ce qu'ils se portassent en toute humanité & douceur auecques leurs subjects, par ce que c'est le seul point qui les faict regner, comme au contraire la cruauté les faict tomber de leur estat, comme tout à point il aduint en cest endroict" (XIV, xxi, 29). Now and then an evil ruler can be reformed. The giant Corbon, whom Amadis d'Astre converts to goodness, is an example. As his name implies, he is basically a good-hearted fellow, but he has been led into evil ways by his brother Radigar, who practiced and preached the doctrine that might is right (XVII, xli).

All princes are taught that they will be called upon to suffer more and lose more than common men. They must be prepared to undertake great enterprises as befits their station. After a bloody battle for which Heleine holds herself responsible, Alastraxerée comforts her: "Considerez que comme les hautz arbres & les tours sont plus exposez à perilz & ruynes: & au contraire, d'autant qu'ilz surpassent les autres en degré de dignité, pareillement doiuent en toute vertu resister ou porter plus magnanimement les influences fatales" (X, xix, 46ᵛ). Throughout *Amadis* it is taken for granted that Fortune is especially fickle with princes, and since they occupy the highest places, they must show the highest courage. The true prince is eager to try the test that has never been passed. Amadis says that all his life he has understood "it is an Article, proper and peculiar to them, that couet the supream place of honour and renowne, to attempt occasions of most danger, and difficultie" (IV, xxxii, 142).

Though princes must learn to expect great troubles, they know more than ordinary joys and glory. *Amadis* is firmly founded on the idea of hierarchy that was taken for granted by medieval and Renaissance society. Scattered through the romance are several long speeches on order in the universe, especially in the state. The wise Urgande gives Oriane a good talk on the subject: "Although wee are all made of one and the same substance, all obliged to vices and passions, yea equall alike to death: yet the omnipotent Lord of all, hath made vs diuerse, in enioying the goods of this world. To some hee giues authority; others are subiect to seruility and vassalage. Some are made poore and very miserable, others enioy aboundance and prosperity, and all according to his owne good pleasure. So worthy Madame, comparing the great blessings you now enioy, with such sorrowes and vexations as you haue sustained, put all your present aflictions into one scale, and your passed fortunes into another, and they will no way be answerable in weight" (IV, xxxviii, 191).[10]

Special problems of the lady in chivalric society—the preservation of her honor, her conduct in a variety of circumstances, and her education—are treated with interest and sympathy. The French version of *Amadis* was obviously designed to attract feminine readers, and many asides are leveled at them. Since the lady's primary duty in the romances is to love and be loved, we may presume that sixteenth-century ladies liked to identify themselves with Lucelle, Diane, Fortune, and the many other love-plagued ladies of *Amadis*.

For the unmarried lady in *Amadis,* even more than for the knight, honor is a matter of reputation. Her good name must be guarded at all times, and the highest praise goes to those ladies who, if they sin, sin discreetly. Scandal is to be avoided like the death. In a highly military society she is, of course, dependent on her knight and to some extent shares his glory. She therefore does not stand in his way when he wishes to go off in search of glory.[11] Since she may be on occasion the reason for his fighting or jousting, she must attend to her beauty and remain worth fighting for. She watches the combats as steadfastly as she can, and she may later in the company of other ladies visit her wounded knight. She may even, as a mark of special favor, help to arm or disarm him—as Shakespeare's Cleopatra helps Antony.

Her problems arise not so much on the field as in the chamber. When her knight is near, her honor is in great danger. Letters may be exchanged, but all must be managed so carefully that nobody knows. Meetings at night in the garden may be arranged, but the lady is wiser if she remains behind barred windows and merely offers her lover a hand to kiss. Above all she must never reveal her feelings in company. Oriane is particularly admired for the way she manages to keep secret her long affair with Amadis. In Book III, after he rescues her from the Romans and a hated marriage, she finds herself in a very dangerous position. Though they have long been lovers and have even had a child, only Oriane's confidantes know about the relationship. But how is Oriane to preserve her reputation now? She and Amadis agree that she must be treated as a prisoner, and Amadis does not see her at all except in the presence of others. She and Amadis are ideal lovers, in part because each is so discreet.

The preservation of chastity until marriage, or at least until a trothplight has been made, is a first essential. On the other hand, a lady should not allow her true love to languish and die unrequited. Cold and unkind ladies of the kind celebrated by Petrarchan sonneteers are often treated harshly in *Amadis*. There is a *via media* between unyielding chastity and illicit love if knight and lady are truly pledged to each other.

If the narrative does not make the moral clear, the narrator is likely to interrupt to point it out. So in the opening of Book I the narrator is concerned lest the brazen conduct of the princess Hélisène give bad example. Hélisène and Périon fall in love at

first sight, and a secret meeting is promptly arranged by her confidante Dariolette. No sooner have they consummated their love
than the author interrupts to talk of the desirability of feminine
chastity and the need for more devotion to religion—"and not
without cause haue I made this little discourse, for it is to the end
that it happen not to them, as it did vnto the faire Princess Eli-
sena" (I, ii, 8). Hélisène is so quickly won that, were it not for
Dariolette, she would have succumbed without extracting a
promise of marriage from Périon.

Ladies must be careful lest they be hoodwinked by unscrupu-
lous males. Knights like Galaor and Rogel thrive only because
there are so many indiscreet ladies. The knight Balays admits,
after trying unsuccessfully to emulate Galaor, that damsels who
say no are more admired by men (I, xxix). The beautiful Lucelle
is a good example of a girl misled by her naïveté. When she has
an opportunity—through the enchantment of the Mirror of Love
—to look into the heart of Amadis de Grèce, her supposedly
loyal lover, she sees there to her astonishment herself and another
woman. When she asks him for an explanation, the guilty lover
conceives an inspired lie. He says that the other lady must be
Venus. Lucelle's suspicions are considerably eased. The narrator
interrupts to comment on Lucelle's innocent acceptance of so
egregious a fabrication and suggests that his feminine readers
would call her not naïve but stupid. He continues: "Mais donnez
vous garde, que sous vne trop grande finesse, vous ne demeurez
encores mieux engulees qu'elle ne fut: aquerrans pour nom de
sotes reputation d'infamie: qui vous seroit vn tresvilain acoustrement" (VII, lvii, 108).

The authors of *Amadis* are particularly fond of the myth of
Danaë as an example of the uselessness of trying to enforce chastity on women. Several ladies in the romance are closely guarded,
but to no avail. Niquée is locked up and kept all her girlish years

from the sight of men, but all precautions are in vain. Niquée herself says that her father should have remembered that imprisoning a woman is like keeping "vne grande quantité de puces, que l'on cuide enclorre dans son poing & sortent neantmoins par la separacion des doitz" (VIII, lxxiii, 136). Heleine is carried off by Florisel despite the steps her father took to keep her from traffic with men. The narrator points up the application to sixteenth-century parents: "Telz inconueniens auons veu auenir de nostre temps, ie m'en raporterois bien a plusieurs peres & meres qui ont mis leurs enfans trop ieunes en religion pensant les diuerter des affections mondaines, mais paruenuz en aage, ont bien monstre qu'ilz en estoient plus desireux que ceux qui ne bougent ordinairement des bancquetz & mondaines assemblees" (IX, lxx, 181^v–182). Parents cannot enforce morality. It must arise out of virtue and represent the free choice of their daughters.[12]

Whether or not ladies took its lessons to heart, *Amadis* was evidently intended to be a force for good. For all its drawbacks as a courtesy book, it is hard to believe that many young ladies or gentlemen in the sixteenth century were corrupted by reading it. Sir Philip Sidney testifies that he knew some who had by reading *Amadis* "found their hearts moved to the exercise of courtesy, liberality, and especially courage."[13] Evil in it there might be, for some, but its emotional force was in the direction of good. Modern readers who consider the work dull must remember that sixteenth-century readers found it tremendously exciting and became deeply involved in it and its characters. Sidney discerned many faults in *Amadis,* but he knew it was wisdom to believe the heart.

An eloquent sixteenth-century defense of *Amadis* as a courtesy book also stresses the emotional impact: "For what a dullarde is he, that wise counsell, vertuous exhortations, friendly admonitions, wittie and subtill persuasions shall not quicken and reuiue?

and how farre without sense is he, whom amiable, fine, and beautifull ladies with their ticklyng and flatteryng wordes shall not awake, stirre vp, and call to their lure, wanton fansie, & feruent loue? What stonie and harde hearte hath he, that with the glittering and twinkeling of the eye, the abundant teares, the dulcet and sweete parolls of his paramour (wherwith this fine flattering booke is infarced) will not be mollefyed and melted? And how depely are they drowned in sorrowe, that with godly and vertuous consolation will not be comforted? What weake and cowardly heartes and stomackes haue they that will not be stirred or moued with the rhetorical & eloquent orations, the vehement persuasions, and liberall promises and rewardes of wise, noble & worthie capitains, pluck vp their harts, inuade their enimies, & (for worthie renoume sake, & immortall glorie) fight stoutly and corageously, as *Amadis,* the king of England & France. . . ." [14]

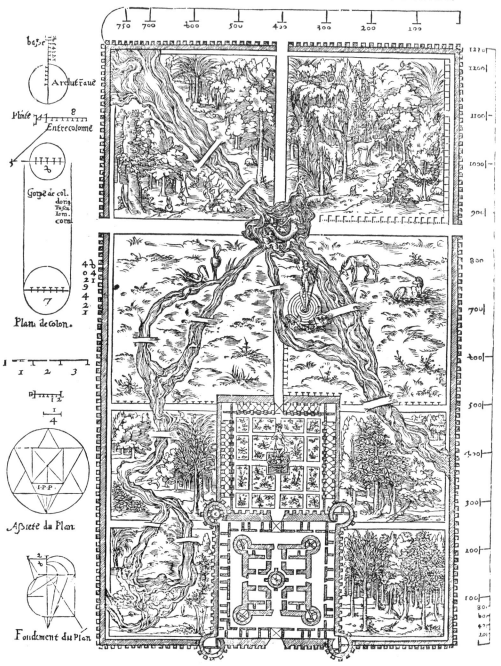

750 700 600 500 400 300 200 100

baſe

Architraue

Pline 8
Entrecolomne

Gorpe de col.
doriq.
Tuſca.
Ionr.
corin.

Plan de colon.

1   2   3
1   2   3

1
2

1
4

I · P · P ·

Aſſiete du Plan.

2
6

Fondement du Plan.

1270
1200
1100
1000
900
800
700
600
500
400
300
200
100
80
60
40
20

V

Structure and Variety

In *Amadis de Gaule* the narrative is arranged in such a way as to exploit the heterogeneity of matter. Knights frequently set out on their quests with no specific destination in view. Though they seek to break an enchantment or free a captive, they may not know exactly where the trouble is, and so they give the horses their heads or let the ship sail where it will. The important thing, the knights all know, is to move. Something of this chivalric philosophy seems to have rubbed off on the many authors. The books of *Amadis* wander through episode after episode, in every direction, and wind and wave or the plodding of a dumb beast bring variety and surprise, along with some monotony and repetition, to a story so fluid that it promised to go on forever.

When he was about to burn the books in his library, Don Quixote saved from the fire the first four books of *Amadis de Gaula* because, he said, this work was the best of its kind. On the remaining books of the cycle, however, he had no mercy. His judgment has been corroborated by later critics, who have by and large praised Montalvo's first four books and damned the rest. The common critical view is that the narrative grows wilder and more aimless after Book IV. As Sir Henry Thomas puts it, Book V "and the succeeding continuations of *Amadís* are for the most part but poor exaggerations of their original. The giants become more gigantic, the monsters more monstrous as time goes on. This is inevitable when each new hero is the son of the preceding hero, and proves himself invincible by overcoming his already invincible father."[1] This attitude may explain in part why there have been in our time so few readers of the romance after Book IV.

Yet Thomas himself takes pains to point out how Book V is anticipated by Montalvo as early as Book III, and there is every indication that Montalvo and the authors of the following books knew in a rough way what they were up to. Though most readers of the later books may feel some sympathy with Thomas' comment and recognize in it some truth, his view is overstated. There are in the later books many new things, themes not touched upon at all in the first four books. Moreover, nobody—not even his son—ever defeats Amadis de Gaule in a fair fight in any of the orthodox versions of the story. As for the compounding of the exaggerations of the first four books, one can only remember that the Palace of Apolidon, the Endriague, and the chivalric feats of Amadis invited imitation, but that in the Renaissance manner it became imitation with a difference.

For the authors who chose to follow Montalvo in writing the romance the narrative pattern was already established by countless medieval romances. By his invention of Esplandian as hero of Book V, Montalvo had pointed out the easy way to carry on with the narrative. Henceforth succeeding narrators merely allowed old heroes to beget new ones. Amadis de Gaule gives way to his son Esplandian, who is followed by his son Lisuart de Grèce, who in turn gives rise to Amadis de Grèce, who is succeeded by Florisel de Niquée, who has a son Rogel, who has a son, and so on.

Since few of the principal figures die, even the most devoted reader must occasionally have lost his way in the maze of family histories and shifting relationships. Add to the chief figures those of relatively minor interest and the modern reader begins to wonder whether he ought not look for help to an electronic computer. One writer on *Amadis* lists two hundred and forty-eight characters in the first five books alone.[2]

Yet so great a number guaranteed variety, one of the principal aims of romance writers. Furthermore, if the proliferation of heroes and their dependents taxes patience and memory in the twentieth century, we may suppose that the case was different four hundred years ago. The sixteenth-century reader, his mind uncluttered by quantities of light reading, must have read these tales of marvelous adventures in exotic places with a concentration reserved in our day for history. Since *Amadis*, like most romances, claims to be based on an authentic old chronicle and its characters are often likened to royal or courtly personages, it must have been read with the rapt attention that makes complexity a joyful challenge.

A given book of *Amadis* is never concerned with the uninterrupted recital of the adventures of a single knight, however diverse or imaginative they may be. In the early books the adventures of Amadis are paralleled by or contrasted with those of his brother Galaor. Lest this doubling become too obvious or too easy for readers to anticipate, a half-brother Florestan makes his appearance toward the end of Book I. As love between Amadis and Oriane ripens, she becomes still another center of interest. Similarly in other books three or four knights or ladies vie more or less equally for the reader's attention. For example, in Book XVII most of the episodes involve one or the other of three heroes: Amadis d'Astre, Lucendus, and Sphéramonde. Each undergoes the same kind of adventures or has a similar experience in love, but the names are different, the locale changes, time is confounded, and so the aim of the romance-writer—unlimited variety—is achieved.

Narrative of such a complex and intricate sort is now somewhat out of fashion, and few modern readers can go very far into the work without feeling their memories bruised like the grass beneath the weight of the Dragon half-flying, half-footing upon Red Cross. What Matthew Arnold deprecated as "confused multitudinousness" was regarded by most Renaissance critics as a chief merit in a long narrative. It is clear that the several authors of *Amadis* went to considerable pains to produce at least a happy confusion. Seldom do they pursue the adventures of a single knight or a group of knights for more than three consecutive chapters, lest the reader become bored. So in Book VII, in the midst of an adventure involving Amadis de Gaule, we are suddenly warned of a change in scene: "Et pour diuersifier & embellir nostre histoire, entendez comme ce pendant se portoient les affaires de l'Empereur Arquisil, duquel noz volumes precedans ont fait si grand mention" (xlvi, 118). So writer transfers reader from the wildly improbable to the deliciously fantastic.

At times the variety of incident becomes overwhelming, and in this respect *Amadis* is closer to Boiardo than to Ariosto. Incident succeeds or overruns incident at a dizzying pace. No less than five colossal shipwrecks occur in Book XIV, and each sends the survivors off in a new direction or effectively interrupts a quest already under way. In Book VII seven great storms at sea divert heroes and heroines to unexpected destinations. A knight who sets out on a mission finds countless obstacles to deflect him from his course, and his journey is usually interrupted many times.

As for structure, it would be unfair to generalize about all twenty-one books, for some, especially the first four, are comparatively well organized, whereas others are chaotic. That a book should have a unifying idea and that the various episodes should be relevant to it in some way are considerations that, while not totally alien, are scarcely native to *Amadis* or its genre. The division into chapters and books has no consistent structural significance.

A book sometimes contains a great central battle or enchantment that serves in a rough way as a unifying agent. In Book XVII the battle at the Château du Fort is the great episode that enables the author to detach his chief characters, Amadis d'Astre, Lucendus, and Sphéramonde, from their separate adventures and bring them together. The climax of the book comes in Chapter lxxi with the victory of the besieged Christians, and thereafter the narrative subsides weakly through twenty more chapters. The center of interest shifts to the love of the Christian knight Arlanges for the pagan Sestiliane and to the discord between Amadis d'Astre and Rosaliane. Many of the last chapters serve merely as an advertisement for Book XVIII, for they pose love problems or start episodes that will unfold in the following volume.

In such a loose, composite structure a shipwreck is a common excuse for a diversion. In Book XVI—the work of Nicholas de Montreux—a shipwreck in Chapter xxi involves several major characters. The author first focuses on the fortunes of Amadis de Gaule as he makes his way safely to shore in Chapter xxi and gets caught up in new adventures in Chapters xxii and xxiii. In Chapter xxiv Montreux leaves Amadis and goes back to the shipwreck to get Esplandian ashore and entangle him in a new set of troubles on land. In Chapter xxv we learn how Amadis de Grèce saves himself from drowning and finds himself cast up on an unknown coast where he encounters more perils. In Chapter xxvi Silves and

Pentasilée are saved from the stormy sea and reach the shores of Egypt. In our last view of the shipwreck in Chapter xxvii we see the rescue of Fortunian and Astrapol.

Now that there are five different parties involved in different adventures in different places, the author can start the interweaving process that will eventually bring all the heroes back together again in Constantinople. But by Chapter xxxii he seems to grow weary of this game, for he ignores the shipwrecked knights and describes the fortunes of Sphéramonde, Amadis d'Astre, and Lucendus for three chapters. In Chapter xxxv he returns to Esplandian and the other shipwrecked knights. In Chapter xxxix he goes back to Sphéramonde and Amadis d'Astre. All this scene shifting seems to be governed by whim alone.

A fork in the road can also serve to disperse the characters. As Amadis and Galaor follow the trail of the kidnapers of Oriane and Lisuart, they come to a division in the road. In accordance with romance custom, Amadis takes one way and Galaor the other. We follow Amadis as he rescues Oriane, and then we return to the fork so that we can follow Galaor through his adventures. This common narrative device is sometimes overworked. In Book XII, for example, five knights—Daraïde, Garaye, and Galtazar and his two brothers—pursue thieving knights who have just robbed the damsel Belenie. By a nice coincidence five roads fan out at a forking of their route, and each knight can choose a separate way.

The unusual twists that can be worked in this kind of pattern— and the elaborations thereon—seem almost endless. In *Amadis,* where a sense of chivalric parody can be often detected, they are sometimes unmistakably comic. So in Book XII as the five knights take their five different roads, the narrator follows Daraïde as he accompanies the victim Belenie. After a time they come upon a fight in which two of the thieves are struggling against four knights. Upon learning that the casket stolen from Belenie is now in the hands of a squire, the pursuers avoid the fight and follow his trail. Before long the four knights overcome the two robbers and also set out in pursuit. Next, Daraïde and Belenie come suddenly upon their friend Garaye fighting against a group of knights who have tried to steal the casket from the squire. In the midst of the confusion the squire, still clutching the casket, rides away. Once again avoiding a fight, Daraïde follows the squire, while the four knights continue to follow him. As soon as Garaye finishes off his opponents, he sets out after the four knights.

This semicomic, disjointed chase is still far from over. Daraïde finally overtakes the squire, who drops the stolen casket and continues to run. The four knights ride up and demand the casket of Daraïde, but he fights them off while Belenie retreats with it. The four, however, kill Daraïde's horse and, leaving him, follow Belenie, whom they overtake and rob again. But now the pursuing Garaye arrives. He kills two of the four knights before his horse is killed, but the two remaining knights ride off with the casket. Daraïde, meanwhile, uses Belenie's palfrey to catch two loose horses. He and Garaye chase the two—only to come upon Galtazar, who, by taking the third of the five roads, has met and killed the two miscreants and recovered the casket (XII, iv–v).

If the reader is by now somewhat confused, he can expect further befuddlement, for the complications which began at the crossroads have not yet been resolved. Galtazar's brothers, who took roads four and five, have yet to be accounted for.

Whatever the reaction of the modern reader to such wild and whirling episodes, the sixteenth-century reader was apparently delighted. Writers of romances worked hard to keep the narrative full of turmoil, wonder, and surprise. In his remarks prefacing the translation of Book XIII Jacques Gohorry writes: "Or pour rendre le Rommanceur sa narration plus plaisante il met en auant choses nouuelles ou non iamais ouyes ne veuës, il la rend plus agreable par admirations, attentes, issuës, inopinees, passions entre-meslees, deuis des personnes, douleurs, coleres, craintes, ioyes desirs ardents. Quant à la disposition, il monte aucunesfois des petites choses aux grandes, autresfois il descend des grandes aux petites, autrefois il les mesle les vnes parmez les autres, & les simples auecq' les composees, les obscures auecq' les claires, les tristes auec les gayes, les incroyables parmy les vray semblables: qui n'est pas besongne de legere industrie."

A romance was a gigantic stew seasoned by marvels of all kinds and fraught with surprises. From this view *Amadis* must be one of the most successful of all romances, for it is of wonders all compact. For one thing, it is an astounding bestiary. In addition to lions, tigers, bulls, bears, panthers, boars, unicorns, dragons, and griffons, all fairly standard in sixteenth-century romances, *Amadis* contains such curiosities as the giraffe ("qui est vne beste ressemblant au Chameau & Panthere"; XX, lii, 216^v), the lionce (which is part lion, part ounce), the grifaléon (the result of a union between a lion and a griffon), and beasts so strange that they cannot be identified. One of the animals that attacks Amadis de Grèce is as big as a horse, has a head like a tiger, tusks like an elephant, a body like a leopard, and claws like a griffon (VIII, xxxix). Near the Palace of Apolidon is a fabulous garden where the Phoenix comes yearly to moult. There live two unicorns as well as "Ciuet and Muske-cattes, which made the ayre . . . extraordinarily sweete," a singing mermaid, and two serpents "bred of his kinde, that watcht the golden Apples in the Garden of Hesperides day and night" (IV, ii, 9).

The romance is also visited by a variety of monsters from the twilight world between animals and men. There are centaurs, cyclops, betusked wild men, dog-faced giants, and man-eating Elestrigons. The Cenofales Barbacans are dog-faced twins who have ten fingers on each hand. At the time of their conception their mother "pensoit auoir affaire auec vn beau & grand chien," and they are born about the size of puppies (XX, lxv). The awesome Endriague, a product of incest, is the mortal habitation of Satan, for "the ponderous weight of a sinne so monstrous, had in such sort alienated naturall disposition: that the foule fiend tooke the place of a reasonable soule, and so caused this hellish procreation" (III, x, 98–99). When Amadis de Gaule kills this monstrosity after a desperate fight, "the deuill came out of his body, causing such a clap of thunder, as all the whole Island shooke with the sound thereof" (III, x, 102).

The sin and terror surrounding monstrous births contrast sharply with the circumstances under which heroes enter the world. Silves de la Selve is conceived under auspices especially mysterious. When Amadis de Grèce and Finistée are cast ashore on a desert isle, they set up Platonic housekeeping. One day Finistée finds "vn fruit de grand saueur qu'elle aporta à Amadis, comme Eue la pomme à Adam" (XI, lxxvii, 128). The fruit makes them drunk and amorous, and they remain so for a month, until all the fruit is gone. When they return to their senses, they have no remembrance of what has happened. When Finistée's appearance begins to change, neither can think of an explanation. Perhaps the fruit has caused the swelling, or perhaps, as Amadis soberly suggests, she has conceived by the same wind that impregnates mares in Spain.[3] Even when the baby is born, Amadis' best explanation is that it must be the product of Finistée's imagination, "que les medecins dient causer d'estranges & prodigieux effetz en nature" (XI, lxxvii, 128). Later the magician Alquif translates the writing on the baby's breast and assures all interested parties, including Amadis' wife, that the birth has occurred without sin on the part of Amadis or Finistée.[4]

There are many other wonders: an isle inhabited only by monkeys (V, xviii); a ring which stanches the flow of blood (XVII, xix); a mirror in which Alquif observes what is happening at a distance (XI, lxxix); Astrapol's ring, which keeps him faithful to Rosalve as long as he wears it (XVIII); meals served by invisible servants aboard a ship manned by mutes (XVII, i); a Caesarian operation performed on a dead woman four months pregnant (XII, xcvii); a valley of love, where knights and ladies lose all sexual inhibitions and all remembrance, and where Zahara thinks she has conceived by the god Mars (VIII, lxxxv); Estebel's magic face-rinse, which makes Balarte look just like Amadis de Grèce (VIII, lxviii); an arch in Persia that is festooned with heads hanging bloodily by the hair (IX, vii); a mantle that works in such a way that its wearer "shall neuer be offended with her husband" (I, xxx, 181); a kidnaper who walks on water (IX, xlii); a garland that will keep a maiden always looking like a sixteen-year-old (XII, iv); water that will keep chaste a maiden who bathes in it and render would-be rapists impotent (IX, ix); a city whose walls rest on water (XIV, xxiv); a disappearing island (XVIII, xc); a shield that makes its bearer invisible (XVII); the Isle of the Cruel, where blood drips off fruit on trees, and where a river of blood flows out of a heart of darkness—a wall of headless men (XIV, xvi). Among his possessions the magician Apolidon had the golden apple that Venus won and the "Pearle (otherwise tearmed the Vnion) which Cleopatra long time had in her possession, after she had quaft off the other in the company of Marke Anthonie" (IV, ii, 6). In Book XVII Lucendus and Fortune have each a mirror in which one can see and hear the other.

The reader is transported to far-off lands and introduced to many strange and wonderful customs. The king of Mont-Libéan prepares a sacrifice of his handsomest prisoners to the gods in thanksgiving for victory (XX, xxxiv). King Bulthazar has blood drained from captive knights and put into goblets. He drinks, and the cups are passed among his knights so that all can drink in token of their indissoluble military union.[5] The tyrannical giant Olampard makes all travelers worship his wife and daughter on pain of death (XIX, xix). The giant Anacléon demands a daily ration of ten lovely maidens for his pleasure in the country where he rules (XVIII, iii). The Elestrigons, who eat human flesh, keep flocks of men and women in the open fields like cattle (XVIII, lvii).

The law of Scotland, which decrees that a woman taken in an extramarital sexual act shall be burned at the stake, is enforced on numerous occasions. In Athens the law is invoked for adulterous wives (XIII, xvi). On the Isle of Sidonie, where all marriage proposals have to be made in public and no one can reject a proposal by a fit suitor, death is the penalty for transgressions (X, xlii). On the Isle of Canabée, an Amazon community, any man who has sexual relations with a woman not his wife is burned alive (XII, lxxxix). Any knight who enters the realm of the Amazon Castora must take a woman for at least two years on pain of death, the children of any such union to belong to the state (XXI, xcix). In Indie men are forbidden to enter certain areas restricted to women (XXI, xxi). On the Isle of Dardanie the people are ruled by the old laws that Lycurgus established in Sparta. There damsels have no dowry but their chastity, and they are kept rigidly apart from men until marriage (X, x). Amazons from Californie forbid men to enter their country, but the unimammians themselves are permitted once or twice a year to cohabit beyond the borders. When they return from battle victorious, they habitually carry the heads of their enemies upon the ends of their lances (V, l).

Processions, tourneys, and festivals are described lavishly—and occasionally *ad nauseam*. In some books, like Book IX, the narrator is obsessed with feminine dress. Even when Florisel disguises himself as a lady, his attire is described in unusual detail, perhaps because as a woman he is said to be "vne seconde Venus" (IX, xlvii, 117). After Zaïr and Abra land at Trebizond, they proceed in state with a large and resplendent retinue, Abra clad in an elaborate dress and riding a strange mount engendered in the Mountains of the Moon, where the Nile has its source (VIII, v).

Similarly when Cléophile comes ashore in style to view the siege of Constantinople, the procession is presented in profuse detail. The women in her train ride "vne espece de cheuaux ayans le col hault & droit comme Dromadaires" (X, xxvi, 56ᵛ). Agrian, the great emperor of Tartarie, and his brother Léopante make a similar grand entrance into Constantinople to attend a tourney (XIV, li). An entire chapter is devoted to the magnificent procession of Cléophile and her followers into Guindaye and to the magnificent costumes in which Diane and Daraïde dress to receive her (XI, xxxiv).

When Queen Zahara enters Trebizond, she comes attended by many lovely damsels, and the author's attention is divided between the opulence of their clothing and its diaphanousness. The magnificent spectacle is accompanied by music. "Et neantmoins celà ne pouuoit tant contenter l'oreille d'l'escoutant, comme l'oeil du regardant demeuroit satisfait: Car ces belles . . . n'auoient sur leurs corps que leurs simples chemises d'vn crespe tant delié, que leur beauté & perfection naturelle n'estoit nullement offusquée: ains pouuoit-on voir à l'ayse & à chacune d'elles deux pommettes au bout rouge, hautes esleuées, & assises sur vn estomac plus blanc, ne qu'yuoire ny que la premiere nege tombée du ciel durant vn fort hyuer. Et qui vouloit baisser l'oeil plus bas, let [*sic*] petit ventre rond & poly, autant qu'vn cristal, faisoit encores souhaiter voir plus outre. Mais vne simple peau de Canepin, qui s'y treuue, veult, qu'il n'y paroisse autre chose que blancheur. Aussi croy-ie que tel obstacle n'y fut oncques aproprié de Nature, sinon de crainte, ou que la Rose & le bouton qui y croist se flestrit, ou que les hommes trop enuieux de si douce fleur la vousissent cueillir & rauir par force d'Amour. Certes celà estoit (ce me semble) beau à regarder, & voudrois bien telle & si louable coustume estre encores au iour d'huy entre celles qui sont dignes de leur reng, pour louër en elles la grandeur de l'ouurier qui les a fabriquées si parfaitement" (VIII, xliii, 79).

While the variety of spectacle, custom, and dress engaged the mind's eye of the reader, the large number of poems, discourses, letters, and speeches tickled his ear. In stylistic versatility and rhetorical vigor none of the other chivalric romances of the century can compare with the *Amadis*. In addition to the complimentary verse that frequently adorns the various books, the French translation features a large quantity of verse. The amount varies from book to book, some volumes containing not a line and others offering a rich assortment.

Beginning particularly in Book VIII, with the wooing of Niquée by Amadis de Grèce, and continuing through Book XIV, poems and songs are prominent in the narrative. The reader learns that "Amadis de Grece estoit bien l'vn des plus parfaitz iouëurs de lut de son temps, & ayant la voix aussi douce & harmonieuse" (VIII, lxvii, 124). Rogel and Agesilan are also noted singers. Book XI contains twelve poems, and Book XII another dozen, mostly *chansons*, odes, and sonnets. All are carefully worked into the narrative framework. In Book XIII almost all the poems are confined to Chapter lvi, where the marriage of nine heroes is celebrated. Léon le Suave even composes a nuptial song for the occasion. After Book XIV poetry and song are less in evidence. Knights and ladies continue to sing, but the songs themselves are not often given, and it is clear that authors and translators felt more at home in prose.

Prose discourses that arise from the passions of the characters— those sorrows, angers, fears, joys, and burning desires of which

Gohorry speaks—are in many ways more interesting than the verse. Indeed many passages seem to be pieces of verse that have been turned into prose.[6] Love is the main topic or inspiration, and the soliloquy is the most common form. Conceits are frequently borrowed from Petrarchan sonneteers, and discourses are often so well developed and so generalized that they can be lifted whole out of context. Most such discourses found their way into *Le Thresor des liures d'Amadis,* where they became the fare of countless readers who presumably were untroubled by the absence of the narrative cocoon.

Important occasions—before a battle, an urgent council meeting, or a time of crisis—usually require speeches, and since important occasions abound in *Amadis,* there are dozens of important speeches. Letters too appear here in profusion. All told, discourses, speeches, and letters are to the flow of narrative rhetoric what shipwrecks and crossroads are to the plot.

As befits so varied a tale, the style has great range. The conventionally high-flown description of a sunrise, so often parodied in anti-romances, occurs in a few instances like the following: "L'Aurore n'eut plustost quitté le lict de son enuielly & chenu espoux, & Phoebus ne fut plustost sorty de sa salle doree, & monté en son estincellant chariot la torche au poing, à fin d'illuminer les cieux, que l'Empereur Amadis de Grece. . . ."[7] But in the light of the great length of *Amadis* and its fondness for rhetorical embellishment, this kind of writing is by no means typical. A diligent search of the romance would probably turn up most of the stylistic affectations to which the genre is prone, but extremes of inflated language are remarkably scarce.

Generally the prose style is subordinated to the needs of the narrative and assumes importance only during pregnant pauses in the action. Then it is frequently eloquent. When an angry letter from Rome contends, in a manner reminiscent of Shakespeare, that

Florisel has committed a crime so great that "a grand'peine vous lauera toute l'eau de vostre mer, d'vne si grande tache & macule," Frandalo in an answering speech manages to sound both biblical— "Royaume diuise en soy ne peult estre perdurable"—and full of peasant hardheadedness—for he sees the Romans "cherchans tousiours cinq piedz en vn mouton" (X, v, 14ᵛ–15). The dialogue sometimes sounds like a parody of chivalric speech, as when Anastarax thus addresses the giant Brosdolf: "Geant c'est toy qui as enleue ma femme & ma fille, comme vn trahistre & voleur: Si me les ren presentement, ou ie te puniray selon tes demerites" (XI, xxx, 54ᵛ). Such examples, however, are unusual, and knights are more likely to address each other in language incisive and urbane.

Some books contain a good deal of proverbial wisdom, and most allude frequently to classical mythology and biblical history. An occasional, almost inadvertent reference to unnatural natural history creeps in, but all twenty-one books would not yield twenty-one instances. *Amadis* shows scarcely a trace of the euphuism which was so popular in England in the last quarter of the sixteenth century, but some of the books come very close to a highly decorated prose of the kind Sidney favored. In spite of the excessive number of clichés and a tendency toward sudden sinkings, *Amadis* is narrated in a very lively style. In range, suppleness, and precision the prose style of *Amadis* is a remarkable achievement.

The frequent intrusion of wit and humor provides a refreshing change of pace for the reader. Indeed, nothing illustrates the superiority of *Amadis* to *The Mirror of Knighthood* or the Palmerin cycle more convincingly than the quantity and quality of its comedy, which ranges from the ironic and intellectual to the broadly vulgar. Most of the knights and many of the ladies have a keen sense of humor, albeit sometimes of a narrowly sixteenth-century cast that modern readers may not find congenial. Many a chapter contains little more than a prolonged merry conversation as knights and ladies jest their way through a tedious ride. Occasionally the sequence of chivalric adventures is broken by the insertion of a fabliau. A few of the comic interludes parody actions that are treated seriously in the rest of the book. Most interesting of all are the passages in which heroes who are usually taken seriously are ridiculed or made to look foolish.

Merry quips and quick answers comprise much of the wit in *Amadis*. In Book VIII a long discussion of love between Amadis de Grèce and a damsel is abruptly terminated when a knight attacks without warning and unhorses Amadis. The damsel looks down at the stunned hero and suggests dryly that perhaps he has been "transporté d'Amour" (xx). On another occasion, when Amadis de Gaule's squire Gandalin, in strange armor, attempts to rescue some kidnaped damsels, he is attacked by his lord, also in strange armor, and a fierce fight ensues. Luckily for Gandalin his helmet is knocked off just as he is knocked down. Amadis, looking down in some perplexity at his prostrate servant, asks in mock surprise: "Ah! Gandalin, est il possible que vous vous meslez de prendre à force les damoyselles! qu'en dira la Contesse vostre femme, si elle le scait?" (VII, li, 130). Gandalin merely rubs his head ruefully and replies that if Amadis treats all his servants so, he will not keep them long.

Understatement is a favorite humorous device in all books of *Amadis*. So common is it that it becomes almost a mannerism. So in a naval fight we read that Falanges beats off attackers and that Florisel "ne se tenoit pas les braz croysez" (IX, lxxi, 184). In another fight at sea Tiron rashly boards Quadragant's ship, "but his tarrying there was longer then he looked for" (that is, he was captured) (IV, 46). After Florisel and Heleine have consummated their love in the garden, the lady Timbrie returns and perceives immediately "qu'ilz s'estoient aprochez bien pres l'vn de l'autre" (IX, lxviii, 179). When Amadis de Grèce breaks into

Mouton's castle, he is threatened with death by a giant standing in a gallery above him. He retorts: "Monstre moy seulement . . . par ou il faut monter vers toy, & ie te releueray du trauail que tu prendrois à descendre çà bas" (VIII, xxxix, 71).

Such wit is occasionally grotesque or cruel. For instance, after the dwarf Miconel falls in love with the giantess Gaurisse, he becomes very jealous of Fortunian, whom he imagines a rival. There is a great deal of jesting about this misalliance, and Claire-Estoille comments that Miconel cannot even look his sweetheart in the face. When Arcalaüs dies, Lisuart urges burial rather than cremation because "son ame aura desormais plus de chaleur, qu'elle n'a eu en ce monde, soit en rosty, ou en bouly" (V, vii, 22). Jokes at the expense of dwarfs, giants, and miscellaneous deformed or maimed creatures abound. When Florisel fights and kills the giant Brostolfe, he bids him go to hell as a messenger for Satan. Florisel's fellows laugh heartily, for in the course of the fight Brostolfe has lost both arms, and the idea of an infernal courier without arms strikes them as very funny (X, lxi).

Dwarfs are almost always timorous—to the amusement of knights. When a dwarf leads Amadis of Gaul to the castle of the dread Arcalaüs, Amadis "tooke great pleasure to beholde his trembling, speaking thus merily to him. Feare not tall fellow, but let vs go down these staires" (I, xix, 125). In Book XI the dwarf Buzando fights a female dwarf, much to the amusement of the onlookers: "c'estoit vn tresplaisant spectacle que ce combat, semblable à celuy d'vn chien & vn chat" (xxxi, 56). A principal source of comic relief in Book IX is the running feud between the dwarf Mardoquée and the rustic booby Darinel.

This kind of humor delights in grotesque descriptions and mockery. After Esplandian has seen a hideous old hag—"vne femme tant vieille, caducque, & ridée, que ses deux tetasses luy deualoient iusques au dessouz du nombril" (V, xxxvii, 101)—he describes her to Urgande in terms of mock admiration: "elle a vn taint frais & delié, qu'a le bien contempler ie ne le vous pourrois mieux acomparer qu'a l'escorce de ces grands ormes qui seruent communément d'ombrages aux carrefours d'aucunes villages de la grand'Bretaigne" (V, xxxix, 109).

The Knight of the Burning Sword trades invective with the one-eyed daughter of Frandalon Cyclops: "Par Dieu ma Dame, si toutes les belles de ceste contree vous ressemblent, on ne iugera iamais que ie soye venu par deça pour y faire l'amour, & moins encor'que vous & moy soions enfans d'vn mesme pere" (VII, xix, 51). When the elder Cyclops comes out to fight, he brandishes a mighty axe, "lourde, pesante, & propre à vn si gentil & gracieux Damoisel qu'il estoit" (VII, xix, 51).

Humorous situations are often interlarded, apparently for variety's sake. Take, for example, the interlude in which Florarlan, called the Knight of the Phoenix, becomes the bone of contention between the youthful Galace and the old hag Palarce. Which of the two shall have him? Does priority belong to age or beauty? The two women finally come to blows over Phoenix, while knights look on and laughingly cheer the combatants (XI, vi).

Comic situations of this kind almost always involve love. When two foolish old knights, Barbaran and Moncan, arrange a nocturnal meeting with two sisters, they are told that the sisters sleep on the top floor of a castle. The only approach is by a rope let down from their room. But Barbaran says that he and Moncan do not mind climbing to heaven to be with such angels, and the sisters finally agree to help haul them up. On the designated night the two old lovers are hoisted halfway up and then left hanging.[8] The sisters let down the carcass of the recently slain Cavalyon, a monster like the Endriague, to hang alongside, and in the morning the whole castle turns out to hoot and laugh (XI, lxxx).

One of the most successful of these interpolations is the fabliau which comprises Chapter xxxii of Book XII. There Rogel and two companions with six damsels arrive at a castle where a wedding celebration is still in progress. The bride is much taken by the sight of Rogel and decides she prefers him to her husband. She prevails upon her maid Gante to take her place that night with the new bridegroom, while she, pretending to be one of the six damsels, creeps into Rogel's bed. Meanwhile, Rogel's squire Sirind has made advances to Gante, who pretends to acquiesce. But at night she gets a black chambermaid to take her place with Sirind, who has generously invited two other squires to share his luck. The details, lurid enough by the best fabliau standards, are neatly managed. The episode is told with zest, the high point coming with the discovery by the squires that their Diana, whom darkness lent beauty, has been eclipsed by the sun.

Comic episodes occasionally parody serious episodes or themes in *Amadis*. The emphasis on the youthfulness of Amadis and his descendants is serious enough, and it lends added force to the humor of the episode in which Barbaran and Moncan are robbed of their horses by a thief who promises to show them the fountain of youth (XI, lix). In similar fashion the enchantment of the duchess of Bavarie is used for comic purposes. This enchantment, wherein the lovers Rosaran and Silverne are immobilized, is able to inform lovers what success in love they are destined to have. When a knight enters the enchanted chamber where the two entranced lovers sit, Silverne is temporarily metamorphosed into the lady he loves, and he can learn from her reactions to him to what extent his love is requited. When a lady enters, Rosaran is similarly transformed into the knight she loves, and she can learn whether she is loved in return. A trickster who captures Daraïde binds him to a chair in a tent and tells him he must, like Rosaran and Silverne, greet all who enter and assure them of the love the trickster bears them (XII, xxiv).

Although such efforts to parody itself are not frequent in *Amadis,* they emphasize the antichivalric flavor that is common in many books. Even the most heroic knights are on occasion made to look ridiculous. In Nicholas de Montreux's version of Book XVI, Amadis de Gaule, still riding into adventure long after his hair and beard have whitened, is laughed at as "ce radoteur vieillard." [9] Amadis de Grèce, in disguise as the Knight of Death, has his horse stolen and is forced to ride the old crowbait left in its place. When he meets the damsel Angelée, she laughs at his appearance, though she admits the propriety of Death riding a half-dead horse (XI, xxvi).

Knights who disguise themselves as women invite embarrassment, and in *Amadis* they never escape it. When Agesilan and Arlanges travel together in feminine attire, Arlanges tries to explain the reticence of his companion by warning the curious that "she" is "touchée." When this explanation is offered in a vain attempt to dissuade an amorous knight whom they meet along the way, he retorts that he does not care whether she is sane or foolish: "ie n'ay besoin des discours de son cerueau" (XI, xvii, 33). In the fracas that follows, both Agesilan and Arlanges are much hampered by their long dresses. After Galtazar de Barberousse falls madly in love with the disguised Agesilan, the latter tries to cure him by telling him the truth. But Galtazar never entirely recovers, and thereafter, whenever he sees Agesilan, the old flame revives.[10]

When Garinter and Manely go ashore on a strange island, their helmets are stolen by monkeys, and they are forced to comic lengths to retrieve them. One expedient is to fashion a crude bow of wood, using as string "la corde de leurs iartiers" (V, xviii, 44).

Though love is usually taken quite seriously, the chivalric habit of fainting is often ridiculed. Amadis d'Astre in the guise of the Knight of Sadness swoons so frequently that his squire has almost given up trying to revive him. One day when he faints at a fountain, a lady asks his squire why he does not throw water in his face. The squire answers that if water were used for every fainting fit, "ie pense que i'assecheroys bien vne riuiere" (XVIII, xxix, 232).

Many of the humorous situations in the romance arise from the machinations of a trickster called the Fraudeur. His avocation is to make fools of knights. A master of disguise, he specializes in stealing their horses and then returning in another disguise to trick them again. In disguise he takes particular delight in hoodwinking knights after first warning them of the subtlety of the Fraudeur. Several of the greatest heroes of *Amadis* find themselves on foot or up to their armpits in a bog as a result of the Fraudeur's trickery. The Fraudeur prides himself on performing the function of an educator, for he teaches knights to be more careful about strangers. After warning Rogel to be wary of tricksters, he so arranges matters that Rogel falls into "vn trou punais . . . lieu si puant & infait, que de son odeur seule il pouuoit donner la mort" (XIII, xiii, 71). Although in the long run the Fraudeur is himself tricked, he helps put chivalric heroes in a new light. He takes the chivalric romance a giant step closer to the world of Don Quixote.

VI

Structure and Repetition

Though *Amadis* may be viewed as a work in which variety has run wild, it is marked also by familiarity, monotony, and repetition. When Sir Henry Thomas complains that later books are but poor exaggerations of their originals, he is clearly not complaining about the novelty and diversity of the romance. He is bemoaning the authors' habit of building the narrative upon itself. No alert reader can wade through many books of *Amadis* without being aware of the recurrence of themes, episodes, and motifs. Since the episodes most frequently repeated are derived from such distinguished literary works as the *Iliad*, the *Odyssey*, and the *Aeneid* or from well-known medieval and Renaissance books, readers are likely to experience a nagging sense of the familiar. The repetition or parallelism in *Amadis* is so constant that it represents a habit of composition and indeed establishes an underlying unity. The surface variety, the wild and whirling narrative, the wonders, the diversity of style, the tragicomic approach—all are in a sense counterbalanced by an underlying similarity. Despite their differences—Rogel is unlike Agesilan or Amadis de Grèce—the heroes have so many traits in common that in important situations they are interchangeable. Repetition and parallelism in *Ama-*

dis conspire with timelessness and ubiquitousness to produce a sense of sameness.

The latter half of Book IX is based on the story of the rape of Helen and the Trojan War. The analogy is loose, and the author is content to keep it so. When Heleine, who is engaged to Lucidor (Menelaus), falls in love with Florisel (Paris), the reader is warned that the consequence will be crueler and bloodier wars than ever were made "pour le rauissement commis par Paris, de la belle Heleine femme de Menelaüs" (IX, lxviii, 175ᵛ). Thus the reader is not surprised when Florisel runs off with Heleine and the abduction provokes a great war between Rome and Constantinople. Nor should he be surprised when Heleine comes upon the walls of Constantinople to watch the fighting. But the author uses the parallel to suit his needs and drops it without apology when it ceases to help him.[1]

Other writers of *Amadis,* noting that the Helen story had been successfully retold, resorted to the myth again in later books. In Book XX Queen Persée comes out upon the walls of besieged Taurique to watch the battles in the plain below. She sees herself as another Helen of Troy and holds herself responsible for the deaths of countless knights. In fact, her situation is only vaguely like Helen's. She has not eloped, and Taurique is not another Troy, but her vision of herself as another Helen elevates Book XX merely by its evocation of the Homeric parallel. In Book XXI the story is repeated once more, this time in duplicate. On the eve of their weddings to two princes, Grisonie and Corinne are carried off by two other suitors to a city named, aptly enough, Dardanie. The king of Silandrie thereupon raises a great army and, following the lovers, lays siege to the city.

In addition to the Helen-Paris tale classical mythology furnishes the framework for several episodes of somewhat lesser scope. Circe is a great favorite, and several women who hold knights captive by force of magic or beauty invite comparison with that famous witch. So Lindanie holds the prince of Palomar enchanted in the Val Amoureux, and Ginolde on her invisible isle preys upon knights who pass in their ships. The myth of Danaë is retold in the stories of princesses who are immured by their parents to keep them from men, and the parallelism with the myth is indicated. So in Book VIII Bazilique isolates his daughter Niquée, and in Book XI Queen Sidonie locks up Diane. The story of the horrendous Laestrygones, who give Odysseus and his men so much trouble in Book X of the *Odyssey,* is recalled in the chapters of Book XVIII that concern the Elestrigons, who inhabit the Isle of the Cruel and live off human flesh. The frame for the tale of Silvan and Licinie in Book XX, Chapter lxx, is derived from the legend of Antiochus of Syria, who loved his young stepmother Stratonice so passionately that his life was endangered. On the advice of an alert physician, who noted that his pulse rate varied according to her visits and departures, he was allowed to marry her.

The Dido and Aeneas story is quite clearly being followed when Queen Florelle falls madly in love with Rogel and tries to keep him in her country by offering herself in marriage. But Rogel, as usual, has other women in mind, and he sails off. As she watches his ship go, her grief turns almost to madness. She dies, and the smoke from her funeral pyre is seen by Rogel at sea (XII, xcvi).[2] In the same book Agesilan rescues the naked Diane just as she is about to be sacrificed to a sea monster (xcv). The tale is that of Perseus and Andromeda, but it would have appealed particularly to those sixteenth-century readers who had read Rogero's rescue of Angelica in Canto X of Ariosto's *Orlando Furioso,* the immediate source of the episode in *Amadis.*

The writers' habit of basing a story in *Amadis* upon Greek and Roman precedent is nowhere better illustrated than in Book XX, where the entire book is a retelling of Heliodorus' *Ethiopian History*.[3] So easily does the Greek romance adopt horse and armor and chivalric manners and so naturally does its elaborate structure blend into that of *Amadis* that the relationship of the two romances has not hitherto been noticed by scholars.

Not only is the reader of *Amadis* often reminded of parallels in Greek and Roman myth and story but he is also often urged to compare characters and incidents with classical or biblical prototypes—even when the similarities are remote and general in nature. Catalogues of classical figures from myth and history turn up in various arrangements to help give an air of weight and learning to the tale. Dido and Medea frequently head lists of loyal but forsaken ladies, and Aeneas and Jason are prominent among the names of fickle and heartless men. The bestiality of Pasiphaë, the terror of Daphne pursued by Apollo, and the tragic love of Pyramus and Thisbe help to give an impression of universality to many stock chivalric situations. Apelles and Zeuxis are remembered as artists who have looked on beauty bare, and a famous portrait of Diane in Book XI is done by a descendant of Apelles. Agesilan derives his name from that of the Spartan king Agesilaus, whom he resembles in manners, and his friend Arlanges is said to be like the great hero Theseus. When Florarlan, who is raised in unusually wild and primitive circumstances, compares his state to that of Paris before he learned he was a son of Priam and Hecuba, the analogy gives him added stature and sets his pastoral upbringing in a new context. The many references to mythology are given solid backing by the intermingling of allusions to such historical worthies as Alexander the Great, Pompey, and Julius Caesar and to biblical figures like Samson, Holofernes, and Nebuchadnezzar.

If the reader is again and again reminded that an episode in *Amadis* resembles a story from antiquity, his recurring sense of the familiar is increased by the romance's heavy reliance upon widely current medieval and Renaissance tales. The Amadis cycle drew particularly upon Arthurian matter. Arthur is frequently alluded to as a warrior who belongs in a class with Amadis and his descendants. In an enchanted rock Léonide sees paintings of King Arthur and the most famous of his knights of the Round Table. Other pictures there portray Charlemagne and his followers. Later in the same cave Léonide sees a statue of Arthur, "qui doit vn iour regner en la grand'Bretaigne" (XII, ii, 7). Arthur and his Round Table seem to be the model for Lisuart and his court in Britain. Lisuart sets out to glorify his reign by attracting to his service the most famous knights of the world, and to Lisuart's King Arthur Amadis plays a kind of Lancelot. The great battle fought between Lisuart and King Cildadan of Ireland is somewhat like that between Arthur and Modred. After the battle Galaor and Cildadan are carried from the battlefield mysteriously by twelve maidens.

In Book IV of *Amadis* Balan's island is marked by a red tower built by Joseph, described as the son of "Ioseph of Aramathia, who brought the Sangreal into Great Brittaine" (xxxiii, 147). The island is destined to pass into the hands of Segurades, who is to live in the time of "Uter Pendragon, Father to king Arthur." Segurades' son is destined to be slain "by Sir Tristram de Lyons, as he conducted fayre Yseult, wife to King Marke, into Cornewall." Segurades' grandson is to be a great friend of "Sir Lancelot du Lake" (xxxiv, 157). Obviously the various authors of *Amadis* feel a strong sense of friendship for Arthur.

Indeed, *Amadis* appears to derive principally from medieval French romances about Arthur and the various heroes of the Round Table. The legends of Tristan and Lancelot have been suggested as particularly close.[4] The idea of a knight disguising himself as a woman in order to gain access to his lady—one of the most unusual motifs in *Amadis*—may be derived from *Tristan*. Iseut, shut up in a tower by Mark, tells Brangien that Tristan can come to visit her "vetu d'une robe de demoiselle," and in that garb Tristan successfully comes and goes.[5] The Tristan story is also recalled in *Amadis* when Queen Sidonie, like Iseut of Brittany deserted by her husband, lingers by the sea, continually looking out for the ship that will bring him back (X, xlvi).

In both matter and imagery *Amadis* is very close to the tales of Chrestien de Troyes. For example, the episode in Book II, wherein Amadis in disguise as le beau Ténébreux is recognized by Mabile from the scar on his face, is probably derived from Chrestien's *Yvain*. There Yvain runs mad for love—like Orlando and, to a lesser degree, Amadis—and lives only through the kindness of a hermit. One day while he sleeps in the woods, a damsel sees him and recognizes him by the scar on his face. Almost all Chrestien's stock phrases and figures of speech turn up in *Amadis,* and there can be no question that Chrestien's tales and *Amadis* are part of a common tradition.

Although the story of Troilus and Criseyde does not attract unusual attention in *Amadis,* Criseyde is mentioned several times in lists of fickle ladies. The story of her treachery is recited in some detail in Book V by the king of Dace, who is trying to persuade Esplandian not to place too much trust in Léonorine: "N'entendistes vous oncques le bon tour que fit Brisaide a Troilus, apres la ruine d'Ylion? Elle l'aymoit tant, qu'elle cuida morir entre ses braz quand elle fut contrainte l'habandonner: & pensoient les Grecz asseurement qu'elle se vousist deffaire: Et toutesfois a peine fut elle hors de Troye, qu'elle oublia du tout son Troilus & transfera ceste vehemente amour, qu'elle luy auoit portee toute sa vie, sur Dyomedes Roy de Trace. O Dieu qu'elle inconstance, qu'elle legiereté! quel fondement sur arene mobile? Ceste malheureuse auoit, sur soy entre autres aornemens precieux que son amy Troilus luy donna par singularité vne paire de gans parfumez, lesquelz elle bailla a son nouueau Dyomedes, vn heure apres sa prinse en signe d'amytié, & du bien qu'elle luy portoit. Qu'eust dit lors Troilus s'il eust esté present? l'eust il peu croire? ie croy que non, & l'eust il veu de ses deux yeux" (V, xxxiii, 87).

Though medieval romance is the strongest influence upon the character and tone of *Amadis,* other kinds of medieval literature also make themselves felt. Reynard the Fox is referred to on several occasions, particularly in connection with the clever magician Arcalaüs. The adventure in which Virgil the necromancer is left dangling in a basket lies behind the trick played on Moncan and Barbaran by the Fraudeur.[6] Even Boccaccio, whose influence on *Amadis* is dim at best, is recalled in Book XVII, when two knights named Tancred and Guischard arrive in the Christian camp to fight against the pagans.[7]

The same book contains an analogue of the old tale of the loathly lady—of which John Gower has a version and Chaucer's *Wife of Bath's Tale* is a cousin. Amadis d'Astre comes upon a deserted village and a countryside terrorized by two fierce dragons. He learns that they are really two lovely girls who have been transformed by a magician. They can be restored to human shape by the knight who dares to touch them with his right hand on face and breast. Many others have tried and failed, the sight of the dragons at close range being almost too much for normal human courage, but Amadis of course succeeds (XVII, lxxxv).[8]

Among the sixteenth-century works echoed in the French *Amadis,* Ariosto's *Orlando Furioso* is most easily distinguished. In fact, since several books of *Amadís de Gaula* were in print in Spain before his heroic poem appeared in Italy, Ariosto may have been indebted to the Spanish romance.[9] The similarities noted, however, are so vague and commonplace as to indicate merely the likelihood that both works drew upon common medieval sources. On the other hand, there can be no question that the

French *Amadis* borrowed extensively from Ariosto. Some of this borrowing has already been indicated by scholars, but a complete record has not yet been made. In his recent study of the influence of Ariosto in France, A. Cioranescu agrees that almost the whole Grifaléon episode in Book XII of *Amadis* is obviously derived from Ariosto, and he adds enough evidence of borrowings of other kinds to suggest that *Amadis* owes Ariosto a debt much greater than has yet been recognized.[10]

Not only has *Amadis* drawn on Ariosto for incident, but it also makes use of various descriptive passages. To those that Cioranescu has pointed out, the following may be added as an illustration of the way Ariosto is used. After Rogero falls into the lap of the seductress Alcina, he undergoes a metamorphosis, which is thus described in Sir John Harington's translation:

> About his necke a carkneet rich he ware,
> Of precious stones, all set in gold well tride,
> His armes that erst all warlike weapons bare,
> In golden bracelets wantonly were tide:
> Into his eares two rings conveyed are,
> Of golden wire, at which on either side
> Two Indian pearles in making like two peares,
> Of passing price were pendent at his eares.
>
> His locks bedew'd with waters of sweet savour,
> Stood curled round in order on his hed,
> He had such wanton womanish behavior,
> As though in Valence he had long bene bred:
> So chang'd in speech, in manners and in favour,
> So from himselfe, beyond all reason led,
> By these inchantments of this am'rous dame,
> He was himselfe in nothing but in name.[11]

This description of Rogero fits the change that occurs in Rogel after he has become infatuated with Queen Florelle: "Son col estoit enuironné d'vn carcan d'esmeraude, ayant double fermail;

l'vn deuant, taillé en vn gros ruby; l'autre derriere, caché souz vn large safir qui rendoit vne merueilleuse clarté: A ce mesme carcan pendoit à vn ruban de soye incarnate, vne medaille de fine Porcelaine enchassée en or esmaillé a petis fueillages, qui representoit au naturel la belle Royne de Canabée qu'il acompagnoit: A chacune de ses oreilles pendoit vn pirope mis en oeuure fort industrieusement: Ses cheueux estoient frisez, crespes, annellez & embaumez des plus souefues odeurs de l'Arabie: ses yeux estincellans, & lascifz; son visage frais & poly; tous ses gestes amoureux & folastres, comme s'il eust seulement esté produit au monde pour faire la court aux Dames, & laisser flestrir la plus excellente fleur de sa ieunesse en oysifues mignardises dans le giron de Damoyselles" (XII, xciv, 233^v–234).

In addition to Ariosto, whose poem furnishes the inspiration for several other episodes in *Amadis,* other poets are invoked by the French translators. François Villon's most famous line is recalled in Book VIII, when Amadis de Grèce meets Lucelle and promptly forgets Niquée, "qu'il ne luy en souuenoit non plus que des neiges d'antan" (xxi, 40). In Book XI Queen Sidonie, at the sight of a portrait of six damsels who have killed themselves for her in a dramatic public fashion, is moved to these words: "Ie suis en paix & en mortelle guerre: ie crains, i'espere, i'ardz froide comme glace: ie vol au ciel, tout estendue en terre, & rien n'estrains de fait & tout i'embrase: en prison suis qui ne s'ouure ne serre: d'vn mesme laz on me lace & delace: Amour m'enferre ensemble & me deferre, m'ayant donné & puis m'ostant sa grace: heur & malheur me suyuent en ma chasse: Ie veux mon bien & à mon mal ie cours: egalement la vie & mort ie suis: voire la vie & la mort ie pourchasse: & veux perir & demande secours: en tel estat pour Florisel ie suis" (i, 2).

Although a French poem is the most likely immediate source for Sidonie's speech, the words can be traced back to a sonnet of

Petrarch (Sonetto in vita 90) which begins: "Pace non trovo et non o dar far guerra." The sonnet was well known in England, for it appears in *Tottel's Miscellany*, and the Englishman who did not read Book XI in French could find Sidonie's speech reprinted in *The Treasurie of Amadis of Fraunce*—but with no indication of its sonnet ancestry.

The discovery that a Petrarchan sonnet, its rhyme scheme still intact, has been put in Sidonie's mouth raises the suspicion that other sonnets and poems may lie buried among the thousands of words of *Amadis*. Certainly many passages in various books sound as though they have been lifted out of other contexts. For instance, in Book XIX Fortunian gives Claire-Estoille a definition of love which he says he heard from a wise man: "Amour est ie ne sçay quoy, qui vient de ie ne sçay où; ie ne sçay qui l'enuoye, en ie ne sçay quelle maniere: il nasquit ie ne sçay comment; & estant soy-mesme confus, il confond les autres: il paist icy & se nourrit ailleurs: il s'alimente de ie ne sçay quoy: il n'estime la louange; il se glorifie en la douleur; & n'a en soy ny raison ny maniere: ie ne sçay pas comme ores il se manifeste, & ores il se cache. Il frappe ie ne sçay comment au milieu du coeur, sans que l'on puisse remarquer ny sang ny playe: celuy qu'il a tue, vit en mourant. Il fait parler du coeur, & non auec la langue: il se taist dedans, & impose silence dehors. Qui scauroit maintenant interpreter ce fol?" (cxv, 381). This seems too carefully composed for its context. The wise man may have been a poet Mambrino Roseo knew. At any rate the theme is common among Elizabethan poets.[12]

The reader's sense, as he peruses *Amadis*, that he has read an episode somewhere before is bolstered by the authors' common habit of echoing themselves and one another. Later books frequently repeat with major or minor alterations tricks of characterization, narrative patterns, or spectacular devices used successfully in earlier books. The repetitions set up mnemonic echoes in the reader and help give an impression of purpose and form that is belied by the rambling structure of the work.[13]

The birthmark is a favorite romance cliché, and many of the heroes of Amadis bear an indelible and often quite extraordinary mark somewhere on their bodies. Léonide and Rogel are led to name their son Sphéramonde because he is born with a sphere imprinted on his left side (XIV, xxv). Falanges d'Astre is so named for a star on his breast (IX, lix). Amadis de Grèce has perhaps the most famous birthmark of all romance heroes. He is born with a flaming sword engraved on his body from knee to breast, and for a large part of his life, his parentage unknown to him, he goes under the title of Knight of the Burning Sword. His son Silves, born in strange circumstances on a desert isle, also bears a red sword on his body. The child Foulgorant is so named because of the mark of a thunderbolt which seems to enflame his left breast. Such marks not only single out knights who are destined for high achievement but are useful in such practical matters as identification. When Amadis de Grèce disguises himself as the maiden Néreïde in order to woo the nearly inaccessible Niquée, he finds it necessary on one occasion to prove his real identity. "Et desboutonnant le deuant de sa iupe descouurit son estomac" (VIII, lxxii, 134).

The birthmarks are sometimes accompanied by, or take the form of, prophetic writing. Argantes, son of Rogel and Fusilée, has a complete prophecy written on his chest (XIII, lii). Amadis de Grèce's famous birthmark contains white characters which go undeciphered for a long time. Finally, after a fight between Amadis de Grèce and his father, in which neither knows the other, the magician Alquif interprets the characters and establishes paternity. They read: "Amadis de Grece filz de Lisuart de Grece et de la Princesse Onolorie." Nascian the hermit is able to baptize

Esplandian by his proper name when he finds the infant, because Esplandian bears his name marked on his body in white letters. Esplandian has other markings—seven red characters—that are for a long while unread. When finally interpreted, they prove to be the initials of the woman destined to be his wife: LFDGEDG (Léonorine, Fille Du Grand Empereur Du Grèce). The fate of many lovers has been written in the stars, but Esplandian may well be the only hero of fiction whose fate in love is enciphered on his body.

Birthmarks are essential in the Amadisian world of secret births and infant exposure or kidnaping. The physical consummation of love before marriage is very much the rule for heroes and heroines. The trothplight is first used in Book I by Périon and Hélisène, and their offspring Amadis is technically a bastard. Thereafter in almost every union the trothplight is used, children are born out of wedlock, and feminine ingenuity is taxed to keep maternity a secret. Just as Amadis, Moses-like, is cast adrift upon the waters and brought up by an alien people, so many later heroes are subject to exposure and strange rearing. Galaor as a child is kidnaped by a giant, and Esplandian, in a manner reminiscent of Romulus and Remus, is adopted by a motherly lioness.

The strain of inventing variations upon the common motif of maternal agitation and infant exposure shows most noticeably in the writers of later books. Often they try to achieve novelty by doubling the ingredients. Thus in Book XIV when the two princesses beloved by Silves and Lucendus secretly give birth to sons at the same time, they turn the babies over to the witch Dragosine for rearing. But she bears Lucendus a grudge and takes the children into the forest to kill them. In the nick of time a lion chases her off. Then the babies are taken up by pirates from Palomar, who hope to regain the favor of their queen by giving them to her, and who manage to feed them on shipboard through the help of a captive lioness (lxv).

Devices like birthmarks, secret births, and infant exposure, overworked as they are in *Amadis,* bring the various heroes closer together and make the ladies sisters under the skin. In the jumble of narrative the reiteration even of such old motifs has about it the charm of the familiar.

Descriptions of wondrous structures also encourage emulation and invention. The marvelous Palace of Apolidon, which is described so glowingly in Book IV, inspired succeeding writers to conceive buildings even more marvelous. Axiane's Palace in Book VII is said to be the equal of Apolidon's, and here Amadis de Grèce and Lucelle break an enchantment in a manner that recalls Amadis de Gaule and Oriane at the Palace of Apolidon and the Forbidden Chamber. The Palace of Axiane is not described quite so vividly as that of Apolidon. Perhaps the imitator recognized the futility of attempting to equal such descriptions as this: "The pauement was of Chrisolite, carued in loue knots, enriched with Corall and Cipres, cut in little scales, and fastened with threds of gold" (IV, ii, 5). In Book VIII a third magnificent edifice, this one called the Tower of the Universe, is built by means of the combined efforts of three magicians, Zirfée, Alquif, and Urgande. This imposing structure, said to be "non moindre que celle de Nembroth" (lix, 111), is described in detail. Later, in Book XI, the Château of Phoebus is described with awe and admiration, and a woodcut is supplied for the curious reader (ii, 3). Like the Tower of the Universe, it is divided into seven sections, each sacred to one of the planets. In succeeding books the reader is introduced to still other marvelous dwellings—like the Palace of Zirzée in Book XVIII (cxxv)—each understood to be superior to the one described before it.

Certain narrative patterns also frequently recur. One of the most memorable episodes in the first four books concerns the falling out of Amadis de Gaule and Oriane. Overcome by jealousy because she believes that he has been unfaithful to her with Briolanie, she writes him an angry letter dismissing him forever from her sight (II, ii). In Book VI an almost exact parallel occurs when Onolorie hears that her knight Lisuart loves Gradafilée and she him. Wild with jealousy, she writes a letter in which she tells him never to come into her presence again (xxix). In Book XVII Rosaliane, angry at what she fancies to be the affection shown by Amadis d'Astre for Artamire, writes a letter commanding him never to appear before her again (lxxvii). In each case the innocent lover rides off disconsolate, disguises himself respectively as le beau Ténébreux, the Solitary Knight, and the Knight of Sadness, and thinks of living out his existence as a hermit. In each case the lady soon has reason to suspect she has been hasty, and she sends a messenger to find her knight and deliver a letter of forgiveness.[14]

The fondness for this plot situation can be explained in part by its sentimental appeal, but it happens also to fit neatly into the alienation-and-return pattern that has always been a favorite in romances. Similarly, many other recurring narrative schemes in *Amadis* have archetypal properties. The confrontation in battle of father and son is very common. Almost every book has also its great enchantment, like a puberty test, to try the mettle of the chivalric hero. Dozens of damsels in distress are distinguishable from one another only by name or the number of attackers. Many a lady is tied to a stake, ready for burning, when her champion appears in the nick of time, and many a dragon or ravening serpent terrorizes a kingdom until a hero comes.

All these narrative clichés are characteristic also of other romances, particularly *Palmerin* and *The Mirror of Knighthood*.

But some of the episodes and twists of plot that recur often in *Amadis* are rare in other sixteenth-century romances and even in medieval romances and so have a special claim on our attention. For instance, the motif whereby a knight disguises himself as a warrior maid, usually to woo a closely confined lady, is used quite often in several books. The disguise itself has a venerable history going back to Achilles' donning of female dress, and *Amadis* could have derived it from *Tristan*. Nevertheless, no other romance has exploited the disguise so thoroughly and so often. Amadis de Grèce first uses such a disguise in order to gain access to the carefully guarded princess Niquée. Later Agesilan and Arlanges copy Amadis' trick, which has by their time become legendary. Both dress as women to make their way into the presence of Diane. In a somewhat different context Florisel adopts feminine disguise. He looks so much like the Amazon Alastraxerée, his half-sister, that he can readily pass for her. Once he dresses as a woman to save Alastraxerée from seizure, and on another occasion he does so to avoid the overardent attentions of Arlande. In all cases the complications resulting from this disguise are thoroughly exploited for their erotic and humorous qualities, and are the ingredients for a central episode.[15]

The knight who is simultaneously involved with two or more ladies, each of whom he wants to marry, is another motif—rare in other romances—which is repeated several times in *Amadis*. Indeed it appears to be a hereditary ambivalence. Early in his career Lisuart is secretly married to Onolorie, but he is also attracted to the pagan Abra, who loves and pursues him ardently. (Abra first appears in Book VIII.) The timely death of Onolorie, which allows Lisuart to marry Abra, also establishes a narrative pattern. Lisuart's troubles recur for his son Amadis de Grèce, who loves Lucelle and the pagan Niquée and for a long while turns like a weathercock from one lady to the other. He finally marries

Niquée, but continues to feel guilty about his duplicity toward Lucelle. But then, in Montreux's version, Niquée dies, and Amadis is able to satisfy both Lucelle and his conscience by a new marriage.[16]

Heredity seems to compound matters for Florisel, the son of Amadis de Grèce. At one point he loves no fewer than three ladies: Silvie, Alastraxerée, and Heleine. Later he becomes deeply involved with yet a fourth, Queen Sidonie. When Silvie turns out to be his aunt and Alastraxerée his sister, Florisel's dilemma becomes more like his father's and his grandfather's. He marries Heleine, who conforms to pattern by dying in time for him to make an honest woman of Sidonie.[17] Florisel's son is Rogel, a philanderer as notorious as Don Juan. But even Rogel cannot escape his ancestral fate. He marries Léonide even though he has promised to marry Queen Persée. The outraged queen swears vengeance and declares war. In the midst of hostilities Léonide suddenly dies, and Rogel is therefore free to keep his word and restore peace.[18] The axiom that ontogeny recapitulates phylogeny is further reinforced when Astrapol, a grandson of Amadis de Grèce, undergoes a similar experience. He marries Rosalve, though he also loves the queen of Clotone. Fortunately he has inherited not only the amorous tendencies of his noted ancestor but also his luck. Rosalve's opportune death clears the way for him to marry the queen and preserve the family way of love.[19]

In most medieval and sixteenth-century romances religion is taken for granted, and so it is in *Amadis*. It supplies a ready excuse for the many holy wars, but, comfortably in the background, it is scarcely ever a matter of immediate concern. The one exception to this generalization concerns the life of the religious recluse. Hermits, of course, are romance commonplaces, but in *Amadis* the reader is often reminded that the hermit's life represents an alternative to chivalric action. Old knights become hermits. Old kings enter monasteries. Princesses disappointed in love—like Lucelle—seek refuge in nunneries. Several hermits are important to the story, especially Nascian in the early books and the kindly bull-riding hermit who advises the Knight of the Burning Sword in Book VIII. Florisel, who is helped by a hermit, secretly uses the hermitage as a base of operations for his seduction of Heleine in Book IX. Knights who suffer reverses in love almost always consider retiring to a hermit's life. In Book XXI the reader meets two hermits, both former courtiers, who have found peace and a sense of fulfillment in isolated prayer. Amadis de Gaule establishes an important precedent in Book II by becoming a hermit in a vain attempt to forget Oriane. Thereafter other knights adopt the same expedient. Amadis de Grèce, torn by love for two women, takes up the life of hermit among the barren crags on which he is shipwrecked. Even the irrepressible Rogel catches the fever and threatens to become a hermit if Persée does not forgive and marry him.

Converting pagans to Christianity is another matter not strange to romances but carried to extraordinary lengths in *Amadis*. The Citizen in Francis Beaumont's *Knight of the Burning Pestle,* one who knows romances well, calls to Ralph to convert Pompiona, daughter of the king of Cracovia,[20] and both *Palmerin* and *The Mirror of Knighthood* take conversions seriously. But in *Amadis* the number of converted pagans is exceeded only by the hundreds of thousands killed in myriad battles. There are numerous instances of baptism by force, as when Amadis de Gaule overcomes the tyrant Madraque but spares him on condition he become a Christian (III, ii). Giants who are suddenly made aware of the shortcomings of paganism when their pagan gods fail them in battle elect baptism in revulsion against defeat.

Love of a Christian knight moves numerous pagan princesses to interest in Christianity. The queen of Clotone, out of love for

Astrapol, is baptized with all her kingdom (XIX, xlv). When Sestiliane becomes a Christian for love of Arlanges, she is seized with evangelical fervor. With the help of Arlanges she converts the king and queen of Mont-Libéan and their entire army (XX, xxxiv). After Florarlan saves the kingdom of Dardanie from the invasion of Madaran, the queen and all her people accept baptism out of gratitude (XI, xxii). Even magicians usually see the light, and a letter from four of them—Alquif, Urgande, Zirfée, and Zirène—refers to them as "bons Chrestiens & catoliques" (XIV, lxx, 97).

There is also more emphasis upon youth and youthfulness in *Amadis* than is usual in romances. This theme, repeated in the various books, was doubtless popular in reaction against the Spanish Book VIII, wherein Amadís died. People wept and proved disconsolate until Book IX appeared with the glad tidings that Book VIII was a mistake. There was not to be another such re-action from readers of fiction until the eighteenth century, when Pamela's marriage caused public rejoicing and the ringing of church bells in English towns. After Book VIII writers felt obliged to keep Amadis alive. And if Amadis, why not his whole tribe? Not only Amadis but all heroes remain vigorous. Again and again father is mistaken for son, even by a wife or sweet-heart, not only because they look alike but because they look the same age. Rosalve thinks her rescuer is Astrapol, whereas he is really Astrapol's father Silves (XVIII, xcvi). Amadis de Grèce is more than once mistaken for his father Lisuart—on one occa-sion with embarrassing results.[21] Until Book XXI none of the important male figures dies, and the final great battle in the East involves some Christian knights well above a hundred years of age.

From birthmarks to marvelous edifices, from conversions to intimations of immortality, the various authors of *Amadis* seem

to feel that motifs that work well on one occasion are bound to improve with repetition. What Sir Henry Thomas calls the "poor exaggerations of their originals" serve as cohesive elements in the vast, apparently structureless, books that comprise the romance. In Book IX when Florisel makes improper advances to Heleine and she asks with mock severity whether the hermit (with whom Florisel is staying at the time) has taught him such tactics, the reader will remember that Oriane asked Amadis de Gaule the same question in similar circumstances in Book II.[22] The memory helps bridge a gap of seven books, encourages the reader to compare the love of Florisel and Heleine with that of Amadis and Oriane, and suggests that for all their individual differences the lives of most men follow remarkably similar patterns. The familiar motifs, which obliterate place and time, fit easily into the timeless and placeless world of romance.

Like all romances, *Amadis* revels in the far away and long ago. But like the blows the knightly heroes take, which are always deadly and yet never kill, place and time are often mentioned and yet seldom matter. The heroes range all the known world and much of the unknown, from London, where Lisuart keeps his court, to "l'Inde superieure," where Amadis d'Astre wanders. Many of the places cited are, or seem to be, familiar—as when the Knight of the Burning Sword lands at "Ciuita Veche, pres Rome." Places like Sicile and Naples are set in the same world with the exotic country of Californie, where the Amazons live, and with the Isle called Cynofale, "ou tout le peuple qui y habite a le visage de chien." Persia, Babylon, Arabia, Palestine, and Trebizond are among the fabled places visited by errant knights, who also make their wonderful way through lands of somewhat less renown like Calidonie, Apolonye, Paphlagonie, Saba, and Natolie. Mounted on his flying beast, Agesilan traverses the world in Book XII, and Silves makes a trip to the Underworld, where he sees the Golden Fleece and Medea's murdered children and fights Jason.

Whatever their names, cities and countries are vague. Buillon, which ought to be in France, seems as remote from reality as the Isle of Silanchie, where Frandalon Cyclops lives with his one-eyed daughter. Places like Niquée and Sidonie seem even more unreal because they are also the names of prominent characters. Others, like the isle belonging to the sorceress Ginolde, disappear like mirages before the eyes of the characters. Constantinople is the great city of the romance, constantly under attack by Moors and Saracens, and as the seat of Amadis de Gaule's descendants, it is a focal point of the fantastic Amadisian world. Most of the quests begin and end in Constantinople, the Cleopolis of this fairyland.

In all the comings and goings in *Amadis*, from Russia to the Mountains of the Moon, time is frequently mentioned. Knights sail for seven or eight days and land on a Monday or a Friday. Night comes and day breaks. Yet time is insignificant. It seldom affects the characters, and they in turn treat it casually. When she is abandoned by Florisel, Arlande is greatly cheered to find herself pregnant, for she looks forward to a son who will avenge his mother. She does not think of the years that must pass before her desire for revenge can be satisfied. Time does not alter love or hate. Nor does it seriously hamper the physical activities of heroes.

Amadis de Gaule seems ageless, and time, which normally transfixes the flourish set on youth, treats him lightly. Born in Book I, he is described in Book VII as eighty years old, though he looks only forty. The youthful Cléophile falls in love with him in Book X, white beard and all, for he is still "fraiz & vermeil comme la rose." In Book XVI, his white beard hanging to his navel, he is still active, though miscreants now think him a bit ridiculous. After Book XVI his name appears less often. He wants to help at the siege of Taurique in Book XX, but he is persuaded to remain in semiretirement. Despite all pleas he insists on being present for the great battle in Alape in Book XXI, and there he dies after a gallant fight against pagans, many of whom are more than a century younger.

Past, present, and future blend with disarming sameness. Although Amadis de Gaule is born shortly after the death of Christ, Arthur is referred to several times as dead—though expected to return; gunpowder is used in artillery and in mines to blow up walls of besieged towns; and it is frequently assumed that the customs and dress of the characters are those of the readers. Knights are sometimes given armor or weapons used by classical heroes like Achilles or Hector, and Silves defeats Jason by using a wrestling hold made famous by Milo of Crotona. Yet ladies are described as wearing their hair in "the Italian style," and the pagans constantly beating at the gates of Constantinople are really the Turks so feared by sixteenth-century Europe.

Future events are often forecast by dreams, prophecies, and omens. Sphéramonde and Amadis d'Astre have visions in which they see the ladies they are fated to love. After Alastraxerée dreams twice that her husband Falanges is calling to her, she takes ship and lets the winds carry her—for her dream gives no hint where he is. Urgande and other magicians make frequent appearances at the various courts to announce impending disasters. As becomes oracular statements, such prophecies are usually couched in terms intended to be unclear or misunderstood. Ominous signs often precede great events. The weather suddenly changes on the day Lucidor's fleet arrives for his marriage to Heleine—a sign of trouble to come—and on other occasions the strange behavior of birds or the appearance of weird fires in the heavens signals disasters.[23]

In the clockless never-never land of romance a dream or prophecy of a future event has approximately the same validity as the event itself. When Rosalve dreams that her long-absent lover will rescue her from pirates, she believes so completely that she immediately arranges to make herself more readily accessible to such marauders (XVIII, xciv). It is no surprise to her when her dream comes true. The repetition that is inevitable in the realization of a dream or prophecy helps bolster the illusion of an underlying design. Over all events in the romance rules the hierarchy of supernatural power—God, Fortune, the magicians—and the reader is constantly reminded that despite confusion in the narrative surface the world of *Amadis* is ordered by a purpose ultimately divine.

Le premier liure de Amadis de Gaule,

Traduict d'Espaignol en François, par le Seigneur des Essars.

Quelz furent les Roys Garinter & Perion, & d'vn combat qu'eut icelluy Perion par cas fortuit contre deux cheualiers: puis contre vn Lyon qui deuoroit vn Cerf en leur presence, & de ce qu'il en aduint.

Chapitre premier.

Eu de temps apres la Passion de nostre Saulueur Iesus Christ, il fut vn Roy de la petite Bretaigne nommé Garinter, instruict en la loy de verité, & grandement decoré de bonnes & louables vertuz, qui eut d'vne noble dame son espouse, deux filles. L'aisnée (mariée auec Languines Roy d'Escoce) communement appellée la dame de la Guirlande : par ce que le Roy son mary, pour la beauté de ses cheueulx, & le grand plaisir qu'il prenoit à les veoir, ne les luy permettoit couurir, sinon auec vn petit cercle ou chapelet de fleurs. De ce Roy Languines & d'elle, furent engendrez Agraies & Mabile, desquelz l'hystoire presente fera souuent mention. L'aultre fille puisnée de ce Roy Garinter, nommée Elisene fut trop plus belle que son aisnée. Et combien qu'elle eust esté maintesfois demandée & requise en mariaige de plusieurs princes & grans seigneurs : neantmoins ne luy en print (pour lors) aulcun vouloir, ains par sa solitude, & saincte vie, estoit communement

A appellée

VII

The Translations of Herberay and Munday

Readers who know *Amadis of Gaul* only in Robert Southey's translation can have no just idea of the impact of the work on English readers of the sixteenth and early seventeenth centuries, for Southey based his English version upon the Spanish, whereas Anthony Munday, who began to publish his translation about 1589, seems not to have known the Spanish version and probably did not even read Spanish. He relied entirely upon the French translation of Nicholas de Herberay, in which he made very few or relatively minor changes. Herberay, on the other hand, made such significant additions to and alterations in Montalvo that his work constitutes a revision.[1] Consequently the four books that Munday finally published in 1619 are worth comparing with their French and Spanish counterparts. The comparison furnishes *in parvo* a social history of the Renaissance in the three countries.

Unlike either *Palmerín* or the *Espejo de príncipes,* which were available in English black letter editions during the reign of Elizabeth, *Amadis* was, except for the first two books, accessible only to those Elizabethans who could read it in a foreign language. Since French was by all odds the modern foreign language most easily read and spoken in England,[2] and since Herberay's translation was widely acclaimed, educated Englishmen turned naturally toward France for news of the adventures of Amadis. As early as 1568 *The Treasury of Amadis of France* in the translation of Thomas Paynell had provided English readers with a sampling derived from Herberay and had thereby whetted the English appetite for *Amadis de Gaule*. Although the possibility that some Englishmen may have read parts of the romance in Italian, Spanish, or even Dutch and German cannot be dismissed,[3] all available evidence points to the French version as the principal source of English knowledge of the romance.

As in Spain and France, *Amadis* appealed especially to court circles in the British Isles. In 1571 the fifteen-year-old Charles Stewart, son of the Regent of Scotland and uncle of King James, began a translation of the French *Amadis* at the request of his mother, but he completed only a chapter and a half.[4] In England Sir Philip Sidney obviously read *Amadis de Gaule* with pleasure. Not only does he praise it in his *Defense of Poetry*, but he imitated it in his *Arcadia*. The enthusiasm of so influential a literary figure was doubtless not lost on those of his circle at court. Indeed, *Amadis* could scarcely help attracting Stewarts and Sidneys everywhere. Designed originally in part to glorify Spanish chivalry and aristocracy, it retained in translation the backward look, sense of dignity, and aloofness from the world of vulgar reality that reflected an aristocratic sensibility.

Munday's translation is uncharacteristically faithful to the French. Critics since Southey have pointed out Munday's faults as a translator, and in the most thoroughgoing study of this interesting, though minor Elizabethan, Celeste Turner [Wright] provides an appendix in which she shows by means of parallel passages what liberties he took in his translation of *Palmerin of England*.[5] Yet, for whatever reason, the translation of *Amadis* is not nearly so highhanded. In fact, the closeness with which the English follows Herberay's French argues both that Munday took his task with more than usual seriousness and that he looked upon *Amadis* with more respect than he accorded *Palmerin*.

To Nicholas de Herberay, Seigneur des Essarts, in the Renaissance court of Francis I, Montalvo's *Amadís de Gaula* with its strong medieval flavor obviously seemed open to improvement, and in his prologue he acknowledges that he has made some alterations. They are not many, and they have not much effect upon the over-all plot, but they are significant. They involve key episodes and important characters, and the final result in the French version is a substantial change in characterization and tone, and therefore in meaning.

Most of Herberay's changes in Montalvo's text involve additions of a rhetorical, erotic, or military sort. Never extensive enough to interrupt the narrative flow, they are apparently meant to render the Spanish romance less medieval. The added rhetoric is designed to make *Amadis* an up-to-date model of wit and eloquence as well as an intricate and varied tale. The erotic touches are presumably the translator's attempt to make Spanish ideas of love-making more appropriate to the French world of the 1540's. The elaborations on military matters are doubtless due in some degree to Herberay's background, for he was an artillery officer in the service of Francis I.

The extent to which the French rendition changes the meaning of *Amadís de Gaula* is particularly apparent where Herberay puts words in the characters' mouths. For example, in Book III, when Lisuart turns his daughter Oriane over to the Roman ambassador who is to take her to Rome to marry the emperor, the parting between the princess and her royal father is treated in Spanish with dignified reticence. But the French—and therefore the English—version enlarges it into a heated scene. Oriane threatens to kill herself and promises her father that, despite all he can do, she will never reach Rome alive: "rather shall the fishes vse their mercy to me, then I will goe to a home that is my hell, or dwel where I can haue no affection or desire." Whereupon Lisuart in a rage threatens: "instead of wiuing you to the Emperor, I will wed you to the Tower, and where you shall see neither Sunne nor Moone" (xviii, 182).[6] All this dialogue is Herberay's invention, and Lisuart's threat that he will marry Oriane to "vne tour" works neatly to Munday's advantage.

This incident illustrates the subtle alterations of characters and meaning that occurred as the *Amadís* became French and then English. Readers come to know characters in a story in great part by what they say. To add words is to enlarge the character. Just this process of enlargement takes place in the scene between Oriane and Lisuart. The primary emphasis in Spanish is on the farewell between a king and a princess. Lisuart, to be sure, is moved to paternal pity. Tears come to his eyes, and he urges those going with his daughter to take good care of her. Yet his behavior and hers are dictated by their sense of royal propriety. In French, however, Lisuart and Oriane are humanized and universalized into obstinate father and rebellious daughter.

An even better example of the humanization of Spanish characters by the addition of French rhetoric occurs earlier in Book III, when Oriane says a tearful farewell to her newborn baby Esplandian. The substance of the following speech appears only in French and English: "Alas little Creature, Heauen enlarge such blessings on thee that thou mayst proue to be as good and vertuous a knight as thy Father, and make the beginning of thy fortunes more prosperous then his hath beene. Alas, I am enforced to forgoe thee, and shewe my selfe towardes thee more cruell, then any Tiger or Leopard to their young ones. For I know not whether thou goest, nor when I shall see thee againe, which filleth my soule with such affliction, as Fortune cannot affoord thee the very least danger, but I shall finde it presented before mine owne eyes. Oh that I could but know the Nurse that shall giue thee sucke; I would entreate her to bee very carefull of thee. For it may come to passe, that she will be so negligent of thee, that before thou canst be able to helpe thy selfe: she may many times leaue thee in the danger of wilde beasts, while she attendeth on slighter affairs, or else sit gossipping with her neighbours, telling vaine tales and fruitlesse fables. Neither can I therein much condemne her, because both she (and many more beside) may iudge thee to be the sonne of some silly woman; and perhaps the best fauour they will bestow on thee, shall be to make thee a Shepheard, or some other flock-keeper in the field, who cannot alwayes be prouident in their paines, but (euen in despight of their vtmost diligence) the Wolfe or Lyon passing by, may make spoyle and bloody ruine" (iii, 29–30).

Oriane is so moved by her own rhetoric that she decides she will not give up her child after all and has to be persuaded anew by her confidantes. Despite its straining after effect and its sentimentality the speech is effective. Moreover, it does so much to make Oriane a sympathetic character that one who has read the story in French or English is likely to resent the relative coldness of her behavior in the Spanish version of this scene. Herberay makes Oriane behave like a mother and renders her giving up her infant son—an act already acceptable by romance standards—acceptable as well by the standards of feeling.

Not all Herberay's rhetorical interpolations broaden our knowledge of character. Some are speeches of a formal nature. Herberay, for instance, adds several pre-battle speeches. The great battle in Book III between King Lisuart and King Aravigne features in

French (and English) a stirring address to the troops by each of the leaders. Many of the speeches put into Amadis' mouth are rhetorical platitudes, but lifeless as they may seem to a modern reader, they helped *Amadis* bridge the literary gap between Spain and France. In Book III, at the court of Constantinople, Amadis meets Léonorine, whose girlish beauty puts him in mind of the beauty of Oriane. In the Spanish, Amadis is moved to tears, but in French and English, he is moved as well to a "priuate imparlance" in which he apostrophizes love as "Oh happy prison," "Oh sweet death," "Oh quick remembrance" (xi, 109). A modern reader may not feel that this addition has done much to bring Amadis alive, but in the sixteenth century it made him at least more familiar, his words labeling him blood brother to the anemic lovers of Petrarchan convention.

Occasionally the added discourses have a familiar ring to readers of sixteenth-century English literature. When Oriane weeps in her room because she has unjustly accused Amadis, she says: "Ah my eyes, no more eies but floods of tears" (II, viii, 44). One recalls Hieronimo's "Oh eyes! No eyes but fountains fraught with tears," and, remembering the dates, wonders if Munday may have consciously or unconsciously echoed Thomas Kyd. But the French version of *Amadis,* which antedates *The Spanish Tragedy* by many years, provides a sufficient answer: "Ah mes yeus, no plus yeus mais ruisseaus de larmes & de pleurs" (II, viii, 18). Perhaps some of Kyd's reading was in the French romances.[7]

Some of the speeches added in French are not particularly well timed. In Book III Amadis' fleet attacks the ships bearing Oriane to Rome, and after a bloody fight Amadis rescues her. In the Spanish account, while the fight rages, Amadis leaps aboard Oriane's ship, breaks down the door of her prison chamber, and kneels to kiss her hand. She embraces him and begs him not to leave her, but despite her plea he returns to the fight. In French and English when Amadis stormed into her chamber, "she glewed her lippes so fast to his, as if she meant they should neuer be parted" (xviii, 184). When they finally leave off kissing, it is to speak at some length, still embraced. Here one suspects that the Spanish author sees the situation more clearly—Amadis, after all, is covered with the blood of battle, and the battle is not over—but Herberay cannot resist the temptation to let the lovers speak the language he and his readers thought proper to lovers, wherever they might be.

In general, the rhetorical additions in French add a great deal of life to the romance, especially to Amadis and Oriane, but the process of bringing a figure more sharply into focus by making him speak can be seen also in many of the minor characters. A good example occurs in Book III, when Salustanquidio, disgusted by the admiration he sees the British show the Greek Knight (Amadis in disguise), whom he is just about to fight, says: "¿Qué es eso, gente de la Gran Bretaña? ¿Por qué os maravillais en ver un caballero griego loco, que no sabe al sino trebejar por el campo?" (xvii). In his version Herberay adds a neat touch by having the Greek Knight put on an exhibition of horsemanship, which further angers Saluste Quide and makes his language much stronger: "Ah sote gents, Bretons ydiots, & de peu étonnés, qui vous meut de faire tant de cas d'vn tel lourdaut mal adroit, qui n'a autre contenance, que de tourmenter vn cheual sans nule ocasion?" (xvi, 62). Munday, in turn, was inspired to improve upon the French: "Fye on ye foolish sottes, Idiots, and beetle-headed Brittaines, what mooues you to this sencelesse admiration, of a blockish paltrie companion, that shewes all the wit and courage he hath, in tormenting a poore horse vpon no occasion?" (xvi, 160).

A comparison of the style of the three passages above indicates what in addition to language has changed in the process of translation. Salustanquidio's anger in Spanish is restrained and moderated. Though he is an enemy of Amadis (the Greek Knight), he is nevertheless a nobleman, and he speaks in a manner proper to a knight. He is haughty, but he is not low in language. His "gente de la Gran Bretaña" is emotionally neutral. In both French and English, however, Saluste Quide speaks more directly and more coarsely. He indulges in invective entirely missing in Spanish and so lowers himself to the level of the people he addresses. By thus debasing Saluste Quide, Herberay makes the fight that follows a great deal more intense.

Inevitably the addition of rhetoric in French leads the translator to make small alterations in the action. Having rendered Saluste Quide villainous by adding insolence to his pride, Herberay can scarcely allow him merely to be defeated by Amadis, as in Spanish. He therefore adds that when Saluste Quide lies senseless in the dust, he is kicked ignominiously in the head by his horse— an indignity commensurate with his base language. In similar fashion Herberay does not permit Oriane simply to complain "Ah mes yeus. . . ." Moved to action by her own eloquence, she attempts to throw herself out the window and has to be restrained by her attendants. In short, the addition of embellished language in the French *Amadis* often changes not only character but action as well.

Important as Herberay's rhetorical interpolations are both for the characters and the tone of the romance, his enlargement of the erotic element suggests that Spanish and French views about sexual love were worlds apart. In the Spanish sex is treated with a restraint that sometimes borders on prudery. In the French it is sometimes treated with a freedom that comes close to being licentious. Yet if the love of Amadís and Oriana is occasionally coarsened in the process of translation, it must be confessed that the narrative is made much more spirited and the characters more credible. In fact, the French handling of the erotic encourages humor and irony by emphasizing the contrast between chivalric ideals and practice.

Herberay is disposed not so much to invent erotic situations as to elaborate upon the less graphic, less verbalized account in Spanish. A sentence in Spanish may lead to much more in French. For example, in Book I, Chapter xxxv, after Amadis rescues Oriane from the clutches of Arcalaüs, they have an opportunity to consummate their love. They do so somewhat tentatively and shyly. Montalvo assures us that not the forwardness of Amadís but the loving kindness of Oriana brings the lovers to this physical bliss. Ever the gentleman, Amadís "fué tan turbado de placer é de empacho, que solo mirar no la osaba." Montalvo makes perfectly clear the pleasure of the knight and his lady, but he cloaks the details behind the standard clichés of romance writers. He tells us that "fué fecha dueña la mas hermosa doncella del mundo" and asks those readers who have had a similar experience to imagine what delights the two characters enjoyed.

The reticence of Montalvo is proper in a romance where the love of Amadís and Oriana is held sacred, but Herberay could not resist embellishing the shining moment. Amadís' Spanish reserve is shattered by the French and English elaboration of the physical: "In the end, though his hands had beene slow in vnarming him, all his other members were in better state, for not one of them but did his duty." Oriana is permitted to keep her eyes closed, but somehow even modesty is made to look like artifice in French and English, for "two little alablaster bowles liuely shewed themselues in her bosome . . . ," and she evinced "in countenance . . . a gracious choller & contented displeasure" (I, 214–215).[8]

In Book II a climactic incident concerns the meeting of le beau Ténébreux (Amadis in disguise) and Oriane at Mirefleur. Once again the Spanish version is comparatively reticent. The lovers kiss and embrace and weep for joy. But the Spanish author stops short of specific details: "¿quién seria aquel que baste á recontar los amorosos abrazos é los dulces besos, las lágrimas que boca con boca allí en uno fueron mezcladas? Por cierto no otro sino aquel que, siendo sojuzgado de aquella mesma pasion y en las semejantes llamas encendido, el corazon atormentado de aquellas amorosas llagas podiese dél sacar; aquellas que los ya resfriados, perdida la verdura de la juventud, alcanzar no pueden. Así que, á este tal remitiéndome, se dejará de lo contar por mas extenso." The author admits that when the lovers retreat later to Oriana's chamber "segun las cosas pasadas que ya habeis oido, se puede creer que muy mas agradable le seria que el mesmo paraíso" (xiii, 141).

The French version, which Munday gives, enlarges this meeting lovingly and explicitly. At first sight the lovers kiss "more then a good quarter of an houre," until at last Mabile (Amadis' cousin and one of Oriane's attendants), "smiling, said vnto Oriana: Madam, I pray you at the least before my cosin do die, let vs haue a sight of him if it please you." Later in Oriane's chamber Amadis is overcome with passion and "left off his wonted modesty, thrusting one of his hands into Oriana her prettie breasts, and the other towards the place by him most affected." This sally Oriane greets with a sense of humor quite absent in Spanish: "My deere loue, I beleeue that the hermit of the poore Rock, taught you not this lesson." Finally "hee had that of her which he most desired, tasting together of the sweete fruit, which they did first sow in the Forrest" (xiv, 91–92). The addition of humor and explicit details has changed completely the tone of the original tale.

This difference in the treatment of erotic moments persists throughout the French and English versions, and Amadis and Oriane carry on in a way that would have surprised readers of the Spanish. On a later occasion Amadis visits his lady in her chamber and finds her with "nothing vpon her but a cloake cast about her." She and Amadis "began to kisse and embrace each other . . .

incessantly," and she finally invites him into bed with her. "Madame (answered he) seeing it pleaseth you so to command me, I will not make it daintee to straine a little curtesie with you. No sooner had hee sayde these wordes, but that hee threwe himselfe starke naked betweene the Princesse her armes, then begunne they againe their amorous sports, performing with contentment that thing which euery one in the like delight doth most desire" (II, xx, 159).

Of all this there is nothing in Spanish except a bare mention of the meeting between Amadís and Oriana. The most startling addition is the element of jocularity. The Spanish sense of sin is gone, and the sense of humor by which it is replaced not only alters the characters of the hero and heroine but goes far to alter the class image which is so strong in Spanish. In the original language Amadís and Oriana have dignity, but chivalric dignity can scarcely stand the test of leaping naked into the arms of a mistress —even if she is a princess. And the mock courtesy with which Amadis accepts his lady's invitation is dangerous in a work where so much depends on a social ideal already outmoded and all too easily mocked.

In his alterations of the love interest in the Spanish Herberay concentrates heavily upon Amadis and Oriane. Had he been interested in mere sensationalism, he might have added considerably to the amorous intrigues of Galaor. But his changes here are relatively slight. Galaor is intended as a foil to Amadis and is depicted as being as unfaithful as his brother is faithful. While Amadis remains loyal to Oriane, Galaor is amorously involved with Aldène, Branduete, Madasime, and others. The most notable addition to the French account of Galaor's adventures is a certain lightness of tone not conspicuous in the Spanish. For example, in Book I after Galaor rescues Branduete, she is so grateful that, as Munday has it, "Diana soone after lost interest in the maiden." The Spanish account is more sober: "descompusieron ellos ambos una cama que en el palacio era, donde estaban haciendo dueña aquella que antes no lo era, satisfaciendo á sus deseos, que en tan pequeño espacio de tiempo, mirándose el uno al otro la su floresciente y hermosa juventud, muy grandes se habian fecho" (I, xxv, 65).

In enlarging on a third element, the military, Herberay must have been drawing on his professional lore as "Commissaire ordinaire de l'artillerie du Roy & lieutenant en icelle." At any rate, he displays a special interest in the use of artillery. Most of the events in *Amadis* are presumed to take place soon after the death of Christ, and the mention of artillery may seem a little strange.[9] But, after all, Ariosto introduced firearms into *Orlando Furioso,* and one does not expect strict chronology in the world of romance.

Herberay stresses artillery particularly in Book IV, Chapter xv, in a full account—not to be found in Spanish—of Lisuart's army on the move: "Betweene the men on horseback and foot, marched a band of Artillerie, with a great number of Pioners, and the Carriage, bearing powder and bullets only. The rest, wherein were the Cordages, Cables, Lanternes, Cressets, Iauelins, Pikes, Shouels, Spades, Bils, Axes, Hammers, Axeltrees, Tents, and all other things needfulll [*sic*] for carriage" (69). The artillery is also prominent in a great battle in Chapter xviii of Book IV, although, in following his source, Herberay cannot let it take credit for the victory.

These whimsical military additions of the French translator tend to explode the world of the Spanish *Amadís.* Confined as they are to Book IV, they do not affect the original tone of the romance as much as the rhetorical and erotic insertions, but they nevertheless have the effect of an alarm clock upon a dream. Lisuart's army on the march, as Herberay describes it, is so obviously up-to-date, and the catalogue of artillery implements is so

complete that the real world of the sixteenth century collides with the dream world of medieval chivalry. It would take a Cervantes, half a century later, to exploit the collision that Herberay and his contemporaries only dimly perceived.

Almost as interesting as his additions are Herberay's deletions. They indicate at least that what he did to the original was neither accidental nor entirely capricious. In the first place, he shortened or excised the moralizing of Montalvo and thus rid the narrative of many pointed interruptions: "semblans telz sermons mal propres à la matiere dont parle l'histoire" (I, Prologue). He also cut out some of the religious allusions—perhaps to dilute the medieval Catholic flavor of the original and render it palatable to French gentlemen of the Renaissance and to those of a Calvinist bent— though he is by no means as thorough in this regard as Munday. Moreover, he made at least one deletion on the ground of fastidiousness.

In accordance with its high seriousness, the Spanish version contains occasional, rather long, moralizations upon the action. In Book III, for example, Arcalaus and Dinarda—who is acting the part of a mute—capture Amadís, Perión, and Florestán by means of a specially constructed room which they lower noiselessly into a dungeon. The author interrupts to allegorize: "A esta doncella muda fermosa podemos comparar el mundo en que vivimos" (vii, 209). The analogy, which goes on for a long paragraph, points out that Dinarda represents the world, and the dungeon is the hell into which those who succumb to the world's blandishments sink. Herberay omits this section entirely.

In Book II Brocadan and Gandandel, two of the courtiers most trusted by Lisuart, speak to him against Amadis, and he half-believes them. In Spanish this episode is followed by a long appeal to kings and lords to be on their guard against the influence of advisors who are interested merely in serving their own futures.

The passage begins: "Oh reyes é grandes señores que el mundo gobernais, cuánto es á vosotros anejo é convenible este ejemplo" (xix, 167). In Book I, near the end of Chapter xlii, a section headed "Amonestación" contains a long discussion of the need for rulers to be mindful of divine sanction. Both intrusions into the narrative are dropped without comment by the French adapter. Other such interruptions are similarly treated or drastically abbreviated.

In accord with his attempt to play down the didactic element in Spanish, at least where it intrudes upon the narrative, Herberay frequently omits moral exhortations against illicit love. Thus the chivalric playboy Galaor appears worse in French and English because the translators do not intervene with admonitions to the reader to avoid scandalous entanglements. In Book I Galaor spends a night with Aldena: "Galaor holgó con la doncella aquella noche á su placer, é sin que mas aquí os sea recontado, porque en los autos semejantes, que á virtud de honestad no son conformes, con razon debe hombre por ellos ligeramente pasar, teniéndolos en aquel pequeño grado que merecen ser tenidos" (xii, 30). Herberay's assumption is clearly that his readers are not interested in being preached to, for this encounter appears in Munday as a night spent "so amorously as they that haue tasted like fortune may conceiue" (xiii, 79).

Of the religious passages or sentiments deleted by Herberay some may have seemed too parochial. An analysis of the additional cuts Munday made in his French source yields some clues to the differing views of religion in Spain, France, and England. For example, in Book III, Chapter ix, Oriane confesses to Nascian, the holy hermit, and tells him of her love for Amadis and of the birth of Esplandian. He is astonished at the news and shocked by her behavior, especially since she is supposed to be setting a good example for her inferiors. He is greatly relieved when she explains that she and Amadis were betrothed, and he gives her absolution. The verb "absolve" is used in Spanish, but it does not occur in the French and English versions, where Nascian's function is rather to comfort and advise Oriane than to forgive sin. Herberay thus quietly removed what might have been a source of annoyance to his Protestant readers.[10]

In Book II Amadis stops at a chapel to pray to the Virgin. In Spanish the prayer appears as follows: "Señora Vírgen María, consoladora é reparadora de los atribulados, á vos, Señora, me encomiendo que me acorrais con vuestro glorioso Fijo que haya piedad de mí, é si su voluntad es de me no remediar el cuerpo, haya merced desta mi ánima en este mi postrimero tiempo; que otra cosa, si la muerte no, no espero" (ii, 112). A prayer to Mary seemed appropriate enough to Herberay, and he keeps it, though he shortens it somewhat: "Dame glorieuse, consolatrice & refuge des affligés, ie vous supplie m'implorer la grace de vôtre fis, & me secourir, prenant pitié de ma pauure ame en céte extremité" (iii, 7). But Munday in 1589 found even this too much. According to his version Amadis, upon arriving at the chapel, "allighted from his horse, entred into the Church, and kneeling downe with great deuotion, hee made his prayers to God" (iii, 16–17).

Impatient with sermons and cautious on religious matters, Herberay shows that his sense of propriety was on at least one occasion offended by the Spanish reading. In Book II Amadís' sword is stolen from his chamber by a giantess and given to Ardan Canila, whom Amadís is shortly to fight. The giantess has been invited to Amadís' room, and when she sees his sword there, she determines to steal it. In Spanish the theft is thus described: "é dijo á sus escuderos é á los otros que allí estaban que se saliesen afuera é un poco la dejasen, y pensando que alguna cosa de las naturales que se no pueden excusar facer queria, dejáronla sola, y ella, cerrando la puerta, tomó la espada" (xviii, 160). This doubtless seemed too vulgar an excuse to Herberay, and his alteration appears thus in Munday's translation: "and to doe the same more cleanly, she walked so long about the chamber, that as Amadis and his people had their backs towards her, she slily drew the sword forth of the scabbard, and held it vp close vnder her cloake" (xix, 130).

Since the emphasis in this chapter has been on the changes made in the first four books of the Amadis cycle in the process of translation from Spanish to French to English, it is worth repeating that the alterations are not extensive or consistent. They tend, on the whole, to destroy Montalvo's unity of conception. Events, characters, background, and tone of the Spanish *Amadís* belong to a dream world, sufficient unto itself, and the didactic and Catholic elements, intended to make that world relevant, make it even more remote. The reader finds himself held at a distance from episodes and characters by a persistent haze, and he may feel that herein lies the chief charm of the work. Amadís and Oriana act and feel, but generally as in a dream. The changes made in the French translation and followed in English are not great enough to destroy the dream world, but they make it perceptible and thus a bit foolish.

VIII

Amadis and Elizabethan Drama and Verse

A precise mapping out of the influence on Elizabethan literature of a narrative so long, rambling, and eclectic as *Amadis de Gaule* is, of course, impossible. One can only read as widely as he can and try to keep his assumptions within the bounds of reason. Spenser's *Faerie Queene*, Sidney's *Arcadia,* and several pieces of Elizabethan fiction have at least one obvious bond with *Amadis*—all are accounts of the adventures of knights—and it is therefore logical to look closely at them for other links. But when the researcher has to enter the labyrinth of Elizabethan verse and drama without the clue of chivalry, his findings are bound to be sketchy or conjectural. The sonnet spoken in prose by Sidonie is a case in point. That Petrarch's sonnet should have been translated into French comes as no surprise, but that it should appear in this form, disguised as prose and put into the mouth of a distressed queen, raises many questions. Is it the work of the translator of *Amadis?* Or did he quietly appropriate someone else's translation? Was it recognized as a poem? Did it have any influence on English versions of the sonnet?

149

Although a look at Elizabethan verse and drama from the view-
point of the French *Amadis* is likely to lead to many such unan-
swered questions, it also turns up one or two small surprises. The
description in Book XI of the ecstatic experience of Arlanges and
Cléophile, a high point in the neo-Platonic variety of love, is so
close in matter and setting to John Donne's poem "The Ecstasy"
that the question of direct influence inevitably arises. The incident
in *Amadis* begins when Arlanges follows Cléophile as she turns
aside from a hunt to muse alone. She lies down on the grass, pil-
lowing her head on her cloak. Arlanges watches and listens as she
soliloquizes about the problem of honor involved in her love for
him, and then he shows himself. He sits down near her and asks
pardon. He asks to kiss her and, permission granted, does so.

"Il tint ce baiser long n'ayant pouuoir de soy retirer du lieu ou
gisoit son cueur, puis elle le repoussa doucement, & se maintin-
drent long temps regardant l'vn l'autre. Lors il saysit ses blanches
mains les serrant & estraignant entre les siennes: Lors souspirs
sailloient des deux bouches longs & drus: les cueurs leurs battoient
comme s'ilz eussent voulu sortir de leurs poitrines pour ioindre
ensemble: le sang montoit aux visages, puis les laissoit pasles &
decoulourez. Ainsi furent vne heure sans parler, Arlanges re-
tournant au baiser, puis se retirant pour repaistre la veüe, comme
si les yeux fussent ialoux de la bouche, remaniant par fois les
mains de celle qui estoit demy morte: en sorte que tous leurs sens
transportez & esperduz donnerent place aux ames de s'unir par
le moyen du corps, demeurans chacun mort en soy & vif en l'autre,
quasi yures de la liqueur de volupté (nommée nectar des dieux)
quasi fondans de douceur comme au feu la cyre, quasi rauiz en
extase, s'embrassans d'vne ardeur gloute, comme s'ilz eussent
voulu estre tous entiers l'vn en l'autre, & par ce moyen iouïssans
du souuerain bien de ce monde, lequel les vrays amans seulz co-
gnoissent. & comme l'imperfection de ceste masse enuelope les

esperitz, tellement qu'vne part prenant plaisir priue l'autre des rayons d'amour, ainsi que le soleil eschaufant & enluminant la terre en vn endroit & hemisphere laisse l'autre en froideur & obscurité: A eux autrement auint & non en façon bestialle, ains estoient leurs sens corporelz comme serfz endormis, pendant que les ames maistresses s'entrecherent & visitent au plus pres que leurs prisons permettent. . . ." After two hours they arise "comme s'eueillans d'vn profond sommeil," and return to the world (XI, lxxxix, 154–154ᵛ).

In substance this is very close to Donne's poem. It is true that Donne's theme, that the ideal is to be achieved only through the actual, is not explicit here, and there are some minor differences as well. On the other hand, the resemblance is unmistakable, and direct influence of *Amadis* upon Donne is by no means unlikely. Yet, since neo-Platonic doctrines were common property and any two descriptions of an ecstasy could have much in common, it is impossible to say categorically that Donne knew the episode in *Amadis*.

The relationship between *Amadis* and John Donne involves another factor. Arlanges is so moved by his ecstatic experience that he writes a *chanson* about it.[1] Although his poem is essentially a repetition of the description in prose, it introduces some new elements. The lovers' tryst is described much more fully. It is a conventional setting—a small garden by a clear brook, shady trees, the sound of rippling water and birds' song, the odor of flowers— and in it the ecstatic union of the two lovers seems somehow less important. Although the *chanson* appears to be further from Donne's poem than the prose interlude, it makes a literary connection with Donne seem almost certain.

It is most probable that Arlanges' *chanson* supplied Sidney with the pattern for the Eighth Song in *Astrophel and Stella*. If so, the *chanson* from *Amadis* has exerted, directly or indirectly, a great deal of influence in English poetry. Morris W. Croll first pointed out that Sidney's Eighth Song and Fulke Greville's *Caelica 75* belong to the same poetic convention. More recently, George Williamson has shown that the convention was used also in the seventeenth century, that Sonnet 3 of George Wither's *Fair Virtue, the Mistress of Philarete,* Lord Herbert's "Ode upon a Question Moved, Whether Love Should Continue Forever?" and "The Ecstasy" of John Donne are all variations upon the pattern first used in England by Sidney.[2] Williamson quotes Croll on the characteristics of the convention as they appear in Sidney and Greville: "the description of a May landscape, the walk of two lovers through 'an enamel'd meade' (in Greville), in a 'grove most rich of shade' (in Sidney), the long silence of both, with nice analysis of their emotions, finally a long casuistic dialogue on love, in which the ardor of the lover is restrained by the prudence of his mistress, or, in Greville's case, by her anger." Williamson goes on to examine the poems of Wither, Lord Herbert, and Donne to show how the convention described by Croll served the later poets. He finds Donne's variations in the pattern most radical and restates Croll's characteristics so that "The Ecstasy" will fit more readily.

Although Sidney was the first English poet to use the convention, Williamson and other scholars have suspected it must have a foreign origin. The *chanson* of Arlanges indicates that they were right. Since Sidney's acquaintance with Book XI of *Amadis* has long been known to scholars of the *Arcadia,* there can be no reasonable doubt that Sidney had read the *chanson.* Most interesting of all, the discovery that Arlanges' *chanson* lies behind Sidney's Eighth Song puts the convention described by Croll and Williamson in a new light. Whatever the exact relationship of Donne to *Amadis,* his handling of the convention no longer looks so radical. Indeed, in view of the heavy neo-Platonic context in which the *chanson* appears, Sidney, whose Eighth Song is an invitation to physical intimacy, emerges as more of an innovator than Donne, whose poem is substantially neo-Platonic.

Whereas the influence of *Amadis* upon English poetry appears to be greater than one would expect, its influence on drama is surprisingly thin. The one certain link I have been able to find is an episode in Book XII that furnishes another analogue to the embarrassingly well-analogued *Much Ado About Nothing*. The episode is a most ingenious variation of Ariosto's tale of Ariodant and Ginevra—so ingenious that it has gone unnoticed hitherto.[3] It is extremely unlikely that Shakespeare ever read the episode in *Amadis*. It deserves attention largely because it is so fresh and lively a retelling of Ariosto's tale.

In *Amadis* the episode takes place on the Isle of Canabée, a region formerly ruled by Amazons and still under Amazon law. Unlike Ariosto's rendition, wherein the law of Scotland is enforced upon unchaste women, the law of Canabée punishes men. It decrees that any man who has sexual relations with a woman not his wife must be burned alive. The knight Brianges, a stranger to the isle, comes upon two knights about to kill a young man. Brianges intervenes, saves the victim, and binds the two assassins. The young man, whose name is Anurge, tells his story. He has been received in the household of Bruzanges, the brother of Queen Florelle. He falls in love with the duchess Polinecque, who bestows upon him many favors—"& m'en alloys presque toutes les nuytz en sa chambre, ou elle me faisoit monter par vne fenestre qui regardoit sur son iardin." Anurge thinks Polinecque is in love with him, but he soon learns that lust is a more accurate word.

One day Polinecque confesses that she wants to marry Bruzanges, and she asks Anurge to help her win him. She insists she also loves Anurge, but differently, and promises him rewards. Anurge thereupon tries to interest Bruzanges in Polinecque, but he is unsuccessful because Bruzanges loves deeply the lady Arfleure and she loves him. When Anurge reports his lack of success to Polinecque, she is furious and secretly resolves to get revenge. She pretends to accept the inevitable, and since she cannot enjoy Bruzanges in fact, she says she will have him at least in imagination. Anurge is to come to her from now on attired in Bruzanges' clothes, she says, and "vous essayerez à le ressembler à vostre possible, en gestes, en parole, & en maniere de faire: & quant à moy en vous receuant par la fenestre de mon iardin, ie m'imagineray que soyez celuy duquel vous aurez l'habillement; de sorte qu'en me trompant ainsi moymesme, ie donneray parauanture quelque soulas à ma langueur" (XII, xc, 219ᵛ).

Polinecque now visits Arfleure and accuses her of trying to steal Bruzanges. When Arfleure argues that he loves her, Polinecque says he has been sleeping with her. Arfleure refuses to believe, and Polinecque offers proof. She tells Arfleure to hide in the garden at night and watch. Arfleure goes to the garden, bringing along her warrior sister Larmelle. Both watch as the lover— apparently Bruzanges—climbs the ladder and embraces his lady. The broken-hearted Arfleure secretly departs the next day, but Larmelle publicly accuses Bruzanges of breaking the law. Queen Florelle orders a trial by combat and begins questioning members of her brother's household. Anurge becomes frightened and goes to Polinecque, who offers to help him escape. Instead she sends two knights along, with orders to kill him.

The order in which the tale is told, the details, and the motivation are all Ariosto's. The name Polynesso becomes Polinecque as Ariosto's men become women and his women men, but otherwise there are no significant changes. The major shift, from a male-dominated society to an Amazon government, is very clever and places everything that happens in a slightly distorted perspective. The emphasis on male infidelity—and its drastic punishment— has about it an Ariostan wryness.

Amadis *and Elizabethan Drama and Verse*

If *Amadis* was ever a source book for English playwrights, as Stephen Gosson says it was, its vogue must have been rather brief, and the plays have not survived.[4] There are, of course, in Elizabethan and Jacobean plays numerous references—most of them uncomplimentary—to Amadis, as well as to Palmerin, Rosicleer, and the Donzel del Febo, but such allusions do not always indicate familiarity. Even illiterates had heard of Amadis. The important question is how many playwrights who mention him knew anything much about him. Ben Jonson, who had a low opinion of chivalric romance, manages a number of derogatory remarks in his plays. In *Every Man out of His Humor* Puntarvolo is so addicted to the trappings of chivalry that he habitually has a trumpet sounded outside his lady's house and addresses her in what he fancies to be knightly idiom when she comes to the window. But no English play, so far as I know, derives its plot from *Amadis,* though some plays—like *The Four Prentices of London*—are chivalric catchalls.

The Knight of the Burning Pestle is heavily indebted to chivalric romance, and doubtless *Amadis* is one of the romances Beaumont had in mind. Yet the allusions and quotations in the play are mostly concerned with *Palmerin* and *The Mirror of Knighthood*, both of which Beaumont must have known well.[5] The title is probably borrowed from the famous sobriquet of Amadis de Grèce, the Knight of the Burning Sword. Moreover, the episode in which Jasper is delivered to Luce in a coffin may be derived from Book V of *Amadis*, wherein Esplandian is similarly borne to Léonorine (V, xxxvi). But the play nowhere demonstrates a close acquaintance with *Amadis.*

Though *Amadis* had very little direct influence on Elizabethan plays, it helped to establish certain narrative and rhetorical conventions. Elizabethan plays are generally romantic, and evidence of a playwright's familiarity with chivalric clichés sometimes turns up in unlikely places. Shakespeare is not particularly addicted to Amadisian chivalry, but again and again allusions to it arise. When Aufidius greets Coriolanus in Antium, he does so in the language of chivalric combat:

> Let me twine
> Mine arms about that body, where against
> My grained ash an hundred times hath broke,
> And scarr'd the moon with splinters: here I clip
> The anvil of my sword. . . .
> [*Coriolanus*, IV, v, 112–116]

In *Amadis* it would be hard to find two clichés more often used. When two knights charge each other, their impact is often measured by the height to which the splinters of their lances fly; and the clash of sword on an opponent's armed body is almost invariably compared to the clash of smith's hammer on anvil. Hyperbole of such an old-fashioned kind may have been Shakespeare's way of alerting his audience to the duplicity of Aufidius. In a play wherein language and imagery are relatively plain, what better way to discredit a speaker than by putting into his mouth an anachronistic and discredited rhetoric?

Generally Shakespeare uses the stuff of chivalry to suit his ends, whether serious or comic. When Macbeth unseams Macdonwald from nave to chaps, he wins himself a place in the history of great blows. Several such are struck in *Amadis,* and every chivalric romance emphasizes the strength of the hero's sword arm. Again, as Cleopatra helps Antony to put on his armor, she behaves not like his Egyptian dish but like an Oriane. Shakespeare makes use of the spectacular side of chivalry in Edgar's challenge in *King Lear,* the tourney in *Pericles,* the etiquette of challenge and reception in *Richard II.* Sir John Falstaff suggests that knighthood could have for Shakespeare a comic aspect. The comic duel in *Twelfth Night* may have come indirectly from *Amadis,* perhaps by way of the *Arcadia.*

Although, as in the case of Aufidius' speech, Shakespeare was capable of using chivalric rhetoric to indicate a character's hypocrisy, he also drew upon it in moments of high seriousness. Thus, when Macbeth asks whether all the ocean will wash Duncan's blood from his hand, he is using one of the commonplace images of *Amadis*.[6] The words of Prince Hal over the dead Hotspur,

> When that this body did contain a spirit,
> A kingdom for it was too small a bound;
> But now two paces of the vilest earth
> Is room enough. . . .
>   [*Henry IV*, Pt. I, V, iv, 89–92]

are very close to the words of Abra upon the death of Zaïr in Book VIII of *Amadis* and represent a convention that goes back at least to Chrestien.[7] Abra says: "Dieux eternelz! . . . que tant amirables sont voz secretz diuins! ayans permis es premiers ans de mon frere, l'entiere obeïssance non seulement des Parthes, mais de tous les circonuoysins iusques à la mer Rouge, & en vn instant l'auez tellement abaissé, que luy dominateur de tant de païs est demeuré vaincu, & si desnué & d'amys & de moyen, qu'en sa mort n'a peu auoir six piedz de terre pour l'inhumer" (xxxii, 59). Whether or not Shakespeare knew *Amadis,* he shared with its authors certain ideas and habits of rhetoric.

There is not a shred of evidence that Shakespeare ever read so much as a book of *Amadis*. Although scholarly caution and scrupulousness would have to grant that *Amadis* is among the conceivable sources of *Much Ado About Nothing*, it is not likely that Shakespeare went so far for what was obviously one of the most common and widespread of Renaissance tales. In *The Winter's Tale* he may have been closer to *Amadis;* that is, if Robert Greene's *Pandosto,* his accepted source, is derived, as has been claimed, from the story of Florisel in Book IX.[8] The interesting question is not whether *Amadis* is the immediate source of either play. It is why *Amadis* is so close to Shakespeare in narrative motifs and tone. Shakespeare's *Tempest,* so far as I know, has never been linked by scholars with *Amadis,* and yet the two have much in common. In Book XVIII, Chapters xc and xci, a ship at sea is caught in a great storm generated by an enchantress who dwells on an island. Through the operation of her magic she brings the ship safely into harbor, puts the mariners on board to sleep, and renders the ship itself invisible. Through her, meals are served by invisible servants.[9] I am suggesting, not that Shakespeare derived his play from *Amadis,* but that both play and romance share a common tradition. *Amadis* is helpful, therefore, because it puts the literary historian in touch with romance motifs and rhetorical flourishes that were available to Elizabethan dramatists.

Amadis and the other chivalric romances must also have contributed to the Elizabethan fondness for hyperbolic villainy. Elizabethan plays feature evil monsters like the Jew of Malta and Aaron the Moor. Such villains may have shaken the rafters as well as the boards, but the playgoer who had read *Amadis*—or *Palmerin* and *The Mirror of Knighthood*—would not have found their malevolence new or surprising. Like Barabbas and Aaron, the villainous Famangomad dies unrepentant and unforgiving: "And although that hee was likewise at the point of death, yet notwithstanding hee had throwne his helmet from his head, holding both hands before his wound, to keepe in his blood, that thereby he might prolong his life, the more to blaspheme God and his saints; not being sorry for his death (as he said) but because that he had not in his life time, destroyed al the churches wherein he had neuer entred" (II, xiii, 88). Famangomad's obduracy is paralleled by that of several other gigantic villains, and his behavior may be taken as a standard of giantly conduct in chivalric romances.

One of the most ferocious acts in *Titus Andronicus* is the rape of Lavinia upon the dead body of her husband. An outrageous rape also occurs in Nashe's *Unfortunate Traveler,* when Esdras rapes Heraclide upon the dead body of her husband. But Elizabethans had no monopoly on imaginative cruelty. Malfadée tells Amadis de Gaule about the heinous injury done her by the giant Mascaron, who had begun by killing her father and mother: "Quant & quant me saisit Mascaron par les cheueux, me disant, que pour me faire plus souffrir il ne m'occiroit comme les autres, ains me forceroit sur les corps de mes tristes parens, pour receuoir plus grande iniure: & ainsi executa il sa dannee & malheureuse volonté, quelque resistance ny menace que ie luy fisse. Puis me donna du pied contre le ventre, me disant: Va chetiue creature, cercher qui t'honore d'auantage, ou te rende le bien que tu esperois à l'auenir" (VII, xxxv, 95).

The bloody banquet in the last scene of *Titus Andronicus* may derive from Seneca's *Thyestes* or the legend of Philomela, but it is also a fairly common medieval and Elizabethan motif. It occurs in *Amadis* when the giant Brandinel and his brother seize two damsels and attempt to force them to submit by making them eat only the bodies and drink only the blood of their own servants. The most difficult aspect of their forced feeding is that the damsels are made to look at the heads of those they are eating—"& entre autres plusieurs de nostre cognoissance" (IX, ix, 26ᵛ).

Marlowe's conception of Tamburlaine may well owe something to the giants of chivalric romance. Certainly Tamburlaine's words and actions would have seemed familiar to Elizabethan readers of *Amadis* and other romances. Just as the dying Tamburlaine burns the Koran, giants in their last rages habitually destroy statues of their gods. When Tamburlaine beards the gods and threatens to make war on heaven, he sounds like an irate giant. In *Amadis* one angry giant roars out: "O Iupiter, comment peulx tu endurer que ceste vile canaille ait meurtry tes Cheualiers & sectateurs de ta saincte loy? Ie te promets & asseure de casser & briser ton image, ne iamais ny à elle ny à toy porter aucune reuerence: te defiant toy-mesme au combat, si tu es si osé que d'y comparoistre" (XVI [Montreux], xix, 61–61ᵛ). When the giant Strangoulam-bœuf is wounded by Fortunian, he curses Jupiter and all that god's kin. If he escapes, he says, "ie monteray & escheleray ton ciel & mesme t'iray rompre la teste au milieu de ta maison" (XVI [Montreux], xxviii, 96). Tamburlaine's use of Bajazet as footstool does not occur in *Amadis*, but the episode has parallels in other romances.[10] The carnage of Tamburlaine's wars, in which horses wade in blood up to the pasterns, recalls the butchery of chivalric battles fought before Constantinople and Trebizond. And the exotic ring of names like Persepolis must have sounded familiar to those in the audience who had read in *Amadis* of the kingdom of Siranquie or of Palomar or Traramate.

Though *Amadis* is not an important source for the plots of Elizabethan plays—or at least not for extant plays—it was nevertheless a principal fount of their stuff, and acquaintance with the romances puts the rhetoric and episodes of the plays in a new light. In a literary form as practical as a play—especially one performed in a public theater—chivalry and knighthood were not likely to be taken seriously, and the trend was toward knights like Sir Andrew Aguecheek. The conventions of chivalry that were still useful could help to patch up a scene, but chivalry as a literary force on the stage was in decline. For evidence that chivalry was still a direct and substantial literary influence we must look to Spenser and Sidney.

IX

Amadis and Spenser's
Faerie Queene

In 1805 H. J. Todd in his *Works of Spenser* suggested that the Mask of Cupid might have been drawn "in a small degree" from "*Amadis de Gaule* and other publications." [1] To this rather vague suggestion Robert Southey gave more direction by proposing that Spenser found his inspiration for the Mask in *Amadis of Greece* (Books VII and VIII of the French *Amadis*). [2] Modern scholarship has not as yet taken either suggestion very seriously. The index of the Spenser Variorum contains only six entries for *Amadis of Gaul*—none for *Amadis of Greece*—the most important of them a reference to an article by Edwin Greenlaw in which he says: "I do not believe that the *Amadis* versions exerted any appreciable influence on *F.Q.*" [3] So flat a statement would ordinarily put an end to further discussion. Greenlaw's investigation, however, was limited to the first four books of *Amadis* in Southey's translation from the Spanish, and in view of that limitation it seems proper to reopen the question.

The probability that Spenser knew *Amadis,* at least in part, is very strong. The great prestige of the romance in France, where it had the approval of members of the Pléiade,[4] would have been sufficient to interest Spenser. Moreover, in England the impact of *Amadis* seems to have been especially felt during the decade of the 1570's. *The Treasury of Amadis of France* was published in England in 1568, and Stephen Gosson lists *"Amadis of France"* as one of the works that helped contaminate the English stage during that decade.[5] There can be no question that Sir Philip Sidney, Spenser's patron and a powerful literary force, read *Amadis* and was considerably influenced by it. Not only was the romance well known in England but its matter was wholly relevant to Spenser, who was at work around 1579 on a version of the *Faerie Queene*. To someone of his interests and imagination *Amadis* could have provided a base for the flight into Fairyland.

To suggest that Spenser must have known *Amadis* is easy enough, but conclusive evidence is another matter. The difficulties are enormous. Both works are long and episodic. Moreover, similarities are to be expected even if Spenser never saw *Amadis,* for both works draw from the vast tradition of prose and verse romances from Heliodorus to Chrestien and Ariosto. The nature of the problem is well illustrated by Arthur Dickson's edition of *Valentine and Orson.*[6] In his introduction he has a list of analogues common to that medieval prose romance and the *Faerie Queene.* The list runs to more than eight pages. Since the French version of *Amadis* must be at least twenty times as long as *Valentine and Orson,* adequate treatment of parallelism would presumably require a book. All questions of the usefulness of such a study aside, the aim of this chapter is less ambitious. I wish to concentrate upon some of the more striking parallels between *Amadis de Gaule* and the *Faerie Queene,* especially those bearing on the Mask of Cupid, in an attempt to ascertain whether Spenser was directly indebted to this chivalric romance.

The problem of determining Spenser's relationship to *Amadis* or any other work is made more difficult by the power of the poet's imagination and the shaping force of his allegory. Spenser was a wide and eclectic reader, and the *Faerie Queene* is an impressive record of his browsing. But what he derived from other men's books he turned to his own uses. In the strange chiaroscuro of his allegory, borrowings often assume new and unusual shapes. Though the *Faerie Queene* is laden with romance commonplaces, Spenser's originality lies in his treatment of stock material. The dragon in Book I is as tried and true a literary cliché as a romance writer could find. A romance would scarcely be proper without at least one dragon. But Spenser turned this worn crutch of hack imaginations into a literary triumph, no small part of which is due to the allegory. What scholar would seriously suggest a literary source for the dragon or for his fight with Red Cross?

On the other hand, *Amadis* presents problems of its own. Not only is it extremely long and complicated, but like the *Faerie Queene* it is indebted to a variety of literary sources. Many of them are medieval, but, for the French version of *Amadis* at least, some are also Renaissance. In a few cases *Amadis* and the *Faerie Queene* were inspired by the same work. For instance, both draw upon Ariosto's *Orlando Furioso*. When both *Amadis* and the *Faerie Queene* make use of the same Ariostan matter, the question arises whether Spenser's use of his Italian source might not have been modified to some extent by his knowledge of an intermediate version. The story of Ariodant and Ginevra is retold in Book XII of *Amadis* and Book II of the *Faerie Queene*. The version of the tale in *Amadis* is so transformed from that in Ariosto that it is not likely to have exerted influence on Spenser. Another episode, the stealing of Guyon's horse in Book II of the *Faerie Queene,* represents more of a problem. There are two or three instances of horse-stealing in Ariosto, but in *Amadis* the thief Fraudeur specializes in horses, to the number of a dozen or more.

Though it is likely in the case of common material that Spenser was influenced by the *Orlando Furioso,* a work he had set himself to surpass, *Amadis de Gaule* remains at least a conceivable source.

Like both Ariosto and Spenser, *Amadis* makes frequent allusions to classical myth and draws more or less directly from Greek romance. The story of Helen of Troy, which Spenser retells in his tale of Hellenore and Paridell, is also retold in Books IX, XX, and XXI of *Amadis*. Could Spenser's redaction have been affected by the versions in *Amadis?* Though the question is unanswerable, the problem it illustrates is real. Since in dealing with Book VI of the *Faerie Queene* scholars tend to speak of the general influence of the Greek romances of Heliodorus, Longus, and Achilles Tatius, it is worth noting that *Amadis* in its habitual omnivorous fashion absorbed much from Greek fiction. Book XX alone contains almost the whole plot of Heliodorus' *Ethiopian History.* Could it be that Spenser derived the Greek pastoral spirit of Book VI indirectly, by way of *Amadis?*

Many of the specific details that the *Faerie Queene* and *Amadis* share are clichés of romance narrative. The composite beast exposed shockingly to view in the stripping of Duessa and the savage man with tusk-like teeth and long ears are standard fare in *Amadis*. The prose romance also tells of many knights who, like Prince Arthur, first see their ladies in a dream. The magic mirror of Merlin, in which Britomart first sees Artegal, has two or three counterparts in *Amadis,* one of them the mirror of the magician Alquif (*F.Q.,* III, ii, 18 ff.; *Amadis,* XI, lxxix). The shape-shifter Malengin, whom Talus captures, has a counterpart in the witch Dragosine, who changes shape repeatedly when she is on the verge of capture (*F.Q.,* V, ix, 16 ff.; *Amadis,* XIV, lx).

The bed in Dolon's chamber, which can be lowered to trap a sleeper, is like beds in *Amadis* used by such treacherous hosts as Arcalaüs and the Fraudeur (*F.Q.,* V, vi, 27 ff.; *Amadis,* III, vi, and XV, xxiii).[7] The seven-headed beast that appears as an ally of Orgoglio has a near relation in *Amadis*, a seven-headed, fire-breathing animal that fights Lucendus (*F.Q.*, I, viii, 6; *Amadis*, XIV, xxxi). The naked damsels Guyon sees sporting in the water near the Bower of Bliss are like the lovely blonde siren Silves espies in a small lake and also like those by whom Sphéramonde is tempted—"bien les regardoit il attentiuement" (*F.Q.*, II, xii, 63–64; *Amadis*, XIV, xxvii, and XVI, xlii, 492). The Well of Life, which cures the wounds and mends the sword of Red Cross, is a somewhat more sanctified version of the fountain which performs a similar service for Sphéramonde in Book XVI (*F.Q.*, I, xi, 36; *Amadis*, XVI, xxxvi, 420).

This list of characters and specific devices could be extended for many pages. But a fuller list would prove nothing except the remarkable durability and ubiquitousness of romance props. It would certainly do nothing to demonstrate a literary debt of Spenser to *Amadis*. Turning to an examination of analogous episodes, one finds a similar difficulty: the commonplace nature of the parallel passages.

One of the episodes of the *Faerie Queene* often discussed in the light of possible or probable sources is the Calidore-Pastorella interlude in Book VI. Pastorella, a girl of noble birth reared by shepherds whom she takes to be her parents, attracts the eye of the knight Calidore. To be near her, he doffs his armor and dresses as a shepherd. He is accepted by the shepherds as one of them, but in wooing Pastorella, he finds himself in competition with the rustic Coridon. One day a fierce tiger attacks Pastorella. Coridon takes to his heels, but Calidore kills the beast with his shepherd's crook. Later he saves Pastorella from pirates who have kidnaped her and helps restore her to her real parents. For this part of the *Faerie Queene* scholars have suggested a number of analogues. *Daphnis and Chloë*, Sidney's *Arcadia*, Greene's *Mena-*

phon and *Pandosto,* and *The Mirror of Knighthood* are among the candidates, and the number should be warning enough of the popularity of this motif in sixteenth-century England.

The early chapters of Book IX of *Amadis* offer still another parallel. There Silvie, a girl of noble birth who thinks she is the daughter of the shepherd rearing her, attracts the eye of the young prince Florisel of Niquée. To be near her, he disguises himself as a shepherd. His chief competitor is Darinel, an arrant coward but a fine rustic musician. One day Silvie is attacked by a passing knight. Darinel runs, but Florisel kills the knight and rescues her. When the rescue is repeated on still another occasion, Florisel becomes the toast of the country clowns. Later, after Florisel is knighted, Silvie is carried off by pirates led by a giant, and Florisel saves her once again. Silvie is eventually restored to her proper parents, and all ends well.

Though Book IX contains this interesting analogue to Spenser's Calidore-Pastorella story, it does not seem a likely source. The parallels are too general and commonplace. The real value of the analogue, I feel, is that it illustrates how difficult it is to make a certain judgment about sources of the prose romances. Of all the analogues mentioned above, the case for *The Mirror of Knighthood* as the source is superficially the most convincing.[8] The point must be made, however, that the episode in *The Mirror of Knighthood* has apparently been derived from Book IX of *Amadis.* Therefore, one who holds that *The Mirror of Knighthood* is the immediate source must make provision for *Amadis* as an antecedent source. Moreover, a question about Spenser's powers of invention arises. If the author of the episode in *The Mirror of Knighthood* derived his version from *Amadis,* why might not Spenser have done so too?

The truth seems to be that the Calidore-Pastorella episode is like Spenser's dragon—a composite of so many clichés of romance narrative that it is almost hopeless to attempt to trace it back to a specific source. For a scholar to choose analogue A as the source because it has ten points in common with Spenser's narrative, whereas analogue B has only nine, not only is naïve but makes Spenser naïve too.

A somewhat more satisfactory relationship can be worked out between the episode involving Britomart at Castle Joyous and an incident in Book XV of *Amadis*. The episode in the *Faerie Queene* begins when Britomart overcomes the six knights outside the castle. When she enters, she is aware of the perfumed and decadent air of the castle, looks at the paintings, and unwittingly attracts the salacious Malecasta, who takes her for a handsome knight. In *Amadis* the knight Fortunian comes upon a castle kept by four lascivious sisters who prey on passing knights. He wins the sisters' admiration by overcoming ten of the castle guards. They invite him into the castle, and conduct him to a perfumed chamber adorned with paintings designed to provoke "lubricité & luxure," while they retire to argue the question which of the sisters is to have him (*F.Q.*, III, i, 20 ff.; *Amadis*, XV, ix).

All told, this episode from *Amadis* is closer to the Castle Joyous incident in Spenser than any analogue yet advanced, but by itself it is not sufficient to prove Spenser's acquaintance with *Amadis*. As in the case of Calidore and Pastorella, one feels that Spenser may not be following a specific source but blending common motifs into a new combination for his own purposes.

A more striking episode is that in Book II, Canto vi, of the *Faerie Queene* in which Pyrochles, burning with the raging fire of his intemperance, throws himself fully armed into a lake. There he thrashes and beats the water and cries aloud in agony. His servant Atin watches him for a while in bewilderment and finally tries to rescue him. In the process he is almost drowned by the frenzied Pyrochles. The incident is memorable, perhaps in part because it contains something of the humor that madmen seem often to have inspired in sixteenth-century poets and dramatists.

It is somewhat like an incident in Book X, Chapters xlvii–xlviii, of *Amadis*. There the knight Zahir comes to a castle by a lake. He sees a fully armed knight in the water beating it madly with his sword, while women from the castle stand by weeping helplessly. When Zahir tries to help, the mad knight kills his horse and goes back to beating the water. Zahir requires the help of two other knights before he can haul the madman out of the lake and truss him up. Zahir learns that the knight has been driven to insanity by his wife's eloping with another man. He beats the water because it reflects his face, and he can no longer bear the sight of himself. The mad knight is later freed by a good Samaritan, but, after killing his liberator, he returns to slashing at the water until he drowns himself. The humor in *Amadis* is more marked and somewhat more grim than in Spenser. Although there are many differences between the two episodes, the main likeness—a mad knight fully armed thrashing in the water—is striking.

Spenser's concern with allegory makes some books of *Amadis* especially interesting, for they contain substantial allegorical episodes. For example, in Book XIV, Chapters xxxiii–xxxvii, Silves undertakes an enchantment that involves five towers, each associated with a virtue. The first tower represents Justice, the second Temperance, the third Charity, the fourth Strength, and the fifth Reason. The towers have to be tried in their proper order, and it is clear that a process of growth is involved for the knight. Each tower is treated in detail, an entire chapter being devoted to the account of Silves' attempt to take possession of it.[9] Much is made of the relative position of the towers, Reason being situated in the middle of a square and each of the other virtues occupying a corner. At each tower Silves meets with adventures appropriate to its virtue. At the first three towers he sees examples of the users and abusers of the three virtues.

The mixture of allegory and chivalric romance and the progress of the narrative, wherein a knight grows in virtue by passing a series of tests, make Silves' experiences analogous to those of the Red Cross Knight and other Spenserian heroes. Although there are few specific resemblances between this part of *Amadis* and the *Faerie Queene,* one is of special interest. When Silves tries the tower of Charity, he finds over the entry a representation of a woman in white giving suck to two infants. Later, inside the tower, he sees Charity on the throne giving a similar demonstration of love.[10] This is very close to Spenser's description of Charissa (*F.Q.,* I, x, 29–31).

In yet another allegorical incident in Book XIX, Lindamart attempts to cross a lake in a boat with a mysterious old lady. The lake is at first calm, but soon it becomes tempestuous, and the boat is in danger of sinking. After the waters have grown placid again, the boat is attacked by monstrous fish of all kinds. Then the song of sirens is heard. An appropriate moralization is made by the old lady, who tells the knight that crossing the lake is like passing through life. Peace is always followed by tribulations in which one must place his hope in God. The attacks of the giant fishes are like "les tentations des diables." The song of the sirens represents the transitory beauty of the world to which man must close his eyes and block his ears. Lindamart's crossing of the lake is generally like the journey of Guyon and the Palmer to the Bower of Bliss. Though Spenser's description is fuller and draws upon a vast wealth of reading, the tempest, the attack by giant fishes, and the song of the sirens are all present (*F.Q.,* II, xii, 2–41; *Amadis,* XIX, xxviii, xxx).

All the similarities between *Amadis* and Spenser pointed out thus far have one of two faults: either they are striking and partial or they are common and vague. None shows convincingly that Spenser was acquainted with the French version of *Amadis*, and, taken all together, they add up merely to a suspicion. But with the Mask of Cupid analogues we enter an area of much greater certainty.

Whether or not Spenser got the idea for the Mask of Cupid from *Amadis of Greece*, as Southey maintained, Spenser's description is very close to that of several processions in the romance. The authors of *Amadis* never hesitated to repeat a favorite motif, and processions involving the god Cupid occur more than once with details more or less like Spenser's. Since analogues for this part of the *Faerie Queene* are scarce, the number of resemblances between the Mask and various passages in *Amadis* is especially noteworthy.

An examination of Spenser's Mask against the background of *Amadis* reveals at least three separate motifs. One is the wall of flame which blocks off the enchanted area from the rest of Fairyland. The second is the transfixed or exposed heart of the victim. The third is the procession or mask of the god. All three motifs are to be found—both together and separately—in *Amadis*.

The wall of flame motif is very common in *Amadis* and not unusual in other romances, though it is not always connected with an exposed or transfixed heart or with a religious procession. Usually it is a barrier—like a qualifying examination. Those knights who pass the initial test are eligible to try the main enchantment. Though a wall of flame is a common first test, various strange or monstrous animals, tempestuous lakes, and enchanted warriors are also favorite initial barriers. Merely passing the first obstacle is no guarantee of success in rescuing the enchanted. In Book VIII, for example, both Niquée and her brother Anastarax are for a while enchanted behind a wall of flame which can be penetrated only by a loyal lover. Though Niquée is disenchanted, her rescuer is powerless to help Anastarax, who has to remain until the lady fated to release him appears.[11]

The motif of the transfixed or exposed heart is also common in *Amadis*. It may involve a knight or a lady or both. In some cases the heart is both exposed and transfixed, and enchantments of this nature almost always include a continuous flow of blood. One of the knights Florisel fights in Book IX, Chapter lvi, has on his shield a portrait of a beautiful lady, a knight kneeling before her with his chest cut open. His heart is plainly visible and mirrored therein is the lady. This is a somewhat unusual instance of the symbolic use of the motif, for it generally involves living persons and much blood. In Book VIII, Chapter xxxviii, Amadis de Grèce breaks an enchantment—without a wall of flame—by fighting his way against invisible opponents through a cave and drawing a sword from the heart of Brizène, the enchanted queen of Alexandria.

In Book XIV, Chapter xvi, the two lovers Paudonie and Filide are transfixed by a single sword and set behind a wall of flame in a château. Silves breaks the spell by passing the fire and several other obstacles and drawing the sword. Similarly in Book XI, Chapter lxxii, Artifire and her lover Rosafer are enchanted in a burning chamber. Both have their breasts cut open so that their hearts are revealed. Each holds the other's heart in hand, their mouths joined. Here, though the hearts are not transfixed, an image of the two lovers is, and they are not released from the spell until Daraïde pulls the sword from the image.

A procession in honor of a god is also common enough in *Amadis*—with or without one or both of the preceding motifs. There is, for example, a long description of the procession and ritual involved in the worship of Alastraxerée on the Isle of Colchos. The chief event in the ceremony is the sacrifice of the hearts of various beasts (IX, lix). In Book X, Chapter xlii, Florisel and Falanges view a strange religious ritual. They see a procession on its way to a temple. A chariot drawn by six unicorns contains twelve heads enshrined in pure gold like reliquaries. Also in the chariot are three girls with bows and arrows. Three knights are led captive. In the temple, before the altar, one of the damsels addresses the idols of Venus and Cupid. She and the other two damsels then kill the captive knights with their arrows. The hearts of the victims are ripped out and sacrificed, while the three executioners play and sing. Then the victims' heads are cut off and displayed.

Anaxartes and his sister Alastraxerée see a ceremony which is even more weird. In Persia they come upon a château in the middle of a lake and watch a procession emerge. In it are twelve damsels, musicians, a knight bearing a bloody sword, four gentlemen, each carrying a silver basin of human blood, four gentlemen, each bearing on a gold plate a human head, and finally gentlemen bearing food (IX, vii).

All these rituals are connected in some way with love. Others involve blood sacrifices to the god Cupid. In Book XVI, Chapter xxxvi, of the Montreux rendition, Amadis de Gaule comes to a château and enters. He hears the sound of music and follows it to a chapel. There he finds an altar on which is placed a statue of Cupid, who holds in one hand a basin of blood and in the other a dart. At the statue's feet are the heads of men and women. A giant enters armed with a scimitar, and then a naked damsel who is being beaten by four knights. Four others play viols while a group of damsels sing beautifully. Two other damsels gather the blood of the scourged girl in a basin. Suddenly the music ceases, and the giant kneels in prayer to Cupid. His orisons ended, he rises and beheads the girl. He collects her blood, pours half into the basin of Cupid and drinks the other half himself—in an attempt, he says, to drown the fire of love. Then he cuts out the girl's heart and divides it, giving half to Cupid and eating the other half himself.

Book XVI—again in the version of Nicholas de Montreux—contains still another ritual of Cupid. In Chapter lxiii Fortunian and Astrapol come to an isle and follow a river of blood to a château. Through a crack in the wall they witness a procession into the courtyard and a sacrifice of six knights and ladies. After the victims have been killed, their tongues are ripped out and fastened to a chain of tongues. All occurs before an altar of Cupid. There is music in the background, and censers are used.

Not all the rituals involving Cupid are quite so bloody. In Book IX Anaxartes witnesses a pageant of Cupid which is connected with an enchantment at the Château of the Marvels of Love. He has first to pass through an entrance full of "bruine & vapeur." Then he has to row across a stretch of water to a palace. He enters a gate and finds himself in a lovely garden where the green grass is sprinkled with flowers and singing birds make melody. Here he sees a throng of men and women, some sad and some happy. In their midst is enthroned a king bearing the arms of Cupid. He announces that Love is lord over reason and shows a pageant of Love's power. He accompanies the pageant by a commentary: "considerez Piram qui se donna luy mesmes la mort, pensant sa bien aymée Tisbé estre expirée: voyez la d'autre part de quel courage elle se transperce du glaiue de son amy mort: voyez les regretz que fait Dido pour son Enée, & en fin se tuë: voyez de quelle cruauté vse Medée en elle mesme pour l'amour de Iason. . . . Voyez Solomon auecques ses femmes & concubines, voyez Dauid auec Vrie: considerez Virgile, Aristote & tant d'autres philosophes. . . . Voyez Paris auecq' Heleine. . . . Voyez l'estrange ardeur de Pasiphae enuers le Minotaure" (xlv, 112^v).

All the above instances constitute a considerable body of material from which it is conceivable that a poet like Spenser might have derived his Mask of Cupid. But there remains another analogue, so much closer to Spenser's Mask in general outline and in many details that it ought to be considered first in a list of possible sources. In fact, the Mask of Cupid is so close to an episode in Book VIII, Chapters lxxxv–lxxxviii, of *Amadis* that direct imitation appears to be the only adequate explanation.

The episode in Book VIII begins with Chapter lxxxv. Amadis de Grèce and Zahara, an Amazon queen, land on a strange island after a storm and ride off to explore it. They come upon a river of blood littered with human hair which is blonde and golden. They follow the river to "vn grand parc," surrounded by a wall. As they continue, they see at intervals mysterious warnings about the cruel vengeances of Love. They also become more and more amorous. At last they pause by mutual consent and seek release in a sexual encounter which is rendered fumbling and funny by the circumstance that they are both in armor. When they resume their journey, they forget entirely what has just occurred. When Zahara later gives birth to twins, she is at a loss of explain the matter except in terms of the intervention of the god Mars.

A hermit whom Amadis and Zahara meet explains some of the mysterious sights they have encountered. They learn that this is the Island of Rodes, and the strange experiences derive from a strange love story. A king named Areïsmino had a lovely daughter Mirabela, who was loved by the giant Monstruofuron. Unsuccessful in his wooing, Monstruofuron sought help from a magician, who then enchanted the area through which Amadis and Zahara have just passed so that Mirabela, in crossing it with Monstruofuron, would fall in love with him. One night the giant kidnaped Mirabela and several of her women. He left them at a fountain and turned back to fight the pursuing Areïsmino, whom he killed with all his knights.

On learning of her father's death, Mirabela stabbed herself; however, the magician, mortally wounded in the fight, made a last magical effort. He enchanted Mirabela so that she would not die and left her women enchanted too, perpetually mourning and tearing their hair. The fountain, reddened by Mirabela's continuously flowing blood, and cluttered by the hair of her women, has become the bloody river which Amadis and Zahara followed. Monstruofuron attempts to keep the enchantment intact by setting up guards and imprisoning all who intrude upon the scene. Once a year, on the anniversary of Mirabela's wound, he kills his prisoners.

The hermit tells them that the château they are approaching is also enchanted. Not only are strange noises heard at night, but the door has remained locked ever since the enchantment began. The hermit also tells Amadis and Zahara that Monstruofuron makes a daily visit to the fountain, where Mirabela bleeds on, frozen in agony.

Amadis and Zahara leave the hermit and go on to the château. In the court they see Mirabela pierced by the sword, her blood flowing into the fountain, and her women lamenting and tearing their hair. The knight and the Amazon now try to enter the château, but the door is locked fast. They hide and watch Monstruofuron as he comes and goes on his visit, lamenting about the tortures of love.[12] As night falls, a great rush of wings brings flocks of night birds; then suddenly, at midnight, lightning flashes, thunder rumbles, and the locked door bursts open. A great torch-lit procession of ladies and gentlemen comes forth, bearing the god of Love in triumph. Four heralds appear, two dressed gaily as Joy and Mirth, and two dressed somberly as Tedium and Melancholy. Cupid is enthroned in the middle of the court, and the assembled throng hears first a proclamation by Joy and then a statement by Tedium. Joy's announcement is greeted by sweet music, but Tedium's is followed by a great wailing, in which the attending night birds join. Thereupon the god of Love and his followers return through the door by which they entered, and the door slams shut as violently as it has opened.

Throughout the ceremony Amadis and Zahara have looked on in amazement. They leave their hiding place briefly to get something to eat and then return to it to await the next visit of Monstruofuron. When he comes, he brings ten prisoners to be sacrificed—for this is the anniversary of Mirabela's enchantment. Amadis leaps from hiding and challenges the giant. In the fierce fight that follows, Monstruofuron is wounded and, before Amadis can prevent him, he pulls the sword from Mirabela's bleeding body. She dies, and he stabs himself.

Although there are many differences between the mask in *Amadis* and Spenser's Mask of Cupid, the similarities are too many and too impressive to be accidental. In each case the vigil of the onlookers is of two days' duration and a door magically barred bursts open at midnight after lightning and thunder and then slams shut after the maskers have retired. Each mask contains the god Cupid as a central figure and a damsel whose heart is magically transfixed. In each the maskers are divided into two groups. Even the river of blood that Amadis and Zahara follow turns up in one of Spenser's magnificent wall tapestries.

It is possible, of course, that the two writers followed, in their separate ways, the same literary tradition. The Court of Love tradition goes back to classical times, and both *Amadis* and *The Mirror of Knighthood* give ample evidence that the tradition still had strength in the sixteenth century.[13] But if we may judge by the number of rituals of Cupid described in *Amadis* alone, the tradition had undergone many transformations. It is therefore unlikely that Spenser could have come so close to *Amadis* if he had not been influenced directly by it. On the basis of our present

178

knowledge of Spenser's sources, it seems to me inescapable that at some time he must have read at least Book VIII of *Amadis*.

Josephine Waters Bennett has adduced evidence that the Mask of Cupid was written earlier than other parts of its canto.[14] If she is right, an early dating would coincide with the general closeness of the Mask to the rites described in Book VIII of *Amadis* and the general distance of the rest of the *Faerie Queene* from *Amadis*. An early dating for the Mask of Cupid would indicate that Spenser had read *Amadis* early, made use of it in a poem about Cupid and his court, and then gradually forgot *Amadis* except for bits and pieces—like the mad knight beating the water—which remained in his memory along with other half-forgotten fragments of other romances.

Whether or not one agrees that the episode involving Amadis and Zahara was Spenser's immediate source, it is worth examination for whatever light it may shed on meaning in Spenser. The mask in *Amadis* is very clearly a triumphal procession. The central exhibit is Mirabela, who suffers because she has rejected Cupid and preferred death to an importunate love.

In one group, led by Joy and Mirth, the maskers sing happily of the bliss of Love and wear green, the color of Hope. Among the happy lovers are Achilles, Thisbe, Medea, Paris, Pyramus, Penthesilea, Dido, and—surprisingly—Narcissus, figures we are not likely to associate with joy and mirth. In the other group, led by Melancholy and Tedium, are those who know only sorrow and discontent, wear the orange-yellow garb of those jealous and thwarted in love, and keep their arms crossed in melancholy. They are the men and women who during their lives scorned Cupid and who now, like Mirabela, know the hell Cupid keeps for those unfaithful to his law. The purpose of the mask is to show Cupid's omnipotence. The proclamation announces that Cupid wants to reward his martyrs who have suffered "pour la foy d'Amour" and punish those "qui l'ont mesprise." Better to have loved like Pyramus, however unfortunately, than never to have loved at all. Amadis and Zahara look on with awe at Love's heaven and hell, and Zahara says that only a madman would scorn Love and his laws.

Seen against the background of the mask in *Amadis*, Spenser's Mask of Cupid bears out C. S. Lewis' interpretation of it. It is a deliberate attempt to demean courtly love or, if that seems too narrow an idea, love that aims at sexual fulfillment, revels in the here and now, holds that passion is sole justification, and observes no laws beyond itself. Spenser's Mask represents strikingly the decay of Cupid's greatness. Although the maskers are in two groups—those who march before Amoret and those who come after—Spenser has carefully removed all semblance of joy. Paradise and hell are almost indistinguishable. Those in the first group, the "elect," have known what passes for love, but Pleasance is clearly a delusion and Hope is rotten at the core. Those in the second group, the "damned," are led by Reproach, Repentance, and Shame. The contrast between the two groups in *Amadis* has been kept by Spenser, but with a basic difference: the only reward of the faithful is Cupid's sneer of cold command.

One is especially aware of how far Spenser's Cupid has fallen. Britomart seems dazed after she sees the splendid tapestries that depict Cupid at the height of his power, when *carpe diem* was the password and Love evoked greatness in gods and men. But the tapestries represent Cupid as he was in pagan times. The Mask, which she gazes coldly upon, shows Cupid as he is in Spenser's day. Gone is the glory, and gone the pagan glorification of that love that reaches but to dust. The Mask is clearly a procession in honor of the cruel, meretricious, and shameful, and Cupid is a god of slaves. Unlike Amadis and Zahara, themselves victims of Cupid and all too ready to pay homage, Britomart hears in her heart

the drumbeats of another kind of love. She is in the house of
Busirane as a representative of an ideal more spiritual and more
powerful, and the ease with which she overcomes Cupid's minion
Busirane is a promise of a new order.[15]

Spenser's Mask is more decorative than allegorical, but his
meaning is clear. Like Mirabela, Amoret has been seized and tor-
tured because she refuses to give in to a seducer. She is not guilty
of lust, nor does she fear sexual love.[16] Unlike Mirabela, she is
saved—for Spenser's Cupid is no longer all-powerful.

A significant detail in Spenser's version is the failure of Scudamour to penetrate the wall of flame. He fails because he is a male
—a husband and true lover—and so is powerless against Cupid,
as husbands and fathers have always been. A man can only attempt to enforce chastity. Acrisius put Danaë in a brazen tower,
and in Book VIII of *Amadis* Bazilique imprisons Niquée to keep
her out of Cupid's toils, but both fathers learn that brazen or
stony limits cannot keep love out. It is better for men to trust
daughters and wives. In a Christian age a woman imbued with
right reason, like Britomart, is of more worth against Cupid than
walls and locks.

X

Amadis and Sidney's *Arcadia*

Though one has to advance arguments to show that Spenser must have read *Amadis*, no such arguments are needed for Sir Philip Sidney. In his *Defense of Poetry* he mentions *Amadis de Gaule* in such terms as to leave no doubt that he had a high regard for the work, even though it "wanteth much of a perfect poesy." Most scholars agree that he must have read some books of *Amadis*, but they disagree about the extent to which his *Arcadia* was influenced. Recent studies of the *Arcadia* have greatly increased the number of other possible sources, and the process has resulted inevitably in increased confusion about Sidney's use of *Amadis*.

The connection between Sidney's *Arcadia* and *Amadis* was first pointed out by Robert Southey, who in one admirably terse—and somewhat offhand—sentence suggested that *Amadis of Greece* (Books VII and VIII in the French version) was the source of Spenser's Mask of Cupid, Shakespeare's *Winter's Tale*, and Sidney's Zelmane.[1] Dunlop's *History of Fiction* picked up Southey's suggestion and indicated the main likenesses between the Zelmane episode and Book XI of *Amadis*.[2] In 1894 William Vaughn

Moody's Sohier Prize Essay at Harvard pointed out in somewhat greater detail some parallels between *Amadis* and the *Arcadia*.[3] Several scholars have since agreed with and, in some cases, expanded Moody's findings. W. W. Greg agreed that *Amadis* appears to be the source upon which Sidney chiefly drew for incidents, and K. Brunhuber and R. W. Zandvoort have largely concurred with Moody's conclusions.[4]

Nevertheless, the case for *Amadis* as a dominant influence on the *Arcadia* has come under considerable attack. Samuel L. Wolff feels that the argument for *Amadis* has been overstated, and he contends that Sidney owed most to the Greek romances of Heliodorus, Longus, and Achilles Tatius. Albert W. Osborn is also inclined to be skeptical about *Amadis* as the primary source. The case for Montemayor's *Diana* as an overriding force in the composition of the *Arcadia* has been advanced by T. P. Harrison, Jr. Marcus S. Goldman admits that the influence of *Amadis* is substantial, but he argues that Malory is an even more important influence on Sidney. In her book on the Palmerin romances Mary Patchell has continued the process of cutting away at the claims of *Amadis* by suggesting that Sidney could have found many of his ideas in the Palmerin cycle.[5]

The uncertainties among modern scholars about the influence of *Amadis* upon the *Arcadia* are best illustrated in two studies of the *Arcadia* by Walter R. Davis and Richard A. Lanham. Davis says plainly that "Book XI of *Amadís de Gaula*" is the source of Sidney's main plot. Yet, having said so, he omits *Amadis* from further consideration and goes on to talk of the *Arcadia* as a pastoral romance in the tradition of Sannazaro and Montemayor. Lanham dismisses *Amadis* out of hand. He admits that "we are glad to know that Book IX [*sic*] of *Amadis* was a specific quarry, but its incidents are hardly unique; if not there, Sidney would have easily found them, or a sufficient substitute, elsewhere."[6]

Part of the explanation for scholarly disagreement about the

Arcadia-Amadis relationship lies in the fact that the case for *Amadis* as a source has never been completely presented. Moody apparently read the first four books of *Amadis* in Southey's abridged English translation from the Spanish and at least part of Book XI in French. In this selective reading he has been followed by others, very few of whom have read any part of *Amadis* outside Book XI. As a result, no one has remarked on the important analogues in Book VIII of *Amadis,* though they are as obvious as those in Book XI. Those interested in advancing the claims of the Greek romances, the *Diana,* the *Morte d'Arthur,* and *Palmerin,* all long and complex works, have understandably not been anxious to become involved in the longer and much more complicated *Amadis.* As a result, scholars who wish to learn what works influenced Sidney can find nowhere a discussion of his debt to *Amadis* which is not either incomplete or tendentious.

Not only has the case for *Amadis* been incompletely put, but, such as it is, it has not been sufficiently emphasized. Osborn, in the course of attacking the source studies of Friedrich Brie and Brunhuber, complains that many of the parallels they point out between *Amadis* and *Arcadia* are commonplaces of romance narrative.[7] He then goes on to suggest that Sidney might have derived many of his ideas as easily from *Primaleon.* Osborn is often quite right, but he never appreciates—any more than Lanham—that *Amadis* does not offer only commonplaces. In fact, for the central episode in the *Arcadia,* the disguise of Pyrocles as Zelmane, *Amadis* is the only source. As Mary Patchell points out, this motif does not occur in the Palmerin cycle as it was translated into English, nor is it in any of the Greek romances, Montemayor, or Malory. The disguise of a knight as a lady is an extremely unusual narrative device and occurs full-blown only in *Amadis.*[8] For this reason *Amadis* deserves a much closer examination than it has yet received.

It is true that Sidney's independent handling of his alleged sources has raised questions. Miss Patchell points out that some episodes in the *Arcadia* are like incidents in *Amadis*, but she notes that there are pronounced differences.[9] Scholars sometimes grow so used to hunting literary squirrels with parallel passages and verbal borrowings that they feel at a loss when confronted by a lion. Sidney boasts that he is not a pickpurse of another's wit, and in general the scholar is struck by his literary independence. But independence is not originality. *Astrophel and Stella* is a very independent handling of the sonnet sequence, but it owes a great deal to French and Italian sonneteers. The *Arcadia* stands in much the same relationship to other prose romances as *Astrophel and Stella* to other sonnet sequences. The scholar who looks for extensive parallelism in plot and for close verbal similarities is certain to be disappointed. On the other hand, there can be no doubt that Sidney knew his literary predecessors and learned from them.

In basing his central narrative upon *Amadis*, Sidney did not so much follow as blend and transform. Because *Amadis* habitually repeats its best plot devices, Sidney was often confronted with two or three variations on a given motif. A comparison of some of the key situations and characters in the *Arcadia* with their counterparts in *Amadis* underscores the point that Sidney's was an art of combining.

A princess is kept in seclusion, usually because of an oracle.

In Sidney's work a king and his family are in seclusion. Alarmed by an enigmatic oracle, Basilius has taken Queen Gynecia and their daughters Pamela and Philoclea with him into semiretirement in a forest lodge. In this way he hopes to avoid the prophecy that Pamela will be stolen away by a prince and Philoclea will be the victim of an "uncouth love."

The motif of a princess in seclusion is very common in *Amadis*. In Book VIII the princess Niquée is kept secluded by her father in a lodge in a forest. A magician and astrologer has learned "par la reuolution & figure de sa natiuité" that any man who sees her will either go mad with love or die within a brief time. Accordingly he has advised her father, the soudan Bazilique, to keep her out of sight.

In Book XI the princess Diane is also kept secluded by her mother, Queen Sidonie, in the Château of Phoebus.

To woo his lady, a lover assumes the disguise of an Amazon.

Pyrocles sees a picture of Philoclea and falls madly in love with her. He disguises himself as the Amazon Zelmane (Cleophila in the *Old Arcadia*) and attracts the attention of Basilius by singing near the forest lodge. Basilius immediately falls in love with Zelmane. Gynecia suspects that Zelmane is a man and also falls in love. Philoclea responds to Zelmane's manifest admiration for her, but then becomes confused and alarmed by the depth of her own feelings.

In Book VIII of *Amadis,* Amadis de Grèce sees a picture of Niquée and is so affected that he almost swoons. To see her, he disguises himself as the Amazon Néreïde. Niquée's father, Bazilique, falls in love with Néreïde at first sight.

In Book XI Agesilan sees a picture of Diane and falls immediately in love with her. He disguises himself as the Amazon Daraïde and, accompanied by his friend Arlanges, who is disguised as the maid Garaye, he makes his way to the Isle of Guindaye. There Queen Sidonie is pleased by the singing of Daraïde and is delighted to add two such lovely ladies to her daughter's retinue. Soon afterwards the beautiful Cléophile comes to Sidonie's court, and Garaye falls in love with her. There follows a great deal of mirth and song among the ladies and an unconscionable amount of kissing. Diane and Cléophile cannot understand why they should feel so deeply the kisses of Daraïde and Garaye.

Daraïde's courtship is broken up by a series of adventures in which, as an Amazon, he can quite properly take part. After one adventure he is shipwrecked and thrown ashore on the Isle of Galdap. Here he meets Queen Salderne, who is normally so closely guarded by her jealous husband, Galanides, that she lives in virtual seclusion. She warns Daraïde to leave, but before he can, King Galanides arrives. The trouble that follows is finally concluded when Daraïde explains that he is a woman—a matter not obvious since he is wearing armor. Whereupon Galanides falls madly in love with him, and Queen Salderne, who is convinced that Daraïde is a man, is more interested in him than ever. When Daraïde changes into feminine attire, he charms the king even further by playing the lute and singing.

A second lover disguises himself as a shepherd to woo a second lady.

Pyrocles' companion Musidorus catches sight of Pamela and, like Pyrocles, falls in love. He disguises himself as the shepherd Dorus and manages to become part of the royal party in retirement. At the forest lodge he is employed as a servant to Dametas and tries as best he can to court Pamela.

In Book VIII Amadis de Grèce has a companion Gradamarte who also assumes a disguise—as merchant. But Gradamarte's disguise is not for love of a lady but to help establish Néreïde in the soudan's household.

In Book XI Agesilan's companion Arlanges assumes a feminine disguise as Garaye, and though his love for Cléophile receives less attention than Daraïde's for Diane, it runs a course roughly parallel. In Book IX Florisel disguises himself as a shepherd to woo Silvie.[10]

The lovers endure frustration and indignities in their disguises.
For a long while both Pyrocles and Musidorus face a series of

embarrassments. Pyrocles' love for Philoclea is impeded by the attentions showered on him by the infatuated Basilius and the amorous Gynecia. He finds almost no chance to be alone with Philoclea. Instead he finds himself "inflamed by Philoclea, watched by Gynecia, and tired by Basilius." Meanwhile Philoclea is troubled by the emotions she feels for another woman.

Musidorus also endures great difficulties. As a shepherd of Dametas, he has to put up with that loud and bumbling fool and pretend to be respectful. Even after he saves Pamela's life, he finds her cold and aloof. Her sense of rank and propriety makes her chide herself for even thinking of a mere shepherd. Meanwhile Dametas' wife Miso and his daughter Mopsa also inflict themselves on Musidorus.

In *Amadis* the disguised lovers also have problems. The disguise of Amadis de Grèce as Néréïde is so successful that Bazilique, though old and impotent, is inspired by young ideas. He is so attentive that Néréïde has very few opportunities to talk alone with his beloved Niquée. The old soudan wants Néréïde always near and even proposes marriage.

Agesilan too knows frustrations. His disguise is so successful that he dares not reveal himself to Diane. He would rather be near her in the dress of a woman than risk the separation from her that he fears revelation would cause.

When Daraïde is shipwrecked on Galdap, his desire is to resume his trip, and Diane is always on his mind. But King Galanides and Queen Salderne give him scarcely a chance to think of her, much less to get away from Galdap. Galanides proposes marriage, an arrangement whereby Daraïde would be queen, though somehow Salderne would retain her title. Queen Salderne proposes adultery.

The lover makes love indirectly.

One of the brightest stratagems of Musidorus is to make verbal love to Pamela while apparently addressing Mopsa. The scheme allows Dorus to tell his whole history and the reason for his disguise.

In Book XII of *Amadis* after Daraïde's disguise has been penetrated, Diane's friend Lardenie intercedes for Daraïde. Diane finally consents to talk to Lardenie as though she were Daraïde. Later Lardenie suggests to Daraïde that he consider her as Diane and pretend he is a knight making love to her. Diane listens while Daraïde plays this game, and she is much moved by Daraïde's sincerity.

An uprising of the people is calmed by the lover-Amazon.

The love tangles of Pyrocles and Musidorus are interrupted by an uprising of the people. The riot is differently motivated in Sidney's two versions of the story, but in the *Old Arcadia* a strong reason is the people's concern for Basilius' safety and their feeling that his retirement is strange and foreboding. The trouble is at last quelled by a speech by Zelmane.

In Book XII of *Amadis* the people become alarmed by cries from the Château of Phoebus, where Diane is secluded. They gather to help their queen and princess, for whose safety they fear. Daraïde makes an address to calm the mob.

In the affair at Galdap, the Daraïde-Galanides-Salderne triangle is interrupted by an invasion led by the king of Gelde.

In addition to these parallels there are other significant points of resemblance between *Amadis* and the *Arcadia*. The character of Dametas probably owes something to the remarkable coward Darinel. Like Dametas, Darinel has illusions of grandeur, even though he is the butt of much chivalric humor. When danger threatens, Darinel looks for a place to hide, and like Dametas, he is very fond of playing on the pipes. His cowardice is so outrageous that knights labor to involve him in a duel with the cowardly hunchback Mardoquée—and it is probably from this hint that Sidney created his comic duel between Dametas and Clinias for the *New Arcadia*.[11]

In addition, Gynecia's sexual advances to Zelmane in the cave, wherein she tears away her clothing and exposes her body, are doubtless derived from Queen Salderne's much more practiced efforts to seduce Daraïde. The differences are significant. Sidney intends Gynecia to be saved. She is a basically modest woman overcome by passion, and so she behaves like a passionate woman, not like a whore. Also, Zelmane's excuse to Basilius that she must perform certain religious rites before she can submit to him is like Néreïde's excuse to the amorous old soudan that she cannot give in to him because she has made a vow of chastity for one year.[12] And the bathing scene in the *Arcadia* may have been suggested by a scene in *Amadis* wherein Diane, taking a bath, asks Daraïde to pour water on her with a pitcher. But Daraïde is so tremulous at the sight of Diane's naked beauty that he finds it hard to concentrate upon his appointed task, and when he pours the water, it misses its target (XI, lxxxii).

It has already been suggested that the trick of Arlande, who by stealing into Florisel's bed clad in Silvie's mantle makes Florisel believe she is Silvie, may have given Sidney the idea for the "adultery" scene between Basilius and Gynecia in the cave.[13] It may also be that the premarital consummation of the love of Pyrocles and Philoclea in the *Old Arcadia* derives from a similar experience of Amadis de Grèce and Niquée (VII, lxxii). At any rate, Sidney's use of such an incident indicates how far under the influence of chivalric narrative he had come, for a sexual encounter between lovers who intend to wed is standard procedure throughout *Amadis*.

In building the central episode of the *Arcadia* out of various pieces of *Amadis*, Sidney is about as independent as a sixteenth-century writer can reasonably be expected to be. His plot is the result of blending, assimilating, and ordering. He does not have a single episode of *Amadis* in mind but at least three—two episodes involving Daraïde in Book XI, which carry over into Book XII, and one involving Néreïde in Book VIII. The thoroughness with which Sidney has taken over the Amadisian material is apparent in the characters of the central episode in the *Arcadia*. Whereas Salderne seems to have been his principal model for Gynecia, Basilius is a blend of Galanides and old Bazilique. Philoclea's name derives from Cléophile, but she is a blend of Niquée and Diane. Pamela's chief model is the cool Cléophile. Pyrocles is modeled on both Amadis de Grèce and Agesilan. Musidorus is probably a combination of Florisel and Arlanges.

Though the characters in the core of the *Arcadia* seem to have been suggested by characters in *Amadis*, Sidney has greatly increased their stature. The impression they make is more vivid partly because they occupy many more pages in the *Arcadia* than do their counterparts in *Amadis*. We see them more and in better focus. They think, speak, and sing more. In both form and content their language is more expressive. More important, they fit the structure of the *Arcadia* in a way that the characters of *Amadis* do not. Whereas the structure of *Amadis* is so loose that it often makes the characters appear inconsequential, in the more purposeful framework of the *Arcadia* the characters become more purposeful, for whatever they do affects the artificial world the structure encompasses. Sidney's real genius was for form.

In examining the various episodes in *Amadis* that Sidney drew upon, one is particularly struck by the extremes the author avoided. In the Daraïde-Diane relationship in *Amadis* the reader is often reminded of a strong undercurrent of Lesbianism, but this is an element almost completely absent in the *Arcadia*. The accident in which Gynecia dislocates her shoulder is really a fortunate fall, for it keeps her from making a Salderne-fool of herself. Though Basilius is carried away by passion, he never becomes so wholly an old lecher as Bazilique, nor does he run mad like Galanides. Even the scene in which Pyrocles in his disguise as Zelmane watches Philoclea bathing in the river becomes less an indictment of Zelmane when Amphialus is discovered looking on from a nearby covert. Somehow two Actaeons, each pursued by his own raging passions, seem less outrageous than one.

Sidney's debt to *Amadis* is not confined to characters and events in the central intrigue of the *Arcadia*. When he rewrote the *Old Arcadia* and enlarged it, he called upon other sections of *Amadis*. Long ago Brunhuber pointed out his use of an episode from Book XI for his story of Pamphilus.[14] In the *Arcadia* Pyrocles is riding through the woods when he hears a cry for help. He comes upon a knight tied to a tree and assailed by nine women armed with bodkins. Pyrocles learns that the captive has made love to all nine women and has abandoned them one by one as a new love came into view.

In Book XI of *Amadis* Daraïde rides through a forest and comes upon two damsels who are beating a knight whom they have tied naked to a tree. Daraïde learns that the knight has made love to both damsels and promised to marry them. As usual with Sidney, in taking over the episode, he has made much more of it. The story of Pamphilus is not merely an isolated, half-comic event as it is in *Amadis;* it is tied in with Sidney's main theme of love and reason.[15]

Still another episode in the *Arcadia,* the meeting of Pyrocles (in the armor of Amphialus) with the coach of Helen of Corinth, has been traced to Book I of *Amadis*. Pyrocles comes upon a coach "drawne with foure milke-white horses, furnished all in blacke, with a black a more boy upon every horse, they al apparelled in white, the coach it self very richly furnished in black & white." [16] With the help of Clitophon he kills or wounds the twelve accompanying knights who refuse to allow him near the coach. When he looks inside, he discovers Queen Helen of Corinth, dressed in mourning and looking with devotion upon a picture of Amphialus. She is so entranced by the image and her sorrow that she has not even heard the noise of the conflict and looks up only when the shadow of Pyrocles falls across the picture. Moody first called attention to the similarity between this episode and that in Book I of *Amadis*. There Amadis comes upon a splendid coach guarded by eight knights who refuse to let him look inside. In a fight he routs or slays them all. He looks inside and sees a beautiful girl in mourning, a "tombe of Marble" beside her (xxii).

This is a significant parallel, but another, from Book IX, Chapter xxvii, should also be noted. There Alastraxerée comes upon a covered coach drawn by an elephant and twelve white horses, a dwarf sitting atop the elephant. Sixteen knights accompanying the coach refuse to allow Alastraxerée near. A fight ensues and she learns, after defeating the entire guard, that the coach carries several beautiful ladies. In Chapter xlix of the same book a similar episode occurs.

Wolff has made much of what he calls "pathetic optics" in Sidney's description of Queen Helen totally absorbed in the picture of Amphialus, and this is an element missing in both analogues from *Amadis*. Wolff asserts that pathetic optics is a device peculiar to Greek romances, particularly Heliodorus, and that Sidney's use of it proves the influence of Heliodorus on him. In fact, pathetic optics is a common trick in *Amadis*, and it is far more likely that Sidney acquired it from his reading of *Amadis* than that he is following Heliodorus. For Helen of Corinth entranced by the sight of Amphialus' picture and disturbed only by a shadow on it, Sidney may well have had in mind the enchantment of Niquée. She is enchanted looking at an image of Amadis de Grèce, perfectly content and oblivious to all as long as nothing blocks her view (VIII, xxiv).[17]

A third point of similarity between the *Arcadia* and *Amadis* occurs in the conditions set by Phalantus for the defense of Artesia's beauty. As Brunhuber has pointed out, Phalantus sets up a picture of Artesia and requires that anyone who challenges him must bring a picture of his mistress, winner to take both likenesses. Since Phalantus is for a long time a winner, he travels with a considerable number of pictures of lovely ladies—described at length in Chapter xvi. This motif seems to be derived from Book VII of *Amadis*, Chapter lvi, when Birmartes similarly defends the beauty of Onorie.

Many other narrative resemblances between the *Arcadia* and *Amadis* might be pointed out or have been noted already. All are either too vague and inexact or so commonplace that Sidney could have come upon them in works other than *Amadis*. For example, Sidney might have derived the idea for the false beheading from *Amadis,* for the romance contains at least two such incidents (IX, xviii; XII, liii). But as Wolff has remarked, the false beheading trick is used also in Achilles Tatius, and it is impossible to be sure where Sidney got the idea. Nor would I wish to suggest that every incident in the *Arcadia* is derived from *Amadis*. That Sidney's debt may be greater than I have indicated is very likely, but where the matter is at all in doubt, I have thought it wiser not to insist.

If Sidney drew heavily upon *Amadis* for incident, it is logical to suspect that the romance influenced the *Arcadia* in other, more subtle ways. What of Sidney's treatment of sexual love, his sense of humor, and his prose style?

Amadis treats sexual love in a frank, sometimes licentious way. Sidney is more reserved in his handling of love scenes; however, it is interesting to note that in revising the *Arcadia*, he apparently intended to play down such sexual license as appears in the *Old Arcadia*.[18] There Pyrocles and Philoclea consummate their love before marriage, and we are given to understand that Musidorus and Pamela would also have succumbed to passion had they not been interrupted by the clownish outlaws. Sidney must have had some second thoughts about the propriety of his lovers' conduct— so far, at least, as one may judge on the basis of his incomplete *New Arcadia*. In any case, his treatment of sexual love in the *Old Arcadia* conforms more closely to the Amadisian code, wherein sexual gratification is almost a knight's prerogative and a lady's constancy is much more important than her chastity. Moreover, an important theme in the *Arcadia*, that foolish, though well-meaning, parents who impose stringent curbs upon mettlesome, but basically virtuous, daughters are really to be blamed for their consequent fall from virtue, is very common in *Amadis*.

Sidney was undoubtedly attracted by the quality of the humor in *Amadis*. Prose romances of the sixteenth century are generally quite sober and take chivalry seriously. *Palmerin* and *The Mirror of Knighthood* have in them occasional moments of comedy, but the reader must look hard and long to find them. Romance humor tends to be verbal—the witty remark of a knight to an irascible giant—and it often comes off lamely in translation. *Amadis*, on the other hand, contains an unusually large amount of comedy, much of it situational. Even such distinguished knights as Amadis de Grèce and Rogel are often made to look foolish, and there is a decided antichivalric cast to much of the fun. The range of comedy is wide, from farce and grotesque buffoonery to neat bits of irony. It is, for example, a nice irony that Oriane's letter dismissing Amadis for infidelity should be delivered to him just as he has proved himself most loyal by successfully traversing the enchantment of the Arch of True Lovers. Generally, however, Amadisian humor is not very subtle. It tends rather to be broad and even grotesque and brutal.

The *Arcadia* is also liberally sprinkled with humor, and much of it derives from *Amadis*. The central disguise motif is often delightful. Pyrocles being wooed by an infatuated Basilius, who has an unregal tendency to fall on his knees and clutch Pyrocles' skirts, retains much of the comedy implicit and explicit in the parallel episodes in *Amadis*. Whether or not Dametas is drawn from the Amadisian Darinel, he is a much tighter and more fully developed humorous figure than Darinel, and Miso and Mopsa keep the reader aware that the *Arcadia* is a comedy.

Nevertheless, Sidney's sense of humor has shocked some modern critics, and words like brutality and callousness have been used to describe it. To our somewhat more democratic age his "humorous" description of the rabble in rebellion is not funny. One of the mob is a painter who wants to get a firsthand view of battle preparatory to doing a portrait of the fight between the Centaurs and the Lapithae—Sidney's sneer at the lofty aspirations of ignorance. In the fight Musidorus with one blow strikes off both the painter's hands, to Sidney's amusement and our horror.[19]

One may defend Sidney, as Myrick does, by pointing out that the rebels are treated with harsh Elizabethan justice.[20] Treason has always been a harsh word. The commoners, after all, attack the king and his family and get only what they deserve. Why expect Sidney, with his aristocrat's sense of degree, to sympathize with these clumsy overreachers?

There are fashions in humor as in clothes. Shakespeare's comedies no longer convulse popular audiences. The antics of bedlamites no longer tickle us mightily. But deformity elicited laughter in the sixteenth century. In his *Defense* Sidney says: "We laugh at deformed creatures. . . ."[21] He goes on to qualify his statement by saying that this is not delightful laughter. But his admission is clearly true. Who more deformed than the cuckold, that horned monster? Yet, who more laughed at in the sixteenth century?

Romances like *Amadis* particularly stress physical deformities. Dwarfs, hunchbacks, and giants of varying degrees of loathsomeness provide a large part of what was considered comedy, and the more deformed the creature, the funnier he is taken to be. Birmartes roars with laughter at his first sight of the dwarf Buzando, who is "la plus layde & contrefaite personne, que Nature produit onques." Cruel humor is very common—a dwarf hung by one foot over a smoking fire, or a giant so wounded that his entrails drag on the ground and he steps on them as he tries to fight. The grotesque battle between Buzando and a female dwarf is intended to be very funny. In his *Arcadia* and in his *Defense* Sidney simply accepts as comic what was generally so accepted. He was, after all, a man of his age, and humor is a sense more social than individual.

Although it would be ridiculous to assert that so elaborate and varied a style as Sidney's is derived wholly from *Amadis*, it would be harder to believe that *Amadis* exerted no influence at all upon the style of the *Arcadia*. The relationship has never been examined in detail, though at least two scholars have suggested its existence. Sir Henry Thomas writes that Sidney may have picked up some of his rhetorical tricks from *Amadis,* and Morris W. Croll mentions as a possible stylistic influence the writing of Feliciano de Silva, who wrote what became in French translation Books IX through XII.[22] Though the problem is much too complicated to be dealt with exhaustively in this study, a few points may be made.

Some of Sidney's rhetorical figures indicate a relationship with *Amadis*. For example, in the *Arcadia* this sentence appears: "This word, Lover, did no lesse pearce poor Pyrocles, then the right tune of musicke toucheth him that is sick of the Tarantula." [23] It is unusual for Sidney to indulge in such natural-history allusions. Nor does *Amadis* make frequent use of natural history, but when Lardenie and Diane try to revive Daraïde from his swoon, music is suggested as a possible remedy. David, they recall, cured Saul by playing, and it is said that music can even cure wounds, as it does "en vne contrée, ceux qui sont piquez des serpens nommez Tarantes" (XI, lvi, 90).

Moreover, in the *Arcadia* Sidney mentions Pamela and Philoclea "about whom, as about two Poles, the Skie of Beautie was turned." [24] The figure is not a commonplace, and it is possible that he was influenced in its use by a similar expression in *Amadis*. There the two poles are the beauties Niquée and Lucelle. The latter says to Amadis de Grèce: "Pensez que nauiguerez desormais entre deux nortz, que quand l'vn apparoistra, vous perdrez l'autre: vostre Niquée est l'Artique, & moy l'Antartique: si vous la trouuez, vous me perdrez" (XI, lxxvi, 127).

Rhetorically, Sidney is also fond of the eyes-hands-heart combination. In the *Old Arcadia* Philoclea says: "Shoulde these eyes guyde my steppes that had seene youre murder? shoulde these handes feede mee, that had not hyndered suche a myscheef? shoulde this harte remayne within mee at every pant, to Counte the Contynuall Clock of my myseryes?" [25] In one form or another —the combination may be eyes-tongue-heart or eyes-tongue-brain—this is a common rhetorical device, much favored by sixteenth-century English poets. Sidney uses a variation of the formula in his "too late dying creature, which dares not speake, no not looke, no not scarcely thinke." And another variation occurs in "But now alas mine eyes waxe dimme, my toong beginnes to falter, and my hart to want force to help." [26]

In one or another form the formula occurs several times in *Amadis,* and it is possible, though quite unprovable, that Sidney was moved to use it by reading it there. For example, Grasandor confesses to Mabila that "the three principall organes of my life, are in most strange and vnusuall distemper: namely, mine eyes, my heart, and my tongue. For as soone as my eyes can but gaine a sight of you: they incite speech, onely to tell you the cause of my griefe; but all in vaine. Then my tongue, hoping to supply that defect: openeth my mouth, but feare preuailing, quickly closeth it vp againe. If then my heart be in heauy martyrdome, I leaue to your owne iudgement, speaking (as it doth) by continuall sighing" (IV, xxv, 111).[27]

One of the marks of Sidney's style particularly noted by his contemporaries was his fondness for such arrangements as "exceedingly sory for Pamela, but exceedingly exceeding that exceedingness in feare for Philoclea," and "the Certeinty of thinges to come, wherein there ys no thinge so certeyne as oure Continuall uncerteinty."[28] Though such rhetoric is not really very common in Sidney, it is extreme, and it is often by a writer's heights and depths that he is most easily identified. Rhetoric of this kind is very close to word play in *Amadis*. When Rogel attempts to seduce Sidère, who is in his care, she reminds him of his honor and duty: "choses si fortes qu'elles sont suffisantes pour forcer les forces desquelles amour vous force pour me forcer" (XII, lxxvii, 193). Later she adds: "ie me mes entierement en vostre sauue garde, à fin que par vostre vertu vous me defendiez de moy contre vous, & de vous contre moy, & encores de vous contre vous mesmes" (XII, lxxvii, 194).

The great bulk of *Amadis* contains numerous examples of high style very close to the elaborate diction Sidney favored. One can perhaps not do better than quote Sardenie's speech to Rogel. She says she is Sardenie, "qui vous donna son amour pour sa hayne, sa liberté pour sa seruitude, son honneur pour son deshonneur, son repos pour son trauail, & son auctorité pour le mespris auquel elle s'est mise, vous venant chercher elle mesme, à fin de vous retrouuer pour vous perdre, & se trouuer perdue pour l'amour de vous, tout ainsi que vous estes perdu pour l'amour d'vne autre: Finablement ie suis celle qui vous ay donné la vie pour receuoir la mort, & qui en viuant, meurs mile foys le iour, pour ne pouuoir mourir" (XII, lxxxi, 201). This kind of rhetoric, which delights in paradox and the play of wit, comes very close to Sidney's style. Since we know that Sidney read *Amadis,* it is unlikely that the stylistic similarities are merely accidental.

All things considered, the influence of *Amadis* upon the *Arcadia* appears to be greater than hitherto realized. Since Moody, scholars have been aware of narrative resemblances between Book XI and the *Arcadia,* but the analogous episodes in Book VIII, noted above, substantially enlarge Sidney's debt. Even the name Basilius Sidney probably derived from that of Bazilique, the soudan of Babylon.[29] Sidney's characters, his treatment of sexual love, sense of humor, and style all appear to owe something to *Amadis.* There can be no question that it is a work basic to an understanding of the *Arcadia.* As a source, it is much more important than Heliodorus, Achilles Tatius, Sannazaro, Montemayor, or Malory, for better than any of them it explains why the *Arcadia* is what it is.

XI

Amadis and Elizabethan Fiction

Some of the attributes of *Amadis* that attracted Sir Philip Sidney may well have alienated other Elizabethan writers of prose fiction. For one who was, like Sidney, bent on writing a prose poem of heroic proportions the French romance, or its equivalent, was useful, even necessary. For the large group of writers who set out to ape John Lyly's euphuistic style a narrative on the scale of *Amadis* was largely irrelevant. The trappings of chivalry—armor, shields bearing heraldic devices, and horsemanship—and the chivalric ideal as modified by Castiglione fascinated Sidney. He himself wore body armor, took part in chivalric tournaments at court, and tried to live in accordance with Castiglione's dictates. The *Arcadia* was directed to a coterie audience who shared his views and attitudes. But writers of less distinguished place, writing for less distinguished readers, could scarcely be expected to share his warmth for the old-fashioned ideals of chivalry, and no other Elizabethan romance approaches the *Arcadia* in spirit or magnitude of conception.

Amadis was clearly the chief influence upon Sidney, but in most other Elizabethan writers of prose narrative the influence of *Amadis* is not so conspicuous and is only with great difficulty, if at all, to be differentiated from that of *Palmerin* or *The Mirror of Knighthood* or other Spanish or French imports. One reason is to be found in the record of English translations. Whereas in the reign of Elizabeth only the first two books of *Amadis* were translated into English, the translation of other romances proceeded more rapidly. The English version of the first book of *The Mirror of Knighthood* was in print by 1580, and the first part of *Palmerin of England* by 1581. The other books of both cycles followed in due, though unchronological, course, and by 1601 all nine books of *The Mirror of Knighthood* and the five books of *Palmerin* could be read in English. In addition, several shorter chivalric romances were translated. The two-volume *Gerileon of England* was translated from French, Book I in 1578 and Book II in 1592. *Palladine of England* (1588), *Galien of France* (1589?),[1] and *The Honor of Chivalry* (1598)—all single volumes—kept knighthood in flower for those English readers who cared. It is, of course, true that all these romances—with the possible exception of *Galien of France*—were influenced more or less by *Amadis*, and that they are all, therefore, vehicles of Amadisian influence in England. But it is an influence somewhat diluted.

The process of dilution is carried further in the English romances written under the influence of French and Spanish imports. Chivalry must have appeared extravagant and of limited utility to English writers for middle-class readers. At any rate, aside from the *Arcadia*, which is something more than a chivalric romance, few writers in England show an enduring devotion to the genre. Only Emanuel Forde wrote more than one full-fledged chivalric romance, and his plots are noticeably less complex and inventive than those in *Amadis* and other imports. Most English writers purged their romances of magic, curtailed the sexual license of knights and ladies, and abbreviated the descriptions of chivalric tournaments and spectacles. They often added a strong dose of moral teaching by stressing Protestant virtue and the importance of trusting in God, and they tried to decorate the narrative with the somewhat tattered remnants of euphuism. Sometimes the chivalry that appears in English romances seems to hark back to Bevis of Hampton or Guy of Warwick and to have only tenuous connections with Amadis and his peers. Richard Johnson and Henry Robarts added an element of patriotism by making their knights English—Tom a Lincoln, the Red Rose Knight—or singing the praises of English soldiers—as in *Pheander* (1595).[2] The unknown author of *The Knight of the Sea* (1600) felt that chivalry was silly and attempted to laugh the chivalric romance out of fashion. Although writers like Robert Greene and Thomas Lodge made extensive use of chivalric motifs, they did so selectively or in such a euphuized way that the chivalric content is almost unnoticeable.

Though few genuine chivalric romances were written in Elizabethan England, the influence of the genre is widespread. Chivalric motifs occur in a variety of prose romances which are by no means chivalric. Writers like Thomas Deloney and Henry Robarts, who wrote fiction to flatter powerful guilds, like the shoemakers and clothiers, do not hesitate to make use of the well-worn clichés of romance narrative. When Jack of Newbury is asked to outfit six men for the king's wars, he furnishes instead fifty horse and fifty foot—"Himselfe likewise in compleat armour on a goodly Barbed Horse, rode formost of the companie, with a launce in his hand, and a faire plume of yellow Feathers in his crest. . . ."[3] Since by Deloney's time money had become a key to knighthood, Jack's metamorphosis from clothier to knight doubtless struck the bourgeois reader as no more than Jack's due.

Similarly, *Haigh for Devonshire* (1600), which deals with the adventures of six gallant merchants, transforms the stuff of chivalric romance to a more mundane purpose. William of Exeter, a merchant, and his friends put on a show for the king that closely resembles a tournament. It lasts for three days, a proper duration, and at the end of each day, in chivalric fashion, a champion is chosen. But instead of knights on horseback in the varied panoply of chivalry we see contestants vie in such common sports as football, hurling, and wrestling.[4]

Many English tales that deal not at all with knights, ladies in distress, and the varied derring-do of chivalric narrative are nevertheless reminiscent of the genre. Both parts of Barnabe Riche's *Don Simonides* (1581 and 1584) are primarily euphuistic, Part I particularly, but there is more than a hint of chivalric influence. In Part I, Don Simonides, bound for Genoa, is shipwrecked. In a deserted country he comes upon a wonderful cave framed by Nature, "as it seemed in despight of Arte." When he enters, he finds that "the Pament was Cristiline, whereon was portratured the wofull passions of Phices, and the crewell meanaces of Iuno, the rare familiarities of Marce and Venus, . . . the angrie Iuno with her seruaunt Argos, the subtill Mercurie with his Oten Pipe, the faire Io in a disguised shape, the flying Daphne in the figure of a Laurel, the wise Apollo pursuyng Cassandria, the Troyan Prophetior refusing his proffer."[5] On the walls are depicted the triumphs of Cupid. All this is very much like exotic settings in the chivalric romances. The tale also involves a shepherd named Titerus and a riddling prophecy. By solving it, Simonides like so many chivalric heroes, frees Titerus from an enchantment of love.

Like *Don Simonides*, many other pieces of Elizabethan fiction borrow narrative motifs from romances of chivalry and combine them in new ways. Robert Greene usually blends chivalric incidents with a liberal infusion of euphuistic rhetoric. His *Card of Fancy* (1584) is heavily euphuistic, but chivalric motifs appear near the end. The father-son combat so much favored in *Amadis* occurs in the fight between Gwydonius and his father Clerophontes. Moreover, in the midst of the fight Gwydonius sees his mistress Castania looking on, and, as so often happens in romances, the sight so inspires him that he overthrows Clerophontes and almost kills him. By winning the fight, Gwydonius wins also Castania, whose hand has been offered as a prize to the victor. Thus *The Card of Fancy*, which begins in a highly conversational mood and abounds in neat antitheses and euphuistic prattle about the fondness of porcupines for staring at the stars, ends in a rush of narrative that is almost wholly chivalric in kind and tone.

The influence of chivalric romance began to be felt in England in the 1570's, but it does not appear strongly in prose narrative until 1580. By that time euphuism was all the rage, and for about a decade most writers of English fiction wrote novels more or less like *Euphues*—almost plotless stories in which what little narrative exists serves only as a frame upon which to hang the incessant discourses. Since the emphasis in the romances of chivalry is on narrative, their influence upon *Euphues*-ridden English narrative was generally beneficial. It is interesting to note in Robert Greene's fiction of the 1580's that his growing sense of structure and his dropping of euphuistic traits coincide with an increasing adoption of chivalric motifs.

The first Elizabethan novel to show a pronounced chivalric bent is Munday's *Zelauto: The Fountain of Fame*, which appeared in 1580. Although *Amadis* may have contributed to this work— Munday mentions Oriana—the most obvious influence is *Palmerin of England*. Munday was at work on his translation of this part of the Palmerin cycle before *Zelauto* appeared in print, and he obviously intended his first novel to serve in part as a herald of the translation to come. In his preface to *Zelauto* he refers to his translation as imminent, and he brings Palmerin himself into

Zelauto to defend the beauty of his mistress Polinarda in knightly combat.[6] Palmerin suffers a crushing defeat at the hands of a woman clad in armor, though the shock of his overthrow is considerably lessened by the circumstance that the warrior-lady is defending the beauty of Queen Elizabeth. As in George Peele's *Arraignment of Paris,* where the golden apple is handed to Elizabeth rather than to Venus, flattery of the Queen brooked no obstacles, least of all the beauty of a goddess or the reputation of a knight. In addition to the combat in which Palmerin participates, *Zelauto* contains another formal chivalric duel, a courtier who has turned hermit, considerable discussion of courtesy, and an attempt to achieve variety of matter and tone—all traits that indicate chivalric influence.

Though Munday took over—largely from *Palmerin*—chivalric motifs, his main debt appears to be structural. Jack Stillinger has pointed out how complicated the structure of *Zelauto* is and has called it a combination "of such disparate influences as euphuism, chivalric romance, the pastoral, courtly love, the jestbook, and the novella."[7] If this judgment is correct, Munday deserves more credit, and his name should be written larger in the history of literature—for he would have created a new kind in Elizabethan fiction. One looks in vain at the writers of English narrative— William Painter, George Pettie, George Gascoigne, John Grange, Lyly, and Gosson—who preceded Munday for any such combination.

But another explanation is more easily made. Far from being a combination of diverse elements, *Zelauto* is in reality a miniaturization of *Palmerin* or *Amadis.* Every element in Stillinger's list except euphuism can be found already combined in *Palmerin of England,* a work that Munday knew intimately. And Munday's euphuism, which is confined almost wholly to his dedication and preface to the reader, is quietly borrowed from the pages of

Gosson's *Ephemerides* (1579).[8] *Zelauto* is the first narrative in English to use the structure of chivalric romance, and it is significant that the work remained unfinished. Munday learned early that a writer of romances always makes provision for additional volumes.

The best examples of the influence of chivalric romance upon the structure of Elizabethan fiction are to be found in the works of Emanuel Forde. Few scholars give him credit for anything but a tremendous—and almost inexplicable—popularity. His three romances *Ornatus and Artesia, Parismus,* and *Montelion* went through numerous editions and continued to be read into the eighteenth century. Many editions were read out of existence, and the earliest edition of *Montelion* is dated 1633, though it was probably first printed in the last years of Elizabeth's reign. The explanation for Forde's appeal to readers is the completeness with which he has imitated his chivalric models. He concentrates upon telling a complex, relatively exciting, and generally coherent story and draws for narrative ideas upon *Amadis, Palmerin,* and Sidney's *Arcadia,* all works of tested popularity. Although Forde's style is occasionally abysmal, it is usually readable. In a style-conscious age it had one great merit: it was kept subordinate to the narrative.

Forde's three romances are merely three different arrangements of the standard clichés of chivalric narrative. *Parismus* (1598), his first work, is his most ambitious.[9] It is the longest of the three and the slowest paced. As in *Amadis* and *Palmerin,* its first part recounts the adventures of the titular hero, but a second part deals mostly with the deeds of his son Parismenos and ends with a vague threat of further continuation. In *Ornatus and Artesia* (1595) Forde wrote a more Arcadian kind of story. The central tale involves the wooing of Artesia by Ornatus, who disguises himself as the lady Silvia in order to have easy access to her. In his third romance *Montelion* (1600?) Forde returns to the formula he has used in *Parismus*, but he adds a touch of humor and seeks to compress and speed up the narrative. For its length *Montelion* is the most complex of the three tales.

Forde's popularity was surely due to his emphasis on plot. Nearly all the tested devices of chivalric storytelling turn up in his romances. The birth of the hero in adverse circumstances, his rearing in a strange manner—the child Parismenos is cared for by a lion—the use of tokens to establish paternity, the heavy dependence on disguise, great battles, jousts, duels, giants, pirates, kidnapings—all these motifs turn up again and again in Forde's stories. The arrangement is episodic. Just when Parismenos and Angelica are preparing for the wedding that, one might presume, will bring the story to an end, she is kidnaped and the tale goes spinning off on a new tack. Forde keeps rhetorical embellishment to a minimum. There are two poems in *Parismus* but none in *Ornatus and Artesia* or *Montelion*. The letters that appear so often in *Amadis,* always given in full, are scarce and much briefer in Forde's romances.[10] The advice to the reader that prefaces *Parismus* makes clear where the emphasis lies: "Expect not the high stile of a refined Wit, but the plaine description of Valiant Knights. . . ."

As usual in such romances, where the occurrences are all familiar, it is often impossible to say certainly where Forde derived his material. *Amadis* does not appear to be so powerful and direct an influence on him as Sidney's *Arcadia* and the Palmerin romances. When Ornatus takes on the disguise of a lady in order to be near Artesia, he is probably following the example of Pyrocles rather than that of Amadis de Grèce or Agesilan.[11] Since many of the other chivalric incidents are common to *Amadis* and *Palmerin* alike, it is more likely that Forde knew the English *Palmerin* than that he went to the French *Amadis*.

Moreover, one incident in *Montelion* seems to be derived from one of the books in the Palmerin cycle. In *Montelion* Praxentia falls in love with the hero, but she is loved by his companion Palian. Praxentia's secret invitation to Montelion is handed by mistake to Palian, who takes advantage of the error and visits her in her chamber at night. The episode is very close to one in Book III of *Primaleon of Greece*. There Padritie, the sister of the king of Lacedemonia, falls in love with Edward, but Edward's companion Bellager is attracted to her. A covert message from Padritie to Edward goes astray, and Bellager takes advantage of the situation by visiting her in the darkness, counterfeiting Edward's voice as Palian does in the similar situation.[12]

Whatever the source of Forde's immediate inspiration—if anything in Forde can properly be called inspired—*Amadis* is a strong, though background, influence. It would be difficult to show that Forde had ever read *Amadis*, even the two books translated into English, but it influenced him indirectly through Sidney's *Arcadia* and, more indirectly and remotely, through *Palmerin*. Perhaps the influence of *Amadis* accounts for Forde's fondness for erotic episodes, which go beyond any in the *Arcadia* or *Palmerin* and set Forde apart among Elizabethan writers of fiction.

Forde's *Ornatus and Artesia* resembles Sidney's *Arcadia* not only in its use of the Amadisian motif of a knight disguised as a woman but in its pastoral tone. Although pastoralism in English literature is often traced back through Sannazaro, Boccaccio, and Montemayor to Theocritus and Virgil, it should be noted that *Amadis* contains a pronounced pastoral strain which in all probability affected Elizabethan fiction. Book IX, in which Florisel for love of Silvie goes to live as a shepherd, mixes chivalry and pastoralism very effectively and is often cited as influential in the spread of pastoralism.[13] Sidney's *Arcadia* was certainly influenced by the pastoral note in *Amadis*, and Spenser's *Faerie Queene* may also have been affected. From Book IX of *Amadis*, *The Mirror of Knighthood* draws a large part of its pastoral content, and from *The Mirror of Knighthood* the English romance *Moderatus* (1595) takes its emphasis on pastoralism.[14]

In *Amadis* the reader is never very far from the countryside. It lies all around. Though it is almost never described, except as a wood or a desert, it is always felt. Knights are often sheltered by shepherds or hermits, and in time of dejection they turn naturally to the woods to brood. *Amadis*, moreover, contains numerous nostalgic expressions of longing for the simple life. When Mardoquée sings a song about the joys of simple rural existence (XI, viii, 17^v), his song echoes Horace and Martial, but it is in tune with one of the great sentimental veins of the sixteenth century. Throughout *Amadis* the knights take for granted the superiority of life lived in the presence of nature, and like Amadis d'Astre, though their duty calls them to chivalry, their hearts are in the woods and fields. Hence the popularity of the recurrent theme of the joys of the hermit's life.

Pastoralism began to appear in English fiction in the 1580's, at about the same time as chivalry. Lodge's short tale *Forbonius and Prisceria* (1583) is the earliest pastoral tale in the English Renaissance. But if Lodge was affected by *Amadis*, he kept his indebtedness well hidden. There is scarcely a trace of chivalry in the narrative. Like Niquée or Diane in *Amadis*, Prisceria is kept in seclusion by her father, and Forbonius takes on the disguise of shepherd in order to court her. As in *Amadis*, it is Forbonius' ability as a singer that attracts the attention of her father and makes the disguise work. Though the resemblances between Lodge's narrative and *Amadis* are broad and general, they probably deserve as much attention as the theory that Lodge was influenced by Sidney's *Arcadia,* which he somehow managed to read in manuscript.[15]

Among Lodge's other prose narratives only *Rosalynde* (1590) deserves to be called pastoral. It is surprisingly pure and has only the most tenuous links with chivalric romances. Perhaps because Lodge followed the fourteenth-century nonchivalric *Tale of Gamelyn,* his story contains a minimum of chivalry. The rescue of Aliena by Saladyne from robbers and the final battle, in which the usurper Torismond is killed, are the episodes that come closest to the stuff of chivalric romance.

Lodge's *Margarite of America* (1595) has been called pastoral, but the pastoral element is almost as scarce as the chivalric in *Rosalynde.*[16] Not a shepherd appears in the story. Yet the novel, which features sensationalism and cruelty on an extravagant scale, is often reminiscent of *Amadis.* In one burst of fury Arsadachus cracks Brasidas' skull, disembowels Diana—"spreading her entrailes about the pallace floore, and seizing on her heart, hee tare it in peeces with his tyrannous teeth, crying, *Sic itur ad astra"*— and, catching his young son by the heels, batters out his brains against the wall.[17] The blood lust is in the spirit of many episodes in *Amadis.*

In addition, *A Margarite of America* makes use of chivalric ritual and processions. A three-day tourney at Mosco, where a hundred pagans and a hundred Christian knights vie for honors, is described in detail. There Arsadachus enters the tilt-yard in a chariot drawn by four white unicorns. Moreover, the palace of the magician Arsinous, which is described with enthusiasm, is like the Palace of Apolidon or the Tower of the Universe. Arsinous has the power of conjuring up a sumptuous banquet and then, after his guest has eaten, making all signs of it disappear. Most interesting is Margarita's sacrifice of drops of blood to the image of her absent lover, in which she seems to be imitating the peculiar practice of Marfire.[18] All told, *A Margarite of America* makes very likely the theory that Lodge knew *Amadis*.

Robert Greene's *Menaphon* (1589) and *Pandosto* (1588) are splendid examples of pastoral romance mingled with chivalry. *Pandosto*, on which Shakespeare based his *Winter's Tale*, is particularly reminiscent of *Amadis*. René Pruvost, who has examined exhaustively the question of Greene's sources, believes that the story of Florisel and Silvie in Book IX of *Amadis* provided Greene with the nucleus for his tale: "The books of *Amadis* gave him the theme of a little princess born in prison and brought up as a shepherdess, who later is wooed by a prince disguised as a shepherd." [19] If Pruvost is correct, then *Amadis* may be said to have influenced Shakespeare's *Winter's Tale*, a proposition which, though scarcely subject to proof, might explain Shakespeare's use of the name Florizel and show Southey right once more.[20]

Like *Pandosto, Menaphon* contains much that appears to be drawn from chivalric romance, but there has never been general agreement about its sources. Samuel L. Wolff has argued for the primacy of Heliodorus, but Pruvost thinks the work is chiefly indebted to Sidney's *Old Arcadia,* which Greene would have had to read in manuscript.[21] In view of his belief that *Amadis* supplied Greene with the central theme for *Pandosto,* Pruvost surprisingly does not mention *Amadis* at all in connection with *Menaphon;* yet this romance has many motifs in common with *Pandosto,* and it is frequently very much like *Amadis*. In fact, the main theme of *Menaphon*—a princess disguised as a shepherdess who is courted by a foolish but well-meaning shepherd and also by a knight in disguise as a shepherd—is very close to the Silvie-Darinel-Florisel story of Book IX. The bumbling Menaphon recalls Darinel not only in his fondness for music but in his persistence in loving a girl far above his station. As in *Amadis*, there are repeated references to the myth of Paris as a shepherd.

The pirate Eurilochus, who wins a pardon from King Agenor by presenting him with the kidnaped child Pleusidippus, recalls the Moorish pirates in Book VII who win a pardon from King Magadan by presenting him with the kidnaped child later known as Amadis de Grèce.[22] Like Amadis de Grèce, Pleusidippus is raised with love by his royal foster father and has intimations of his princely birth by his thirst after glory.[23] The climactic fight between father and son in *Menaphon*—a motif that Pruvost says "is rarely found in traditional novels of adventure" [24]—is a commonplace in *Amadis* and, among others, involves Amadis de Grèce and his father (VIII, li).

My intention here is not to show that Lodge and Greene derived their pastoral romances chiefly from *Amadis*. *Pandosto* and *Menaphon*, and to a lesser degree *A Margarite of America*, are compounded of chivalric and pastoral motifs so commonplace as to be scarcely traceable to their origins. But *Amadis* ought to be more generally recognized as a considerable influence on Greene and Lodge and especially on the form that the pastoral romance took in Elizabethan fiction.

So widespread in the Elizabethan period are chivalric and pastoral motifs that parody was sooner or later inevitable. It appears in Elizabethan fiction somewhat earlier than is generally believed. The first part of Cervantes' *Don Quixote* was not printed in Spain until 1605, and its influence was not felt in English fiction for almost a decade. Shelton's translation began to appear in 1612, but it was not completed until 1620. Robert Anton's *Moriomachia* (1613) is the earliest example of Cervantes' influence upon English fiction, but it is not, as its most recent editor has called it, "the first of its kind in English." [25] *The Knight of the*

Sea precedes Anton's work by thirteen years, and, since it also antedates *Don Quixote,* it deserves more attention than it has received as an antiromance.

Amadis made attacks upon romances of chivalry easy by being itself a considerable repository of antichivalric sentiment. The dignity of even the greatest heroes is not always held sacred, and some of them appear occasionally as very foolish indeed. Sidney's *Arcadia* picked up something of this tone, and one of the aims of the work was apparently to show how ridiculous love can make even the best-balanced knight. Pyrocles in feminine guise is made to feel most uncomfortable and ludicrous, and Musidorus, whom love has led to pose as a shepherd, has to listen patiently to lectures by Dametas on the proper way to dung a field. Moreover, the duel between the two cowards Clinias and Dametas was widely regarded as a comic masterpiece. *Moriomachia* ends on a similar note—a comic fight between the Knight of the Sun and the Knight of the Moon—and Anton makes clear that he has in mind not only the fight between Don Quixote and the barber but also "the battle between Clineasse and Dametasse." [26]

The criticism of knights and knighthood which is so prominent in *Amadis* and is at least latent in Sidney also engages Nashe's attention in *The Unfortunate Traveler* (1594). Chivalry enters the life of Jack Wilton when he meets in his travels the earl of Surrey, lovelorn for his Geraldine. At Florence, Surrey defends his lady's beauty against all challengers, and the tournament, seen through the unsympathetic eyes of Jack, gives Nashe an opportunity to lay on with a vengeance. To Jack the splendid trappings and armorial wit of chivalry are merely ludicrous. One of the challengers is the Knight of the Owl, "whose armor was a stubd tree ouergrowne with iuie, his helmet fashioned lyke an owle sitting on the top of this iuie; on his bases were wrought all kinde of birdes, as on the grounde, wondering about him; the word,

Ideo mirum quia monstrum: his horses furniture was framed like a carte, scattering whole sheaues of corne amongst hogs; the word, *Liberalitas liberalitate perit.* On his shield a Bee intangled in sheepes wool; the mot, *Frontis nulla fides.*" [27] The contest itself is an exhibition of almost total ineptness, all except Surrey being either cowardly or unskilled.

The Unfortunate Traveler is antichivalric only by the way. Nashe clearly does not consider chivalry a very lively threat to Elizabethan sanity, and the earl of Surrey is soon allowed to drop out of sight. *The Knight of the Sea,* however, is an attack on a fairly large scale. Its principal fault is that it attacks too much. Not only does the author have in mind *Amadis, Palmerin, The Mirror of Knighthood,* and other works of their kind, but he aims too at Sidney's *Arcadia* and the euphuized romances of writers like Robert Greene, Thomas Lodge, and Henry Robarts. An attack on so many fronts is difficult to maintain, particularly when the parody is contained in a narrative which must be kept somewhat coherent. The chief weapon of the anonymous author is exaggeration, but it is hard to exaggerate successfully the faults of a genre whose very medium is hyperbole. Moreover, *The Knight of the Sea,* for all its attempts to be outlandish, comes close to being interesting in its own right. It is far more engaging than some parts of the Palmerin cycle, and many contemporary readers may have missed completely its burlesque.

The Knight of the Sea makes fun of many of the staple narrative and stylistic patterns of the romances. The birth of a hero in adverse circumstances, his distinguishing birthmarks, and his perilous survival as a baby, all are made to look ridiculous. When Almidiana gives birth to a son at sea while she is a prisoner aboard the ship of the giant Ortolomorgantell, she and her companion discuss what is best to do.[28] If she keeps the child, Ortolomorgantell may sacrifice him to his "heathenish God Metrath Agorah" or he may keep him as a slave. The two women therefore decide—like Hélisène and Dariolette in the case of Amadis—they will commit the child to the mercy of the sea: "Perhaps some nature-incited Dolphin, wil on his back take pitie on him? Who knows that? were hee Aryon, he could not without an harpe be saued: or had he an harpe, being he could not vse it, it were boot-lesse. . . ." Almidiana kisses the child on the breast "whereon by Nature were liuely depainted the billowes of the Ocean; which by his hearts panting waued vp and downe like the maritime deepe." [29] This startling birthmark and the conditions of his birth lead Almidiana to christen him Oceander, because the name signi-fies in Greek "a man of the Ocean," and when Oceander is later found and brought up by the queen of Carthage, she calls him the "gentleman of the sea"—the same designation given Amadis in like circumstances.

The Knight of the Sea is most clearly a burlesque in its handling of verse. The romance habit of interpolating frequent poems in the text—*Arcadia* and *Rosalynde* are the English works best known for this trait—is made to look especially ludicrous. For instance, a standard subject of romance verse is the beauty of a mistress, and a poem frequently takes the form of a catalogue of charms, from golden hair to ivory feet. Both *Amadis* and the *Arcadia* contain verse of this kind.[30] In *The Knight of the Sea* Kalander, whose wife has been treacherously slain, frequently walks at night near her grave, "where taking her goulden haired head, from forth of a little coffin," he utters a verse lament that follows the conventional scheme in praising her cheeks, lips, eyes, and so on.[31] In similar outrageous parody Allva's dying father curses her in four quatrains and a couplet, and later when Troglador beats her to death, he writes her verse epitaph in her own blood.[32] When the wicked Tantanez tries to seduce the lovely and happily married lady Ericlea, he sends her a poem which contains the following lines:

> For I determin'd am, thy fruit
> Of beautie for to take;
> Or missing narrowly my marke,
> To make the Tree to shake.[33]

Ericlea's sense of honor is apparently fortified by this doggerel, and she rejects Tantanez—also in verse.

Sidney's *Arcadia* comes in for a surprisingly large share of satire. Sidney's use of the inkhornism *monomachy* is derided in Olbiocles' determination to engage in a "monimachye or single combat." Characters with names like Kalander and Basileon are apparently hits at the *Arcadia*, especially since Basileon is a lustful king. Moreover, the story of Tirindantes—the name is variously spelled —seems to be intended to remind the reader of Sidney's Tiridates and his part in the Plangus-Erona story.[34] The attack on the *Arcadia* suggests that the author of *The Knight of the Sea* detested all romances and made no allowances for differences in merit.

The stylistic unevenness of *The Knight of the Sea* is probably to be explained in large part by its attempt to burlesque some of the salient deficiencies of romance style. The book is shot through with inkhorn words like *refruition, iction, procellious, auskult, soboline, houseld, insidie, eyegazers, sight-reave, speech-bar,* and *perpendancy.* The author often inflates his narrative by elaborate circumlocutions. A tongue becomes on one occasion "thoughts legate," and on another "cogitations Embassadour," and a girl's lips become "Rubilike fine closurets." The sun is "the days illustrator" or "Climenes Parramour."

The first sentence drags the reader *in medias res* and sets a standard of rhetorical inflation which is many times bettered in the succeeding pages: "As soone as the bashfull mistresse of the morning, from the windowes of the East (mounted in her golden Chariot) had sent forth her radiant blushes to illuminate the darksome foreheade of night-shadowed Cosmos: The illustrious Prince of Graecia, Olbiocles . . . poasted with all the speede possibly hee could, from the vnsuspecting Court of Rubaldo." In the mixture of styles in the mock-romance even euphuism is not ignored. Moreover, *The Knight of the Sea* is lavish with marginal notes— some in Latin and one in Greek—apparently intended to ridicule the tendency toward excessive moralization which is apparent in English romances like *Moderatus.*

By its somewhat subdued euphuism and by its marginal notes— completely absent in the Peninsular romances—*The Knight of the Sea* shows that insofar as it involves criticism of style it is the style not of the foreign romances but of their English imitators at which it aims. To be sure, *Palmerin of England* in Munday's translation has some euphuism in it, but it was added by Munday to take advantage of the vogue then new. The euphuism is to be found mostly in the early pages, but it soon thins out, for euphuism is not at all suited to a work so long and adventure-ridden. Munday's later translations of the Palmerin cycle are almost completely free of euphuistic turns, and the English translation of *The Mirror of Knighthood* is similarly untainted.

If one were asked to choose a sentence typical of the style of *The Mirror of Knighthood* or *Palmerin* in English translation, he perhaps could not do better than the following: "And when they knewe that those worthie knightes were their friends, they were verie glad and reioyced to see them, and did open vnto them the gates of the citie, & very much meruailed at the other knight that came with yᵉ three Princes, for that they saw the great slaughter which hee made amongst his enimies with his sword in his hand, and when these foure knights sawe the gates of the Citie opened, they did retire by little & little vpon the bridge, vntill such time as their enimies did leaue off following them, as well for the mortall blowes they gaue them, as for the great harme they receiued by them which were vppon the walles of the Citie, so that they had time at their pleasure to enter into the Citie, and when they were within they shut the gates, and receiued them with great ioye, and carryed them before the Queene, whose ioy was so great for the returne of these three Princes, that I am not able to expresse it, for that her comfort and hope that she had in them was verie much, and their imprisonment was a grieuous corsie [*sic*] vnto her heart." [35] It is the writer's, or the translator's, presumption that the sweep of action will carry the reader along through the maze of the sentence, safely past the triple-turned "they," into the presence of the queen. For Elizabethans used to the more elaborate prose of Lyly, Sidney, and Nashe, this kind of sentence must have seemed woefully drab, lacking not only structure but also wit. On the other hand, the idea of style as an element subordinate to matter, however unfashionable that idea was in narrative prose, had about it a certain inescapable good sense, and, willy-nilly, chivalric romances helped establish it in England.

It is manifestly impossible to talk with much exactness about the influence of chivalric romance upon the prose style of Elizabethan writers of fiction. Robert Greene has already been mentioned as a writer whose style becomes less ornate as the matter and structure of his romances become progressively more chivalric. That the change in Greene's style was due, at least in part, to his increasing accent on narrative seems very likely. An even more striking instance occurs in the case of R.P.'s *Moderatus*. The work begins in highly euphuistic fashion. But in Chapter X the narrative suddenly shifts from the vein of courtly love to that of chivalric pastoralism, and the prose style undergoes a corresponding change from decorated to plain.

Other writers of prose narrative show a similar tendency, and a large number of Elizabethan romances are written in two discrete styles. Henry Robarts' *Defiance to Fortune* (1590), a male counterpart to Nicholas Breton's *Miseries of Mavillia* (1597), makes lavish use of a somewhat diluted euphuism in speeches and moralizations, but the narrative portions are generally plain. In *Pheander*, where the chivalric matter is considerably enlarged, Robarts' euphuism has almost wholly disappeared and his ornateness has become merely a tedious complexity.

Emanuel Forde, who furnishes the best examples in English of chivalric structure—Sidney's *Arcadia* excepted—often writes in a manner that comes very close to that of chivalric romances in English translation, and the assumption that he learned from foreign models how to write as well as what to write seems reasonable. His style has been roundly criticized. Margaret Schlauch has written: "As to the style and manner of presentation, these too are artificial and cumbersome in the extreme. . . . His sentences may be long, but they are innocent of the fashionable decorations of the time: they show complexities without balance or other coherent pattern; endless subordinations without plan." [36] A similar criticism might be made of the English translations of *Palmerin* and *The Mirror of Knighthood*.

A reader who examines Forde's style for himself can find numerous examples that corroborate Miss Schlauch's criticism. But he will also find many passages which do not. For Forde, like so many of his contemporaries, has two styles. One is his pell-mell narrative style, which so often reads as though it were written in a single burst, unpremeditated and unimproved. But the other, somewhat more careful, is reserved for discourses and letters.

Although Forde's first style fits Miss Schlauch's description, his second does not. For example, when Ornatus is banished from Phrygia and his mistress Artesia, he laments in the conventional

Was-ever-man-so-unlucky fashion: "Was ever more fortunate and suddenly miserable than I am? Could ever any man whatsoever, attain more heavenly felicity and happiness than I did, by being possessed of Artesia? And now again most accursed, being thus far absent from her, and banished my native soil, into a strange country, ready to be famished and devoured by wild beasts, or that which is worse, never likely to see Artesia again. How could any man contain himself from desparateness, being so miserable as I am? How can I withold my hand from injuring myself, when by doing it I should be rid out of a wretched life? What should I doe? Which way should I go? Here I am in a desolate and unfrequented place, where no human creatures inhabit but wild beasts; without food, without weapons, in womans apparel, and without hope of comfort. Shall I stay here, then shall I be famished; shall I leave this place, and travel further, then I go further from my beloved, and meeting with some ravening beast, may be devoured. Now being hungry, I want food, and there is none, unless I will eat the earth, leaves of trees, or roots of the grass. Well I will seek my fortune, be it good or ill. . . ." [37]

Although this soliloquy can scarcely be called a model of rhetoric, it is better than Miss Schlauch's blanket indictment would indicate. Forde is much too fond of the rhetorical question, but a reader has no trouble in following the sense. An idea of order is discernible. The rhetorical questions are confined to the first half of the speech, and the second half is a summing up of the practical problems of Ornatus' predicament. An ingenious critic might even argue that the lack of rhetorical balance is psychological, insofar as it reflects the confusion in the mind of the speaker.

Sometimes Forde's second style attains a level of eloquence. For example, in *Montelion* Constantia disguises herself in peasant garb and steals out of the palace to join her lover Persicles outside the city. "Constantia hauing past thus far without escape, thought not to be long in going to the appointed place, but feare and hope hastening her steps, she sometimes ranne, and sometimes went: and then againe looking behind her, as if some had pursued her, ran vntill she gate a sight of the tree, where vnder likewise she espyed her Loue, who before that beheld her, but in that habite knew her not. To whom she approacht so nigh, that he noting her well, knew her, and with that embraced her in his armes, saying: My dearest Loue, a thousand times Welcome, and more desired of me, then all the riches of the World: for euer shall this day be blest, and the houre of this our happy meeting accounted Fortunate: Let all that weare this habit be happy, and enioy their most desired content: and let this tree wheresoeuer growing, be esteemed aboue many others: For that it was the appointed place of our meeting. Let the Euening be the most pleasant time of the day for Louers meetings: and let all those be Fortunate in their meetings, whose hearts harbour constant Loue." [38] This passage and others like it show that Forde in his third romance was groping toward a style of his own.

But Forde does not often achieve the biblical sonority one hears in the passage just cited. This is his high style, reserved for moments of high emotion, where other writers might call upon Lyly or Sidney. Generally Forde's prose is flatter, like that in the English translation of *Palmerin* or *The Mirror of Knighthood*. Not only has he taken over the stock ingredients of the chivalric plot, but he has absorbed chivalric prose style as well.

Thus chivalric romances from Spain and France, which are all to a greater or less degree dominated by *Amadis*, exerted upon Elizabethan fiction a pressure that goes beyond the mere use of plot motifs. The emphasis in sixteenth-century English fiction upon variety—which has often led commentators to talk of the varied influence of *novelle,* pastoral romances, jest books, and courtly love—can be accounted for in large part by the structure of chivalric romances. Elizabethan interest in pastoralism in prose fiction goes hand in hand with interest in chivalric motifs and probably derives from romances like *Amadis.* The antichivalric undercurrent in Sidney and Nashe, another by-product of *Amadis,* leads to burlesque on the scale of *The Knight of the Sea.* Finally, the style of Elizabethan fiction flattens out after 1590, partly perhaps in reaction against the extremes of euphuism and arcadianism, but partly too under the impact of chivalric romances in English translation.

Conclusion

Since this is the first book-length study to deal either with the whole of *Amadis de Gaule* itself or with its literary impact on Elizabethan England, it has had to be content with describing and mapping out a work essentially unknown to English readers. Robert Southey's abridged translation of the first four Spanish books, the only English version readily available, represents only a small part of the cycle's immense bulk. If one thinks of the romance as an integral work—and obviously there are objections to such a view—it is surely one of the longest and most entangled prose narratives in any modern Western European language. The great size of the cycle, and the fact that in its entirety it is available only in the rare book rooms of a handful of libraries in the world, stand in the way of reader or commentator, and a first study like this can be only partial and tentative. Much remains to be done.

The French version of *Amadis*—rather than the original Spanish or the important Italian—has been taken as central because the drift of this study is toward England. Although Chapter VII attempts to sketch the relationship between the first four books in Spanish, French, and English, that chapter is intended only as an indication of social, religious, and literary differences. All evidence hints that the later books in those languages may differ from one another in even more striking ways, but for the purposes of this book those differences are irrelevant. Whatever its sources, it is the French *Amadis* that the Elizabethans knew, and that had to be our starting place. The complete record of variations in the romance from one language to another is matter for another, larger book.

The Elizabethan bias accounts not only for the second half of this book but also in some degree for the episodes, characters, and motifs discussed in the first half. The episode involving Zahir, for example, is brought in only because it is reminiscent of the story of Pyrochles told in Book II of Spenser's *Faerie Queene,* and a scholar who approached *Amadis* from another literature would perhaps find it unexceptional. Similarly the person of Darinel gets attention mostly because of his resemblance to Dametas in Sidney's *Arcadia,* and ecstatic love is dwelt upon because of its connection with Donne's "Ecstasy." A scholar who read *Amadis* against a background like Ronsard's *Françiade* or Boiardo's *Orlando Innamorato* would presumably make a different series of choices. The significant point is that *Amadis* is such a large repository— or midden—of literary themes that it is not difficult to imagine several books based on it with no more than minimal repetition.

The choice of a literary point of view has pushed the social and historical implications of the romance into the background. For example, it would be interesting to know what parts of *Amadís de Gaula* spring from the realities of fifteenth- and sixteenth-century Spain and what are vestiges from another age or are largely fanciful. Miraflores, the favorite refuge of Oriana in time of stress, must of course be the famous Carthusian monastery near Burgos, completed during the lifetime of Montalvo, in 1488, and its name would have drawn from Spanish readers a response entirely different from that it excited in readers who had never heard it. Those books of the Amadis cycle that originated in Italy doubtless have not only social but literary relationships that have remained unexplored. Even the excellent books of Eugène Baret and Edouard Bourciez on the socioliterary relations of the French *Amadis* could be considerably expanded by a scholar who, unlike them, began by reading the entire cycle.

Because of the nature of the task nothing in this book is less conclusive than the account of Amadisian influence in Elizabethan literature. A romance that contains parallels to "The Ecstasy," the Mask of Cupid, and the main plot of *Much Ado About Nothing* may well hold other nuggets still unrecognized as gold. Moreover, the influence of *Amadis* extends in England well beyond the reign of Elizabeth. Despite the antichivalric intent of books like *The Knight of the Sea, Don Quixote*, and *Moriomachia*, Amadis lay a long time adying in seventeenth-century England. Munday's 1619 edition of the first four books was meant to be only the beginning, for he announced in his separate preface to Book III that he hoped to translate all the other volumes in due time. Much later in the century, in 1652, Francis Kirkman translated Book VI; and Books V and VII, translated by two different anonymous writers, were published in 1664 and 1693 respectively. In addition, in 1640 appeared a long and grotesque translation of an Amadisian compilation called *The Love and Armes of the Greeke Princes. Or, The Romant of Romants, Written in French by Monsieur Verdere, and Translated for the Right Honourable, Philip, Earle of Pembroke and Montgomery, Lord Chamberlaine to his Majesty.* This is a translation of *Le Romant des romans*, an original work by Gilbert Saulnier, Sieur du Verdier, that attempts to bring to-gether—and one can only sigh at the writer's ambition and te-merity—the adventures of all the Amadises, Don Belianis, and the Knight of the Sun. None of these books had any discernible literary impact in England, but they indicate that some tiny sparks of life still flickered in Amadis. Indeed, although Amadis apparently expired in eighteenth-century England, his ghost must have stalked the study of Sir Walter Scott.

A work so important in the sixteenth century and so long-lived in various literatures does not deserve its present obscurity. It is, to be sure, excessive in length, inconsistent in quality, and outmoded in technique. Yet, in its time it was a model of prose style in Spain and France. A work so important in the dissemination of neo-Platonic ideas, pastoralism, and antichivalric satire surely belongs in the intellectual history of its age. However tempting it may be for modern readers to see *Amadis* as merely a literary curiosity, a vast, almost unreadable jumble of episodes that stands as a fitting monument to sixteenth-century taste for the fantastic, such a view is clearly unjust and unhistoric. In the company of the *Orlando Furioso*, the *Faerie Queene*, and Sidney's *Arcadia*, *Amadis* stands in the literary center of its century.

Appendices

Genealogy of the Chief Characters in *Amadis de Gaule*

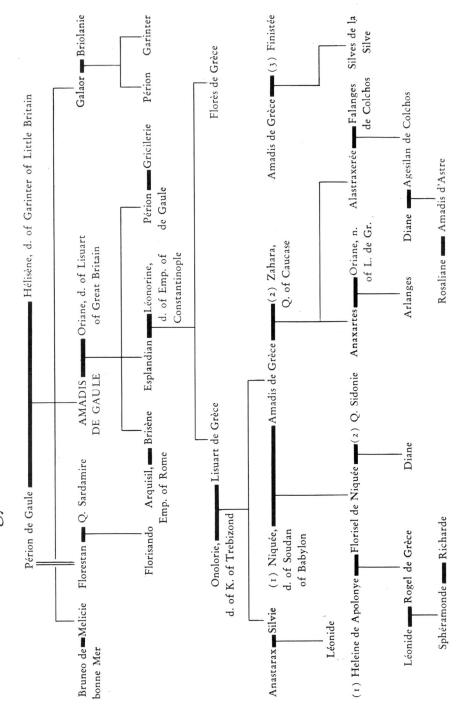

Appendix A

Glossary of the Chief Characters in *Amadis de Gaule*

Agesilan de Colchos The son of Falanges and Alastraxerée and one of the chief heroes of Books XI and XII. Some of his most memorable feats are his killing of the monster Cavalyon and his various adventures on the flying Grifaléon. His love for Diane, whom he woos in disguise as the Amazon Daraïde, is a motivating force in most of his adventures.

Alastraxerée An Amazon queen, the daughter of Amadis de Grèce and Zahara. Because she is conceived under mysterious circumstances, she is thought to be the daughter of the god Mars. She is worshiped as a divinity by Falanges, the ruler of Colchos, whom she later marries. A prominent character in Book X.

Alquif A prominent magician who aids Amadis de Gaule and his descendants in the later books. As such, he serves as a male Urgande.

Amadis d'Astre The son of Agesilan de Colchos and Diane who becomes a hero in Book XV and in following books. His mistress is Rosaliane.

Glossary of Characters in Amadis de Gaule

Amadis de Gaule The nominal hero of the entire cycle, he does not die until Book XXI. He is the first son of King Périon of Gaul and Hélisène, daughter of King Garinter of Little Britain, and the circumstances of his birth, education, and amorous involvement serve as models for later heroes. He is the chief figure of the first four books but continues to reappear in later volumes.

Amadis de Grèce The son of Lisuart de Grèce and Onolorie and therefore the great grandson of Amadis de Gaule. As a child, he is stolen by Moors and brought up at the court of King Magadan of Saba as a pagan. He is undoubtedly the greatest hero of the Amadis cycle after Amadis de Gaule. (See Ardante Espée.)

Anaxartes The son of Amadis de Grèce and Zahara and twin brother of Alastraxerée. An important character in Books IX and X.

Apolidon The wise and learned ruler of Firm Island before Amadis de Gaule comes to it. Apolidon has left behind a marvelous palace and enchantments, like the Arch of True Lovers and the Forbidden Chamber, which measure a knight's and lady's fidelity in love.

Arcalaüs The great villain of the first four books, he repeatedly tries to overthrow King Lisuart and kill or injure Amadis de Gaule.

Ardante Espée, Chevalier de l' Amadis de Grèce is first known only by this title because he is born with a burning sword emblazoned upon his body. He takes the title while he travels in search of his identity. (See Amadis de Grèce.)

Arlanges The son of Anaxartes and Oriane (not Amadis de Gaule's Oriane) and the friend of Agesilan de Colchos. He disguises himself as the damsel Garaye in Book XI and falls in love with Cléophile. With her he shares an ecstatic experience.

Arlanges (Arlange) The hero of Book XX who seeks to rescue the lady Sestiliane from the temple in Mont-Libéan where she is cloistered.

Bazilique The soudan of Babylon and father of Niquée. He falls madly in love with Amadis de Grèce in disguise as Néreïde.

Beau Ténébreux One of many disguises of Amadis de Gaule. As le beau Ténébreux (Beltenebros), he resides on Poor Rock with a hermit and wastes away in melancholy because Oriane has dismissed him from her service.

Cavalyon Like the Endriague, the Cavalyon is a monster, the product of incest. He is the offspring of the witch Gregaste and her son. Part horse, part man, with the claws and limbs of a lion, he is killed by Daraïde in Book XI.

Cléophile   The queen of Lemnos and a descendant of Priam. She comes to visit Diane in Book XI. She is attracted by Arlanges in his disguise as Garaye and experiences with him the ecstatic mingling of souls.

Damsel of Denmark   The loyal and devoted lady who serves Oriane throughout the first four books.

Daraïde   The chief disguise of Agesilan de Colchos in his attempt to gain the love of Diane. He dresses as an Amazon.

Darinel   One of the few commoners mentioned by name in *Amadis*. He first appears in Book IX as a suitor of Silvie and rival of Florisel de Niquée. A bumbler and a fool, he is tolerated in large part for his ability as a musician and singer.

Dariolette   As Hélisène's confidante, she arranges for King Perión to come secretly to the princess' room at night. Thus her name became synonymous with bawd in the sixteenth century.

Diane   The daughter of Queen Sidonie and Florisel de Niquée and the heroine of Books XI and XII. She is placed in a tower built by Cinistrides the magician so that she will never be seen by a man. She is wooed and won by Agesilan de Colchos in his disguise as Daraïde.

Endriague   The monstrous product of an incestuous union between the giantess Brandaginde and her father. He is killed by Amadis de Gaule in Book III.

Esplandian   The first son of Amadis de Gaule and Oriane and the principal hero of Book V. He reappears in later books and through magic means lives as long as his father.

Finistée   A girl who loves Amadis de Grèce but resigns herself to a purely spiritual relationship when she sees her love can never be requited. Through the properties of a strange fruit that he and she eat on the Solitary Isle, she gives birth to Silves.

Florisel de Niquée   The son of Amadis de Grèce and Niquée and a chief hero of Book IX and subsequent books. He falls in love with the shepherdess Silvie and for a while is known by his title of Knight of the Shepherdess. When he elopes with Heleine de Apolonye, he brings on the great war between Greece and Rome that occupies most of Book X.

Galanides   The king of Galdap. He is so jealous of his wife Salderne that he does not allow her to talk to men except in his presence. He falls in love with Daraïde and later goes mad and dies.

Garaye   The name Arlanges takes when he disguises himself as a woman in order to keep his friend Agesilan company.

Gradafilée   She loves Lisuart de Grèce even though she knows he loves Onolorie. When Lisuart needs a knight to fight for his cause in a duel, she fights disguised as a knight. Lisuart is so moved by this instance of love that he wishes he were free to love her.

Grifaléon   This flying beast, the result of union between a lion and a griffon, derives from Ariosto's *Orlando Furioso*. Originally trained by Patrifond, it is later taken by Agesilan de Colchos, who uses it in several adventures. Like a crane, the grifaléon needs a run of four or five steps before it can become airborne. It first appears in Book XII.

Heleine de Apolonye   The daughter of Birmartes and Onorie, she is one of the prominent heroines of Books IX and X. Like her prototype, Helen of Troy, she triggers a great war between the Romans and Greeks when she runs off with Florisel de Niquée just before she is supposed to wed the Roman Lucidor.

Hélisène   The daughter of King Garinter of Little Britain. When King Périon stays at her father's palace, he and she fall in love at first sight. She becomes the mother of Amadis de Gaule and, after marriage, of Galaor and Melicie.

Léonorine   Her reputation for beauty is so great that Esplandian falls in love with her before he even sees her. She is the daughter of the emperor of Constantinople, who retires and turns over the rule to her and Esplandian after their marriage.

Lisuart   The king of Great Britain whom Amadis de Gaule serves and whose daughter Oriane he marries.

Lisuart de Grèce   The son of Esplandian and father of Amadis de Grèce. The principal hero of Book VI, he is also prominent in the following books.

Lucelle   The daughter of the king of Metz and the first love of Amadis de Grèce after he rescues her in Book VII from Frandalon Cyclops. Their love is later much complicated by the fact that Amadis de Grèce falls in love with Niquée.

Mabile (Mabila)   One of Oriane's trusted attendants.

Néréïde   The name under which Amadis de Grèce masquerades when he woos Niquée. Néreïde is supposed to be an Amazon, but "she" is so attractive that Niquée's father falls in love with "her."

Niquée The daughter of Bazilique, the soudan of Babylon. She is so lovely that men who see her either die or go mad. Her father keeps her sequestered among women. After she elopes with Néreïde and marries him, she gives birth to Florisel.

Oriane (Oriana) The daughter of King Lisuart of Great Britain and the principal heroine of the Amadis cycle. Her love for Amadis de Gaule sets a pattern generally followed throughout the cycle by other heroines. (There are several other heroines later called Oriane.)

Périon The king of Gaul, father of Amadis de Gaule, Melicie, Galaor, and Florestan.

Persée The queen of Perse who both hates and loves Rogel. To get revenge upon him for betraying her love, she joins the pagan attack upon Christendom in Book XIX.

Rogel de Grèce The son of Florisel de Niquée and Heleine de Apolonye and a prominent hero in Books XI, XII, and thereafter. He is the most amorous and fickle of all the heroes, and the record of his loves is stressed as much as his feats of arms.

Rosaliane The beloved of Amadis d'Astre. Their love is recorded mostly in Books XVII and XVIII.

Salderne The queen of Galdap and wife of the jealous Galanides. She sees through Daraïde's disguise and falls in love with him. She is thus a prototype of Queen Gynecia in Sidney's *Arcadia*.

Silves Often called Silves of the Desert because he is born on a desert island to Amadis de Grèce and Finistée. Since his father and mother have been rendered amorous and unaware by a strange fruit, much is made of the fact that he is born of a sinless sexual union.

Silvie The daughter of Lisuart de Grèce and Onolorie. She is kidnaped in childhood and brought up as a shepherdess. In this state she attracts such suitors as Florisel. Her adventures are contained mostly in Book IX.

Sphéramonde The son of Rogel and Léonide and one of the chief heroes of Books XV and XVI. He loves Richarde and later marries her.

Urgande Urgande la desconnue, a chief seeress of the Amadis cycle. Her magic powers keep Amadis de Gaule and all his clan alive, and she frequently visits court to make oracular prophecies.

Glossary of Characters in Amadis de Gaule

Zahara   An Amazon, Queen of Caucase, who falls in love with Amadis de Grèce in Book VIII. Because of a strange amorous experience she shares with him she gives birth to twins whom she thinks must have been engendered by the god Mars.

Zahir   A relatively minor character from Books IX and X who travels with Fénix and Astibel of Mesopotamia. He has a memorable adventure with a madman in Chapters xlvii and xlviii of Book X.

Appendix B

Chanson d'Arlanges

After Arlanges and Cléophile experience a neo-Platonic ecstasy in Book XI, Chapter lxxxix, he writes the following song to her:

CHANSON D'ARLANGES

Arlang par foy, trauaux & larmes,
Liura telz assaux & alarmes
A Clyo, que de son dur cueur,
Par temps amollit la rigueur.
   Et qui eust esté la cruelle,
Voyant mourir l'amy fidelle,
Qui sa vie n'eust rachetté,
Fust ce au pris de sa chasteté?
   Ce fut au secret cabinet
D'vn delicieux iardinet
Que costoyoit vn cler ruisseau,
D'vne viue & argentin' eau.
   D'autre costé le verd bocage
Le couuroit de son frais ombrage:
Dont les oyseaux au bruit & son
De l'onde, accordoient leur chançon.

239

Chanson d'Arlanges

La terre estoit là par fleur mainte
D'odeur pleine & de couleur painte
Mais tout effaçoit vne rose
Qui par Amour y fut eclose.

    Arlang trouua Clyo s'amye
Sus l'herbette moll' endormie
De qui ses yeux tant se repurent
Que du tout eblouys en furent.

    Elle tiroit souspirs diuers
Tesmoins de ses desirs couuers,
Et dormant reclamoit par fois,
Arlang, Arlang de foible voix.

    Ce mot le fait à terre fondre,
Ou d'vn baiser luy va respondre
Decouurant la blanche poitrine,
D'ou sortit vn'odeur diuine.

    Son beau sein doucement vndoye
Comm' au riuage la mer quoye,
Comm' vndoye vn champ de haut blé,
Par le vent battu & souflé.

    Clyo s'eueille au baiser prendre,
Qui n'est pas ingrate à le rendre,
Entr'ouurant l'oeil dont elle voit
Celuy à qui seul le deuoit.

    Tandis que la vermeille bouche
Des amans l'vne l'autre touche:
Les espritz sont confus ensemble
Tant corps de pres à corps s'assemble.

    Les deux ames ne sont plus qu' vne
Spirans vne haleine commune,
Et sont par vnion d'espritz,
Les membres de fureur espris.

    Car l'ame d'Arlang au corps entre
De Clyo iusques en son centre:
Et l'ame de'elle en luy se range
Pour à la sienne faire eschange.

    A chacune semble plus beau
Que le sien, ce logis nouueau
Et luy plaist y faire demeure
Quoy que viuant là, en soy meure.

Chanson d'Arlanges

Làs quand falut l'ame rauie
Reprendre sa premiere vie,
Que sa naturelle maison
Luy sembla horrible prison?

Vrays amoureux seulz vous sçauez
(Qui de ce miel gousté auez)
Comme vne double volunté
S'vnit confite en volupté.

Venus (de qui tiens ma victoire)
Pour en consacrer la memoire,
Ie pendz à l'autel de ton temple
Vn cueur iumeau de deux exemple.

Appendix C

Heliodorus and
Amadis de Gaule

Book XX of *Amadis* is heavily indebted to the plot of the *Ethiopian History* of Heliodorus. An outline of the plots of the two works follows:

Ethiopian History

When he comes to worship at the Temple of Apollo, Theagenes sees the priestess Chariclea and falls madly in love with her. He is especially struck by her beauty when she takes part in a magnificent procession. With the help of the priest Calasiris, he runs off with her. But the ship they take is captured by pirates, who in a rough sea land on a beach near the Nile. The pirate chief Trachinus falls in love with Chariclea and decides he must have her, but Pelorus

Amadis de Gaule, Book XX

The knight Arlanges, who has long sought his lady Sestiliane, finds her cloistered in a temple, her memory erased by magic. He watches a great procession in which she shines. Through the unwitting help of the priest Osimenide, Arlanges rescues his lady. But the ship they take is attacked by pirates, and all on both ships are killed but Sestiliane and the wounded Arlanges. Grappled together, the two ships drift ashore, and the Nabateans come to loot

Heliodorus and Amadis de Gaule

his lieutenant also wants Chariclea. The two fall out, and the pirates take sides. A terrible fight on the beach leaves all dead except Chariclea and the wounded Theagenes, whom she tends. Egyptian robbers come but think Chariclea must be a goddess. They loot the ship, taking all they can carry, but they are put to flight by the approach of another gang of robbers. The new gang takes the booty and the lovers with them into their refuge in a marsh. There Thyamis, the bandit chief, decides to marry Chariclea. When he proposes, she speaks of Theagenes as her *brother* and says that the marriage would have to be postponed until she can give up her vows as priestess. Thyamis accepts her conditions and tries to stay out of her way so that he will not be tempted. At this point the robbers are attacked.

By the order of Thyamis, Chariclea is hidden in a cave, but when the fight goes badly for the robber band, he retires to the cave to kill Chariclea, for this is the way barbarous people act. Entering the cave in the dark, he stabs a woman he takes to be Chariclea and then tries to make good his escape. Meanwhile Theagenes and another Greek have escaped. They return to the hiding place in the marsh, find the cave, and therein come upon a dead body. Theagenes

them. They seize everything movable and take the lady and her wounded knight with them. But on the way the Nabateans are attacked by another troop and run off, leaving Sestiliane and the wounded Arlanges. The leader of the second band of robbers takes Sestiliane and Arlanges to their refuge on a craggy mountain. There Lucard the bandit chief falls in love with Sestiliane and asks her to be his wife. She accepts, but expresses concern for the health of her *brother* and tells Lucard that she has sworn not to marry for a year. He agrees to respect her oath. Lucard's band is attacked by Egyptians led by the Duke of Corvanie.

Lucard puts Sestiliane in a cave where she will be safe during the fighting. When the fight seems to be lost, Lucard rushes to the cave to kill her, for if he cannot have her, he is determined that no one else will. But in the dark he kills a female servant instead, she and Sestiliane having changed beds. Arlanges, who has escaped the slaughter, returns to the cave at night and finds his mistress. They slip out, taking some of the treasure they find in the cave.

Heliodorus and Amadis de Gaule

thinks the dead woman is Chariclea, but as he mourns over her, he hears the voice of his mistress in another part of the cave. They set out for a nearby town.

But they are captured and separated. After many adventures Theagenes finds himself in the army of Thyamis besieging Memphis, where Arsace, the lovely but wanton wife of Oroondates, resides. She catches sight of Theagenes and is immediately seized by lust for him. Peace is made, and Chariclea is reunited with Theagenes before the jealous eyes of Arsace, who sends for her trusted bawd Cybele. After consultation with Cybele, Arsace arranges for Theagenes and Chariclea, who are still pretending to be brother and sister, to lodge in the palace. But Theagenes remains unmoved by Cybele's hints. When the bawd finally puts the proposition plainly, he refuses. Cybele even asks Chariclea to try to convince her obdurate brother. Arsace is much upset.

Meanwhile Cybele's son Achaemenes comes home. He recognizes Theagenes and Chariclea as the former slaves of Thyamis and falls in love with Chariclea. He goes to Arsace and tells her, asking Chariclea's hand as a reward, for as slaves Theagenes and Chariclea cannot refuse. But Theagenes still refuses Arsace and finally consents

Arlanges makes a reputation as a warrior by helping a village against its attackers. The wife of the duke, a wanton woman named Adamantée, sends for him. She falls madly in love with him at first sight and has him lodged in the palace near her. She sends her bawd Tessale to sound out his feelings toward her. Arlanges tells his problem to his "sister" Sestiliane, and both agree that death is preferable to infidelity. He tells Adamantée that he cannot love her because of his sense of duty to the duke her husband and the king of Egypt, her brother.

Tessale's son comes home and recognizes the brother and sister as the former slaves—or prisoners of war—of Lucard. When he hears of Adamantée's problem, he tells her she can demand, not ask, and begs for Sestiliane's hand as reward. The lovers stall for time as Sestiliane pretends to plead Adamantée's case with her brother.

Heliodorus and Amadis de Gaule

only if she will first allow him to marry Chariclea. When the lust-ridden Arsace agrees, Achaemenes in a rage rides off to Oroondates and tells him all. In the meantime Arsace plans to kill Chariclea. Cybele puts poison in a cup, but, when the cup is switched, she drinks the poison herself. Chariclea is accused of murder and condemned to be burned at the stake. But the fire does not harm her. Before another attempt on her life can be made, order comes from Oroondates that Theagenes and Chariclea are to be sent to him. Arsace kills herself.

On the way to Oroondates the two lovers are taken by a force of Egyptians, and ultimately fall into the hands of Hidaspes, the king of the Ethiopians. Chariclea is joyful when she learns in whose hands they are, for she knows Hidaspes is her father. The lovers are to be sacrificed to the gods in a group of ten youths and ten maidens, but Chariclea does not make herself known immediately, since her proof would be meaningful only to her mother Persina. On the day of the sacrifice, when her mother the queen arrives, she tells all and saves not only herself and Theagenes but all the other prisoners as well. Moreover, the Ethiopians give up the practice of human sacrifice.

Tessale's son grows angry when his suit seems not to prosper. He rides to the duke and tells him the whole story. The duke sends for the prisoners, his messenger arriving just in time to save Sestiliane from a trial for murder—for the frantic Adamantée has poisoned Tessale and accused Sestiliane of the deed. When the lovers are led away, Adamantée kills herself.

The duke is defeated in battle by the king of Mont-Libean, who takes Arlanges and Sestiliane, intending to sacrifice them to his gods. But Sestiliane is not distressed, for the king is her foster father. Twenty prisoners are to be sacrificed, but Sestiliane does not reveal herself until the queen arrives. On the day of the sacrifice she makes her identity known to the king and queen. Then she pleads for the lives of the other victims. So moving is her plea that the custom of human sacrifice is abandoned.

Appendix D

The Mask in
Amadis de Gaule

In Book VIII, Chapter lxxxvii, Amadis de Grèce and Zahara wait in the courtyard for the coming of midnight. Meanwhile they talk of what they have already seen:

"Et ainsi deuisans arriua la nuict acompagnée de tenebres & obscurité, durans lesquelles fut entendu vn bruit & battemens d'aelles venant de loing, qui continua vn grand quart d'heure & plus, & tant qu'ilz entreuirent descendre autour d'eux vne infinité de Chouettes, Effrois, Hibouz, Chauuesouriz, & autres oyseaux nocturnes, faisans telz & si estranges & lamentables criz qu'on n'en eust sceu iuger que malheur & dangereux presage, attendu mesme qu'enuiron l'heure du mynuit mille esclairs, mille tonnerres & vapeurs de feu furent ouïz & veuz en l'air, estimans & Amadis, & la Royne, que le ciel, la terre, & tous les elemens ensemble deussent terminer & prendre fin. Car il tomba vn tel brandon de feu auec vn si horrible & espouuentable retentissement de foudre, que force leur fut d'eux prosterner la face contre bas, & vint cest esclat donner à trauers les portes de la chambre enchantée, à l'ouuerture de laquelle trembla si fort le palays, que ce fut grand' merueille qu'il ne se tourna le dessus dessouz. Toutesfois rien ne s'en dementit, ains cessa

246

seulement le bruit qu'auoient iusques adonq' continué les oyseaux malheureux. Et furent veuës plus de cent Dames, & Damoyselles sortir de la chambre ouuerte leans en leurs mains torches & flambeaux allumez deuant le dieu d'Amour, que l'on portoit en triomphe droit à l'estang acompagné d'vne infinité de peuple. Specialement de quatre Heraux, ou Roys d'armes, deux desquelz vestuz de cotes gayes & plaisantes, representoient ioye & liesse: & les deux autres de couleur morne, ennuy, & melencolie. Maints Roys, Cheualiers, Dames, & Damoyselles les suyuoient pas à pas, dont la plusgrande partie estoient signez par leurs noms qu'ilz auoient escritz sur leurs chefz. Entre lesquelz furent recogneuz. Achilles, Tisbée Narcise, Medée, Paris, Pyramus, Pantazilée, Dido, & autres vestuz de satin verd. Ceux la certes portoient visage & contenance heureuse & trop plus contente que ceux, qui parez d'vn iaune orengé alloient apres les bras croisez, monstrant à veue d'oeil, le peu de conte qu'ilz auoient tenu en leurs iours de ce petit Dieu, auquel on presenta droit au mylieu de la court, vne chaize couuerte de drap d'or, dans laquelle il s'assit commençans a sonner vne infinité de haultsboys, cornetz, lucz, violons, & autres instrumens, au son desquelz ces biens & parfaitz amans (dont nous auons parle) donnerent signe de grande allegresse, faisans separer d'eux (& retirer en dueil & tristesse) les vestuz de iaune tout au plus pres de Mirabela, & deuant elle les genouz prosternez en terre sembloit qu'ilz participassent en sa douleur. Quand l'vn des Heraux à la cotte gaye, commanda faire silence, & à haute voix publia la proclamation, qui s'enfuyt.

À l'acroissement de la gloire, & heureuse augmentation de plaisir, de ceux qui pour la foy d'Amour ont souffert. Et à l'iniure, & acroissement de la peine des autres qui l'ont mesprisé. Nostre dieu veult maintenant magnifier le bien des siens, & le mal de ses contraires: faisant sçauoir à tous, que le guerdon d'Amour se donne & retribue par l'effait d'oeuures amoureuses, non par le merite de beauté ingrate.

Puis se teut, & recommencerent les ioueürs d'instrumens leur musique si harmonieuse, qu'Amadis & la Royne, ne sentirent onques vn tel plaisir (ce leur sembla qui continua quelque espace, & iusques à ce que l'vn des Roys d'armes d'ennuy, fit la seconde proclamation criant à haute voix. Pour rengreger la peine de ceux qui (desdaignans l'amour) ont vsé de cruauté se continuera chasque nuit telle cerimonie, au desplaisir des vns & contentement des autres: car ainsi le veult & commande nostre Dieu: faisant iustice du tort & sacrifice que l'infante Mirabella s'est preparé contre soy mesmes.

Ce cry acheué, elle, & les vestuz d'orengé se mirent à lamenter & plaindre comme s'ilz eussent bruslé en viues flammes, & les oyseaux nocturnes à faire leur bruit acoustumé tant que le dieu d'Amour & sa suite retournerent d'ou ilz estoient sortiz se refermans les portes auec aussi grande impetuosité comme elles s'estoient ouuertes. Et toutesfoys les oyseaux ne se teurent pourtant, iusques au point du iour qu'ilz reprindrent leur vol & s'eslongnerent de Mirabella, laquelle se cruciant & tourmentant tousiours de plus en plus, mit telle compassion en Amadis qu'il ne se peut tenir de dire à la Royne, Vrayement le Cheualier par qui la pauurette doit estre deliurée, est grandement tenu à Fortune. Sur mon Dieu (respondit elle) ie n'eusse iamais pensé Amour auoir telle puissance qu'il nous a fait cognoistre ceste nuict & à veuë d'oeil. Bien, certes, est hors du sens celuy ou celle, qui contredit à son vouloir ou desdaigne ses loys & ordonnances" (164–164^v).

Notes

Chapter I: The Literary Background of *Amadis de Gaule*

1. Sir Henry Thomas, *Spanish and Portuguese Romances of Chivalry* (Cambridge, 1920), p. 147. To this useful and learned work I am greatly indebted, particularly in this chapter, for bibliographical and background information.

2. "All these writers copied without scruple or conscience of any kind what they had read in other books of the same class; they did not even take the trouble to change the names." Pascual de Gayangos, *Libros de caballerías,* Biblioteca de Autores Españoles, XL (Madrid, 1909), lv, n. 2.

3. *Ibid.,* p. lv. See also Thomas, *Spanish and Portuguese Romances of Chivalry,* pp. 89–90; 125–126.

4. In his *Romance of Amadís of Gaul,* Supplement to No. 17, *Revista de História* (Sociedade portuguesa de estudos históricos, Oporto) (1916), p. 31, Sir Henry Thomas corrects Gayangos' genealogical chart.

5. Thomas, *Spanish and Portuguese Romances of Chivalry,* p. 55.

6. *Ibid.,* p. 82.

7. Don Guerau Despes, the Spanish ambassador in England in 1569, declared that ladies and gentlemen at the Spanish court called their queen Oriana in praise and admiration. See Roy C. Strong, "Queen Elizabeth I as Oriana," *Studies in the Renaissance,* VI (1959), 254.

8. M. Menéndez y Pelayo, *Orígenes de la novela,* Nueva Biblioteca de Autores Españoles (Madrid, 1905), I, ccxii.

9. Miguel de Cervantes Saavedra, *Don Quixote,* Part I, Ch. 11, p. 233.

10. For an account of the German continuation, in which the adventures of Amadis' descendants are carried into the Americas, see Maximilian Pfeiffer, *Amadisstudien* (Mainz, 1905).

11. Quoted by Thomas, *Spanish and Portuguese Romances of Chivalry,* p. 213, n. 2.

12. For references to these and other pageants drawn from chivalric romances and Greek mythology see W. L. Wiley, *The Gentleman of Renaissance France* (Cambridge, Mass., 1954), pp. 64, 69; Gabriel Mourey, *Le Livre des fêtes françaises* (Paris, 1930), Ch. 2.

13. Wiley, p. 116. Here Wiley is echoing the comment of Edouard Bourciez, who writes that *Amadis* "devint le bréviaire, où la Cour de Henri II apprit à penser et à exprimer ses sentiments . . ." (*Les Mœurs polies et la littérature de cour sous Henri II* [Paris, 1886], p. 63).

14. François de La Noue, *Discours politiques et militaires,* ed. F. E. Sutcliffe (Geneva, 1967), p. 162. Quoted by Wiley, p. 117.

15. The prolonged interval was doubtless mostly attributable to the mood of the reading public after the death in 1559 of King Henry II. Since he was

killed while taking part in a tournament at court, a considerable pall fell upon French chivalry and its literary manifestations. Sir Henry Thomas suggests that Henry's death explains why Paris ceased to be the center for the publication of chivalric romances (*Spanish and Portuguese Romances of Chivalry*, p. 216).

16. According to Thomas, the 1578 translation of Chappuys is taken from Mambrino Roseo's commentary on the Spanish Book XII (*Spanish and Portuguese Romances of Chivalry*, p. 202). Dull and generally irrelevant, it is by all odds the poorest—with the possible exception of Book VI—of the entire Amadis cycle in France. All references to Book XV in this work are to Tyron's version.

Both versions of Book XVI contain some matter in common—for example, the breaking of an enchantment by Sphéramonde and Amadis d'Astre—but there are numerous discrepancies. Since Chappuys' version makes a much better connection with Books XV and XVII, it is presumably canonical. Montreux's work may be an original addition, or it may owe something to Mambrino Roseo's supplements.

17. Strong, p. 255.

18. See particularly the prefatory letter of Jacques Gohorry in his translation of Book XIII.

19. Gayangos notes this confusion in his edition of the first five books (*Libros de caballerías*, p. 198n.).

20. Walther Küchler, "Eine dem *Orlando Furioso* Ariosts entlehnte Episode im französischen Amadisroman," *Zeitschrift für französische Sprache und Litteratur*, XXXIV (1909), 274–292. Küchler points out that between Chapters clxvii and clxviii of the Spanish the French translator inserted matter taken from Ariosto. In his *L'Arioste en France* (Turin, 1963) A. Cioranescu cites this article and adds other borrowings in *Amadis* from Ariosto.

21. Quoted by Thomas, *Spanish and Portuguese Romances of Chivalry*, p. 210, n. 3.

22. For numerous instances see Pauline M. Smith, *The Anti-Courtier Trend in Sixteenth-Century French Literature* (Geneva, 1966).

23. This is a central point in Cioranescu's *L'Arioste en France*.

24. Most students of the Spanish *Amadís de Gaula* use the title to refer to the first four books only. Book V is known by the name of its hero Esplandián. And in acccordance with Spanish practice, in which the narrative of Books VI and VIII is ignored, Book VII is the book of Lisuarte de Grecia, Book IX that of Amadís de Grecia, Book X that of Florisel de Niquea, Book XI that of Rogel de Grecia, and Book XII that of Silves de la Selva. In the French translation, however, the narrative does not correspond to the Spanish book number after Book V. Thus Spanish Book VII is French Book VI; and Book IX, the Book of Amadís de Grecia in Spanish, becomes in French Books VII and VIII and so renders the title by hero ambiguous. Similarly Spanish Book X becomes in the French version Books IX and X, Book XI becomes French XI and XII, and

Notes

Book XII becomes French XIII and XIV. As a result, a scholar who refers to *Amadis of Gaul* may be talking about the first four books only, or he may mean the entire cycle.

25. The plot of *Amadis* is so fraught with episodic byways, some of them of more charm than the main narrative, that a résumé cannot do it justice except by going far beyond the limits of useful brevity. The first four books, structurally the tightest books of the cycle, are most commonly summarized. Thomas gives a four-page condensation of the action of the first four books in his *Spanish and Portuguese Romances of Chivalry* (pp. 44–47), but his account is so curt that it is not very helpful. John Colin Dunlop's *History of Fiction* (rev. Henry Wilson, London, 1896) attempts, more ambitiously, a summary of the entire twelve books of the Spanish cycle. This condensation requires twenty-one pages (I, 358–378), and since even that measure of brevity is achieved only by a ruthless cutting of key episodes and characters, I am driven to believe that an adequate brief retelling of the French *Amadis* would require at least forty pages. See Appendix A, however, for a genealogical table and glossary of the chief characters.

Chapter II: *Amadis* as a Book of War

1. It has been suggested that Gaul may signify Wales rather than France. For a recent discussion of the problem see Edwin B. Place, "Amadis of Gaul, Wales, or What?" *Hispanic Review*, XXIII (1955), 99–107.

2. In *Les Mœurs polies*, p. 81, Edouard Bourciez notes that battles in *Amadis* are often recounted in realistic fashion and do not differ noticeably from the records left by sixteenth-century soldiers and commentators.

3. Despite the claim made in Book XIII, Chapter xxxvi, Greek fire is used earlier in *Amadis*. In Book X, Chapter xxix, the Greeks prepare chariots with Greek fire for use against the elephants in Lucidor's army.

4. Where quotations from *Amadis* occur in English, as here, they are taken from one of the books translated by Anthony Munday and printed together in 1619.

5. In these fights Agesilan is following closely the adventures of Rogero and Astolfo in the *Orlando Furioso* (Cantos X and XXXIII).

Chapter III: *Amadis* as a Book of Love

1. For an account of such criticism in Spain, France, England, and other countries see Thomas, *Spanish and Portuguese Romances of Chivalry*, Chs. 5, 6.

2. Menéndez y Pelayo, *Orígenes de la novela*, I, cxxvi; Cioranescu, *L'Arioste en France*, I, 25.

3. In defense of Falanges' worship of his lady it should be said that Alastraxerée is reputed to be a demigoddess, the daughter of Zahara and the god Mars.

Notes

4. The episode occurs in Montreux's Book XVI, Chapter xiii. It is a continuation of an affair that begins in Book XII, Chapter xii, though Montreux has somehow changed Marfire's name to Marfise.

5. Cf. *Orlando Furioso*, Canto VIII, 49–50.

6. See *Amadis*, XII, xcv, 231. The entire episode is taken over from the *Orlando Furioso*, Canto X, wherein Rogero carries the naked Angelica on the hippogriff.

7. Niquée is so lovely that every man who sees her falls madly in love with her. Her father has to keep her isolated and entirely in the company of women—except for the dwarf Buzando, who is inevitably infatuated by her. Niquée's brother, who sees her accidentally, does not recognize her as his sister, for he has never seen her before.

8. The episode is found in Montreux's version only, in Chapter lxi. The enchantment in Chappuys' Book XVI has a completely different origin.

9. Galtazar's love becomes so obvious—Galtazar is growing thin and sickly—that Daraïde finally reveals he is really Agesilan. The revelation cures Galtazar, but not entirely. "Car chacunefois qu'il la regardoit à l'impourueuë, il sentoit rallumer en son cueur les mesmes flames qui l'auoient au parauant embrasé pour son amour; demeurant en vne continuelle angoisse, iusques à ce qu'il fust reuenu à soy, tellement qu'on l'eut peu comparer à ceux lesquelz sur la nuyt ayans veu quelque estrange fantaume, ou estans eschapez de quelque dangereuse rencontre, tremblent encores de peur à chasque foys qu'ilz les recitent, ou qu'elles leurs retournent en la memoire" (XII, xii^v). ["For whenever he looked at her unexpectedly, he felt flaring up in his heart again the same flames that had formerly consumed him for his love; he remaining in continual anguish until he was restored to himself, in such manner that you could have compared him with those who, having seen at night an unearthly ghost or escaped from some dangerous adventure, still tremble with fear every time they tell about it or the memory comes back to haunt them."]

In *The Honor of Chivalry* an episode obviously derived from the above arouses much merriment. Don Contumeliano falls in love with Belianis, who is disguised as a woman. Belianis reveals himself as a man, but magic is required to remove the pain from Don Contumeliano's love. Every time he sees Belianis, "his pulses and spirits would beate, with alteration, like one strooke with an vncoueth feare" (p. 160).

10. Niquée dies only in Montreux's Book XVI. In the other books she remains alive, and Amadis de Grèce does not marry Lucelle.

11. For a more detailed description of this experience and its similarity to John Donne's "Ecstasy," see Chapter viii below and Appendix B.

12. It is significant that Books XI and XII, which contain several substantial passages of neo-Platonic love, are both dedicated to Diane de Poitiers, whose name is often associated with neo-Platonism in France.

Notes

Chapter IV: *Amadis* as a Courtesy Book

1. Bourciez, *Les Mœurs polies*. Eugène Baret, *De l' "Amadis de Gaule" et de son influence sur les mœurs et la littérature au XVIᵉ et au XVIIᵉ siècle* (Paris, 1873). Cioranescu, *L'Arioste en France*, pp. 27–28.

2. Edwin B. Place, "El *Amadis* de Montalvo como manual de cortesanía en Francia," *Revista de filología española*, XXXVIII (1954), 151–169.

3. This is an idea often repeated. In Book XIV Agrian refuses to beg for his life, though he is helpless. He says: "je te dy que celuy seul se peut appeller vaincu, qui par lascheté ou couardise laisse à faire son deuoir" (lvii, 79). ["I tell you that he alone can be called beaten who out of slackness or cowardice fails to do his duty."] See also VI, iv.

4. In this motif *Amadis* is probably influenced by Chrestien's story of Lancelot, hooted at as the opprobrious Knight of the Cart. For the story see *Le Chevalier de la charrette*, ed. Mario Roques (Paris, 1958), ll. 345 ff.

5. Episodes of this kind recall Ariosto, who is fond of placing knights in embarrassing positions. Cf. *Orlando Furioso*, Canto XX, 143–144.

6. Thomas, *Spanish and Portuguese Romances of Chivalry*, Ch. 1. See also Edwin B. Place, "Fictional Evolution: The Old French Romances and the Primitive *Amadís* Reworked by Montalvo," *PMLA*, LXXI (1956), 521–529.

7. The education of Silves is described in detail in Book XIII, where the utility of learning is particularly stressed: "Or combien que l'exploit des armes semble seul digne d'vn Prince, voire d'vn simple gentilhomme qui en doit faire principale profession: Toutesfois il y doit adiouster quelque bonne cognoissance des lettres politiques & historiales mesmement vn grand Seigneur (afin qu'il ait dequoy payer, comme l'on dit) en compagnie des autres princes & ce point d'honneur, sur ceux qui moins en sçauent, & sur les inferieurs, par dessus lesquels il doit auoir autant d'auantage de sagesse & prudence, qu'il a de puissance & commandement . . ." (ix, 45–46). ["Now although the exercise of arms alone seems proper to a lord—indeed to a plain gentleman, who ought to make of it his chief vocation—nevertheless he ought to add to that a good knowledge of history and politics, especially one who is a member of the high nobility (so that he may have enough substance, as they say) in the company of other lords and so that he may have a certain advantage in repute over those who know less and over his inferiors, beyond whom he ought to have as much more wisdom and prudence as he has power and authority. . . ."]

8. Montalvo must have liked Amadis' wit too, for he uses much the same situation later in the same book—Chapter xiii—this time putting the flattering remark in the mouth of Florestan.

9. Cioranescu, I, 24.

10. One of the chief demands upon chivalric heroes is the restoration of law and order in areas where tyranny and anarchy prevail. Even after killing the giant or monster responsible for the trouble, the hero invariably remains long

enough to appoint a new governor and to see that law is reestablished. It is at this point in the narrative that a moralization is frequently made. In Book IX, Chapter x, Anaxartes writes a letter to the inhabitants of a valley hitherto subjected to tyrannic rule. He explains that order in the state is a reflection of God's order in the universe.

For a more general discussion of hierarchical order see Book IX, Chapter lxii, where Florisel talks of the order and harmony of Nature and the principle of Universal Love.

11. "Les femmes de ce temps-là estoyent de coeur genereux & viril: & sachans que les cheualiers leurs maris, auoyent pour leur but, la gloire & honneur en recommandation, elles n'osoyent pas les empescher en leurs grandes entreprinses" (XIX, cxix, 392). ["The women of that age were noble and stout of heart; and knowing that the knights their husbands for their goals held honor and glory above all, they did not venture to hinder them in their great quests."]

12. Parents are warned that it may be wiser to expose their daughters to the ways of the world rather than to strive to keep them innocent. In Book IX, Chapter lxviii, after Heleine surrenders to Florisel, the author comments: "Et Voylà, lecteurs, comme il en print à ceste Princesse, laquelle tous les iours voyoit faire & oyoit le seruice diuin dans l'abaïe, ou le Roy son pere l'auoit mise, pensant la destourner des mondaines affections, mais ie croy (& est à presumer) s'il l'eust tousiours tenuë aupres de luy en sa court entre toutes les delices & mondanitez, qu'elle n'eust esté si viuement assaillie de concupiscence & encores moins vaincuë." ["And there you may see, readers, how it fared with this princess, who every day of her life saw and heard mass celebrated in the abbey where the king her father had sent her, thinking to turn her from worldly pleasures, but I believe (and it is to be supposed) if he had kept her always near him in his court, among all the delights and social gatherings, she would not have been so sharply attacked by concupiscence, still less conquered by it."] And the idea is repeated in Chapter lxx.

Young ladies should have an opportunity to converse in the company of others of both sexes. The educational value of honest conversation is discussed by Amadis d'Astre and a lady in Book XVII, Chapter xxviii.

13. *Defense of Poetry*, in *The Prose Works of Sir Philip Sidney*, III, 20.

14. "To the Reader," *The Treasury of Amadis of France*.

Chapter V: Structure and Variety

1. Thomas, *Spanish and Portuguese Romances of Chivalry*, p. 67.

2. Grace S. Williams, "The Amadis Question," *Revue hispanique*, XXI (1909), 52–58.

3. The idea of the wind as an impregnator was not unusual in the sixteenth century and before. Spenser's Orgoglio, for instance, is fathered by "blustring Aeolus" (*F.Q.*, I, vii, 9). In *The White Goddess* (New York: Vintage, 1958),

Notes

pp. 486–489, Robert Graves discusses the currency of the idea and traces it back to Lactantius.

4. The writing on Silves' breast reads as follows: "Silues Du Desert, Filz D'Amadis De Grece Et De Finistée, Sans Vice Ny Offence De L'Vn Ne De L'Autre" (XI, lxxxi, 136ᵛ).

5. The custom is supposed to be "a l'exemple de Catilina en sa coniuration contre Romme" (XIII, xxxi, 207).

6. For an example of a Petrarchan sonnet printed as prose see below, Chapter VI.

7. This kind of rhetoric, which is parodied by Cervantes and others, is more obvious in other romances of chivalry.

8. The episode recalls one of the medieval tales about Virgil the necromancer. See below, Chapter VI, n. 6.

9. The episode occurs in Chapter xxiii (79), but only in the version of Montreux. Otherwise Amadis de Gaule is always treated with due respect.

10. Evidence that this was regarded as a comic episode is furnished by a parallel in *The Honor of Chivalry*. There Don Contumeliano falls in love with Belianis, who is disguised as a maid. Later Belianis has occasion to tell others about his embarrassing tangle. "And when hee spake of Don Contumeliano, they coulde not stand for laughter" (p. 163).

Chapter VI: Structure and Repetition

1. Though much is made of the Troy parallels, the Heleine-Florisel episode is also very much like the Amadis-Oriane story in Books III and IV, for which no Trojan precedent is claimed or implied. Oriane is engaged to the Roman Lucidor, but she is carried off by Amadis, and the act is followed by a great war.

2. Cf. *Aeneid*, Book IV.

3. For an outline of the plots of the two works see Appendix C.

4. See Williams, "The Amadis Question," *passim*.

5. The episode is contained in *Le Roman de Tristan et Iseut,* traduction du roman en prose du quinzième siècle, ed. Pierre-Honoré J. B. Champion and P. Galand-Pernet (Paris, 1958), p. 86.

6. The episode is in Book XI. Moncan is pulled up first by a rope let down "comme on dit de Virgile en la corbeille" (lxxx, 133). For the tale alluded to here, see Domenico Comparetti, *Virgilio nel medio evo* (Florence, 1895), II, 248, "Comment la demoiselle pendit Virgille en la corbeille."

7. See *The Decameron*, Day 4, story 1.

8. The story is probably derived from Boiardo's *Orlando Innamorato,* Book II, Cantos XXV–XXVI.

9. Pio Rajna, *Le fonti dell' "Orlando Furioso"* (Florence, 1900), p. 155 and *passim*.

10. Cioranescu, *L'Arioste en France,* I, 360–362.

11. *Orlando Furioso*, Canto VII, 46–47.

Notes

12. The example best known in English is probably Romeo's attempt to define love in *Romeo and Juliet*, I, i, 196–200. Robert Greene also has a poem on the subject in *Menaphon*, p. 104.

13. *Amadis* on occasion echoes *Palmerin*. Although generally the current of influence flows from *Amadis* to the other chivalric romances, the trend does not apply to the later books of *Amadis*. Books XIX and XXI are influenced slightly by the Palmerin cycle. In *Palmerin d'Oliva* Palmerin cures King Primaleon of a strange malady by bringing him water from a fountain on Mount Artifaeria. The mountain is mentioned in *Amadis*, Book XIX, Chapter xxxix; and in Book XXI, Chapter vi, Dorigel emulates Palmerin's feat by going to a mountain to get a herb called "Pinearee, en langue Indienne," which cures the queen of Orgestre of a mysterious malady.

14. The repetition in Book XVII carries over into Book XVIII and is complicated further there. Amadis d'Astre, in disguise as the Knight of Sadness, is confused with Lucidamor, who is also masquerading as the Knight of Sadness because he too received an angry letter from his lady dismissing him from her sight. Since Amadis d'Astre and Lucidamor resemble each other, they are mistaken one for the other by messengers from their respective ladies, who have discovered that their jealousy was unfounded. Chapters xxix to xxxviii in Book XVIII follow the story of this confusion, which ends with each knight changing his title to the Knight of Happiness.

15. The disguise of a knight as a lady occurs only in Books VIII, X, XI, and XII. In later books the device is reversed, and several Amazons unintentionally win the hearts of ladies who take them for knights.

16. Niquée dies only in Montreux's Book XVI.

17. Florisel's love problems begin in Book IX, at the end of which he elopes with Heleine. She dies in Book XIII, Chapter xxiii.

18. Rogel is the most notorious of all chivalric lovers, and the record of his amorous exploits makes up a large part of Books XI through XIV. Léonide dies in Book XIX.

19. Astrapol's problems in love are largely the concern of Book XIX.

20. Francis Beaumont, *The Knight of the Burning Pestle*, IV, ii, 40.

21. In Book VIII, Chapter xlvi, Abra mistakes Amadis de Grèce for his father Lisuart and carries on in such a way that Lucelle grows jealous. Amadis finally convinces Abra that she is mistaken, but he admits that this is the second time he has been confused with his father.

22. Heleine says: "Comment mon amy, l'hermite vous a il aprins ceste leçon" (IX, xciii). ["What is this, my love? Has the hermit taught you this lesson?"] Cf. the remark of Oriane quoted below in Chapter vii.

23. The most impressive celestial manifestation is the fiery sword that appears suspended above the city of Constantinople in Book VI, Chapter xii. Ominous flights of birds are seen in Book X, Chapters xxx and xxxi, just before the great battle between the Greeks and Romans.

Notes

1. This conclusion is, to some degree, at odds with that voiced by Place, "El *Amadís* de Montalvo como manual de cortesanía en Francia." He quotes Herberay's prefatory statement in Book I: "Et si vous apperceuez en quelque endroict que je ne me soye assubjecty à le rendre de mot à mot, je vous supplye croire que je l'ay fait tant pource qu'il m'a semblé beaucoup de choses estre mal seantes aux personnes introduictes en regard es meurs et façons du jourd'huy, qu' aussi pour l'aduis d'aulcuns mes amys. . . ." He then quotes several passages from *Le Thresor des liures d'Amadis* (1559) and compares them with Montalvo's original. He concludes that Herberay follows his Spanish source slavishly and that Herberay's claim to have changed and improved the original is pretense.

Actually, Mr. Place and I are not far apart. He concentrates on the similarities between Montalvo and Herberay, whereas I am interested primarily in the differences. I do not understand why Mr. Place uses *Le Thresor* to demonstrate Herberay's indebtedness. The full text of Books I through IV of the French *Amadis* provides a more just indication, for it shows how the relatively few changes made by Herberay affected the characters of the French tale.

2. In his recent study of Spanish fiction in English translation, *The Golden Tapestry* (Durham, N. C.: Duke University Press, 1963), pp. 35–36, Dale B. J. Randall discusses the role of French as an intermediary between source language and English readers.

3. When the English traveler Fynes Moryson arrived in Lübeck in 1593, he bought a copy of Book XIV of the German *Amadis* to help him brush up on the language. In his *Itinerary* (1617) he recommends *Amadis* to his readers because it is available in so many languages and because the translators are "Masters of eloquence." (Quoted by Thomas, *Spanish and Portuguese Romances of Chivalry*, pp. 236, n. 1, and 268.)

4. Randall, p. 55.

5. Celeste Turner Wright, *Anthony Mundy: An Elizabethan Man of Letters* (Berkeley: University of California Press, 1928), App. III.

6. In Herberay's translation Oriane prefers "plutôt tomber en la mercy des poissons, que demeurer en lieu ou ie n'ay desir, ny affection." Lisuart threatens: "au lieu de vous marier à l'Empereur, ie vous feray espouser vne tour, ou ne verrés de vôtre vie Soleil, ny Lune" (III, xviii).

7. Kyd might, of course, have read Oriane's impassioned lament in *The Treasury of Amadis of France*, where it is translated "Ah, my eyes no more eyes, but streames of teares and weepings . . ." (p. 15). But by Kyd's time the expression had become a commonplace in both French and English literature.

8. As usual, Munday is closely following the French translation, where Oriane "monstroit deux petites boules d'albastre vif, le plus blanc et le plus doulcement respirant que nature feit jamais" (I, xxxvi).

9. Montalvo's version also mentions artillery.

10. It is interesting to note also that in neither of the first two books, which appeared in the reign of Elizabeth and shortly after the defeat of the Armada, does the word "Mass" appear. Munday translates it as "service." By 1619, however, when the edition of the first four books was published, the word appears in Books III and IV. Munday's qualms may or may not reflect general attitudes.

Chapter VIII: *Amadis* and Elizabethan Drama and Verse

1. The *chanson* is given in full in Appendix B.

2. George Williamson, *Seventeenth Century Contexts* (Chicago: University of Chicago Press, 1961), pp. 63–77.

3. In *The Sources of "Much Ado About Nothing"* (New Haven: Yale University Press, 1950) Charles T. Prouty lists eighteen sources. See also John J. O'Connor, "Three Additional *Much Ado* Sources," *Essays in Literary History*, ed. Rudolf Kirk and C. F. Main (New Brunswick, N. J.: Rutgers University Press, 1960), pp. 81–91.

4. The influence of *Amadis* would most probably appear in heroical romances, and according to Alfred Harbage, *Annals of English Drama*, rev. Samuel Schoenbaum (Philadelphia: University of Pennsylvania Press, 1964), eleven heroical romances were performed between 1570 and 1581. Of them only *Clyomon and Clamydes* (1570) is still extant.

5. In *The Knight of the Burning Pestle*, I, iii, Ralph reads from *Palmerin d'Oliva* and shows a very close knowledge of *The Mirror of Knighthood*. He refers to the army of "fourteen or fifteen hundred thousand men . . . that the Prince of Portigo brought against Rosicleer. . . ." Since this is an accurate reference to a war in Book III, Beaumont's knowledge of *The Mirror* was not merely superficial.

6. The image has been traced back to Sophocles, *Oedipus Tyrannus*, ll. 1227–1228. Seneca also uses a similar conceit in *Hippolytus*, ll. 715–718, part of which John Studley's Elizabethan translation renders as follows:

> . . . not Neptune graundsire grave
> With all his Ocean foulding floud can purge and wash away
> This dunghill foule of stane. . . .
> [*Seneca His Tenne Tragedies*, The Tudor Translations
> (London and New York, 1927), I, 162]

7. Cf. Chrestien, *Yvain*, ll. 2092–2094.

8. René Pruvost, *Robert Greene et ses romans* (Paris, 1938), p. 301.

9. This is, however, not unlike an earlier episode in which Alquif appears in a Prospero-like role. In Book X, Chapters lxxviii and lxxix, Alquif arranges through his magic a tempest that brings a ship of knights and ladies to his isle.

10. It occurs in the first part of *Gerileon of England*. See John J. O'Connor, "Another Human Footstool," *Notes and Queries*, n.s. II (1955), 332. It also occurs in the anonymous English romance *The Knight of the Sea* (1600). There

Notes

when the giant Grand Cardigan comes ashore, Oceander sees him prepare to climb into a chariot drawn by two lions "and vnder his feete in steede of a footestoole, to lye an armed knight" (p. 122).

It is interesting also that in Forde's *Parismus*, when Andramart kidnaps Laurana and tries to persuade her to marry him, he offers her among other things a chariot of gold, "wherein thou shalt be drawne by kings" (p. 160). Much of Marlowe—*Tamburlaine* in particular—has a great deal in common with chivalric romances.

Chapter IX: *Amadis* and Spenser's *Faerie Queene*

1. H. J. Todd is quoted by Jewel Wurtsbaugh, *Two Centuries of Spenserian Scholarship* (Baltimore, 1936), p. 149.

2. Robert Southey in the preface to his translation of *Palmerin of England* (London, 1807), pp. xliv–xlv.

3. Edwin Greenlaw, "Britomart at the House of Busirane," *Studies in Philology*, XXVI (1929), 123.

4. Book IX contains complimentary poems by Jean-Antoine Baïf and Etienne Jodelle, and Book X has an ode by Joachim du Bellay.

5. Stephen Gosson, *Plays Confuted in Five Actions*, reprinted in W. C. Hazlitt, *The English Drama and Stage* (London, 1869), p. 189.

6. *Valentine and Orson*, ed. Arthur Dickson, Early English Text Society, No. 204 (London, 1937).

7. Arcalaüs has a bed "fixed vpon a vice or screw, to bee let downe and mounted againe (without any noyse at all) into a dungeon of twenty fathome deepe" (*Amadis*, III, 54). In Montalvo's text it is not the bed but the room (*cámara*) that moves down to the dungeon, and the three knights who are Arcalaüs' victims sleep in three beds. For whatever reason Herberay read *cámara* as though it were *cama*. He translated the word into French as *lict* and put the three knights into a single bed. Munday, as usual, follows Herberay faithfully.

In Book XV, Chapter xxiii, Amadis d'Astre and Sphéramonde are also trapped by a trick bed.

8. Dorothy F. Atkinson, "Busirane's Castle and Artidon's Cave," *Modern Language Quarterly*, I (1940), 185–192.

9. The chapter recalls an allegorical episode in Book IX, Chapter liii, where five ladies are described—Reason surrounded by Temperance, Prudence, Justice, and Force.

10. The woman is "toute vestue de blanc, qui entre ses bras tenoit deux enfançons, & par grande douceur les allaictoit du laict de ses blanches & belles mamelles, & sur sa teste auoit vn escriteau, qui disoit: la Pieté" (XIV, xxxv, 44ᵛ); ["all dressed in white, who held in her arms two infants and with great tenderness nursed them with milk from her fair white breasts, and on her head she had a sign that read Charity."]

11. He is not liberated until Book IX, Chapter xxx. His enchantment, called the Hell of Anastarax, is the center of attention in the first half of Book IX.

12. For the French version of the episode which follows see Appendix D.

13. See especially C. S. Lewis, *Allegory of Love: A Study in Medieval Tradition* (New York: Oxford University Press, 1936), Ch. 1.

14. Josephine Waters Bennett, *The Evolution of the "Faerie Queene"* (Chicago, 1942). On the basis of enjambment tests she thinks the Mask of Cupid was reworked by Spenser. She points to the apparent changes of personal pronouns. It is interesting to speculate that Spenser's original version may have been modeled directly upon the mask in *Amadis* and that when Spenser incorporated it in the *Faerie Queene* he added the wall of flame to keep Scudamour out and so enlarge Britomart's role. Mrs. Bennett also considers the possibility that Spenser may have derived the episode from *The Mirror of Knighthood,* and she refers to Dorothy F. Atkinson's article, "Busirane's Castle and Artidon's Cave." But like almost everything else in *The Mirror* the Cupid rituals there are drawn from one place or another in *Amadis.* None of them is half so close to the Mask of Cupid as the episode from Book VIII of *Amadis.*

15. Busirane is a remarkably colorless villain, but the reason for such a characterization is clear. The real villain is, of course, Cupid, and it is the primitive force of Love that Spenser wants to emphasize. Thus it is Cupid, not Busirane, who takes part in the Mask. Busirane is merely Cupid's mortal representative, but he is a necessary character because Britomart, who must be victorious, can scarcely be expected to conquer Cupid.

16. In *The Kindly Flame* (Princeton University Press, 1964), p. 77, Thomas P. Roche, Jr., suggests that "the House of Busyrane is presented as if it were an objectification of Amoret's fear of sexual love in marriage." I think this is an over-ingenious reading that makes a strange psychiatric case out of the Venus-fostered Amoret.

Chapter X: *Amadis* and Sidney's *Arcadia*

1. Robert Southey in the preface to his translation of *Palmerin of England.*

2. Dunlop, *History of Fiction,* I, 372.

3. William Vaughn Moody, "An Inquiry into the Sources of Sir Philip Sidney's *Arcadia.*" Unpublished manuscript in the Harvard College Library.

4. W. W. Greg, *Pastoral Poetry and Pastoral Drama* (London, 1906), p. 150; K. Brunhuber, *Sir Philip Sidneys "Arcadia" und ihre Nachläufer* (Nuremberg, 1903). R. W. Zandvoort, *Sidney's "Arcadia"* (Amsterdam, 1929), and Mary Patchell, *The Palmerin Romances in Elizabethan Prose Fiction* (New York: Columbia University Press, 1947), give descriptions and evaluations of Moody's findings.

5. Samuel Lee Wolff, *The Greek Romances in Elizabethan Prose Fiction* (New York: Columbia University Press, 1912); Albert W. Osborn, *Sir Philip Sidney*

en France (Paris, 1932); T. P. Harrison, Jr., "A Source of Sidney's *Arcadia*," *University of Texas Studies in English*, VI (1926), 53–71; Marcus S. Goldman, *Sir Philip Sidney and the "Arcadia*," Illinois Studies in Language and Literature, XVII (Urbana, 1934); Patchell, *The Palmerin Romances*.

6. *Sidney's "Arcadia"*: Walter R. Davis, "A Map of Arcadia: Sidney's Romance in Its Tradition," and Richard A. Lanham, "The *Old Arcadia*" (New Haven: Yale University Press, 1965), pp. 384–385. (Two works in one volume.)

7. Osborn points out, for example, that Edward disguises himself as a gardener in *Primaleon of Greece* in order to be near Flerida. He thinks this is as good a parallel with Musidorus' disguise as can be found in *Amadis*. Miss Patchell has carried this argument a bit farther, but the case she offers for the influence of the Palmerin cycle is not convincing.

8. The failure to take into account both the rarity of Pyrocles' disguise and the importance of *Amadis de Gaule* as a source leads Mark Rose to a serious misunderstanding of Sidney's intention in the *Arcadia*. See "Sidney's Womanish Man," *Review of English Studies*, XV (1964), 353–363.

9. Patchell, p. 127.

10. It is very likely that Sidney got the idea for Musidorus' disguise as a shepherd from Book IX of *Amadis*. Since Sidney wanted to give Pyrocles and Musidorus fair play—he is very careful to let neither conquer the other—he did not want both disguised as maidens. The same disguise could have led only to repetition or to a virtual ignoring of the suit of one, as in *Amadis*, where Agesilan-Daraïde gets almost all the attention.

11. The enmity between Darinel and Mardoquée is frequently played upon in Books IX and X. They first come to blows in Book IX, Chapter xxxii, and thereafter keep up a continuous feud. In Chapter xxxiv Heleine arranges a wrestling match between them, but since both are cowards, blows are generally less frequent than words.

12. Cf. *Amadis*, VIII, lxxiii, and Sidney, *Works*, II, 40.

13. Brunhuber (pp. 14–19) was the first to note this parallel. It is also pointed out by Wolff, p. 318.

14. Cf. *Amadis*, XI, lxxii, and Sidney, *Works*, I, Ch. 18.

15. Walter R. Davis, "Thematic Unity in the *New Arcadia*," *Studies in Philology*, LVII (1960), 123–143.

16. Sidney, *Works*, I, 64.

17. For Wolff's definition of pathetic optics see *The Greek Romances*, pp. 177–179.

18. K. O. Myrick, *Sir Philip Sidney as a Literary Craftsman* (Cambridge, Mass.: Harvard University Press, 1935), pp. 288–289.

19. Sidney, *Works*, I, 313.

20. Myrick, pp. 263–264.

21. Sidney, *Works*, III, 40.

22. Thomas, *Spanish and Portuguese Romances of Chivalry*, p. 77. Croll's comment is cited by Zandvoort, p. 188.

Don Quixote is high in his praises of the style of Feliciano de Silva: "For the smoothnesse of his prose, with now and then some intricate sentence medled, seemed to him peerlesse; and principally when he did read the love dalliances, or letters of challenge, that Knights sent to Ladies, or one to another; where, in many places he found written the reason of the unreasonablenesse, which against my reason is wrought, doth so weaken my reason, as with all reason I doe justly complaine on your beauty" (I, 24).

23. Sidney, *Works*, I, 58.

24. *Ibid.*, I, 360.

25. *Ibid.*, IV, 274.

26. *Ibid.*, I, 181.

27. See also *Amadis*, VIII, lxix; IX, xxiv.

28. John Hoskins praises the first of them in his *Directions for Speech and Style*. See *The Life, Letters and Writings of John Hoskyns*, ed. Louise B. Osborn (New Haven: Yale University Press, 1937), p. 130.

29. Bazilique derives obviously from the Greek word for king, Βασιλεύς, and the name may have given Sidney the idea—not altogether unusual in chivalric romances, though more common in other literary kinds—of using descriptive names derived from Greek roots (e.g., Gynecia, *woman;* Philoclea, *love of honor;* Pamela, *all honey*).

Chapter XI: *Amadis* and Elizabethan Fiction

1. *Galien of France* is no longer extant. It was translated by Anthony Munday about 1576 and is listed in Francis Meres' *Palladis Tamia* (1598) as among the romances harmful to youth.

2. See Robarts' dedication of *Pheander* to Captain Thomas Lea. See also in the story Thelarchus' stirring speech on behalf of soldiers, who are not sufficiently honored in "Thrace" (sig. G).

3. Thomas Deloney, *Jack of Newbury*, in *The Novels*, p. 30.

4. Henry Robarts, *Haigh for Devonshire*, Ch. 15.

5. Barnabe Rich, *Don Simonides*, sig. M4 ff. My copy lacks a title page.

6. See Anthony Munday, *Zelauto*, pp. 47–49. Palmerin is not mentioned by name, but all readers are presumed to know whose mistress Polinarda is.

7. *Ibid.*, p. xxvi.

8. Munday's borrowing has been noted by William Ringler, *Stephen Gosson* (Princeton, N. J.: Princeton University Press, 1943), p. 129.

9. In the epistle to the reader Forde calls *Parismus* his first work, but *Ornatus and Artesia* seems to have been first in print.

Notes

10. *Ornatus and Artesia* is a partial exception. It gives the full text of several letters between the lovers.

11. In *The Palmerin Romances*, p. 99, Mary Patchell points out several other resemblances between *Ornatus and Artesia* and the *Arcadia*.

Forde's *Parismus* is even more clearly indebted to Sidney. At one point Laurana is kidnaped by Andramart and taken to the Isle of Rocks. When she rejects him, he asks his sister Adamasia to intercede for him. She treats Laurana with great cruelty—without Andramart's knowledge—and the whole episode is very much like the treatment of Pamela and Philoclea by Cecropia.

12. Emanuel Forde, *Montelion*, Chs. 18–21; *Primaleon of Greece*, III, v.

13. Patchell, p. 99; Thomas, *Spanish and Portuguese Romances of Chivalry*, p. 75.

14. The author of *Moderatus* is known only by his initials R.P., though several attempts have been made to identify him. The romance is so close in matter and tone to *The Mirror of Knighthood* that it seems very likely that the author is the same R.P. who translated Books III and IV. The interested reader should see especially *The Mirror*, IV, xv, xxii, xxvii, xxviii, and *Moderatus*, Ch. 15.

15. N. Burton Paradise, *Thomas Lodge* (New Haven: Yale University Press, 1931), p. 77.

16. *Ibid.*, p. 120.

17. Thomas Lodge, *A Margarite of America*, p. 218.

18. *Ibid.*, p. 188; *Amadis*, XVI (Montreux), xiii.

19. René Pruvost, *Robert Greene et ses romans* (Paris, 1938), p. 301.

20. As Mary Patchell points out (p. 114), Shakespeare may have derived the name directly from *Amadis*.

21. Pruvost, p. 349.

22. *Amadis*, VII, i; *Menaphon*, pp. 66 ff. See also *Amadis*, XIV, lxv.

23. Cf. *Amadis*, VII, xx, 56, and *Menaphon*, p. 80.

24. Pruvost, p. 345.

25. *Short Fiction of the Seventeenth Century*, ed. Charles C. Mish, The Stuart Editions (New York: New York University Press, 1963), p. 45.

26. *Ibid.*, p. 78.

27. *The Unfortunate Traveler*, in *The Works of Thomas Nashe*, II, 273–274.

28. The name Almidiana is itself a parody upon the names of romance heroines, for Diana compounds are much in favor. For example, Claridiana is a heroine in *The Mirror of Knighthood*.

29. *The Knight of the Sea*, pp. 19–20.

30. *Amadis*, XII, viii, 30; Sidney, *Works*, I, 218–222.

31. *The Knight of the Sea*, pp. 82 ff.

32. *Ibid.*, pp. 12 ff.

33. *Ibid.*, p. 66.

34. Cf. *The Knight of the Sea*, pp. 39 ff., and Sidney, *Works*, I, 232–236.

35. *The Mirror of Knighthood*, II (*The Second Part of the First Book*), fols. 62–62ᵛ.

36. Margaret Schlauch, *Antecedents of the English Novel, 1400–1600* (London, 1963), p. 173.

37. Emanuel Forde, *Ornatus and Artesia*, in *Shorter Novels*, II, 60–61.

38. Forde, *Montelion*, sigs. D3–D3ᵛ.

Translations

Chapter I: The Literary Background of *Amadis de Gaule*

p. 11. Likewise, if you would understand clearly, you may perceive therein another meaning designed to praise for brilliant deeds the King, his sons, and his noble ancestors; for Perion and Amadis ruled in our Gaul and indeed triumphed. By Perion, then, and Amadis and their children so wise and bold, the puissant King of France is meant, and all the royal blood from them descended. . . .

Chapter II: *Amadis* as a Book of War

p. 25. the man who does not strive to be valorous in this life and by his valor to assist and provide for others is less to be esteemed than . . . brute beasts.

p. 28. The Pope at Rome, all the consistory of cardinals and the whole clergy prayed God almost without cease for the Christian victory, and throughout Europe many processions were held.

p. 29. several rams and machines such as were used in ancient times to batter and shake the city walls.

p. 31. equipped with augers and wimbles . . . went down secretly to pierce the enemy vessels, which then little by little took in water and during the fight went to the bottom.

p. 33. because his head was like a mastiff's.

p. 34. more stubborn than old mules and, hot for their destruction, like two strong stags in their rutting season.

p. 36. in short it was a beast that had been created in hell rather than on earth.

p. 37. whoever did not see him up close could smell him a mile away.

with which sometimes he would tear and dismember men alive.

he vomited forth froth like an angry old cur, filling the whole room with vapor and smoke that poured out of his horrible gullet.

to emit a thick smoke from his mouth and nostrils.

p. 38. fire and smoke from his nose and ears.

that there issued from his nostrils and mouth a great thick smoke, as from the mouth of a furnace.

bellowing like an enraged bull.

a sticky, foul venom.

p. 39. made it roll like a bowling ball.

p. 40. he made fly the arm of one, the head of another; one fell with a leg lopped off, another with his head split to the teeth; yet another fell senseless as though he had been struck by the falling sickness.

more than ten thousand pagans flew into the air, arms, heads, legs, and bodies scattered.

p. 41. Here one saw pale Death going around with his scythe, busying himself on every side; one heard the horrible screams of the wounded who were dying, the lamentations of those who pitied them, the cries of those who were begging for help to restore them, and finally the clash of arms, the whinnying of horses, and the sound of the trumpets, terrifying to the cowardly and pleasing to the brave.

Chapter III: *Amadis* as a Book of Love

p. 44. a fire of straw, no sooner lit than out.

he was transported to the third heaven (which is the sphere of Venus).

p. 45. was used to seeing him fall in such faints.

threw himself on the grass, where he tossed and turned in distress.

bathed in a cold sweat.

I resemble Prometheus, whose liver, which grows back as fast as it is gnawed away, serves as an everlasting food for the hawk of the Caucasus.

the blood drained from his face, and he grew pale as a corpse.

Translations

Ah, God, God! Must the reward of faithful love be like this?

p. 47. whoever looked at her (conquered by Love) would either lose his senses or die in a short while.

his mind grew troubled, and he began to do so many foolish things and to make such hideous grimaces that they locked him up in a room.

p. 48. To have given his will to his lady (said Don Brianges) and to be unable to rule himself by any other will than hers, meanwhile loving her utterly with all his heart. It is in this way (said Don Rogel) that we are supposed to love God, not women.

a relic . . . that has touched the shrine of the body of our holy Prophet Mohammed.

p. 49. Love is not subject to the laws of men.

and others without number named in histories both ancient and modern.

Because he who loves . . . is entirely powerless and has to do the bidding of the passion that rules him.

p. 50. it is thus decreed by the heavens.

from a maiden she was made a woman.

renewing several times the combat of love.

p. 51. he immediately grew so bold that, kissing her, he moved his right hand up onto the nipple of her breast, which he fondled bare, forgetting himself with this move, and no wonder: because Love and good will consenting to the passionate opportunity that presented itself, his lust for her caused him to push back her gorget of crepe so far that his eye could enjoy on the sly what her clothing was supposed to hide.

so that gaining ground little by little he went from kisses to fondling her nipple and indeed he would have gone further . . . if shame, prodded by honor, had not interfered. . . .

he wanted, in kissing her, to get at her breast, and lower

p. 52. And for this reason, they two being alone and the door well barred, he undertook, without long pleading, to come to the point whereat he aimed, if all things had favored his aim as much as he wished: but inasmuch as impotent Old Age deprived him of the strength of his arms, it had left him still less his potency in other areas. . . .

Nevertheless his curtal, unbridled and unstabled, flopped at every encounter, being so deadened because of the years passed that the more he shook the bridle or troubled it, the less it was at his command, without as much as making a semblance either of leaping or of kicking up its heels, keeping its head always lowered, for the feeble old body responded not at all to such lust.

enough to move a Narcissus or Hippolytus and all the austere and crabbed philosophers who abhor the functions of nature.

handled him under the bedclothes and redoubled her kisses, dry and moist, in all sorts of ways.

p. 53. Those who have had a similar experience may supply the rest, and the others, beginners, ought to reckon that not for the third, the fourth, even the sixth encounter, were they willing to consider themselves jaded or spent, but rather, continuing and pausing for breath, they fell to talking.

he kissed her and fondled her so sweetly that the fire almost quenched by their previous efforts was rekindled in all its vigor, without their being able to extinguish it utterly at the time in such a way that it did not come back twice as strong.

after having bestowed on her a good morning neither more nor less than she had been wished a good night

p. 54. upon coupling with his wife, he engendered in her by force of imagination a creature so strange and monstrous that from the navel down he had the shape of a bull and for the rest that of a man, except that he had two horns on his head, four arms, and four hands.

p. 55. sucking the honey of her crimson mouth.

A girl to be in love with a girl, alas, what is this but to be in love with the moon? Alas, Pasiphaë was never so unlucky for having loved a bull, though it was a beast unworthy of her affection. Nor Myrrha likewise in her incestuous love. Nor Pygmalion in love with his statue, which Venus quickened and animated.

and that Sappho, the lyric poetess, had been in love with Amytone and Atthis and that her people were more prone to this kind of love than others.

p. 56. so much power had the soul to aid the healing of the body.

p. 57. Which makes me believe that among all the loves and loyalties that have ever been called to memory, even among those most impassioned by the arrows of the little god, who ever gave proof of their attachment, this damsel ought to have first place.

by force of love the heart and the body where the gentle soul reposes, and the spirit so perfect.

We are like two lutes attuned to the same notes, so that when one is sounded, the untouched strings of the other (which is just opposite) vibrate and stir the straw you may place upon it.

p. 58. if it is true that bodies used to be double, we are the halves separated and now joined again better than ever.

so that what is left of me is truly feminine and has no more masculine potency towards other ladies than if I were a real woman.

we wish to leave the shadow and with all our senses embrace the real truth.

Because being so like of body and soul, they join in perfect union, as of two in one, which the ancients called androgyne, which nothing may ever possibly separate or disjoin.

p. 59. if I were not Amadis d'Astre, I would prefer to be no other than this shepherd. . . .

Chapter IV: *Amadis* as a Courtesy Book

p. 62. a multitude of beautiful maxims useful for instruction that are scattered throughout, the ornament of our French language; the justice that is so naturally depicted there in the punishment of giants; the generosity of princes and knights in helping and providing for the afflicted and for those who experience unhappy turns of fortune; the compassion for ladies and damsels; and a multitude of fine deeds of honor and courtesy.

p. 63. whence one can gather or glean that the wicked in the presence of the good can by their example be led to act as they should and to change their evil natures into good ones.

p. 64. true, imperishable wealth is the renown of the virtuous person for good and heroic deeds.

p. 65. therefore I think I am issued from royal blood, or an illustrious line; whereof my heart often bears witness by the exalted and **dangerous** undertakings to which it summons me.

p. 67. as your Doctor of the Roman Church very well put it, he is not without blame who exposes himself to a certain danger.

p. 68. Knights, it seems to me that you have a hard enough game to master without putting yourselves in danger of having each to deal with odds of two to one.

his present glory augments my past glory.

p. 71. And if you perceive somewhere that I have not constrained myself to render it word for word, I beg you to believe that this is as much because many things seemed to me to be unbecoming to the characters introduced in regard to the manners and fashions of today as. . . .

p. 72. for he understood this language very well, as he did several others which he had learned as a little boy from his father on the deserted and Solitary Isle.

p. 73. like one who knew all languages.

he acted more like a subject than a lord in his observance of the laws.

Because such was the opinion of the great king Amadis in the education of the princes of his blood, to render them so gifted and learned that their subjects would willingly obey them, knowing them to be so worthy of the rank and place they held; and that when they found themselves among strangers they would by their virtue win preeminence everywhere.

Although he was a knight-errant in the world, he always stole a bit of time to devote to the reading of some book, being so well read in matters of Holy Scripture that he seemed a great theologian; he was equally well versed in ancient history, by reason of which in his everyday talk and conversation he acquired great honor. . . .

p. 75. begins to kiss him and interpose her wanton leg.

that he was affected by a privy illness that robbed him of the power to do her such service.

p. 76. In order to teach those who would rule,/The good way of ruling all well.

not prolix, does not use affected or high-styled language.

because a prince can have no worse enemy than a sycophant.

p. 78. Which ought to be a fine example to kings, that they should bear themselves with all humanity and gentleness towards their subjects, because this is the only principle that makes them rule, just as, to the contrary, cruelty causes them to fall from their estate, precisely as it happened in this case.

Consider how the lofty trees and towers are more exposed to perils and ruin; and, on the other hand, how just as they surpass others in degree of dignity, so they ought with all their might to resist or bear more magnanimously the forces of destruction.

p. 81. But be on your guard lest by too clever a piece of cunning you are gulled even more completely than she was, winning instead of the name of fool a bad reputation, which would be a very ugly get-up for you.

p. 82. a great number of fleas that you think you have trapped in your fist, and yet they escape through your fingers.

Such misfortunes have we witnessed in our day; I could just take the word of several fathers and mothers who placed their children in religion when they were too young, thinking to divert them from worldly affections, but they, come of age, amply showed that they desired such things more than those who ordinarily do not budge from banquets and society functions.

Chapter V: Structure and Variety

p. 88. And to diversify and embellish our story, hear meantime how the Emperor Arquisil's affairs were progressing, a man much mentioned in preceding volumes.

p. 91. Now the romance writer, to make his tale more delightful, sets forth new things or things never heard of or seen; he makes his tale more pleasing with wonders, expectations, unlooked-for events, mingled passions, repartee, sorrows, angers, fears, joys, burning desires. As for the ordering, he ascends sometimes from small things to large; at other times he descends from the large to the small; sometimes he blends them one with the other, and the simple with the complex, the dark with light, the sad with the gay, the incredible with the probable: which is not work of an easy sort.

p. 92. which is a beast resembling a camel and a panther.

p. 93. thought she was having to do with a fine big dog.

a fruit of fine flavor that she brought to Amadis, as Eve the apple to Adam.

which the doctors say causes strange and prodigious effects in nature.

p. 96. a breed of horses having a long straight neck, like dromedaries.

And yet that could not so well please the ear of the listener as the eye of the beholder was satisfied. For these beauties . . . had on nothing but their simple chemises of so sheer a crepe that their beauty and natural perfection was in no way obscured; rather one could easily see on each of them two little red-tipped, high-thrusting apples of breasts set on a bosom whiter than ivory or the first snow fallen from the sky in a hard winter. And if someone wished to lower his eyes, the sight of the little belly, round and glossy as a crystal, made him long to see even further. But a single piece of fine lambskin fixed there decreed that nothing but whiteness should show. Moreover, I think that such an obstacle was never adopted by Nature, except through fear either that the rose and bud growing there should fade or that men too desirous of so sweet a flower should want to gather and ravish it by force of Love. Truly that was (it seems to me) beautiful to look at, and I should like very much to see so laudable a custom today among those who are worthy of their rank, to extol in them the greatness of the Creator who has made them so perfectly.

p. 97. Amadis de Grèce was surely one of the most accomplished lute-players of his time and had a voice most sweet and harmonious.

p. 98. Aurora had no sooner left the bed of her aged and hoary spouse and Phoebus had no sooner left his golden hall and climbed into his sparkling chariot, torch in hand, to light up the heavens, than the Emperor Amadis de Grèce. . . .

p. 99. all the water in your ocean will scarcely wash you free of so heinous a blemish and stain.

A kingdom divided against itself can not endure.

always hunting for a sheep with five legs.

Giant, it is you who have kidnaped my wife and daughter, like a traitor and robber. Now return them to me at once or I will punish you according to your deserts.

p. 100. Ah, Gandalin, can it be that you are mixed up in ravishing damsels? What will the Countess, your wife, say when she finds out?

did not keep his arms crossed.

that they had come quite close to each other.

p. 101. Just show me . . . the way up to you, and I will save you the trouble of coming down here.

his soul from now on will have more heat than it had in this world, whether it is roasted or boiled.

it was a most enjoyable spectacle, this fight, like one between a dog and a cat.

a woman so old, tottering, and wrinkled that her two flabby dugs hung down below her navel.

p. 102. she has a fresh and delicate complexion that, upon close consideration, I could not compare better for you than to the bark of those great elms that commonly serve as shade for the squares of some villages of Great Britain.

By God, my lady, if all the beauties of this land look like you, one would never think that I have come here to make love, and still less that you and I are children of the same Father.

massive, weighty, and fit for so goodly and gracious a young gentleman as he.

p. 104. this foolish old fellow.

I have no need of intercourse with her brain.

the string of their garters.

p. 105. I think that I would dry up a whole river.

a stinking hole . . . a place so rank and poisonous that by its odor alone it could kill a man.

Chapter VI: Structure and Repetition

p. 108. for the rape by Paris of the lovely Helen, wife of Menelaus.

p. 111. who will someday rule in Great Britain.

p. 112. dressed in a damsel's robe.

Did you never hear of the good turn that Briseida [Criseyde] did Troilus after the fall of Ilion? She loved him so much that she thought she would die in his arms when she was forced to leave him; and the Greeks assuredly thought she was determined to kill herself. And yet scarcely was she out of Troy when she entirely forgot her Troilus and transferred this burning love, which she had borne him all her life, to Diomedes, king of Thrace. O God, what inconstancy, what fickleness! what a foundation on shifting sands! This unfortunate girl had on her, among other precious ornaments that her lover Troilus gave her especially, a pair of perfumed gloves, which she presented to her new Diomedes one hour after her capture in sign of friendship and the good will she bore him. What would Troilus have said then, had he been there? Could he have believed it? I think not, even if he had seen it with his own two eyes.

p. 114. His neck was encircled by an emerald carcanet with a double clasp, the one in front cut in a great ruby, the one behind hidden under a large sapphire that gave off a marvelous luster. On this same carcanet there hung from a ribbon of carnation silk a medallion of fine porcelain enchased in gold enameled with little clusters of leaves, which represented to the life the lovely Queen of Canabée, whom he accompanied. At each of his ears hung a pyrope very painstakingly worked. His locks were curled, frizzled, twirled, and anointed with the sweetest perfumes of Araby, his eyes sparkling and lascivious, his countenance fresh and gleaming, all his gestures amorous and wanton, as though he had been created only to pay court to ladies and to let the most excellent flower of his youth fade away in slothful dalliance in the bosom of damsels.

p. 115. whom he remembered no more than the snows of yesteryear.

I am at peace and in mortal war; I fear, I hope, I burn cold as ice; I fly up to the sky, while all stretched out on the ground; and indeed I clasp nothing and I embrace everything; in prison am I which neither opens nor shuts; with one lace I am laced and unlaced; Love shackles me and unshackles me, having given me and then removed his grace; fortune and misfortune follow me in my chase; I want my good and I run to my evil; I am at once life and death; indeed life and death I pursue; I wish both to die and to ask for help; in such a state am I for Florisel.

p. 116. Love is I know not what that comes from I know not where; I know not who sends it, I know not in what way; it was born I know not how; and being itself confused, it confounds others; it feeds here and is nourished elsewhere: it sustains itself on I know not what; it cares not for praise; it glories in sorrow; and has in itself neither reason nor form; I know not how, now it shows itself and now hides. It strikes I know not how in the heart's core without anyone's being able to note either blood or wound: the one it has killed, lives dying. It makes one speak from the heart and not with the tongue: it keeps silent inside and imposes silence outside. Who now would know how to understand this madcap?

p. 117. And unbuttoning the front of his tunic, he exposed his breast.

p. 126. where all the inhabitants are dog-faced.

p. 136. O, my eyes, no longer eyes, but rivulets of tears and weeping.

p. 137. What is this, people of Great Britain? Why do you marvel to see a mad Greek knight who knows only how to gambol about the field?

Oh, foolish people, silly Britons, astonished over little, what moves you to make such a fuss over such a clumsy lout, whose only boldness is to torment a horse without cause?

Chapter VII: The Translations of Herberay and Munday

p. 139. was so confused with pleasure and shyness that he did not dare even look at her.

the loveliest damsel in the world was made a woman.

p. 140. who would be able to recount the amorous embraces and the sweet kisses, and tears that were mingled together there, mouth to mouth? Surely no one would be able to treat it but him who, being overpowered by that same passion and burned in like flames, has his heart tormented by those pangs of love, pangs which those already grown indifferent, the verdure of their youth lost, cannot comprehend. So that, deferring to such a one, I will leave off telling it in more detail.

according to what you have already heard about these doings, one can believe it would have been much more agreeable than Paradise itself.

p. 142. they two tumbled a bed that was in the palace, where they set about making her a woman who was not one before, satisfying their passions, which in so short a period of time, each one gazing at the other's flowering and beautiful youth, had grown very great.

p. 144. such sermons seeming ill suited to the matter of this tale.

to this fair mute damsel we can compare the world in which we live.

p. 145. O kings and great lords who rule the world, how germane and proper for you is this example. . . .

Galaor sported with the damsel that night at his pleasure, and no more need be recounted to you here, because in such cases, which do not conform to the virtue of pudicity, a man ought rightly to pass lightly over them, holding them in that small esteem that they deserve.

p. 146. Our Lady Virgin Mary, consoler and restorer of the afflicted, to you, Our Lady, I commend myself that you may intercede with your glorious Son to have pity on me; and if it is His will not to alleviate my body, to have mercy on this my soul in these my last moments, for nothing else if not death do I hope for.

Glorious Lady, consoler and protector of the afflicted, I beg you to beseech your Son to grant me grace and to succour me, having mercy on my wretched soul in this extremity.

and she told her squires and the others who were present to go out and leave her for a while, and they, thinking she wished to perform one of the inexorable bodily functions, left her alone, and she, closing the door, took the sword.

Chapter VIII: *Amadis* and Elizabethan Drama and Verse

p. 150. He held this kiss for a long time, having no power of his own to retire from where his heart lay; then she gently pushed him away, and they remained a long while looking at each other. Then he took her white hands, clasping and fondling them between his; thereupon sighs, long and hard upon one another, came from their two mouths; their hearts beat as if wanting to leave their breasts to mingle together; the blood rose to their faces, then left them pale and wan. Thus they remained an hour without speaking, Arlanges kissing her again and then drawing back to feed his gaze upon her, as if his eyes were jealous of his mouth, reclasping the hands of her who was half dead; so that all their senses, transported and amazed, gave way to the souls to be joined by the medium of the body, each remaining dead in himself and alive in the other, well-nigh drunk with the liquor of sensuous pleasure (called nectar of the gods), melting with sweetness like wax in the fire, rapt in ecstasy, embracing each other with greedy passion as if they had wished to be wholly one in the other, and in this way enjoying the sovereign good of this world, which true lovers alone experience. And since the imperfection of this flesh envelops the spirit in such a way that one part taking pleasure deprives the other of the beams of love, just as the sun warming and lighting up the earth in one place and hemisphere leaves the other in cold and darkness, to them it happened otherwise, and not in bestial fashion; rather their corporal senses were like sleeping thralls while the souls, supreme, caressed each other and visited at the closest proximity their prisons would allow. . . .

p. 151. as if awaking from a deep sleep.

p. 153. and I used to go almost every night to her room, to which she had me climb by a window that looked out on her garden.

p. 154. you will try to be as much like him as you can in gestures, in speech, and in your ways; and as for me, in receiving you by the window of my garden, I will pretend that you are the man whose clothes you will be wearing; so that in thus deceiving myself, I will perchance give some solace to my languishment.

p. 158. Eternal gods! . . . how wonderful are your divine secrets! Having granted unto the early years of my brother's reign the complete subservience not only of the Parthians but of all the neighboring peoples, even as far as the Red Sea, likewise in one instant you so brought him down that he, the lord of so many countries, was left conquered and so stripped of friends and wealth that in his death he could not have six feet of earth to bury him.

p. 160. Forthwith, Mascaron seized me by the locks, saying that to make me suffer more, he would not kill me like the others, but would rape me on the bodies of my wretched parents so that I would receive greater outrage; and so he carried out his damned and miserable will despite whatever resistance or threat I made him. Then he kicked me in the belly, saying: go, caitiff creature, find someone to honor you more or to give you the good things of life that you hoped for in the future.

and among others, several of our acquaintance.

O Jupiter, how can you have permitted this vile canaille to murder your knights and followers of your holy law? I solemnly promise you to break and smash your statue, and never offer any reverence to it or you, challenging you yourself to combat—if you are so bold as to show yourself.

p. 161. I will climb and scale your heaven, and I will even go break your head inside your very house.

Chapter IX: *Amadis* and Spenser's *Faerie Queene*

p. 175. consider Pyramus who killed himself, thinking his beloved Thisbe was dead; see there on the other side with what courage she transfixes herself with her dead lover's sword; see the lamentations Dido makes for her Aeneas and finally kills herself; see what cruelty Medea uses on herself for love of Jason. . . . See Solomon with his wives and concubines, see David with Uriah; consider Virgil, Aristotle, and so many other philosophers. . . . See Paris with Helen. . . . See the strange passion of Pasiphaë for the Minotaur.

Chapter X: *Amadis* and Sidney's *Arcadia*

p. 198. the ugliest and most deformed person Nature ever made.

p. 199. In one country, those who are bitten by serpents named Tarantulas.

consider that you will navigate from now on between two poles, that when one is in view, you will lose the other: your Niquée is the Arctic and I am the Antarctic: if you find her, you will lose me.

p. 200. matters so forceful that they are enough to force the forces by which Love forces you to force me.

I place myself entirely in your safekeeping so that by your valor you may protect me from myself against you and from you against me, and even from you against yourself.

who gave you her love instead of her hate, her freedom instead of her servitude, her honor instead of her shame, her repose instead of her travail, and her esteem instead of the scorn to which she has been subjected, coming to search you out herself so as to find you again in order to lose you and to be lost for love of you even as you are lost for love of another. Finally I am one who has given you life in order to receive death and who, while living, dies a thousand times a day for not being able to die.

Bibliography

LE PREMIER LI-
ure de Amadis de Gaule, qui
TRAICTE DE MAINTES ADVENTV-
res d'Armes & d'Amours, qu'eurent plusieurs Cheualiers & Dames, tant du royaulme de la grand
Bretaigne, que d'aultres pays. Traduict
nouuellement d'Espagnol en Françoys par le Seigneur des
Essars, Nicolas de
Herberay.

Acuerdo Oluido.

Patere, aut abstine.

Nul ne s'y frotte.

Auec priuilege du Roy.

1 5 4 4.

De l'Imprimerie de Denys Ianot, Imprimeur du Roy en langue Fran-
çoyse, & Libraire Iuré de l'Vniuersité de Paris.

Editions of 16th and 17th Century Works Cited

THE AMADIS CYCLE

So many editions of the various books of *Amadis de Gaule* were published in the sixteenth century that it is astonishing indeed that so few have survived. Yet complete sets of the cycle are scarce, and in my reading, done over a period of several years, I have depended upon a variety of editions, from lavishly decorated folios to missal-sized texts. I used Hugues Vaganay's modern edition of Book I and the Rutgers University Library copies of Books II, III, IV, V, and VII. Books VI, VIII, IX, X, XI, XII, and XIV I read in a microfilm copy furnished by the Folger Shakespeare Library. For the remaining volumes I relied upon the Princeton University Library, which has a complete set.

I have refrained from supplying the complete texts of the title pages of all the books of *Amadis de Gaule* cited in this volume. Instead, I offer a facsimile title page from a very early folio edition of Book I, which, together with the woodcut illustrations from other rare folio editions in the Folger Library and the New York Public Library, suggests the fine quality of the Parisian printers who first produced *Amadis de Gaule*. As a further sample, here is the text from the title page of the Folger Library's 1548 folio edition of Book VIII: *Le Huitiesme Liure d'Amadis de Gaule, auquel sont recitées les hautes prouesses et faitz merueilleux d'Amadis de Grece surnomme le Cheualier de l'ardante Espée: Mis en*

Bibliography

Françoys par le Seigneur des Essars N. de Herberay, Commissaire ordinaire de l'artillerie du Roy & lieutenant en icelle, es pais & gouuernement de Picardie, de monsieur de Brissac, Cheualier de l'ordre grand Maistre, & Capitaine general d'icelle artillerie. Acuerdo Oluido. [Printer's mark.] *Auec priuilege du Roy. À Paris. Pour Vincent Sertenas Libraire, tenant sa boutique au Palays en la galerie, par ou l'on va à la Chancelerie, & au mont saint Hylaire à l'hostel d A'lbret* [sic]. *1548.*

In the following list of French editions cited, except in the case of Book I, the entry for each book contains the name of the translator, the place of publication, the name of the printer or bookseller, and the date printed.

Garci Ordóñez de Montalvo, *Amadís de Gaula* [Books I–V]. Edited by Pascual de Gayangos. *Libros de caballerías.* Biblioteca de Autores Españoles, Vol. XL. Madrid, 1909.

The Ancient, Famous, and Honourable History of Amadis de Gaule . . . Written in French by the Lord of Essars, Nicholas de Herberay . . . [Books I–IV]. London, 1619.

Le Premier Livre d'Amadis de Gaule. Publié sur l'édition originale par H. Vaganay. Société des textes français modernes. Paris, 1918.

Book II. Nicholas de Herberay. Antwerp: Iean Waesberghe, 1561.

Book III. [No title page.] [Nicholas de Herberay.] [Colophon: Antwerp:] De l'imprimerie de Christophle Plantin, 1560.

Book IV. Nicholas de Herberay. Antwerp: Guillaume Silvius, 1573.

Book V. Nicholas de Herberay. Antwerp: Guillaume Silvius, 1572.

Book VI. Nicholas de Herberay. Paris: pour Vincent Sertenas, Libraire, 1557.

Book VII. Nicholas de Herberay. Antwerp: Guillaume Silvius, 1573.

Book VIII. Nicholas de Herberay. Paris: pour Vincent Sertenas, Libraire, 1548.

Book IX. Claude Colet [and Giles Boileau]. Paris: pour Vincent Sertenas, Libraire, 1553.

Book X. I.G.P. [Jacques Gohorry, Parisien]. Paris: pour Vincent Sertenas, Libraire, 1555.

Book XI. I.G.P. Paris: pour Vincent Sertenas, Libraire, 1559.

Book XII. Guillaume Aubert de Poitiers. Paris: pour Vincent Sertenas, Libraire, 1556.

Book XIII. I.G.P. Lyon: François Didier, 1577.

Book XIV. Antoine Tyron. Antwerp: Iean Waesberghe, 1574.

Book XV. Antoine Tyron. Paris: Iean Parant, 1577.

Book XV. Gabriel Chappuys. Lyon: Benoist Rigaud, 1578.

Book XVI. Gabriel Chappuys. Lyon: François Didier, 1578.

Book XVI. Nicholas de Moutreux [*sic*]. Paris: Iean Poupy, 1577.

Book XVII. [Gabriel Chappuys]. Lyon: Estienne Michel, 1578.

Book XVIII. [Gabriel Chappuys]. Lyon: pour Loys Cloquemin, 1579.

Book XIX. Iacques Charlot. Lyon: pour Loys Cloquemin, 1581.

Book XX. Gabriel Chappuys. Lyon: pour Loys Cloquemin, 1581.

Book XXI. Gabriel Chappuys. Lyon: pour Loys Cloquemin, 1581.

The Treasurie of Amadis of Fraunce. London, 1568.

OTHER WORKS

Anton, Robert. *Moriomachia* (1613). In *Short Fiction of the Seventeenth Century*, edited by Charles C. Mish. The Stuart Editions. New York: New York University Press, 1963.

Ariosto, Lodovico. *Orlando Furioso*. Translated by Sir John Harington. London, 1634.

Beaumont, Francis. *The Knight of the Burning Pestle*. In *Elizabethan and Stuart Plays*, edited by Charles Read Baskervill, Virgil B. Heltzel, and Arthur H. Nethercot. New York, 1934.

Cervantes Saavedra, Miguel de. *Don Quixote*. Translated by Thomas Shelton (1612). The Tudor Translations. London, 1896.

Chrestien de Troyes. *Yvain*. Edited by Wendelin Foerster. Halle, 1912.

Deloney, Thomas. *The Novels of Thomas Deloney*. Edited by Merritt E. Lawlis. Bloomington: Indiana University Press, 1961.

Forde, Emanuel. *Montelion*. London, 1633.

———. *Ornatus and Artesia*. In *Shorter Novels: Jacobean and Restoration*. Everyman's Library. London, 1930. Vol. II.

———. *Parismus*. London, n.d.

Greene, Robert. *Menaphon*. In *Menaphon and A Margarite of America*, edited by G. B. Harrison. New York: Oxford University Press, 1927.

The Honour of Chivalrie. London, 1598.

Hoskins, John. *The Life, Letters and Writings of John Hoskyns*. Edited by Louise B. Osborn. New Haven: Yale University Press, 1937.

The Knight of the Sea. London, 1600.

Lodge, Thomas. *A Margarite of America*. In *Menaphon and A Margarite of America*, edited by G. B. Harrison. New York: Oxford University Press, 1927.

Bibliography

The Myrror of Knighthood: The Second Part. London, 1583.

The Mirrour of Knighthood: The Second Part of the First Book. London, 1585.

Munday, Anthony. *Zelauto: The Fountain of Fame.* Edited by Jack Stillinger. Carbondale: Southern Illinois University Press, 1963.

Nashe, Thomas. *The Unfortunate Traveler.* In *The Works of Thomas Nashe,* edited by Ronald B. McKerrow. London, 1904. Vol. II.

P., R. *Moderatus,* London, 1595.

Palmerin d'Oliva: The First Part. London, 1637.

Primaleon of Greece . . . The Third Book. London, 1619.

Riche, Barnabe. *Don Simonides.* London, 1581.

Robarts, Henry. *Haigh for Devonshire.* London, 1600.

————. *Pheander.* London, 1595.

Le Roman de Tristan et Iseut. Traduction du roman en prose du quin-zième siecle. Edited by Pierre Honore Champion and P. Galand-Pernet. Paris, 1958.

Sidney, Sir Philip. *The Prose Works of Sir Philip Sidney.* Edited by Albert Feuillerat. 4 vols. Cambridge: Cambridge University Press, 1912 (reprinted 1963).

Spenser, Edmund. *The Poetical Works of Edmund Spenser.* Edited by James C. Smith and Ernest de Selincourt. New York: Oxford University Press, 1912.

A Note on Secondary
Sources Cited

The number of books and articles dealing directly with the Amadis cycle as a literary phenomenon or with its influence on English literature is very small. Sir Henry Thomas' *Spanish and Portuguese Romances of Chivalry* (Cambridge, 1920) is the most useful general study. Although, as its title indicates, it is concerned with other romances in addition to *Amadis*, it is indispensable for historical and bibliographical information.

Much of the scholarship available is devoted quite properly to the Spanish *Amadís*. Unfortunately the modern edition of the first four books of *Amadís de Gaula* by Edwin B. Place was not completed when I began this book, and I have had to rely on the older edition of Pascual de Gayangos, which appears as Vol. XL of the Biblioteca de Autores Españoles, *Libros de caballerías* (Madrid, 1909). In addition to the first four books of *Amadís de Gaula* it contains *Las Sergas de Esplandián.* Gayangos has a long informative preliminary essay.

The comments on *Amadís* of the great Spanish critic and scholar M. Menéndez y Pelayo in his *Orígenes de la novela*, Nueva Biblioteca de Autores Españoles (Madrid, 1905), are concerned with literary values and are pronounced with a memorable combination of passion and authority. Although a relatively small number of pages in that book are devoted to *Amadís,* they represent the best literary criticism of *Amadís* yet written.

A study by Grace S. Williams, "The Amadis Question," *Revue his-*

panique, XXI (1909), 1–167, and Edwin B. Place's "Fictional Evolution: The Old French Romances and the Primitive *Amadís* Reworked by Montalvo," *PMLA,* LXXI (1956), 521–529, investigate the origins of *Amadís* in medieval romances; and Place's "Amadis of Gaul, Wales, or What?" *Hispanic Review,* XXIII (1955), 99–107, considers the problem of geography in the Spanish version of Montalvo.

Dale B. J. Randall's *The Golden Tapestry* (Duke University Press, 1963), a study of Spanish fiction in English translation from 1543 to 1657, explicitly omits chivalric romances from consideration, but the book has a number of helpful asides on *Amadis.*

In *Le fonti dell' "Orlando Furioso"* (Florence, 1900), Pio Rajna suggests that *Amadís de Gaula* was a source for Ariosto, but his references to *Amadís* are few and scattered.

Most of the scholarship on the French *Amadis* is concerned not with the romance itself but with its social and literary influence. Eugène Baret, *De l' "Amadis de Gaule" et de son influence sur les mœurs et la littérature au XVIᵉ et au XVIIᵉ siècle* (Paris, 1873), and Edouard Bourciez, *Les Mœurs polies et la littérature de cour sous Henri II* (Paris, 1886), are still valuable commentaries on the influence of *Amadis* in France. W. L. Wiley, *The Gentleman in Renaissance France* (Cambridge, Mass.: Harvard University Press, 1954), has few specific references to *Amadis,* but it is excellent for its evocation of the society in which *Amadis* flourished.

An article by Walther Küchler, "Eine dem *Orlando Furioso* Ariosts entlehnte Episode im französischen Amadisroman," *Zeitschrift für französische Sprache und Litteratur,* XXXIV (1909), 274–292, points out how Book XII of the French *Amadis* has borrowed some of the plot of the *Orlando Furioso.* A. Cioranescu's two-volume-in-one study *L'Arioste en France* (Turin, 1963) has much to say about *Amadis* as a forerunner of Ariosto in France.

Hugues Vaganay, *Amadis en français: Essai de bibliographie* (Florence, 1906), contains title pages, prefatory material, chapter headings, and illustrations from sixteenth-century French editions of Books I through XII. The book is particularly useful in that it reproduces woodcuts and gives the modern reader an idea of the care and expense lavished upon the early folios.

Some valuable commentary on *Amadis* comes as *obiter dicta* in special studies on Sir Philip Sidney. William Vaughn Moody's unpublished Harvard essay "An Inquiry into the Sources of Sir Philip Sidney's

Arcadia" is the first detailed examination of the influence of *Amadis*—especially Book XI—upon the *Arcadia*. In *Sir Philip Sidneys "Arcadia" und ihre Nachläufer* (Nuremberg, 1903), K. Brunhuber discusses *Amadis* along with other romances; and R. W. Zandvoort's *Sidney's "Arcadia"* (Amsterdam, 1929) is a sound reexamination of Moody's evidence. Several studies of the *Arcadia* are skeptical of Amadisian influence: Samuel L. Wolff, *The Greek Romances in Elizabethan Prose Fiction* (New York: Columbia University Press, 1912); T. P. Harrison, Jr., "A Source of Sidney's *Arcadia*," *University of Texas Studies in English*, VI (1926), 53–71; Albert W. Osborn, *Sir Philip Sidney en France* (Paris, 1932); Marcus S. Goldman, *Sir Philip Sidney and the "Arcadia,"* Illinois Studies in Language and Literature, XVII (Urbana, 1934); Mary Patchell, *The Palmerin Romances in Elizabethan Prose Fiction* (New York: Columbia University Press, 1947).

A recent provocative study, *Sidney's "Arcadia"* (New Haven: Yale University Press, 1965), incorporates two works: Walter R. Davis, "A Map of Arcadia," and Richard A. Lanham, "The *Old Arcadia*." Although the name of *Amadis* scarcely occurs, Davis recognizes it as a principal source, whereas Lanham dismisses the matter of source as inconsequential.

René Pruvost, *Robert Greene et ses romans* (Paris, 1938), discusses *Amadis* as a probable source for Greene's *Pandosto;* but the latest study of Elizabethan prose fiction, Margaret Schlauch's *Antecedents of the English Novel, 1400–1600* (London, 1963), disregards chivalric romances.

Index

Index

Index

Index

Index

Index

Index

Index

Index

This book was set in Garamond Linotype and printed by offset on Warren's #1854 Medium manufactured by S. D. Warren Company, Boston, Mass. Composed, printed and bound by Quinn & Boden Company, Inc., Rahway, N. J.